A
HAUNTING
SMILE

A
HAUNTING
SMILE

A NOVEL BY
CHRISTOPHER G. MOORE

Heaven Lake Press

Distributed in Thailand by:
Asia Document Bureau Ltd.
P.O. Box 1209
Bangkok 10110, Thailand
Fax: (662) 665-2587
Web site: www.heavenlakepress.com
E-mail: editorial@heavenlakepress.com

First edition 1993 by White Lotus
Second edition 1999 by Heaven Lake Press
Trade paperback edition: copyright © 2004 Christopher G. Moore
Printed in Thailand

Jacket design: Jae Song
Author's photo: copyright © 2004 Pamela Hongskul

Author's web site: www.cgmoore.com
Author's e-mail: chris@cgmoore.com

ISBN 974-92214-8-6

To the memory of Rene Magritte
whose perspective
provided the needle and thread
to weave the haunting
and the smile

Special thanks to Timothy Mo,
with his sure novelist's eye
selflessly provided guidance
pointing out flaws and weaknesses
that haunted the original text and
in the process granted that most
precious of all things:
A second chance to get it right.

May 19, 1999

If the Party could thrust its hand into the past and say of this or that event, *it never happened*—that, surely, was more terrifying than mere torture and death?

George Orwell,
Nineteen Eighty-four

One shall seek nothingness only to find a way out of it and one shall mark the road for everyone.

Elisa Canetti,
The Conscience of Words & Earwitness

INTRODUCTION

Before 1992 I had heard the sound of gunfire in a city. In May 1992, there were days of gunfire and days of bloodshed. Bombed out police kiosk and telephone booths left busted and black. Pickup trucks prowled Sukhumvit Road with armed men in the back. Curfews kept most people off the street. One felt anything could happen. A stray bullet lodged in the roof of my bedroom. Witnessing death marks a man. The images and feelings are one that I still carry forward. Sanam Luang was packed with tens of thousands of people. They came by bus, car, motorcycle, and by foot. They were from all walks of life. What I remember most were the large number of middle class people among the people sitting on the short grass and listening to the speakers and the bands. The middle-class in most places is known for its apathy. Politicians rarely can turn them out in large numbers to vote. Protesting in an open field with the threat of violence, real and present, is a quantum leap beyond exercising the vote. It was mind altering to see eighty thousand people standing up for what they believed was just and right. That took courage and commitment. You have to push hard to get people to leave the comforts of their office and home to gather in a place where they may die. That happened in 1992. I was there and saw it myself.

In *A Haunting Smile*, I wanted to capture what most authors covering a battlefield seek to communicate: the chaos, madness, and horror. I also wanted to place the violence in May 1992 onto a larger historical canvass. A lot of recent non-fiction has well-documented the violent nature of a species that is only 13,000 years away from the hunter-gather tribe and bands. Only five thousand years ago we had learned to read and write. We have a much longer history of killing than reading. It seems we've been programmed for blood letting. Especially when the "other" is not one of "us"—not a member of our band or tribe.

In Thailand, the culture embraces ghosts and erects spirit houses as a place to provide offering to appease the spirit of a place. I wanted to bring ghosts from another place and time into the story as a counterpoint. As the events of May 1992 unfold, the ghosts of Cortez and Montezuma patrol Patpong and the battlefields. Harry Purcell, whose family had an ancient history of selling guns—helicopters, tanks, heavy artillery—has a deep understanding of the reasons behind the death and destruction. The generals, politicians and influential people are the buyers.

Warriors count their women, like heads taken in battle, as another token of power.

Warfare and prostitution are connected. Each leads to an inevitable personal destruction and creates psychological games to prevent guilt. I was much taken by the games of war and the games of love, the weapons used in both, and the way language makes men and women use different vocabularies for desire, pain, and victims. I threw myself into May 1992 like someone who couldn't swim, diving into the deep end of a pool. I sought to make a connection between the East and the West. The challenge was to do this within the context of an overall narrative that at heart was fiction.

There are observations that I believe still hold largely true in *A Haunting Smile*, as when Harry Purcell wrote, "In Asia the underdog has tank-tire tracks over its back, and was kicked into the gutter with a jackboot. To be an underdog in the East was a sign of weakness, failure, lack of support and at the first sign someone had slipped and fallen, this was not an opportunity for compassion, to offer the helping hand—no—this was the precise time to launch the attack and finish off this animal before it regained its strength..."

A dozen years later, looking back at these and other observation in *A Haunting Smile*, and the bloody events of May, I wonder how much anyone has learned? Or if we are capable of learning, whether we can accept our basic nature. Ignoring such knowledge comes with a terrible price. Distorting such knowledge corrupts our language, what and who we are, and how we can live together. From the upstairs skull bars of Patpong to the temples of skulls of the Aztecs, the story remains the only account in fiction to recall the events of bloody May 1992 and to ask the question of what that time said about us and what lessons, if any, we have learnt. Perhaps the answer is that some lessons can't ever be learnt and that each generation must let blood again because it is our destiny to repeat our mistakes.

We have moved from year of the Monkey 1992 to the next year of the Monkey 2004. The monkey is agile, tricky and resourceful. An opportunistic creature, one that lives in extended bands with a strict hierarchical system. The distance between them and us is very small. I wait for the right moment twelve years from now, in the next Monkey year, 2016, I'd like to revisit the events of May 1992 and once again explore the issue of missing people and the violence that takes them away into the night. I was on the scene in 1992 and in 2004, and I hope to see where another year of the Monkey takes us next.

Christopher G. Moore
Bangkok,
June 2004

PART 1
THE UNEXPECTED ANSWER

1

DEE lay on her back beneath a ceiling fan which was slowly rotating overhead. The room was small, old, worn and cluttered. The windows were open, and mosquitoes buzzed through. There was no breeze and the air hung heavy with smoke drifting from the coils. Tuttle lay next to her, and he raised his hand, held it, then slapped a mosquito dead against his arm. His hand came up smudged with his own blood splashed from the tangle of wings and legs.

"Your blood, Tut?" she asked.

Holding his wrist she examined his fingers by candle light, licked his fingers clean of the blood.

"Taste good," she joked.

He said nothing as she lay back on the pillow.

Mosquito coils were at the four corners of the side by side bamboo mats. But the mosquitoes made their way through the smoke for an airborne strike. He touched his hand wet from her tongue against his thigh. They were naked, glistening with sweat from making love, rivulets of sweat dripped from Dee's belly. Tuttle reached over and felt her wet, smooth hip touching his own. What in the world could ever feel more secure than this moment? That touch, a knowing brush of the fingers? The answer was there was none; no prison could ever more securely hold a man within the four walls than a beautiful, kind, loving woman moments after the act of love-making. A few feet away a slender yellow altar candle melted down on a piece of white coral collected from Koh Samui. The flame danced over her flat belly; illuminating the peach fuzz swirling like a spiraling universe flowing from her navel. Outside there was an odd sound (he knew the sounds of her apartment). Distant laughing voices of children. And some unknown hand had struck the gong in the *wat* a few doors down. Perhaps it was the children, playing in the night.

"Why you go, Tut?" asked Dee, her face in the shadows.

"You're tired of Dee? You not think I'm young any more. Do I talk a lie? Why you not stay, Tut?"

He was listening to the gong. A long silence followed. He lay with his hands cupped around the back of his head. Her hand came down, fingers running down his thigh, touching to his knee.

"I cannot," he said. This was the night of his prison break; his sprint into freedom. Like all escapes, this one had been planned to the last detail. The rope flung over the high wall of domestic tranquillity was an old one—writing. Writers wrote to launch their escape; the license to invent a life started with destroying oneself. The endless reinvention exhausted Tuttle as he looked ahead, think-ing it was like running the hurdles—each a mile high. To stay would have ended not only the escape, but the race to outrun boredom and smuggle lust from youth into middle age and beyond into that unknown territory of the elderly.

She sensed his uneasiness. But, at the same time, she tried not to sound resentful; they had been through the same discussion for over a week, and no matter what questions had been asked or answers given, neither one felt satisfied the other understood.

"You say before, you can always do. You decide, then you do. You not say that?"

He had told Dee that she could choose her fate; that it was up to her to decide what battles she would be willing to fight, when she would go to battle, and what she wished to die for. And now, on his last night in Bangkok, she had proved herself an able, bright student. She had done exactly as he had preached; and he had used an excuse of the kind he had reproached her for using.

How could Tuttle explain this need to break the bond which held them in peace? Comfort and pleasure ran deep in the blood; relatively few were born free of this weakness. It required courage and in the world the attribute most talked about and least met with was found in this one word—courage. The ultimate courage?

3

Seize the knife and cut the muscle, flesh and bone growing the two naked thighs into one, locking them to the day and night like the small animals turned to rock in the piece of coral at his shoulder. Dee had been born into a world where survival was everything; overcoming discomfort and suffering accounted for the striving, the hunger to succeed, the irresistible force of the day. Here was a divide that neither could cross into a realm of mutual understanding; the gap was too vast, powerful, and the consequences clear—self-destruction in the end. Because it would end, it had to end in a flame as hot as the solitary altar candle. No Asian woman—maybe no woman—could comprehend how a man could abandon her for an ideal. Women were far too practical to throw to chance an ideal of life when life itself was breathing on the mat next to them, attached to the bone, and the bone to the soul.

"It's that *farang*," she said the word, hitting a nasty note of blame. "Addison. He make you crazy. I know. I hear you talking, talking. You think Dee not understand English. But I understand. Addison, he make you feel bad. Why? I don't know. But I think you should forget him."

"It's more complicated than Addison. There are other things," said Tuttle.

"Then tell me this other thing."

"Nothing happens which I don't expect. Someone strikes a gong at the *wat*. And children at two in the morning laughing. But it's not enough." He wished there was a way to make her understand.

She raised herself up on an elbow, and looked at his face.

Looking, looking, she thought to herself. *Farang* looking for what? She had listened carefully to what he said and this is what he meant—nothing but a question with an answer which excluded her. Men looked all their lives for things which were in front of their eyes. Things which women saw. Why were men so blind?

"The accident. A break in the line of continuity. Then you must choose to repair or abandon the break. To start again. You go or you stay. Run away or call for help. Unbroken continuity is a writer's death sentence. How can I explain so you can understand?"

"You think too much. It gives me a headache," she said in Thai. "Men don't make sense. I read the Thai newspapers. I know every-thing happens fast now. I see what the generals say. I see what the

politicians say. I think most of them lie. Cheat. But I'm a simple girl.
I don't even speak English. Because you only speak Thai."

His kayak and gear were packed in the corner. He was going off
alone to Nan Province and the Nan River. Alone. The sluggishness
of habit, of routine living had made him a prisoner of his comforts
and pleasures. He had stopped thinking, seeing, wondering. Addison had said as much. And as much as he hated this *farang* who
was living with his daughter, he could not deny that Addison had
hit the mark. Since Tuttle's book of short stories had come out, he
had fallen into habits which had allowed him to take a great deal
for granted. A big mistake, he thought. All that had been alien,
strange had come to merge into the ordinary. From one end of
the day to the next, he knew each face, sight, sound, and smell of
Bangkok. He could have been anywhere in the world. The only
difference was without substance—a gong at the wrong time of
day, children's voices—half-singing, half-laughing—at some distant
game. Such a marginal difference was not enough. That was the
horror of an ordinary life—it swallowed challenge and courage
and without them what meaning came from looking from Monday
to Tuesday and beyond? What kind of *farang* voluntarily chose to
live in Bangkok? No other city in Asia had such a large contingent
of volunteer residents. What had brought them searching in such a
city? Many found the ultimate contradiction in their journey—those
who had believed Bangkok was one of the few places where a
new identity might be forged. They soon discovered the ordinary
routines in life didn't amount to a new person. Their old identity
waited in the bars and clubs looking for a chance to reclaim them
body and soul. What they rarely admitted was that their way of
living had become not much different from the one they had fled
in horror and disgust.

What a human being was required to do, his test, was by his
strength to resist the great pull of the ordinary which made the
senses stupid, dull, and predictable. There was more lurking to
gut the human soul—the terrible, ugly head of sentimentality, all
tongues, eyes on sticks, and spitting fire under a tranquil mask of
calm. Herding people like cattle by force of appeal to their emotions
ranked as a crime against humanity. It was the underlying cause of
the great crimes recorded in modern history. Sentimentality was the

definition of modern horror. What he wished for was the courage to cast himself back into the disturbances and chaos of living—to cut the lifelines, the safety cables. Break the continuity and restart a story yet to be discovered. You either sink or swim, he thought. At the same time what was he doing? His hand brushing the concave belly; this fertile valley of shadow and light—this landscape which promised itself wholly and forever to his touch. His fingers on her moist pubic hair, he paused. If he delayed his trip one more day, so what? But he knew this trick of the mind; this feeling which ran from his fingers and eyes to his brain. If he stayed, then it would be another life. The existence of a writer caught in his sluggish routine; he could make a living writing advertising copy, magazine articles or TV scripts. He could make a decent living. Buy the life flourishing in the high-rise towers in Bangkok. He withdrew his hand from her stomach. He breathed in deeply.

"I know," she said. "You go."

"I should go now," he said.

"You stay until morning. It's okay. I wait you."

"Don't wait me," he said.

"Never mind. You come back. I know you."

He shook his head. She knew his weakness too well. Maybe he would crawl back like a dog, hungry, cold, lost, looking for comfort. Hoped not. He drew himself up and dressed.

"If I say this hurt me very much, you stay?"

"No."

"I say I kill myself, you stay?"

"No."

She was crying and angry, the reality of separation; the amputation done, nothing was left but to stare with horror at the wound.

"I hate you. I never want to see you. I hope you die. Not slow. I want you to die. Drown on that fucking river. I go look at your body, and I laugh." She hurled the piece of coral with the candle still burning at him. It struck the wall with a loud whack, shattering into a hundred fragments.

A few minutes later he was gone, down the stairs, out the small courtyard and into the street. She had turned her head and curled up under a sheet. Neither one said goodbye.

He walked through Banglamphu, carrying his collapsible kayak and gear. He had willed himself out the door, against the instincts of his blood and some deeper pulse which would anchor him to Dee's side forever. There was an old joke at HQ—the all-night joint on Sukhumvit where Tuttle was a regular—about experiencing a coyote morning. Like a coyote with its leg caught in a steel trap, the punter wakes up with a terrible hangover and finds a old, over-weight, dragon-lady he can't remember dragging out of HQ and can't remember anyone else ever taking, sleeping on his arm, trapping him under layers of upper arm blubber, exhaling her garlic fumes in his face, giving him the choice of waking her and making love or chewing his arm off and slipping away. What wasn't a joke, was to chew off some vital part of oneself held within a woman as beautiful and soft and loving as the laughter of children at play. Why was he in the street? Because of an ideal. Because of a conversation—more a confrontation than a conversation with an American DJ named Denny Addison who had struck him dead center. Without a connection with the brutal, the distorted, and deprived—without touching the margins, living on the outside, the circumstances of life would never reveal themselves for what they truly were. Innocence and sentiment appeared like children's tender, rising voices outside a room where a candle burned. What those little cries of delight masked were the traps waiting. How many lives over how many generations had fallen through this void, thinking the embrace would break the fall? Something was waiting to change his life; river people waited for him in Nan Province. Each time he made a journey, he thought of the people living lives unconnected with his own, and how soon they would touch, and nothing would ever be the same again. This adventure of discovery of some life beyond his own, a life which would collide and forever change his own, was enough for him to extinguish the altar candle, roll up his bamboo mat, and, listening to her curses in silence, close the door and walk down the stairs.

There was that gong again.

The children's voices didn't follow. Perhaps they were asleep now, or running off to another hideaway where their games couldn't be detected. He walked around the corner and found a taxi to take him to the train station. On the way, he remembered something Harry Purcell had said.

Purcell, a gun-runner, from a family of gun-runners, had told Tuttle the lesson of life was threefold, "First sacrifice comfort, then blow up the bridges of familiarity, and finally detonate all bunkers of respectability. Once the sky clears from the dust and shards of metal, glass and stone and all that hate, fear, and curses of betrayal drain away, you can invent a new beginning. Once you have that chance, you are one up. Who in life takes the chance to invent a new life? I sell guns to people who put these inventors of life against a wall. They stuff a cigar in their mouth. Not a Havana but a cigar nevertheless. Next comes the blindfold and the signal to the squad. It's over like that. You feel nothing, I'm told. The generals admire such courage. They envy it, and what you envy you ultimately fear and hate. And it is a short step to believing this object of hatred is a monster out to destroy the security of the nation. The generals wear their uniforms, issue their orders, and buy their weapons waiting for the day when they have to destroy men like you. Nothing personal. My family are like middle men between the generals and their targets. You've got bull's eye written all over you. Take a chance, Tuttle. Give yourself a nice, long head start. Who knows how far you may get before some major lowers his sword as you stand before the wall?" Purcell grinned widely, lighting a Havana cigar, his Zippo lighter shooting a tongue of flame into the air.

2

THE UNEXPECTED ANSWER

A Denny Addison Documentary Film
Running time: 46 minutes
Black and White

THE screen credits roll—Director & Writer & Director of Photography & Editor—Denny Addison. The film is a grainy black and white in the style of the 40s film noir.

The camera angle reveals a female form stripped to the waist before a full length mirror. She stands facing the mirror, touching her nipples with long, slender fingers, the nails painted. Her name is Meow. She twirls a wet Q-tip into a plastic cup and slowly works the wet end of the Q-tip over an erect nipple. The size 36" breasts are smooth, firm, and large; breasts which appear sculptured, a little too perfect—not objects that have come straight from the manufacturer but objects that have been modified substantially once the model left the showroom, and then daily polished with hot wax. She wears an ordinary expression as if she were putting on make-up.

"Instead of studying English tonight, you're going to work?" asks a male voice off camera. Asanee's naked upper body moves into the frame.

Meow glances up, finding Asanee's face and breasts filling the mirror, and smiles. Their eyes lock like cats on a roof, backs raised, then the spell is broken as Meow licks her lips, shrugs, breaks the eye contact.

"I go make business," says Meow, dipping the other end of the Q-tip into the solution and dabbing her other nipple. The cotton end of the Q-tip moves deftly. She blows on her nipple until the glistening surface dries to a dull bone-dry invisible patch. The nipples are in working condition, that is crucial.

"Do you tell customers that you are a *katoey*?" asks the male voice.

Meow laughs. "Of course not. Maybe you think I'm ashamed. But that isn't the reason. I tell man I was born a man, too, then change to woman. *Farang* don't like. They will not take you if you say *katoey*." She stares directly into the camera, sticking out her tongue and turning her face into an evil mask of lust. "You make film of what I say and my face. Maybe you show the police. And police catch Meow." She returns to the mirror and her Q-tip ritual.

"Are you afraid of the police?" asks the male voice.

"I no like the police," she says. "Asanee show herself. She your girlfriend. So maybe I'm not too afraid. You hurt yourself if you show film to police."

"Do you like men?"

"I love men." Her eyes sparkle.

"What do you love about them?" asks the off-camera voice.

"Their money," whispers the *katoey*.

"Is that why you rob them?"

"Who say I rob man?"

There is a long silence as the camera continues to roll.

Asanee breaks the silence.

"The Q-tip is dipped in an Upjohn tranquilizer," Asanee says.

"I think I have nice tits," says Meow. "*Farang* men like them very much. They tell me, Meow your tits very beautiful. I say thank you. You want to touch them? Can. You want to go with me? Can."

"Where do you take men?" asks the male voice.

"Short-time hotel near Patpong."

"Tell me what it's like," says the male voice.

Meow sets her jaw, looks over at Asanee and then over her shoulder and into the camera. She brushes her painted fingernails over what one imagines—the film is black and white—are dusky-colored nipples which, falling along the spectrum from black to white come out a kind of washed-out gray.

"I sit on the bed. *Farang* he sit beside me. I say, you can touch them. It's okay. Then he touch me. Then I say, you can lick them. It's okay. I think you like to lick them a long time. His tongue touches here. And then here. I know five, ten minutes he fall asleep. Pass out like he's very drunk."

"That's it?"

"I take his watch. Rolex is very good if not a fake. He have a gold chain, I take. I want his money. All of it. Baht, dollars, pounds. Sometimes a customer has traveller's cheques and credit cards. I take them, too. *Farang* make it very easy. They keep everything in one place—a money belt. One-stop shopping, my friend say. She make a joke. She say, I ever meet this Upjohn, I thank him for making this drug."

The camera never moves from a fixed location. And Meow and Asanee slowly move around the room like sleep walkers, sometimes moving off camera, then reappearing.

"But if you studied English you could get a real job," says Asanee. "You wouldn't have to sell yourself."

"I have a real job," says Meow. "I like my work." She purses her lips into a pout in the mirror.

"Do *katoeys* believe in democracy?" asks Asanee.

"Bet your sweet ass we do. I vote to cut off my cock. Hold election one time. Then no need to vote anymore," she says.

"What you do is a crime."

The *katoey* raises an eyebrow. "I don't think so. We are a poor country. *Farang* very rich people. They come to our country for boom boom. Isn't that a crime in their country? So why everyone say we are bad? No one make *farang* come here. No one tell *farang* go to hotel with girl. No one tell your boyfriend with camera to make this film. He decide. It's up to him."

Asanee does not respond and lights a cigarette, tilting her head, her forearm covering her exposed breasts, the elbow of her other hand resting on it. She lets the smoke curl from her nose and mouth.

"Denny, I've had enough of this shit. I want to stop," says Asanee, looking at the camera.

"Are you bored?" asks the male voice.

"I'm not in the mood," replies Asanee.

"What are you feeling?" asks the male voice.

"Hungry, tired, bored. I want to sleep. We've been doing this for hours. Can't we stop?" asks Asanee.

There is total silence. The *katoey* combs her long, black hair, pursing her lips in the mirror.

"You want to know how I do it?" asks Meow.

"Not really," says Asanee.

"You're lying," says Meow.

She cups her left breast in her hands and offers the upright nipple to the mirror. She makes another face, pouting lips, eyes half-closed in simulated pleasure. She turns back to face the camera. "Like this. With a little music and wine. I know enough English. Isn't that clear?"

The camera freezes on her. She slowly lowers her head, her long tongue darts from her mouth like a snake. She hisses, her tongue coming within striking distance of her own drug-painted nipple. "Then I say, oh, you look tired. Maybe you sleep a little first. No problem, Meow wait you. Listen to music. *Farang* have tired eyes like Asanee," says Meow, looking into the camera.

Asanee storms off camera, cursing, and there is a sound of a door slamming off camera.

"Your girlfriend go away. I think she's pissed off. But I think she come back. Because you tell her it just a movie about Meow that make her a little crazy. She want to be a star. All ladies want to be star like Madonna. When you a big star other lady jealous. They want to cut you. Make you pain."

"Why are they jealous?" asks the male voice.

"Movie star has a lot of money. When you have money you can do whatever you want. No one can stop you. You can make a man do this, and he do that. He have no choice. Because he know Meow have power. When you have power people fear you. I want people to fear me. When you make fear you can have anything you want. No one can say no to you. Everyone want you. So I go with many men. Like a movie star. I take whatever I want."

The voice-over resumes:

"Meow is one among a half-dozen *katoeys* enrolled in an English language school in Bangkok. She never feels guilty because her English is poor. During the day when she feels like it she goes to the school and studies English. If she improves her English, she feels more confident hustling men. But she is easily distracted. Her real interest lies in the fine art of tranquilizer concealment. Her knowledge of drugs has given her a high standard of living. She knows she could never work a regular job. Meow knows what it takes to gain the high ground. To make people fear her."

The film ends with Meow using a Q-tip on her nipple, pouting her lips and making long, sustained groans.

"When you have power people fear you. I want people to fear me. When you make fear you can have anything you want. No one can say no to you."

This last line of Meow's speech is repeated in an echo chamber.

"No one can say no to you."

3

DENNY Addison's documentary film about the *katoey* won an award at a small independent film festival in Mexico City. What his film failed to disclose in the credits was a piece of vital information: that the location of the shoot was Robert Tuttle's English language school in Bangkok. Meow was a student at the school. Asanee was Tuttle's daughter, and she had been living with Addison for nearly one year. And Addison had not received the permission of Tuttle or anyone else at the school to shoot this film. He talked Asanee into his scheme. On a Sunday afternoon, Tuttle turned up at Asanee's apartment.

"Denny's not here. He's out on location," said Asanee.

Tuttle sat on the sofa, holding a glass of cold water. On the table was a golden reel inscribed with Addison's name for best short black and white film—*The Unexpected Answer.* The gold paint had peeled off at the base of the statue, making the golden reel look like a derelict ferris wheel abandoned in a field of high weeds.

On the black walls of the apartment hung hand-painted wooden masks, movie posters, framed out-takes from several of Addison's documentary films, including one of Asanee stripped naked to the waist. Addison's collection of tank shell casings had paper flowers drooping over the side; his other war collections included military handbooks, flight manuals, flight helmets, shoulder holsters. Piled on the floor were art books about Asia and sex magazines from all over the world.

Tuttle stared at the photograph of Asanee on the wall.

"You don't mind that Addison shows this picture?" asked Tuttle.

"You asked me before."

"A spontaneous narrative image. That's Addison's explanation. I keep waiting for an answer that makes sense. All I see is a naked picture of my daughter," said Tuttle.

She rolled her eyes and tried to control her anger.

"Let's not get into this again. We just end up fighting about nothing. And we are never going to agree. I know you don't like Denny's work. But he thinks you're jealous of his art. His success."

Tuttle set down his glass of water.

"I don't understand how holding a camera on a *katoey* and his girlfriend and rapping about drugs, sex and rock 'n roll is art. He's done nothing original. He points a camera and calls himself an artist. He convinced you to strip before a camera."

"You wrote about me. And let the world know I worked as a bar girl. Wasn't that exploitation?"

"It was a story. Denny wouldn't know a story if it hit him in the face."

"He's interested in situations. Reality. Not fiction. People want to relate to the real world. Your generation just doesn't get it. Denny's art is for young people. Young people like to watch situations. They get off on seeing reactions to situations. Stories are old-fashioned. They don't entertain people. They're boring. He said, she said. Blah, blah. No one cares in the real world what they said or think. Denny says, they take too long to read. Reading is so artificial. You can't see the action, you only see words. Besides it's all made up in the writer's head. Denny says he doesn't know anyone who's into taking the time to read a whole book. Like he says, you have to remember someone did this on page 10 and something else on page 84. It's a drag. But when you film situations, just let it happen naturally, you don't get lost. You can see what's happening—the faces, the emotions—and hear the voices. You feel what you see. Not that Denny doesn't respect you. He's read some of your stories."

He was listening to his daughter begin sentence after sentence with "Denny says," and wondering if he could ever rescue his daughter from herself.

15

"Denny has it all figured out. Every answer," said Tuttle.

"That's not really fair. But he's right about one thing."

"Which is?"

"You've been in Thailand all these years and maybe you've stopped being curious. Going out and making new situations. Denny says the art is in selection. By choosing me, he made an artistic choice. You hang out at the school or at HQ. Fine. No big deal. But don't you ever want to try something new? Challenge yourself?"

4

A S Tuttle huddled in his kayak on the Nan River, tongues of fire streaked across the sky, winds boiled the surface of the water, spreading small white, wakes against the bow. Tuttle was unshaven, his nerves all jingling and jangling like an HQ regular who's gone riding bareback, rolling back afterwards as if he had ducked out of a cowboy gathering around a campfire; all worried about whether he had climbed onto an HIV-positive pony. Tuttle's face matched the grayish mask—the kind worn by cowboys who didn't saddle up the HQ Termites before climbing on and going hell bent for leather into the night. From his face, Tuttle might have been a john glossy-eyed after a long, wet suck on a tranquilized nipple. As he watched the flames, he wondered if he'd ever see Bangkok again. He closed his eyes, extinguishing the flame and in his mind's eye saw a group of regulars sitting with the hardcore at HQ. Sex had become an angry, nightmarish last round-up and HQ the last corral. The old-time riders let their booze talk about how they wanted to die with their boots on and their gun blazing. HQ sexual talk had gone wild west. The girls kept their cool; they were pros who showed a little pink gum, some uneven teeth, the color of their skin never turned gun-metal gray. *Katoeys* for instance—who were neither girls nor boys—maintained their color consistency even with sleep-inducing drugs smeared on their nipples. Gray was the color of desperation. No one ever sucked gray because it evoked a repellent death image.

Tuttle's legs had gone numb in his kayak, and he was thinking this was how death prepared the body for the final exit. Here was where it would end, he thought. Waiting to be killed and what thoughts were in his mind? Not self-pity, fear, or resignation, but Addison's damn film and the last wish for one more night at HQ. Addison had summed up the main message of the documentary as: Never stick anything foreign into your mouth without a lab report clearing the way. Life had come to this point where he was drawing on this kind of wisdom. A cold chill found the center of his back and hiked up to his neck like an insect with electric feet. Tuttle's legs felt cramped as if the blood no longer flown in or out; a couple of stumps attached to his ass.

And he watched the red sky shooting flames from another flare which flown thirty meters away on tiny parachutes. He was punchy from lack of sleep, feeling the kayak rocking, that cradle-like rock which made grown men turn green. A wimp, a nerd, a geek kind of guy whose face flashed neon gray before sloughing off into a greenish terror. He never figured himself for that kind of guy. But he had vomited in the bottom of his kayak and over the legs which had no feeling. Too little sleep, the flares, his near miss with eternity, his role in a killing, the image of the bands of *katoeys* setting up johns on Patpong. Who wouldn't barf up their guts and then some?

He wiped his mouth. His throat had gone dry and scratchy. He remembered the fear of being under fire from his days covering the Vietnam war. The first lesson of the battlefield was a simple one—any man who had another man killed instantly felt the addiction of slaughter; the feeling of supreme power to kill another person. But no one could have predicted until that moment whether he liked that feeling. Or if he felt at all. He was not in this league, he thought. When he shivered, his teeth bucked like a rodeo horse inside his mouth. The lines of the *katoey* in Addison's film flooded back into his mind:

"When you have power then people fear you. I want people to fear me. When you make fear you can have anything you want. No one can say no to you."

When he woke the darkness had returned to the sky; a flat, seamless blackness. It was the river which was on fire. A ring of fire bouncing on the water's surface. The river pirates had returned with kerosene. No more than twenty meters from his kayak a wall of flames burnt. He heard the pirates' voices far off, the firing of their M-16s in the reeds, then near, and then they had gone again, laughing and joking. As if the flames had allowed them to recover some lost dignity. He froze, sitting motionless as the heat of a fire made him sweat. Tuttle sat startled, his face wet, thinking about the dead man in Bangkok as he paddled. He clapped his hands. An hour passed as he sat under his poncho, slipping in and out of sleep, the smell of fire in his nostrils. He almost tipped the kayak over. Half-crouching, he pulled back his poncho, clapping and shaking his hands as a light streak, a razor-thin, crooked smile ran like a fault line along the horizon then vanished in fog.

"Fuck you and your documentary situations, Denny Addison," he screamed, and then collapsed, hitting his head on the kayak. He lay sprawled out, blood spilling from a gash in his head. He listened to the water against the kayak, feeling himself breathing and feeling numb. He inched forward, dipping his hands into the river and splashing his face. He saw his blood.

"I'm here," he shouted, the water and blood dripping from his chin.

He wished the pirates would return. Let them do what they had set out to do. Select the situation. Finish it. But the river pirates had gone and there was no reply to his anguished cry.

As hard as Tuttle tried as the first dawn cracked the water surface with light, he could find no color on his hands. He knew what he felt. He shoved his arms up to the elbow in the river. He held them under water, clutching his hands into fists, releasing them. Would they ever feel clean again? This time as he pulled his dripping arms from the Nan, his red-rimmed eyes saw flesh but felt the presence of fresh blood.

With wet fingers wrapped around the wooden paddle, he squeezed down hard, shutting off his own blood, then he pulled the tip of the paddle through the shimmering water. He felt a chill start at his shoulders and run down his back until the shiver bunched him up, doubling him over on his kayak. He hadn't slept in forty-eight hours. He had prize-fighter eyes, slits which blinked as if the next punch was on its way. He wanted to be home. The Nan River had claimed him, rocking and spraying him. For several days he had been alone on the river, his paddle dipping below the surface. He had disappeared from Bangkok. Alone on the river he glided, moving at his own speed and under his own power. His journey was disrupted by the pirate attack, the fire on the water, his cracked skull. He laid his paddle across the kayak and waited. He saw—or thought he saw—an object, a stone, and then another, floating in his wake. An hallucination, he thought. His eyes no longer completely shut or opened; he had reptile-like lidless eyes. He leaned forward in his boat. "What is this?" he thought. And then, "Why is this happening to me?" The two questions every journey throws up without any possibility of answer.

Objects moved over the surface of the water towards him; studded round, smooth objects bobbing on the surface of the river. He thought the fire had unleashed debris. A fine morning mist filtered the light on the river, turning water and sky into a sheen of crystal overhanging the horizon. He had the feeling of vertigo; someone who had lost his direction, and had been set adrift along an axis without any reference to north or south, or up and down.

He glanced at the shoreline where the shadows of thick palm trees and reeds were swallowed in shadows and mist. He paddled again, this time slowly, looking for shelter, watching and listening, as if searching for an edge. The tip of the paddle struck one of the floating objects. His first reaction was disbelief: stones don't float. He discounted what his eyes reported as floating. He told himself the stones were an illusion created from water, mist, and light on a mind numbed after hours of paddling. He thought back to the day before in a dreamy replay: picking up in his binnoculars again the two Thais in singlets and shorts who had rifles—M-16s—and ammo belts hooked over the shoulder. They'd gave chase in an old boat with a small outboard engine leaving a trail of dirty blue smoke, closing in from about two hundred meters behind his kayak. He remembered how the sudden terror had charged him as he paddled, the crack of the rounds, the awful splash of water ten meters behind and to his left. What an irony, he had thought. He had fled from Dee's apartment to the river. Travel allowed him to shed one identity in order to find another. Being fired upon was the best reason why people rarely abandoned their comforts. Asanee had been right about that much—even though most of what she had said had sounded like something learned from Addison—Tuttle had fallen into a routine life.

As he followed a bend in the river, he had enough of a lead to duck out of sight and lose the pirates. His refuge was near a bank covered with a long bed of heavy reeds as high as elephant grass. They could have searched for days in those weeds and never have found him. The pirates had raised their rifles and pointed flashlights along the shore. Twice, three times they fired randomly into the shadows. This was gunfire born of frustration and anger. They cursed him in Thai. After an exhausting hour or so of cutting through the weeds the pirates left.

The morning after pirates had tried to kill him, Tuttle's kayak drifted in thick weeds. He blinked hard, realizing he had survived; he awoke as if he had been dreaming of death and stones which floated. He bent down and fumbled among the stones, found one and lobbed it like a baseball. It struck the surface of the water and disappeared for a second before it returned. It floated. He stared at it as if he could through force of will compel the stones to sink to the bottom of the river. "Floating stones," he cried out. This was insane. But as he looked around his kayak, he saw more floating stones bobbing along the surface. It was as if he had entered another universe where the ordinary rules of physics had been altered. For several kilometers, he touched the floating stones with the tip of his paddle. Finally, he leaned over the side of the kayak and plucked another one of the stones from the warm water. After several hours, he had determined to fill the bottom of his kayak with stones. He turned one of the objects over in his hand, dropped it on the pile, examined another and for the rest of the day he continued to marvel at this inexplicable act of nature. He thought how he would explain this phenomenon to his friends and colleagues in Bangkok. At first, they would laugh at him. But he had the proof, he thought, looking down at the oyster-shell-like objects.

Floating stones. He had been dreaming, but this wasn't a dream. Or was it? Was he really dead and this was another place? He pinched his hand and felt the pain. He had recovered enough samples to give to many people. In his mind, Tuttle compiled a list of places to which he would send a sample—international institutes, research labs, famous universities, and later, he dreamed about the TV coverage, seminars, panel discussions and scientific papers which would follow. So much for Addison and his documentary film about *katoeys*; he had an image that had never been seen before anywhere. He would be at the center of the controversy as the discoverer of stones which floated on water. As he handled the floating stones, Tuttle thought of Harry Purcell, whose gun- running family had supplied the Spanish Conquistador Hernan Cortez, Purcell and his tale of how Montezuma had been dispatched with a stone hitting his head. In 1519, Cortez wrote in a dispatch to the King and Pope that three days and nights passed before Montezuma died. What would Purcell make of this kind of stone? Suddenly he wished Harry Purcell, who had suggested the trip on the Nan River, had joined him on the journey.

Tuttle navigated his kayak toward signs of a village along the bank of the river. A column of smoke rose from behind a thick wall of palms. The villagers were burning one of their dead. A young boy in shorts watched him from the bank, then ran away to the village and spread the alarm.

"*Farang, farang, farang*," the boy cried.

"*Khon* Thai, *khon* Thai, *khon* Thai," shouted Tuttle in return.

The boy looked stunned. It was one thing to call a *farang* a *farang* but a *farang* calling a Thai a Thai was something never imagined possible. The *farang* must have understood his words. His face went red and he raced away, tucking, twisting, and finally disappearing in the foliage.

He reappeared ten minutes later in the company of the headman and several curious village elders. The boy pointed at him. This was the chance for a trial run, Tuttle thought. The people who lived along the Nan River would be the first to witness his "floating stone" presentation. He had rehearsed what he would say before the cameras for one day and night. Only there was no one with a camera along this stretch of the river. After dinner, as they sat around a fire which burnt in one corner of the headman's bamboo hut, Tuttle pulled a stone from his pocket. He held it out as a gift. A show of gratitude to his host who had offered him food, shelter, and conversation. Why should he reserve the floating stones only for the multi-degreed people in black robes? Tuttle asked for a bowl of water which the headman's daughter duly brought. She set it in front of Tuttle. He waited until all eyes inside the hut had focused upon him. Only then did he delicately lower the stone into the bowl. He held his breath but it didn't sink; just like the stones on the river this stone floated in the bowl.

The villagers did not gasp in disbelief, register any panic, as their eyes focused on the stone. In such a remote village, Tuttle doubted that even the elders had ever seen more than a handful of white faces. The villagers examined his gift, then looked up at Tuttle without betraying any hint of surprise or fear. Tuttle turned the stone over. Still this caused no reaction. They didn't seem to get the significance of what he was trying to show them. Several more moments passed.

He decided upon another demonstration. Turning back to the bowl, he dropped one of the objects into the water.

"It floats," he said. "The stone I dropped into the bowl did not sink. You understand? The stone is floating like a boat."

They stared at the bowl and then at Tuttle, talking among themselves.

"You can touch it. It won't hurt you," he said, passing several of his finds to the villagers.

The villagers now looked at one another, passing the floating stones along the line, when the first laugh began as a lone rifle shot. Soon the room erupted like a firing range in an uproar of wild, uncontrolled laughter. The headman's mouth spread open into a nervous smile as he leaned over and poked the object with his finger. The headman was the host; this was his hut, and he, above all, owed Tuttle as the guest a degree of respect; but cultural duty was insufficient to suppress the laughter which shook the headman's body and turned his face red. The blue tattooed tiger on the headman's chest appeared to be running as the headman's chest rolled with waves of laughter. Everyone in the hut doubled over in laughter, their faces blood red. Tuttle watched as all around him dissolved into breathless laughter. He stood grimly clutching his floating stones. Each time villagers saw Tuttle's perplexed, solemn expression they again relapsed into laughter until not one of them was able to catch his breath and tears streamed down his cheeks. Tuttle avoided their faces, and stared at his feet; he didn't know what to say. He waited until the headman caught his breath and then asked him a question.

"Why does the floating stone cause so much laughter?" asked Tuttle.

The headman wiped the tears from his eyes.

"Because you call them floating stones," said the headman, a hiccup of a laugh belched up from his belly.

Robert Tuttle thought he had done a bad job of translation.

"How would you call them?" asked Tuttle.

The headman stared at a floating stone in the bowl and picked it up with his fingers. He held it and continued to stare at Tuttle.

"Not stones," said the headman.

Tuttle took the object from the headman's fingers.

"Then what are they?"

"Cremated bones. Someone die. The family have the bones burnt. They throw the bones in the river. Finished."

The story the headman told him was a relatively straightforward one. After a cremation in a village the remains of the deceased were tossed into the river. The answer as to what lay in the bottom of Tuttle's kayak was not what he had expected. He had collected the scattered bones of the dead. For miles he had fished out the floating stones, thinking how he would challenge man's conceit that gravity, nature, and existence could be fully understood. Robert Tuttle smiled at the mess of bones. He had been suckered in like a Patpong tourist on a *katoey*'s tranquilizer-laced nipple. He understood that he had not seen or understood anything. The world flipped over from levels of understanding to levels of ignorance.

So much had changed in a week. He was on the river paddling a kayak. Pirates had come within a few meters of killing him. Then he sat in a bamboo hut, smiling, showing his teeth, and passing to a headman his discovery of floating stones. As the headman flashed a blue-gummed smile, Tuttle tuned in his shortwave radio to the BBC World News. An English voice read the news. He caught the word—Bangkok. The military had moved against demonstrators. Bangkok was in chaos. He listened, not moving, not breathing, as the news described the death toll among the civilians. He worried about Asanee, his daughter; she would have been at the huge open grounds near the Grand Palace which bore the name of Sanam Luang—here was the flashpoint where troops, according to the BBC, in full battle dress, had opened fire. First the troops had fired into the sky, shooting at the stars, and then suddenly they lowered their weapons and took aim at the crowd. All he had to clasp onto—these objects of potential fame—had turned out to be human remains. And as the laughter from the headman and his cronies died down, Tuttle realized that all he had were these floating stones in a sea of death rising around him on every side.

5

Tuttle had followed a watery trail of death. The bones had followed him on the Nan River. He stood beside his beached kayak and stared at the bottom at the large catch which had been destined to change his life. Tuttle laughed. What if the river pirates had captured a *farang* who was a bone stealer? Would they have fled in fear or killed him as they had planned? Had the pirates planned as carefully as he had, then he would be dead, he thought, as one by one he tossed the bones into the river, and watched them bobbing in the eddies.

The bone fragments had been transformed in fire into objects that appeared to be pitted gray stones with white sparkling pinpoints of light. The smooth shards were unlike anything he had imagined as the skeletal form upon which human beings were hung or as the final remains left after the flesh had departed. His kayak contained the residue of life; once the bones had been attached to flesh, blood, organs, and had experienced pain, pleasure, regret, and had recalled, joked, hated, loved, wept and fucked. What survived of that experience, then, if all these narrative elements had become detached from life? Such experiences, like heirlooms, passed into living people's imagination and memory.

Harry Purcell—a hardcore HQ cowboy of a time before bare-back riding became a game of Russian roulette—believed the HQ species of male was hot-wired for danger and high-risk bucking horses. They sat around the table listening to the jukebox and exchanged cigarettes, ideas, beer, theories, whores and concepts such as whether the short-time Hotel Playgirl on Soi 11 had better towel service and mirrors than the Happy Day which was hidden away on a lane off Soi 31.

Tuttle threw the cremated bones into the river and felt a shudder of horror—he thought of that instant each time he walked into his daughter's apartment and saw the naked picture Denny Addison hung on the wall. One of the flat bones skipped over the water three times, leaving little ripples. A few feet behind him some villagers squatted in the dirt watching him skip bones across the river. He felt their presence. He lobbed another smooth bone into the river and watched the ripple spread out. Tuttle told himself sooner or later he would find the strike zone. Only a few more bones were left in the boat. One of the villagers slid down to the bank and watched this World Series close-up. One villager handed Tuttle a half-empty bottle of pure white home-brewed whiskey. Tuttle took a drink, wiped his mouth. The liquor burnt all the way down his throat. He thanked the villager, he pretended to shake off two, three signals from the invisible catcher, then wound up and drilled his last bone.

"Home run," he said to himself.

He did a little dance on the river bank. The villagers laughed and clapped, but some looked fearful and ran away, thinking Tuttle was drunk from the home brew. Only Tuttle wasn't drunk. The game was over.

"Why are you afraid?" asked Tuttle.

One of the villagers who didn't run, a boy in a dirty T-shirt and shorts, told him, "This place here has a curse." The boy tapped the dirt with his hands.

"I landed on a cursed place?" asked Tuttle.

The boy smiled at him and nodded.

"And I should be afraid?"

Again the boy nodded.

"Tell me about the curse," said Tuttle.

The boy told him the story of Daeng, a village girl who had once been attacked by a dog on the very spot. When he talked with the old woman who cried hot tears about the whereabouts of her daughter Daeng and confirmed the curse, he knew his journey had been rewarded with a purpose. Here was a gap in the continuity of the life of this old woman and the village; and Tuttle got it into his head that he could find a way to repair what had been broken.

Tuttle climbed into his kayak and with the paddle pushed away from the muddy bank. Not long after, his kayak caught up with the human flotsam he had thrown from the river bank. His paddle dragged through a cluster of the bones. It made a weird knocking noise, like someone clicking their tongue in disapproval. How many dead had surrounded his kayak? He marveled as he looked around. His kayak was encircled by floating bones. He pulled his paddle clacked against them in the water, laid it across his kayak. Some village boys ran along the bank, shouting, *farang, farang.* The old woman struggled to keep up with the boys, she ran flat footed, running with her dress hiked up to her knees. She started to fall behind, she kicked the dust with her foot, cupped her hands around her old cracked lips and cried,

"Find my Daeng, *farang*," she cried. Then she was out of sight as his kayak followed a bend in the river.

Half an hour downstream, he switched on the shortwave. The bone escort had broken up, vanished. He sought comfort from the sound of an English voice broadcasting the news from London.

"This is the world news," said the voice.

Top billing was killing in the streets of Bangkok.

He turned up the volume. More than bareback riders were at risk; the city had exploded.

An unexpected answer to the request for the generals to step aside. Who would have expected the military to be killing demonstrators in Bangkok? Expectations become warped with questions and answers, he thought. He had not expected the Army to open fire on the demonstrators. This was madness. There were no details. No names of those who had been killed. He listened closely, moving the shortwave radio to his ear. He had picked up a familiar voice—George Snow who was reporting from the Royal Hotel. Snow was in a room overlooking the Paan Fah Bridge. This was a live feed to the BBC half way around the world. How had Snow ever in a zillion years landed this with the BBC? In the background was the akkkakkk of automatic gunfire.

"Soldiers have once again opened up on demonstrators in Bangkok. We have no confirmed figures. The number of killed and injured appears substantial. From what this reporter can see—"Akkkkakkkk. "Shit. Sorry about that. Someone put holes in my wallpaper. The soldiers are firing directly into the crowds outside the Royal Hotel. I have just had an unconfirmed report that the numbers of dead and wounded are running into the scores. Maybe the hundreds. This is George Snow, reporting from the Thai capital, Bangkok."

Snow was back in Bangkok and on the air. Getting himself on the BBC would make him insufferable for months. The BBC report ended. Why end? He was in the middle of nowhere. Didn't the fucking Brits in London understand that the rest of the world news didn't matter? Why had they cut off Snow? Why not let him continue to report until . . . until Tuttle was back in Bangkok? Until he could confirm what had gone wrong in a street demonstration at Sanam Luang—trace the path of the soldiers' bullets. File a report on that fraction of a second between the pull of the trigger and passage of life irrevocably into death.

6

As the late afternoon sky cooled to a burnished copper, Tuttle was on the highway with his gear, hitching a ride back to Bangkok. A ten-wheel truck pulled to a stop and he climbed in. The driver was wild-eyed on Captagon—"Dr. Cap"—and planned to drive non-stop until he reached the capital. Half an hour later, Tuttle dozed in and out of sleep. In his dream he saw Harry Purcell and Denny Addison squatting, as the villagers had done earlier that day. Addison was filming Tuttle with his kayak stuffed with floating bones. Harry was joking, drinking and glancing down at him. Tuttle pulled himself up on one elbow and inched closer to listen to their conversation. Harry was explaining something in a hushed tone. Putting the shortwave radio next to his ear, Tuttle could hear Snow reading a script written by Harry Purcell.

"Cortez surveyed the vast salt lake and everywhere he looked he saw the floating bodies of the Aztecs who had tried to escape the slaughter. The Aztec shamans had read omens before Cortez arrived. The water in the rivers had boiled. Perhaps what they had seen was the salt lake boiling with the bodies of their own people. Rivers, lakes, and oceans boiling with the dead. The omen surfaced once again . . . all seers will remember the Aztec's prediction about the invasion of Mexico and into the East—the omen predicted an invasion of a new force of ideas into Thailand. Bodies will again be buried in water."

Twelve hours later, it was pitch dark outside when Tuttle woke from the dream, and looked out the window. Lights along the highway streaked into a patchy blur as the truck hurtled at great speed.

Insects were atomized into blood dots with antennae smashed on the windshield. Dr. Cap had kept the driver wired high. His eyes were wide open, the whites having turned yellowish, his hands a little shaky on the wheel but this went with the territory where Dr. Cap worked his magic. He stared through the blood. Dr. Cap pushed the driver's foot hard on the gas pedal, jamming it flush to the floor for hours and hours. Until they had reached the outskirts of Bangkok, where the driver eased up on the gas. Tuttle sat upright, yawning, and switched on the shortwave radio; the newscast reported more than twenty demonstrators had been killed the night before in Bangkok. The worst of not knowing was imagining where and how Asanee must have spent the night. Christ, she would have made a point of being at the head of the killing line. Why couldn't his own daughter be more like Meow the *katoey*? Rub her nipples with powerful drugs, go for personal gain, leave the politics of dying to the idealists.

The headman had said crazy things. One or two things had stuck in his memory as he returned to the river—his kayak had been filled with the spirits of the dead. This was an omen, the headman had said. Omens brought dreams, and they brought fresh death. The young boy said he had landed on a cursed spot. The headman was no longer laughing. The bones in the mind of the headman were living entities. They had sought out Tuttle for a reason. What reason? That was for Tuttle to discover on his return to Bangkok. The unexpected answer was awaiting him in HQ where the working girls of the night were taking a political stand. Or so one or two said.

For a purple an HQ girl would oblige you and read any script you wanted to hear about any subject you held dear. For a few moments he forgot about the young runaway from the village—Daeng, the girl with the half-moon scar, the girl who had been connected to the curse on the village river bank.

7

Tuttle rolled down his window. The night air was muggy, thick with an organic, rancid, decaying smell and as hopeless as a dead man's promise to pay his debts. Bangkok streets were stripped clean of the great night throng of bodies; nothing much moved along the deserted road as the truck entered the city. He rolled the window back up and watched the empty, dark streets. Traffic lights had been broken, and glass was scattered across the streets. The truck rumbled down the ramp off the Expressway, and the headlights swept over the sign marking the Din Daeng exit. There was a strange quietness. The metal gates of the shop houses had been pulled down; behind the padlocked gates, people continued their uninterrupted existence of eating, sleeping, fucking, complaining and dying. They huddled together, waiting for the storm to pass. Then Tuttle saw the first sign of violence in the shadows—smashed public call boxes the umbilical phone-cords coiled on to the pavement. Few people were on the street; those he saw walked quickly, turning around, looking for someone following. The buses, taxis, and tuk-tuks had been swallowed up by forces unseen and unheard; all that remained was the street litter—suggesting people had come and gone. The faces he saw were drawn, tense; the land of smiles had disappeared, and its place was a strangely new expression—faces of fear, faces of the frightened and confused.

There was a distant sound of gunfire and the driver stopped his truck and told Tuttle he was turning back. Dr. Cap had made the driver edgy, his Adam's apple bobbing up and down in his throat.

Heading back upcountry was the driver's instinct; at least in the country, you knew who wanted to kill you and why. The driver had been listening to the Thai radio; the military radio station said that Bangkok was safe, the Army was in control, and that a few troublemakers causing the disturbance would soon be apprehended. It didn't look that way from the truck. "Bangkok has gone mad," said the driver, as they watched a pick-up packed with plainclothes men open fire on a Honda motorcycle. Tuttle thought this was the most sane statement the driver had made during the entire journey.

The radio announced a curfew. Anyone found on the street would be considered hostile and all means would be used to stop such a person.

The driver pulled over to the curb, reached over and opened the door.

"This is where I get out, I guess," he said to the driver, offering him money. The driver looked terrified, shook his head, and popped another Dr. Cap before he reached over and slammed the door. Tuttle, with a five-hundred-baht note stuffed in his hand, watched as the large truck make a ten-point U-turn, almost tipping over. Then the shattering crunch of gears, as the truck accelerated down the street.

The killing had not stopped as Tuttle walked along streets too silent and empty of people. As he approached the Soi Asoke intersection, another pick-up truck with men in the back opened fire on a motorcycle rider. M-16s sounded from his left. Several rounds whizzed overhead. He heard the roar of an unmuffed motorcycle at full throttle. He saw the headlights of a pick-up, and then the driver gunned it through the intersection. Muzzle flashes from the M-16s streaked through the sky. He thought about the fire on the river. An omen. The pick-up vanished. It was over in an instant. Had any of the bullets found the target? He would never know, he thought, as he walked down Sukhumvit Road. He had decided to seek refuge at HQ. This was the place where information could be obtained; the hardcore would have heard some news of the true status. All the lights had been broken at Asoke. The police booth had been gutted and blackened by flames. The distant sound of gunfire was easily within earshot as he ran across Asoke. He wished his daughter was as near. He quickened his step. He had come back from a river of floating stones to a city filled with violent death.

A few taxis were parked in the alley behind HQ. There were few people waiting for the dawn. The lights from the hotel behind disclosed an empty, narrow passage devoid of life. The hardcore called it the "Alley of Revenge." Personal revenge was part of HQ life, part of the grand scheme of things. An HQ girl was rumored once or twice to have stuck a knife into the guts of a middle-aged *farang*, then twisted the blade; it was the twisting part which rang true. Revenge waited for a *farang* who violated the hardcore cardinal rule—never promise love in a moment of passion, and then take another girl the following night. The violation caused a girl's face to shatter into a thousand pieces and there was only one way to recover that face. . . . Every hardcore knew the outer limits, beyond which the journey down the alley to HQ was his trip to the gallows, a condemned man with no right of appeal. It would be over before he knew what or why. But she would make certain that he knew who.

It was after five in the morning when Tuttle passed through the back entrance of HQ. Several girls were putting on make-up before the cracked mirrors. On their right a couple of drunks, propped up with one arm pushed against the yellow tiled wall, staggered as they pissed into ancient stalls, squinting at old, faded oil company decals, and talking in low tones about spending the night holed up in HQ.

One of the girls spotted him in the mirror. She dropped the bar of soap in the sink. She looked surprised, all nerves as she held her wet hands up in a *wai*, they dripped water onto the floor.

"Papa, we think you dead."

Her friend, smoking a cigarette, looked more together. "No one see you in a long time. We think maybe the Army kill you dead. Bang, bang," she laughed, her red mouth open in the mirror.

This was HQ. One girl gave the traditional *wai*; the other had given him the verbal bird.

Tuttle, who fitted the HQ hardcore profile, had been absent from the scene for months. Denny Addison had started the Papa business. Tuttle despaired of the fact that Addison had turned him into an HQ clown with a red nose, white face, bushy eyebrows—Addison was living with his daughter, exploiting her, flashing her nude photos on the walls of their apartment. He had consigned Tuttle's writing to the ash heap of history, and converted Tuttle into a father figure for the working girls. The HQ girls had started to call Tuttle, "Papa." They giggled, turned coy, and ran away laughing. Asanee said it had nothing to do with Denny—defending him as always—that being called Papa was revenge on the hardcore by the new generation. One night strolling down the alley, the HQ girls flipped in their image perception of him.

"A spontaneous narrative shift," as Addison called it. One night you strolled through the back entrance of HQ, a desirable customer, a young man, and the next night lightning struck, the image changed, the situation in which they saw the man altered irreversibly, converting him into that most dreaded of HQ categories. He had become one of the "old guys."

He had been tagged as he passed the sink, "Papa Tuttle." The words knocked Tuttle off his feet. His status was destroyed not only with the girls but inside his own perception about his place inside the ring of space time.

"Papa Tuttle," another girl said at the stairs, pulling at his arm. "I'm scared, Papa."

"Everyone's scared, Lek," he said, giving her a brief hug.

"*Sia jai*, Papa Tuttle," said another girl, threading her arm through Tuttle's. Little girls with sad hearts and smiling faces. They were sorry he had become old so suddenly. Just the other day, he was Tuttle, the young man coming down the stairs. . . . Now the Army was killing people in the streets. Everyone and everything had been turned upside down. Tuttle had been a center of gravity at HQ, he had gone missing in action, and he had become an old man. Yeah, the HQ girls huddled in a terrified clump, clinging to each other. They didn't care who was right or wrong; it didn't matter, such distinctions never had any meaning to lose. They lived from night to night, flashing their smiles, holding in their rage, hopelessness, and depression; and working the floor, hoping to latch onto a romantic john, one who believed the girl actually liked his personality, charm, jokes, and good looks. It wasn't difficult for the girls to exploit such men. Tuttle had seen the scene played out hundreds of times. But on many nights no such johns were around. The HQ girls nervously circled around the tables of hardcores. Men they knew. And far worse, men who knew the score. These *farang* bargained the fee for sex, and ordered off the old-hand sex menu in advance of taking the girl. The hardcore had become hardcore once he could no longer be exploited by love or sentiment. A hardcore was a person cured of romance.

A constellation of forces had swept through all of Tuttle's relationships and through Thailand, as he had paddled down the Nan River, packed up his kayak, and hitched a ride back to the city. The city had changed. Gunfire gave a new weight to the night. He looked around the nearly filled room. Sex was not on anyone's mind. This was no happy homecoming. No one at HQ had seen Asanee or her friends. He didn't know if she was alive or dead. Or if some soldier was riding her bareback before firing a round into her head. He wanted to find his daughter and tell her about the floating stones. She would laugh with him and the world would once again come right.

"You know a girl from Nan named Daeng?" he asked one of the old crones, who hustled young girls from the bench near the main door.

She smiled, "Her face cut here?" She drew a half-moon-shaped scar on her right cheek.

That was her. And the old crone told Tuttle the story of how she had left HQ the night before. It seems Snow had checked into HQ briefly, and found the old crone who just happened to have a new girl she was breaking into the business. The new girl's name was Daeng. Snow had asked the old crone, "Short-time or all night?" and the old crone had whispered something into Daeng's ear, and she had blushed. The regular had asked Snow how much he was going to pay for a fresh girl.

"The usual purple plus taxi fare."

"She's a new girl," the old crone had said.

"She had a kid? I don't want her taking off her clothes and finding her skin looks like it's been transplanted with corduroy."

The old crone had said, "She no have baby."

Daeng had said nothing, looking away at the floor. It was the same old script old crones taught the new girls.

"Okay, okay. Then I'll keep her until the shooting stops. Think she can handle that?"

The old crone hadn't answered immediately. This was a line she hadn't heard before; what did it mean, until the shooting stops? Anyway Daeng was warming up to Snow who had worked his hand onto her knee under the table. A fresh girl, a new girl never warmed up with a knee massage; they recoiled in fear and embarrassment. "Free room and board," said Snow. "Grass and rock 'n roll. What else does a girl want?"

Snow, who had perfected a professional stringer's instinct for knowing when and where world-class Asian massacres were about to happen, had returned from America. Snow was reporting live from the site of the slaughtering outside the Royal Hotel. And his HQ Termite, Daeng, was curled up under the sheets, crying. She claimed to have seen a ghost. She refused to get out of bed and get dressed.

"A ghost, hey?"

"*Farang* ghost," sobbed Daeng.

"*Farang* ghost, huh? Why not a coke, maybe a big, fat hamburger from room service?"

Intense bursts of gunfire raked the air on Rachadamnoen Avenue. Snow crouched near the window, watching the action below. He looked back at Daeng, who lay completely covered in the white sheet.

"Hey, don't take it personal. The soldiers ain't necessarily shooting at you," he said.

She didn't take this as comfort and her silent crying turned into a wail.

"You don't believe Daeng," she said, referring to herself in the third person like most bar girls.

"Forget about ghosts. Think like a normal HQ girl; about going home," said Snow. "Your mother and father, and brothers and sisters. Everyone happy in Daeng's village, they are all waiting to see you."

It didn't work. She was a strange girl, thought Snow. What Snow didn't know was that Crosby, a friend from the old days of teaching English at Tuttle's school, another HQ regular who cruised the fast lane, had arrived from England the week the Army had marched in the street and started shooting people who were claiming they knew better than the Army the meaning of democracy. It was a hell'va a thing to die for in the streets of Bangkok, Snow thought. But man, what a story. And the bucks from filing. The BBC didn't pay peanuts. And he was filing like crazy to every bureau, radio and TV station he had ever strung for.

The Thai political troubles had flushed out Snow, and then Crosby; brought them back, as if they could sense the doom, smell the blood before it was let, and the fear and hopelessness of those who stayed in the streets after curfew, as if they knew the stakes of those willing to fight M-16s with their bare hands. There were not a lot of regulars in the crowd of newcomers who circled around HQ. Then Tuttle appeared out of nowhere and a couple of HQ girls dragged him by the arms over to their corner booth. Half a dozen were squeezed like spiders inside the booth; several of the girls were already drunk on Mekong. Their eyes a filmy yellow, they threw back their heads and laughed. One hiked up her dress and showed her product. Another grabbed at her crotch and squealed with laughter. It was early in the evening at HQ and already a booth of girls were all wet mouths and dry eyes, engines going full throttle and ready to ride.

Tuttle spotted a mobile phone on the table.

"Where did this come from?" asked Tuttle.

"Papa, don't ask."

"I want to phone a friend," said Tuttle.

Toom, a girl from the old days, a cigarette hanging from her mouth, pushed the phone across the table.

"You buy me a beer."

"I buy you all a beer. Just one thing." He let his voice trail off.

"Who you wanna take tonight?" asked one of the girls. She was heading straight to the price of the round of beers; only she got her price wrong. "Maybe Oh, or Joy, or Dee? Who you think is a sexy girl?"

"Stop calling me Papa," said Tuttle.

Using the mobile phone, he punched in the number of the Royal Hotel. The girls pawed at him. One licked his earlobe, leaving a trace of Mekong. The hotel line was busy the first two dozen times, and then, finally he connected. No surprise. Everyone in the Royal Hotel was filing like bandits. Story after story was going out across the world. The hotel switchboard operator put him through to Snow's room as if the gunfire in the distance did not exist.

"Hey, what's happenin', man?" asked Snow, hearing Tuttle's voice on the other end of the line.

"That's what I want to know," said Tuttle. "And have you seen Asanee?"

"Haven't seen her. But I've not been lookin'. I kinda hope she's not out there tonight. You hear the M-16s?"

The gunfire rumbled over the crackling line. And, above the gunfire, Tuttle heard the terrified cries of the HQ girl. Snow glanced over at the girl whose scream was hardly dented by the pillow she pulled down over her head.

"Why do I always pick screamers?" asked Snow, watching her squirming under the sheet.

"What are you doing to her?" asked Tuttle.

"Not as much as I would like. An HQer and she doesn't like the gunfire. Can't say I blame her."

"Can I to talk to Daeng?" asked Tuttle.

His question caught Snow off guard.

"Hey, man, what's this about? How did you know her name? And don't tell me you took her in '78," said Snow

A loud sound of banging on the door drowned out his voice.

"What's the problem?" asked Tuttle.

"Shit, it's not room service," said Snow.

The loud, thwacking sound which earlier had been body pumped against body had become boots kicking in the door. The sound carried through Tuttle's mobile phone. Then muffled, angry Thai voices. Men with strident voices—the voice which raises the hair on the back on your neck—shouted orders. An officer walked over to the bed and ripped away the sheets. Daeng, curled naked in the fetal position, eyes squeezed, arms wrapped around her breasts, resumed her wailing. For Snow it was difficult to remember how her body had swelled with intense passion; but sexual passion had collapsed, bled away and she had become like some poor animal led on a rope to the slaughterhouse. He thought how pitiful and small she had become. To see her lying on the bed as if she had been broken, bent, subject to a terror eating away until she could only whimper. This girl who had sold her womb was now looking for a womb to crawl into and leave this world not as a corpse but as a fetus.

One of the soldiers knocked the phone away from Snow and shoved him against the wall.

"Hey, man, what's the problem? I'm press. I'm a journalist. You want to see my press card? And that's my wife you are abusing. Leave her alone or. . . .". The soldiers paid no attention to Snow and he didn't know what kind of threat would attract their interest. Under the circumstances, the answer was probably none. Fear was on their side and not his. He leaned around one of the soldiers and picked up the phone.

Tuttle was screaming into his ear. Snow put the phone to his ear and listened. "What are they doing, Snow?" But he received no reply; Snow couldn't think what to say to Tuttle. So he kept on listening to Tuttle's frantic pleas for information while the soldiers wrapped his HQ sweetheart in a sheet and passed her out the door like laundry.

"She's not registered in this room," said the officer, looking through her wallet and pulling out her papers. "What's your wife's name?" he asked in a firm, clear voice that comes with being heavily armed and with the right to use force. He stared at Snow as he looked up from the house registration paper.

"Daeng," said Snow.

"And her family name?"

Snow grinned. "So I lied. We are just going steady."

"Press card," snapped the officer. "Give me your press card."

The grin came off Snow's face and he spoke into the phone while looking at the officer. "Damn, wouldn't you know it. My press card expired. I'm renewing it tomorrow. You can verify me with my boss. He's at the BBC in London. Be there or be square, as my boss likes to say."

Snow handed the officer the phone. He pressed it to his ear and listened, not once taking his eyes off Snow. Two of his soldiers stood in the doorway. Daeng had vanished.

"Touch a hair on his head and the British marines will shoot your ass," said Tuttle.

The Thai officer slammed down the phone and stared at Snow. Something about the officer's eyes Snow couldn't read; searching eyes, looking for a way to say something that just couldn't be placed into words.

"Didn't buy it, huh?" asked Snow.

"You've seen what's happening outside. Tell the world what's happening in Bangkok. You must help us. Because journalists are all we've got. You understand?" asked the officer.

"I'll do my job," said Snow, and flipped the officer a salute, saying to himself, "Man, why am I saluting this guy?"

The officer nodded, turned and walked through the door with his men one step behind. Snow heard the soldiers knocking on the door to the room next to his.

"Fuck me," murmured Snow. "Who would have figured it?"

8

Farangs straggled into HQ looking pale, scared out of their minds. They were seeking the comfort of strangers on a night of death; they ordered drinks at the bar and found empty spaces at the booths and tables. None of the girls complained they hadn't been taken out for a short time. No one wanted to leave the scene. One of the few times in HQ history when HQ girls and customers found fear of death had blotted out the usual fears attending a commercial sexual transaction. They were witness to an original story, a secret story, the real story of death of people just like themselves. Bangkok had become a war scene and rife with rumors. Some units of the Navy were about to launch a counter-coup. Elements of military units were marching into Bangkok from the North, and then from the South. Some had reached Soi 71. Rumors of war pushed out rumors of sex.

The usual suspects were in town for the show. Guys like Snow and Crosby, who flown in before the first shots were fired, would have come anyway; they had a sixth sense about war, and like a rainmaker knew within twenty-four hours when the first showers would fall—metal showers of bullets, aimed head-high, and they knew that they would survive as they always had done in the past. They believed they were immortal. That was a mistake many had made rushing the Army units.

Harry Purcell came into HQ at five thirty in the morning smoking a big hand-rolled Havana cigar. He found Tuttle slumped inside a booth with several HQ regulars.

"I thought you were upcountry," said Purcell.

"I just lost a girl I was looking for, and I can't find Asanee. Other than that, I'm having a great night."

Harry Purcell smiled. "You been listening to Radio 108.3?"

Tuttle shook his head.

"Didn't think so. Addison is on the air. Asanee's working a radio hot line."

"Thank God, she's safe," said Tuttle.

"I don't think I said that," replied Harry Purcell.

"It's Addison. If anything happens to her . . ."

"You will be too late because it will happen to everyone at the radio station," said Harry Purcell. "About your lost girl, I see you've found some replacements." He blew a cloud of cigar smoke to the ceiling.

"Soldiers pulled her out of Snow's room at the Royal," said Tuttle. "What's going on, Harry?"

Harry's eyes lit up. "It's called command crisis,"

"Harry, what are you talking about? People are getting shot in the street. And you talk about a command crisis."

"My family has supplied the command system for more than four hundred years," said Harry Purcell. "We understand Command. How Command thinks. We understand the fear of command, and this has been our strength in the arms business. What does Command fear most? It fears most losing command to others. And what is the heart and guts of a command system? Command never has its orders questioned. Insubordination is questioning. Insubordination is a step from treason, which is punishable by death. This is the reason the killing starts; it explains why the killings continues—massacres are used to cleanse people of the urge to question."

9

The deciding factor in hiring Ross to investigate Addison had occurred after Tuttle had a run-in with Denny Addison. It was unexpected. Addison had turned up at Tuttle's English school on Sukhumvit Road to pick up Asanee after she had finished teaching. They had been seeing each other for several months, and Asanee had decided to move in with Addison. She wanted her father's approval. But she was like her father—strong-willed. Once she had made up her mind that Addison had become her companion there was little Tuttle could do to change it. After the formalities, five minutes into the conversation, Addison made his move.

"You see, Bob, the problem with writing is all the time you waste doing it," said Addison, sitting back in a chair opposite Tuttle's desk. "The way I see it, Bob, is you have to sit and type and type. That must make you crazy. And you've got no feedback. People need immediate feedback and gratification. You want to know if you're pushing the right buttons. So I make my style of documentary. I'm working with people. I can kick back and ask funky questions everyone has always wanted to ask. And I'm off camera. It's easy. But you have to select the right situation and the right people for the situation. Once you've done that, hey, you've scored, Bob."

"You must have a favorite writer?" asked Tuttle, swallowing hard. What Tuttle hated was being called Bob. His name was Robert.

"My favorite writer? William Burroughs. Who else is there? And *The Naked Lunch*, hey, you gotta read it many times before you get what Burroughs was trying to do. Burroughs is the man. He scrambled words and sentences, made mashed potatoes with verbs and nouns. But he got what he was after—these incredible images. He was an image maker. He painted with words. He used words as his lens. And he did massive amounts of drugs. You've got to love a guy like that. He's pure. After you've read Burroughs, forget the rest. Maybe there are some other good writers out there. But who cares? The work you've got to go through to find them. It's torture. It's not worth it, Bob. The reading time cuts into your babe time. And anything that cuts into babe time is a major crime. Burroughs liked babes. Yeah, yeah, I know he killed a babe in Mexico but that can happen to anyone. Too much drugs. It fucked him up. But he communicates what you've got to do. You have to create images. Words are a drag. A camera is better. Load the film, and watch. Sooner or later you stumble on something and go, wow, that's a direct hit. A score in the zillion category. You can't ever get words to do that. Unless, of course, you're a Burroughs. But how many Burroughs are there? One, man. You can't improve on him. So you do your own thing. Hang out with your babe, watch TV, eat pizza, maybe go for a swim. Keep it simple and easy. Asanee tells me you write stories or something, Bob."

"Something with words," said Tuttle.

Robert Tuttle had thought hard about how to remove this Burroughs disciple from his daughter's life. Ross had a plan to deal with the Denny Addison problem. His idea was to gather evidence showing that Addison was incapable of being faithful. Tuttle had gone back to Ross's office and found that Ross had gone. Ross was sitting in the bar below. Tuttle went up to him and asked him if he had found anything to confirm the suspicions that Addison was screwing around. Tuttle wasn't certain what he wanted Ross to dig up; all he knew was he had an uneasy feeling that Addison was the kind to sleep around.

"Of course, he fucks girls. He didn't come here for the clean air and safe streets," Ross had said. That was before he started the investigation and discovered Addison had a paranoid fear of AIDS and had done very little sleeping around.

"Okay, he doesn't take girls short time. Then find out Addison's racket. What's his scam?" asked Tuttle.

"What if he's clean? Then what do you want to do?"

The way Ross asked the question had a certain meaning in Bangkok. Clients wanted pretty much the same final solution for a person who was causing them a problem.

"Nothing," said Tuttle.

"We could make him into a drug dealer. Get his ass busted. Life in a Thai prison is roughly equivalent to death in America," said Ross.

"Forget it. Forget I ever mentioned this guy. His business is likely as clean as his sex life. Send me a bill. I'm good for it."

"Let me have a look around. Then if I find anything I'll send you a bill," said Ross. "Otherwise, consider it on the house."

Tuttle wanted to avoid having Ross take an extreme action. It wasn't so much fear of getting caught or moral objection as the dread that something would go wrong; that Ross would fuck it up and Addison would emerge stronger, meaner, and more determined to destroy what remained of his relationship with Asanee. Tuttle had this feeling of *sang horn jai*—a premonition that something would go wrong. Although Ross was quite drunk by the time Tuttle had tracked him down, he understood that some clients were tortured by conscience, and other clients had a narrow threshold for inhuman cruelty. Tuttle was the scholarly type, Ross had thought. He expected him to be tortured. He expected Tuttle would come back. When Tuttle came into the bar, looking like he was about to vomit, Ross was ready to handle the situation. He had his story about the floods and the strange fish in reserve. The story always worked on clients who sweated from conscience flashes.

"Let me tell you a fish story about that," said Ross.

"I don't want a fish metaphor," said Tuttle. "I want to talk about Denny Addison."

"Fuck that. I'm tellin' you about a fish."

Later Ross's fish story had returned from Tuttle's memory on the Nan River with all those floating bones. Ross was a dozen drinks into the evening, and as Tuttle approached him, Ross had transformed himself into a hard-boiled private eye persona.

"You know it's great," said Ross. "Man, it's bitter. I could write real bitter. If I was in a tight spot and it was the only way I could get out, I'd say, give me a piece of paper and a pen. You want bitter? Then I'll write beyond bitter. You don't know me. I can write vicious. Real street mean stuff."

He looked straight ahead, throwing back a drink, he brought his glass down hard. This was his way of easing into the story. He talked in a low growl of a voice—one which suggested the speaker might be a man accustomed to violence

"Where's Rusty Reagan?" asked Ross. He paused as if the question was being put to a real person, and then continued. "And don't tell me he's not inside. Because I'll call you a liar. Any man who is open on this day is a *jek*. You hear what I called you, Wing? A *jek*. If there was a baht on the road you'd be open for business, finding a way to get that baht in your pocket. Then I looked around and saw his mob was standing behind him. Tough-looking dock-worker types. I thought if Rusty's inside this hole, he's in real trouble. I pushed my way through Wing and his men and surveyed the area. I looked into the back room. It was empty. Okay, where's Rusty Reagan? I knew I wouldn't get a straight answer. When one of his men tried to blindside me with a chair, I put him away with a sidekick to his groin. He doubled up like an oyster feeling the tip of the knife touch the shell. I turned to Wing, and said, the trouble with a *chek* is that you don't have the guts to take a man on face to face, you've got to have pond scum try and hit him from behind."

"That's not a story about a fish," said Tuttle.

"That story is about courage. You have to understand courage before hearing the fish story. Trust me. Besides it was a great story. You should have recorded that story. You should have a camera like Addison. I would be great on film. Telling that kind of story is what people want to hear. True life, hard-boiled conversations about real men in fear of their lives."

Ross's technique was to soften up a client who was racked with regrets, lapses of courage, doubts about his competence. He found it was successful to start with a minor lesson about bitterness and courage. The main story for those who were on the verge of losing their nerve came from the rainy season horrors. It related to a fear that struck terror into the hearts of certain Bangkok residents: a fear beyond the pollution, drugged mad motorcyclists, careless tuk-tuk drivers, political unrest, or armed robbery. The fear had a name: sewers. More precisely, the greatest fear was the one chance in a million of falling into an open sewer during the rainy season. Once the monsoon rains pelted the streets a thick gravy of brown water backed up ankle deep into the sois. Thieves often stole manhole covers for the scrap metal value. Many people were forced to walk out of their sois during the rainy season—they went to work, for food, or for cheap sex—the journey out was like a jungle patrol working a heavily booby-trapped rice paddy. Two *farangs* several years before had disappeared in a sewer on Soi Asoke. The sheer force of the rapidly moving water pulled them down the hole as if water had carried them down the sink hole of a giant bathtub. A few miles downstream the police and bodysnatchers recovered their bodies. Just two regular guys on their way to getting laid, fate sucked them down an open sewer and coughed them up to the surface dead.

Ross was the kind of person who befriended only people who refused to succumb to his sewer-death fear. Some people liked people surrounding them who shared their fears, who reconfirmed that insanity and misery caused by hidden secret traps set in every-day life, someone to whom they could rage and cry out against the unfairness of so much personal danger and risk. Not Ross. He wanted people who climbed into the belly of the beast without blinking an eye as if to say, there is nothing to fear but fear itself.

One of Ross's friends, Lek, had experience working the sewers of Bangkok. Lek was a sewer diver. His specialty was the sewers near the gem dealers' district off Silom Road. Lek spent his days panning for gold dust in the sewer waters. Once in heavy rains Lek was trapped in the sewer and nearly drowned. He managed to stay alive by finding a small air pocket and the rain stopped with several inches of breathing space to spare. Two days later, Lek was back in the sewer on a cloudy day panning for gold. Ross liked the fact that this brush with death hadn't dissuaded Lek from his appointed task. Fuck the polluted water, fuck the rains, and fuck the shit—just keep panning for gold. Lek sometimes found strange fish living in the sewers, which brings us closer to Ross's fish story.

When Bangkok sois flooded, which happened every year despite efforts to dig up sois and main roads and install storm drains, the wild life of the sewers floated to the surface. The sois were filled with fifteen different kinds of catfish and many kinds of snakes. The brown water teemed with schools of fish and tangles of snakes like a school child's drawing of a bad dream. Tuk-tuk drivers and street vendors sat on the high ground and fished the sois. Later they ate catfish that had grown to maturity—shit-eating fish which survived on the bowel movements of gem merchants, tourists, touts, bankers, beggars, peasants and whores.

The German owner of Lucky Lucy's Bar, Wolfgang, caught a one-foot-long fish that looked like a cross between a carp, a goldfish, and a catfish—an entirely new genus of fish: *Shitemper Sewertums*, which was the name Ross called the strange fish. It was anyone's guess how such a living thing could have emerged on this planet short of eating a steady diet of clogged shit and cross-breeding across species. Wolfgang had the fish put in a special tank. Two days later he left Bangkok on a visa run to Penang. He left instructions with his maid. The strange fish was to be cleaned every day during his absence. Wolfgang had visions of fame with this fish. He felt about *Shitemper Sewertums* the way Robert Tuttle later had felt about his floating bones. Both assumed their names would be recorded and immortalized in science. The history of science was the ultimate notebook in which people fought for a mention, a footnote containing their name for the discovery of a plant, a fish, a star, a solar system, the beginning of time and why it left no bones.

Wolfgang had several ideas on how to best capitalize on the creature and the international fame which the creature promised. He thought that the best approach would be writing a letter to a university. Then he changed his mind, because he was, after all, a merchant and not a scholar, and then he thought he would sell the creature to a large foreign aquarium or build a special tank and put the fish on permanent display at Lucky Lucy's as a way of attracting publicity. Tourists would flock to his restaurant to see a half-dinosaur creature which had emerged from the sewers of Bangkok. After talking with Ross and many other friends, Wolfgang decided to keep the creature in his bar and restaurant and use it as an excuse to boost the price of the Pirate's brunch to 95 baht.

Wolfgang was gone for three days. Each day the maid removed the fish from the tank and with a scrub brush and a bar of soap cleaned the fish. The fish died on the second day. The maid sold the fish to a street food vendor for fifty baht and fled Lucky Lucy's with Wolfgang's toaster, coffee maker, and staple-gun. She was never heard of again. As they say in the City of Angels, she fled the scene of the accident. When Wolfgang returned to Bangkok, he was heartbroken. He had invested his heart and soul in a new business venture with this creature as his partner. The creature had been the dream of a lifetime. The fish was no longer a fish. This fish meant everything in the world to Wolfgang. A one in a million chance to break out of the ordinary in life; for others to recognize that Wolfgang counted, should be paid respect, honored, and noticed. The food vendor was not to be blamed. She had bought what she thought was a fish; surely a strange fish, but nonetheless a fish. Those who bought fish that day in front of Lucky Lucy's Bar were hardly to blame for eating *Shitemper Sewertums*. Indeed, Ross said that *Shitemper Sewertums* was one of the most delicious fish he had ever eaten in Bangkok or anywhere.

All that remained of *Shitemper Sewertums* were some bone fragments. How could Wolfgang be certain those bones were from his creature—the creature he had found and belonged to him—as opposed to being the bones of a strange, ordinary fish? The short answer, given by Ross, was that he couldn't. Wolfgang was advised that he had two choices: offer a reward for the return of either the absent maid and/or *Shitemper Sewertums* or wait until the rains came and hope he might be able to capture another creature of the same species. Every rainy season, Wolfgang searched for another *Shitemper Sewertums* but God had apparently made only one. Wolfgang never found a second one. Every resident had heard Wolfgang's fish story and imagined him knee deep in the shit water near the sewer opening, camping out and waiting for the same kind of fish to return. Wolfgang was glad to tell the story to anyone who would listen. Since only Ross and the maid had seen the fish, Wolfgang had put himself in the position of buying Ross beer anytime someone new didn't believe his sewer story and Ross had to be brought in as Wolfgang's lawyer for verification. Ross always ended the story by telling the newcomer that *Shitemper Sewertums* was the most tender, tasty fish he had ever eaten in his life. Every time it flooded Wolfgang was outside Lucky Lucy's in short pants with a fishing net sifting through the dirty water looking to find a fish like the one his maid had cleaned into the next life.

By the time Ross had finished his story about *Shitemper Sewertums* the bar was about to close. He ordered a final drink as Tuttle leaned in close.

"About Addison," whispered Tuttle.

But Ross cut him off. "You can't force a *Shitemper Sewertums* out of a sewer. But if one comes out of its own free will and turns on you, then you either master the courage to kill the sonofabitch or let it drag you back into the sewer with it. Addison is a *Shitemper Sewertums*. I think we should put him in a tank or eat him." The last drink came and Ross raised his glass to Tuttle. "But what do I know?" There was a sparkle in his eye. "On the other hand, what you think you know about Thailand and weird people like Addison? A piece of free advice . . . forget you have this knowledge, and let me take care of the fishing gear. Addison won't get away. I can take that sonofabitch."

10

Crosby was inside HQ. His worn black briefcase was stuffed with several glossy color brochures of T-shirt projects, sales projection figures, financing schedules and, zipped into a side pocket for special expat customers, was an English produced two-hundred page catalogue. The "Bird Book," as he called it, was bait. What Crosby called his customer list. It was well thumbed, dog-eared, and filled with London (King's Road) telephone kiosk name cards—Luscious & Juicy, Fresh & Fruity, Ripe and Ready; Naughty Miss Tease Loves to Please, Open Late Tottenham Ct. Road; Come Play with Me, 42" Firm Bust; Kim Busty Blonde, Mon-Fri from 1.00 pm.

He thought of the Bird Book as a deal closer for non-exclusive rights to sell his T-shirts in England. The best salesman required motivation; Crosby had developed the profile of the ideal *farang* salesman—university educated (redbrick university), over 40, divorced from two white women, an aging baby boomer who was looking for that last chance for romance with a stunningly beautiful, exotic, erotic Asian lady. The Bird Book contained two hundred pages of snapshots. Asian girls, along with their basic, bare-bone details, including age, breast, waist, and hip measurements, hobbies, interests, languages, horoscope, address and a P.O. box number. There were photos and descriptions of Thais, Chinese, Malays, Javanese, Koreans, and Filipinos in the catalogue.

Crosby knew how to find the new face buried deep in the HQ *farang* crowd.

"I don't know about being your representative agent in England. I've never sold shirts before. I work for an estate agent. I mean,

I know nothing about clothing," said the *farang* across the table from Crosby. He was an Englishman from Leicester, who had just finished his second divorce.

"You like Thai women?" asked Crosby.

He nodded.

"England's filled with Asian women," continued Crosby. "And Englishmen who would pay any amount of money for a little memory of Bangkok. This isn't clothing; it's about remembering the good times. It's really quite simple."

"If it were simple, then you would do it yourself," said the Englishman.

"As you can see, I'm a manufacturer," said Crosby, flipping through the T-shirt catalogue at a table with this *farang* who fitted the profile. "These are the export quality. This is the quality sent abroad. Look around this room. You see my T-shirts being worn. Now examine the Bird Book. When you go back, then you have an excuse to talk to all of these girls."

The *farang* looked at one picture of a girl in front of an old brick semi-detached house with dark clouds in the background. It made him shiver. The girl was wrapped in a long scarf and wore a thick coat. Her face looked red from the wind. "They look different in England," he said.

"She's a beauty. You'd sell her a bundle of shirts," said Crosby.

"I thought you said the market was for Englishmen?"

Crosby winced. "My friend, the Thais buy them for Englishmen, and for themselves."

One of the regulars in her late 20s, a slash and burn application of lipstick on her lips, green eye shadow, and long, false nails—a shark—came swimming alongside the table, flashing a torso fin. Like Crosby she could smell the scent of money about to come loose and she came in for the kill. She wrapped her arms around the *farang*'s neck. Crosby recognized the girl; she had recently returned from a year in Germany. She looked down at the catalogue.

"That's Toom," she said, pointing at one of the snapshots.

"You know her?" asked the *farang*.

"She work here two, three years. And that is Noi," she said, turning the page, "and Koy, Lek, and . . . I forget her name."

"Why did they leave?" asked the *farang*.

"Boyfriend or husband take them away."

"Then why are they in this catalogue?"

The girl laughed. "They make business."

"What kind of business?" asked the *farang*. "T-shirts?"

She laughed again, shaking her head. "Same as here. Maybe their husband, he knows. Maybe not. Depends on many things."

The *farang* locked eyes with Crosby who regretted what he figured was a blown sale.

"These demonstrations at Sanam Luang. Things could turn quite nasty," said the *farang*. "I can't say people back home will be in any mood to buy T-shirts with obscene messages about Thailand."

"The Thais are the most gentle people in the world. In a couple of days it will blow over. And the messages aren't obscene."

"You really don't think this problem with the military is a problem?"

Crosby smiled, shaking his head. "Toom, tell this gentleman whether you are scared."

Toom nudged in closer to the *farang*, running her hand down his leg. "Thai people never afraid. Maybe *farang* afraid. But I say, why afraid? There is no trouble in your country? Where is perfect? You show me on a map the country called Perfect, then I go there with you."

The *farang* studied the brochure again. "I'd like a dozen T-shirts with 'No family connections. No education. No prospects of work. Call me hopeful,'" he said. "And two dozen of these." He pointed at the brochure as Crosby wrote up the order.

"You sure?" asked Toom.

"One hundred percent," said the *farang*, as Crosby slid the contract across the table.

Floating bones heading toward the sea.

11

The last thing Snow expected as he huddled near the window, his eyeglasses on the end of his nose, a phone to his ear, filing a report with a newspaper in San Francisco, was that Daeng would return, that he would ever see her again. He tried to comfort himself that he had only taken her short time, and that she had been taken by her own people and there was little he could do to intervene on her behalf. But return she did. Wrapped in the white hotel sheet, looking like a figure from the back row of the chorus in a Greek tragedy, she came through the door, walked over to the bed, and sat down. Snow pushed his glasses up and stared at her as if she were a ghost.

"You okay?" he asked, walking across the floor on his knees. Nothing appeared to be missing.

She didn't answer him.

He reached her feet and laid his head on her lap, looking up at her face in the darkness.

"They hurt you?"

She shook her head.

"They asked you questions?"

She nodded.

"Like what you were doing naked with a *farang* at the Royal Hotel?" asked Snow.

She nodded again, and stroked his hair with her fingers.

"You're pissed off at me," he said.

She gave nothing away.

"Because I didn't believe your ghost story." Then it struck him. "My, God, the soldiers believed it, right?"

She smiled and said nothing, tugging at his ear, wrapping a thin strand of hair around the lobe.

"Okay, okay, I'm an asshole. Tell me what you told them. What did the ghost look like? Did it have a name? A belly? A beard? Was it naked or did it wear clothes? What's the story?"

Her hand stopped playing with his hair.

"Cortez," she said.

"Cortez?" asked Snow.

"The ghost tell me its name," replied Daeng.

Snow sighed, then groaned, struck the floor with his heels like a small child having a fit of temper. He had a good idea about this ghost which wasn't a ghost but a correspondent one floor below named Jack Howrey, a VOA hustler, a part-time guy, who had spent ten years in Costa Rica and sometimes used a fake Spanish name after smoking grass when he picked up bar girls. Howrey was a free-lance whoremonger; his sense of humor hungered for nightmarish visions, simulated torture, and paranormal tricks like bending spoons and disappearing cards, and was fed by uneducated country girls. Jack fine-tuned the connection between magic tricks and getting laid. He got laid a lot because he made girls scared and laugh at the same time.

"This Cortez talked to you?"

Daeng nodded. Sure, this was definitely Howrey fooling around, the scumbag, thought Snow.

"Yes, sir, he talk to Daeng," she said.

"What did Cortez the ghost say? You go with me short-time? Boom, boom. Snow not know? You have beautiful body? You like me like monkey like banana?" Snow was getting himself worked up over the possibility someone had been poaching his short-time girl who ten minutes before he had already written off as a casualty of the insurrection in the streets; he covered an urban street war from his hotel window, a young Thai Army officer had asked him to help the demonstrators and get the news out about the killings, and the officer had returned his girl—all this had happened to Snow at the Royal Hotel. Yet what was fixed inside Snow's mind as the

HQ girl was knotting his hair in braids? How had Howrey pulled this ghost trick off? That was what was on Snow's mind.

Daeng waited until Snow's face had stopped twitching. "Cortez say to me. I don't know how to say. Daeng not understand."

She had his interest at an all-time high level. Snow lifted his head from her lap. He lay back on the bed, the lights off, listening to the gunfire, staring at the ceiling.

"This ghost didn't have a mole on his chin?" asked Snow.

She shook her head. The room fell silent except for the gunfire outside in the streets. This time the M-16s sounded farther away; Snow guessed the shooting was coming from the direction of Sanam Luang.

"What did he say that you didn't understand?"

"Cortez say to Daeng, auspicious time for human sacrifice. He say this many, many times. I still hear Cortez saying this, and I don't like." She touched Snow's shoulder. "What does sacrifice mean? And what does human mean? *Mai kow jai.*" I don't understand.

Snow squeezed his eyes tight.

"So why didn't you ask Cortez to explain?"

She cocked her head to the side. "I did."

"And?"

"He say in Thai—*phairee phinat.*"

"What the fuck is that in English?"

"I don't know how to say in English," she replied.

Snow blinked at her in the dark room. A ghost who spoke English and Thai. What the fuck, he thought. Howrey didn't speak Thai. Snow who spoke fluent Thai didn't have the vaguest idea of the meaning of *phairee phinat*. Maybe it was a designer drug you smoked or snorted, he thought.

"It makes a good lead, Daeng," he said after a long pause. "Next life Daeng born as a war correspondent. What about this as a lead? The carnage in Bangkok streets, like a human sacrifice, has left blood stains that will take years to wash away."

It was a reasonable start after a couple of years away from his trade. A much better lead, he found out long after that night, would have been the English translation of the military plan called Enemy's Destruction—or *phairee phinat*. That night inside the Royal Hotel an HQ girl named Daeng and a room full of generals sitting across town seemed to be the only live people aware of the phrase. How did Daeng ever snag onto that piece of inside information outside of his hotel room? He hated being scooped by a rookie. And whatever happened to Daeng once she left his room two hours later? Would she ever return? He doubted it.

PART 2
THE TREASON OF IMAGES

1

Four or five of the village dogs slept fitfully, their paws curled up snout high, hind-legs kicking the dirt beneath a hut on bamboo stilts. From another hut a child's cry echoed as if the child clung to the sides of the night and was afraid to let go. Tuttle thought of the Blues. Music which arose from poverty, pain and despair; a soundtrack of suffering. Tuttle marked the beat and waited as an old woman with a heavily lined face squatted on the wooden planks; she spread a bamboo mat under the mosquito net. Her fingers had aged into talon-like hooks; fingers shaped like cooked chicken feet. Her old, moist eyes watched as Tuttle crawled under the net. An old man, his face turned to the wall, snored under a net across the open room. Outside the hut, in the distance a motorcycle roared on an unlit dirt road. The headlamp light swept through the cracks in the bamboo slats like a prison beam across an empty yard and disappeared, returning the room to total darkness. After the old woman slipped away, Tuttle lay back under the mosquito netting. His eyes slowly adjusted to the pitch dark; through the cracks in the wall, he slowly picked out an umbrella of stars and the moon outside. In the fields beyond the village, the crickets and frogs were singing. A wind swept off the Nan River, rustling the fronds of the palm tree beside the well—the well pump had been paid for in cash by a bar girl who had gone to work in Bangkok. The headman had explained earlier in the evening the pride of the girl's mother. She no longer was required to lower the bucket and slowly pull it hand over fist to the top. She had achieved a certain kind of status.

As the old woman made his bed she showed Tuttle a photograph of her daughter. All the vital family documents were inside a canister with the words—"Hand Grenade MKII Cont. M41A1"—stencilled along the side. The canister contained the family birth certificates, household registration, and childhood photographs. These were the records of each family member's life. Proof they had lived, gone to school and died. The birth certificates were on rough, crude paper with a blue Garuda stamped at the top. He stared for a long time at the photograph of the bar girl, who was about twelve years old at the time of the photo. Where had this past gone? She had left it a long time ago. He thought about the water pump she had bought for her family. As he lay under the netting, he slid closer to the wall and stared between the cracks. He could hear the river, and see the stars. He thought about that twelve-year-old girl who was now nineteen and tried to multiply the number of customers she must have serviced to have saved enough to buy her mother's water pump. Machinery like a water pump was a luxury; for the rich, for those with girls who could raise the cost. Driving the water from the earth to the surface wasn't a free trip. Raising water for drinking, bathing, and washing had a special measurement—a bump and grind math formula every bar girl had learned by heart.

Tuttle thought about the old woman who had made his bed; her back bent like a longbow, this dignified woman with the scarecrow face and chicken-feet hands was about his own age. They had been born in the same year. Had drunk water year in and year out. Only the cost of the water had been different. In that here and now moment, he felt himself breathing. Another memory rose and fell. This time he saw his father's face and remembered that his father was dead and he was the next generation to stand in that line. He and the old woman were now at the head of the queue, waiting, watching their breath, protected from the mosquitos and exposed to everything else.

Tuttle considered what his life would have been if his father been born a villager on the Nan River. More likely than not, he would have squatted on the floor next to his father; his father would have finished his dinner of sticky rice and fish meal, tipped forward without a word, passing out from too much drink. Tuttle's sisters would be working in Bangkok bars, and it would take days, if not weeks, to track them down; his mother would have been outside starting the electric pump on the well. His records and one photo would have been kept inside a canister marked "Hand Grenade MKII Cont. M41A1." And when his father died, slumped over and stopped breathing, ancient belief and superstition would have kicked in—his lifeless body coiled up on the dirt floor, he would tell himself, was not dead, his body retained the soul like the canister retained the past. Lying on a mat, a floating stone's throw from the river bank, Tuttle felt light years away from Bangkok. In the village, the soul of the deceased charted a path into a new canister, another set of papers and photos, finding a source of water and a means to pump it from the ground, a never-ending cycle of birth and death, until the distant point beyond time when enlightenment occurred.

That night in the village beside the Nan River, the idea of enlightenment seemed as distant as the stars from a world where slaughter was going on in the heart of Bangkok—Sanam Luang. The foreign radio reports pounded home the message: massacres and death squads—no one is safe—shoot to kill. No one passes Go without a uniform or a Benz. These news flashes circled around the world, broadcasting eye-witness accounts of violence, of killings, executions, and murder.

Tuttle was in bed when the headman's second in command lifted the net, grinning and holding up a bottle. He invited Tuttle to drink with the headman and the boys; it was an offer he could not refuse. About half a dozen figures sat around, passing a bottle and lighting hand-rolled cigarettes. Tuttle sat next to the headman. He watched the old man drink half a glass of homemade booze—the kind that could make you go blind—and then belch, shake his head, shiver, and refill Tuttle's glass with the clear liquid. The old man had a dirty little secret he had kept from the *farang*. He spoke to Tuttle as one would speak to a child who had not just suffered a bad education but had emerged with crippling, deformed views of life and death.

"When a man dies of a heart attack, what do you believe?" asked Tuttle.

"Heart attack? No problem. The spirits not leave when the heart stops."

This was the view of a man who had laughed until tears streaked down his face because a *farang* had mistaken a kayak filled with bones for one filled with stones. But somehow the headman retained the emotional edge. He had proved that simple common sense always won. Well, almost always. Until the soul processed itself into the next life the spirit stayed inside the body like a floating stone stayed on the river. Denny Addison had divided the world between those who asked the question off camera and those who looked into the lens and gave answers. Not a story, but a narrative situation, wandering and sniffing from one territory to another, smelling its way along like a soi dog, stopping to lift its leg and make a claim.

The old woman had so thoughtfully handled the contents from that canister as if the essence of her daughter were inside. How could that tender moment ever appear as an image on TV? It couldn't. Her gnarled hands touching each item as if it were a sacred relic. These paper reminders of her daughter's existence; it was the only evidence that this self had ever passed through her womb and into the village. The headman eyed him as if Tuttle had no understanding of the inner workings of life on the river. Why was this *farang* staring at the old woman?

"Spirits? How many entities of the afterlife are we talking about?" asked Tuttle. The old woman sat alone in the corner, away from the men, clutching her hand-grenade canister.

"There are three spirits," said the headman matter of factly, as if any other number were crazy. Tuttle was thinking about the water pump the prostitute's cash had purchased, and wondering if the old woman had sold her daughter into the sex trade.

"Three what?" asked Tuttle, snapping his head around.

"Spirits. One of the flesh. An invisible force. And one of the bones. You don't die until each spirit leaves."

Somehow the old woman didn't seem like the type who would sell her daughter for a water pump—but you never knew, he thought. A girl left the village. The spirits stayed in the body and departed in their own sweet time.

"Bottom line," Tuttle started to say. "When does the last spirit skip out of the hand-grenade canister?" asked Tuttle.

The old man chuckled.

"When the pin is pulled," said the headman.

"Of course," said Tuttle. "And you throw it as far away as you can and hope none of it flies back as a ghost. Timing is everything."

This the old man didn't readily agree to.

Westerners, sensed the headman, were hard-wired with a defect—a sense of time urgency, time knowing, time worrying. Or as the headman thought, "Why the *farang* always in the big hurry?" Always how long does it take for the pot to boil, the fish to cook, the girl to fuck; look at the watch, take out a calendar and count the days and months and years. Where is this place called time? Show it to me. Give me a picture of where it dwells. The *farang* paced from wall to wall, thinking, how much longer do I pace? Where is my destination, and when will I get there, and how will I recognize it once I arrive? This strange *farang* with the boat filled with bones had confided that his father had died of a heart attack out of sight in a distant, strange, unknowable land. He examined the face of Robert Tuttle, thinking could such a man understand that spirits existed outside of time; that spirits don't run according to time schedules like buses, trains, and planes. He lived in a village sandwiched between a muddy river and a jungle. He watched silver-bellied planes flying overhead. He had taken a train two times. But he was a rare exception. For his fellow villagers, outside life was remote, cut-off, and isolated—the surface of the moon was as close as Bangkok and the men who paid them for a vote.

"We all blow up in the end," said Tuttle. Ever take a calculator and compute the odds of making it off the planet alive? There were no odds, he thought. There was no chance.

The old man shrugged his shoulders, smiling with a blackened rack of teeth in wet gums.

"The woman's daughter. Why did she go to Bangkok?" asked Tuttle.

The headman's eyes grew larger, the laugh lines around the eyes a twist of wrinkles and folds of skin, sallow from local brew and smoking. "She very beautiful," said the headman. "Beautiful girl in Bangkok do very good."

"Money for water pumps," said Tuttle.

"For house, for many things."

The villagers smoking and drinking on the floor were not fools; they knew the score—the value of a beautiful village girl, the price of chickens, water buffalo, rice, boats, guns. They drank around a radio at night. The government radio station had jammed them full of lies about the shootings. When Tuttle had showed up, they hung tight, watching him on the river, and wash up on their shore. The government radio warned them about the forces of darkness—a "Third Hand"—and when a *farang* with a boat filled with bones of the dead claiming he had discovered a miracle arrived on their banks—could they be sure this was not the "Third Hand" on the run from Bangkok or on the run to Bangkok?

So the headman thought again, how long does it take to find out what this *farang* really intends? Were the bones a trick? Were they an omen? Some of the villagers had been scared and didn't want Tuttle spending the night in the village. Two of these villagers had rifles and had tried to rob a *farang* earlier on the river. He had escaped with magic like a devil of the water. The headman offered him a bed in his own house. He had been on a train a couple of times; he knew of the outside world, he suspected the "Third Hand" might be crazy talk. He knew the men who had tried to kill Tuttle. He wanted to study this devil of the river up close and took a chance that a man who had lost his father was not a sly, river spirit but a flesh and blood *farang*.

A bone collector was asking about the timing of spirit release. He proved himself a potential Third Hand. If the headman killed Tuttle, no one would ever know. He smiled and watched the *farang* with bloodshot eyes and a three-day growth of beard.

"You don't say, now, Uncle Lek's last spirit has found its way into the next world?" asked Tuttle. This was like asking what is the best part of the day; or thinking a day has any best part to ask about.

He granted this much to the *farang*; he had escaped two of his best men who were ambush specialists—men who rarely missed. But this Robert Tuttle had vanished in the air, or so they said; only to reappear in their village.

"Maybe many years," replied the headman.

"The corpse of the person doesn't become dead for years?" asked Tuttle.

"Not the same as saying it stays alive," said the headman.

Tuttle liked the old man.

"The flesh rots from the skeleton. We wait. Flesh drips like the rain. What time of day does the flesh rain start? When does it end? How long does it take for a drop of flesh to hit the ground? I don't know when. Maybe a Monday, or a Saturday. It all depends."

"Depends on what?" asked Tuttle.

"If there is a wind blowing. Or a hot day. A door may slam hard somewhere. Something slips. A bird flies. How does it go? I don't know how to say. But I once saw this fall," said the headman, rolling up his sleeve and squeezing the upper muscle of his biceps. "Fall from my father's arm. He was kept in the hut by the river. A water buffalo walked past and drank from the river. This fell off my father." Again the headman tugged at his biceps. "Interesting, I think. Water buffalo comes and part of my father goes back into the soil."

Tuttle wondered if this was the booze talking. He looked at the old man and his cronies, two of whom had passed out and lay like scarecrows dumped in a back room. The upstairs had begun to stink of piss, fish paste, and Mekong whiskey. Only the headman and Tuttle remained sober; they had been talking while the others passed the bottle. The survivors of the hard drinking discussed the water buffalo which had gone to the river that day part of his father's spirits had returned to the earth.

One of the men spoke. "Hammer a wooden stake through the asshole. Flesh go to the earth. Fast. Fast. Water buffalo too slow." Then he passed out, hitting his head on the floor. He was the last of the river pirates. Lights out. They had showed up to drink with the man they had tried to kill—a guerrilla gig which hadn't succeeded. The two remaining villagers laughed. Tuttle couldn't figure if this was irony, malice or simply a joke about how water buffaloes and spirits inter-react on the Nan River. He showed no expression and this made the villagers laugh even more. This, after all, was the *farang* who arrived with more bones than any villager had squirreled away for the rainy day when a bone spirit was needed for one of those heart-to-heart conversations that only a bone spirit could understand. He had defeated the pirates once again. They slobbered on the floor. Tuttle, devil of the river, talking about spirits, bones, and whores was not someone you took your eye off, thought the headman. Why had he really come?

What did he really want? Was he a Third-Hand character hatched from the river? Before the old man could think of a single answer, he passed out on the floor.

Tuttle, left alone, finished his home brew and crawled back under his mosquito net. He lay on the mat, having visions of zombies rising in a B-grade horror movie, walking stiff-legged along the shore of the Nan River, coming into view as the kayak came around a bend, and there, above the horizon, dripping flesh droplets. Drip, drip. One drop at a time for months and years until the bones are clean of flesh, and the fat tissue, muscle, the lungs, heart, and miles of intestine have melted drop by drop into the earth, releasing the spirit of the flesh back to the earth. A treason of images.

The next morning the villagers awakened with fuzzy heads, wishing they had never touched a village whiskey bottle. They found their *farang* guest at the edge of the village listening to the BBC World News on his shortwave radio. In Bangkok the Army had opened fire on thousands of demonstrators at Sanam Luang. The pro-democracy demonstrators had been fleeing when the soldiers opened up with M-16s. Volley after volley had dropped them; shot in the back, they collapsed in the street. He couldn't believe what he was hearing. Parts of Bangkok were set aflame. When the BBC report ended, Tuttle found the headman standing in the doorway smiling.

"We show you how we send the bone spirit," said the headman.

People have been killed in Bangkok, Tuttle wanted to say. But they already knew that people had died in the city.

Bangkok was located in another world with New York or London—and news of the deaths filtered through the post-hangover numbness; shit, some people got killed, blown away, as the villagers had a great party. Shit, the *farang* river devil was still alive. Tuttle was starting to spook them. Ever since he arrived in the village, the news from Bangkok had gone from bad to rotten. The old woman had been kneeling beside his net as Tuttle opened his eyes. She *waied* him, touched her head to the floor, as if she were making a prayer to him, this devil the villagers couldn't kill. She was crying, her face a spongy, leaking mask of despair. Her chicken-feet hands clawed at her eyes as if she might tear them out.

"I worry about Daeng, my daughter. Maybe she die," the old woman who was Tuttle's age had wailed. "She come to me in my dream. She very cold, she say. She say she feel the curse. Daeng say she miss me but can't come home now. That Daeng love her mother very much. More than the whole world, and she hopes that the electric pump helps her." She had handed Tuttle the old photograph of the girl. "You look for her, okay? I pay you, okay?" She had six red hundred-baht notes crumpled up and pressed against Tuttle's hand.

"I'll look for her."

"She works in Soi Cowboy."

And did the old woman have any idea what was on Soi Cowboy? Or what Daeng was doing there? She was a bare-back riding machine for travelling cowpokes. The old woman had sold her baby down the river. Peddled her ass for the water pump and now had her weepy regrets that her investment might be in danger on the firing line.

Tuttle had refused her money.

"I can't promise anything. She could be any place. But I'll try." The old woman didn't want to hear this; but it was from the heart, so she had accepted the only chance she had. Tears burst out of her eyes, splashing on her blouse. Soon big, fat wet spots covered the old woman.

Now the headman reappeared with a couple of villagers and insisted that Tuttle follow him. The headman was not going to take no for an answer. Back in the village, Tuttle went into a hut and watched a villager gathering bones. Tufts of hair were still attached to the skull and some weathered leather hung loose like old stockings on the femur.

"You come and watch. You see something you not forget," said the headman, his head throbbing from a massive hangover. One of the villagers with a long jaw and crooked teeth had gathered the bones and carried the remains in clay jars to an oven at the far end of the village for cremation. On the way to the oven, the old woman with the daughter named Daeng selling her ass in a Soi Cowboy bar ran up and grabbed his elbow. She said nothing but wouldn't let go. He pulled her along. Somehow his presence was a comfort to her; he was someone who had been to Bangkok, and someone who was returning, a *farang* who would help her. The old woman made Tuttle think about Dee—the woman who had thrown the heavy piece of coral at his head. And missed. She lived near Sanam Luang; she would have heard the gunfire and would have been afraid. Dee would have cried, wishing Tuttle were with her.

Snow's radio report had been blunt: soldiers had opened fire and shot people dead in the street. Snow had reported from a window in the Royal Hotel. A mass of people and—Asanee, Dee, Daeng might have been flesh dots in the center of this moving target of humanity fleeing the guns of May.

When Tuttle and the villagers reached the oven, the long-jawed man put the bones inside and struck a match. Soon he had a roaring fire going. The village men smoked hand-rolled cigarettes, squatted in the dirt, spat and drank liquor, belched, farted, laughed, drew pictures in the dirt with sticks. Later the long-jawed man and the headman gathered the shards of burnt bone and fashioned them into the shape of a person. The headman, his hands covered with ash, grinned, his broken, black stubbled mouth agape. This was bone art, bone drawing, bone finger-painting. The headman had decided that morning not to kill Tuttle. He wasn't certain why; it was a feeling that killing this *farang* was bad luck. It would extend the curse the boy at the river bank had alluded to. Besides the old woman had delivered to the headman a five-hundred-baht note in return for his pledge not to kill the *farang*. So she hugged her *farang*; she would allow no harm to come to him. This *farang* had promised to find her daughter, a cash-cow, and there would be more purples if the *farang* found Daeng and returned her to the village. It was an offer the headman didn't have the heart to turn down. He played the role of a spirit bone artist for this *farang*. His act of re-creation—the godlike reconstruction of the human form in bone ash—had the purpose of releasing the soul and the long-jawed man had given him twenty baht to help in the ceremony. It was proving to be a profitable day.

Tuttle remembered that sonofabitch Harry Purcell and his crazy research on Cortez's horror at watching the Aztecs and their rituals. Cortez was another devil, an intruder from the outside, with some heavy black Catholic magic working for him. The main Aztec temple was located in Temixtitan. Inside, the Aztec priests created effigies from seeds and vegetables—grand figures, Cortez had written in a dispatch to Charles V—which had been kneaded together with the glue of blood. Human sacrifices. Like an Army shooting its own people in the back. The Aztecs, like the Thais, like everyone else, used animal sacrifices to protect their idols and worship their soul gods high in the private towers above the city. The Aztec animal was a human being.

After the long-jawed man and the headman had finished with the reconstituted figure in cremated bones—Tuttle recognized a bone head, bone arms, legs, back, and feet—the ritual was over. He touched the bone man's head. The two river pirates fled the scene, afraid that this river devil would touch their heads and send them straight to hell. Tuttle hadn't drunk enough rough whiskey the night before; he was taking the whole thing seriously. So what did Robert Tuttle see as they stood back? A bone person which the headman told him still retained the spirit of the dead man. But the person was not yet dead, this little story spun by the old headman, buying some time as his mind flipped back and forth on the decision to kill Tuttle or to take the old witch's money and let him go free. There was no contradiction for the headman. It was perfectly consistent: take the money and kill Tuttle. Why not, he thought? That was before Tuttle had knelt down and passed his finger over the bone man on the ground. There was no fucking way the headman was going to kill this *farang* now. It would curse the village to kill a man who had participated in the ritual. Finished with playing in the ashes, dirt, and charred bone, Robert Tuttle and his shortwave radio were Bangkok bound.

An hour later the other relatives of the dead man came along and joined the long-jawed man. The kin loaded a bamboo tray with a spade, a garden hoe, paper, and tobacco, and carried it to the side of the bone person. The tray was dropped and the things scattered on the ground with the tray bouncing, then rolling to a stop against Tuttle's leg. The bone spirit had taken the objects with him on his final ascent. He had given Tuttle one final tug on the pant leg to say goodbye, joked the headman. He was in a good mood now. The indecision was a thing of the past. He peeled off a red and sent an assistant to buy some Mekong. Tuttle watched the ritual. The headman held up his hands and pronounced the dead

The Treason of Images

man really, truly, absolutely, not fingers crossed behind the back, dead, wasted, gone, no longer on earth, in another place; his three spirits at last had left and gone to the place where spirits dwelt. The headman, lost in thought, wondering about the possibility of squeezing some more money out of the old woman. He believed it was possible. She was loaded; everyone in the village knew she had money hidden. He worked up a scam. The old man took her aside and told her that Tuttle had guaranteed the old woman's whore of a daughter would be returned. The curse would be broken. But he left it vague—he wouldn't promise Daeng would come back alive. The old man had screwed this old widow countless times; as far as he could remember the whore's father had died in Saudi. What he remembered was the exact place on the river bank Daeng's father had cursed the ground and the village.

"You not forget?" asked the old woman, running like an old crow beside the river. She chased after Tuttle as he pushed off in his kayak. "You promise. You break. You die. You die."

"I won't forget," he shouted back.

He watched her fade until the jungle swallowed her.

I won't forget the bones, he thought.

Paddling his kayak on the river the old woman's voice stayed in his ears. "You die. You die."

Harry Purcell had written a passage in *Cortez's Temple*, his latest contribution to the centuries-old Purcell chronicle, and as previous members of his family had done, he had allowed himself the liberty of expressing some personal opinions about bones and human sacrifice. Harry had been born into a family of gun-runners on his father's side and Chinese bandits—generals, anyway—on his mother's side; people who sold arms to the best of families, clans, and tribes, and those who sold guns and those who used them had joined their children in marriage. Both families had looked far into a future when East would be fused with the West. Harry was part of the raw fusion material—an alpha male who knew how to read when a hunting pack was ready to attack. In the killing business, no one knew more than Harry about the hunting games, wolf-pack hunger, the personalities of the leaders, the way hierarchies shifted and became unstable. The lesson of the family chronicle was that no matter how ugly things got they could always become uglier.

Challenge the alpha male in any human pack and you heard the same words century after century—"You die. You die." Those words over the centuries had been spoken, squealed, snarled, or whimpered, and when spoken by the right member of the pack, were taken as a call to arms, and a call to arms was a fresh order for weapons which the Purcells would fill. As Harry's father used to say, "Everywhere around the world you find the scar of the alpha wolf . . . seek and you will find it by holding up a mirror."

2

CORTEZ'S TEMPLE

by

Harry Purcell

After the collapse of Saigon in April 1975 the American Government fought a POW "Bone War" with the Vietnamese
Government. A major appointment with history was kept. The
Vietnamese communists had not only defeated the Vietnamese
capitalists and their allies; they stored away the bones of the dead
American soldiers who the American Government had sacrificed to
the gods of progress, democracy, and shopping centers. Vietnamese,
mainly peasants, the forward troops who had scavenged bones
from Cambodia, Laos and Vietnam, were born merchants. They sold
bones to bone collectors representing Americans who, too, believed
their soldiers were dead but not yet dead. The bone war became
a proxy spiritual war. The terms of engagement were clear, as was
the military objective—no peace until the return of the last femur.
Until that day, the soldiers' spirits remained alive, waiting, unable
to escape until the bamboo tray with a TV guide, a Mickey Mouse
watch, a Big Mac hamburger, and Elvis Presley tapes was dropped
on the ground beside the bone man.

In 1519 the Spanish waged a spiritual "Bone War" with the Aztecs.
The Spanish won that encounter.[1] Cortez commanded 900 troops
(and 150,000 local allies). His troops torched the forty-tower Aztec
temple in Temixtitan, their seed and blood idols, and hundreds of

thousands of human skulls the black-robed priests had collected. The Spanish cremated the temple skulls; but there is little evidence they intended to release the spirits of the dead Aztecs. The Spanish Conquest had a high kill ratio: Cortez and his men murdered 240,000 inhabitants of Temixtitan. The Americans lost less than 60,000 in Vietnam. The Vietnamese lost hundreds of thousands; maybe millions—they spent far less time counting their dead.

The Spanish inflicted this high kill ratio without the attack helicopters.

---

[1] Family legend has it that the Purcell family supplied the arms for the Cortez expedition. The Purcells had promised helicopters and supplied a design. But the chopper was never built or delivered. The weapons and supplies which did reach Cortez cost him an average of less than one cent per kill. Cortez did very well from the deal. The Purcell family did extremely well from the deal. It put them in the arms business.

[2] In 1519 Leonardo da Vinci died (assisted in death by the hand of a Purcell) at his Chateau at Cloux. At the time of his death, according to family legend, Lenny headed the Purcell R&D weapons development program. He had designed a helicopter, a parachute, an aeroplane, a basic steam-driven river gunboat. Lenny was years ahead of his time. But he had no heart for killing. He had an artist's heart, and a Purcell plucked it from his chest.

3

In 1978 Tuttle had a walk-on part in a Hollywood movie shot in Bangkok. This was a memorable year in the City of Angels; *The Deer Hunter* was shot in Bangkok and went on to win four Oscars. Everyone thought it was Vietnam. Who knew the difference? In the film, there was a famous, unforgettable Russian-roulette scene with De Niro and Christopher Walken, sweating, eyes bloodshot, and wearing rags. They played the parts of American POWs held by the North Vietnamese like animals in tiger cages. The North Vietnamese soldiers let these human animals play with guns. This scene created for all time the myth of bitterness—that Americans had been left behind, betrayed to play Russian roulette in the presence of laughing monkey-brained victors. The Pentagon received a great deal of political heat after the Oscars and had no choice but to make the appropriate inquiries about tiger cages and POWs. The next year, Tuttle met Harry Purcell who had been hanging out in the city, getting laid as often as possible. Harry's respectable cover was a university research project. The kind a funding committee selects because it promises to improve understanding of primitive cultures. Harry studied magic and the death rituals of the hilltribes; these people had lived for generations in the north of Thailand.

Harry disappeared for several weeks at a time on his upcountry fieldwork assignments. He was studying the hilltribe cult of bones and his Bangkok house was full of cardboard boxes of old human bones.

Harry was dressed in a rice farmer's shirt with a peace symbol stitched over the heart and a pair of ragged shorts. He squatted

Asian style. Beads of sweat dripped down his hairless chest; and his hair was matted, unwashed, and twirled into ringlets. He existed on a daily diet of rice and fish paste wherever he lived. Harry could move from the world of an English university to a mud hut river village without ever changing his tailoring or diet. In '79, Tuttle took Harry for an eccentric Englishman who hadn't realized that Empire had ended, the sun had set, and that the time was arriving to make a dash to a more promising land.

"Why do men have trouble talking about their relationships to one another?" asked Harry. "Now, if we were two women, I would already know how you feel about your mother, how old you were when a flasher first showed his equipment to you on the way home from school, whether you had cramps before your period, and your views on oral sex. Do you swallow or spit?"

"You're something of an expert on women," said Tuttle.

"A rank amateur exploring a temperamental tribe."

The frogs on the edge of the pond in Harry's garden began croaking. The overgrown grounds had a wild feeling, the appearance of being in the jungle.

"What drawer do you keep your underwear and socks in?" asked Tuttle. "Do you squeeze your toothpaste from the top or the bottom? Do you snore? Have you ever farted during a lecture?"

Harry Purcell smiled. "No, you don't quite have the hang of it. Women ask relationship questions. Men ask object questions. Like whether you enjoyed taking a woman from behind, missionary style, your views on blow-jobs, hand-jobs, masturbation and any fantasy stuff about whips, chains, animals, children, and the dead. When was the first time you masturbated? When was the last time? Do you worry about your cock size? What kind of porno turns you on? And so forth. But since we are men, what do we talk about?"

"How do you like to take your women, Harry? Sunny side up? Or do you flip her over and take her from behind?" A hardcore question if there ever was one.

Harry's eyes lit up and he struck a match and passed it over a fat Havana cigar. He sucked on the cigar, his cheeks billowing in and out like a forge, coughed, covered his mouth with a hand, then handed the cigars and matches to Tuttle. His bony chest dripped with sweat beneath his unbuttoned shirt.

"I take women who like to be fucked from behind. On all fours. Do you think that's peculiar?"

Tuttle shook his head, letting the smoke curl from his nose.

"Good, because it is the absolutely, one-hundred percent natural position for our species. Evolution sculpted our sexual organs for taking a woman from her ass end. When your cock becomes hard have you ever taken time to study the angle? That angle is the point at which our two tribes merge."

Tuttle broke out laughing. "An anthropologist with a hardon theory."

"Yes. But a serious theory. The why for the male cock curves pointing north."

"Like an Aussie boom-boom boomerang."

"A powerful, loaded weapon," said Harry, leaning over and scribbling a note on a piece of paper. "A penis is a sexual boomerang. Or the original inventor of the boomerang studied the angle of his own erection; or that of her boyfriend. When you throw a boomerang right, it always comes back. And the female vagina, when you've got her on all fours, curves upward."

"And your Doggy fucking cult wishes to declare war on all missionary positions?" asked Tuttle.

"We tolerate all positions. But acknowledge that a rear attack is our evolutionary heritage. It's in our bones," replied Harry, sucking his cigar and reaching up to pull a bone out of the box. He tried to stand it on end but it tipped over on the bamboo mat.

"Why are you playing with the bone?" asked Tuttle.

Harry looked up from the femur.

"Woman talk a different sex talk from men. You asked me how I like to fuck a woman. I choose women who like to get fucked from behind. And before I can re-light my cigar you are spinning metaphors about boomerangs and I am doing the same thing. It's better playing with bones. We can't pry ourselves away from our technology and metaphors. That's what we men cling to. Women don't give a dead cat's bounce worth of energy about anything other than the here and now."

Tuttle thought for a moment and persisted. "But, you, Harry Purcell, are playing a live cat's game with these bones."

"It's business," smiled Purcell, not wishing to divulge the arms deal which rested on turning up MIA bones.

"What are you really doing in Bangkok?" asked Tuttle.

"Writing a paper on hilltribe culture," said Harry.

"I might be stoned but I'm not that crazy," said Tuttle.

"Just fucked up," said Harry.

"From behind or totally fucked up?"

"I had the chance to study women when I pimped for the family business," said Harry.

"Pimped? Gun-runners pimp?"

Harry traced his finger along the edge of a femur bone.

"Helicopters, tanks, heavy artillery require buyers in the right mood. Our buyers—generals, politicians, influential people—expect to get laid. They command it. They give an order for a blond or a red head. You want to sell tanks, you better give them what they want."

Tuttle leaned back. "You see *The Deer Hunter*?"

"About five times," replied Purcell.

"I had a walk-on part."

Purcell smiled. "I thought I recognized you. You're a star."

"Blink and you would miss me."

"Blink and you won't see the bullet which hits you," said Harry.

The encounter set a pattern of conversation—a way of expressing thoughts—which was to be repeated many times in the years which came later. The tropical birds sang from wooden cages hanging from nearby trees as they sat in the short grass beside the pond and Harry licked the Havana cigar before lighting it. Bangkok was where Harry always returned. No matter that he had an important university position, or that he searched for bones, or made arms deals on the side. It was in Bangkok where Harry waited for new appointments with history. Guns and bullets were the invitation card for these appointments. Bangkok was the only place where he could be absolutely himself and no one concerned themselves about his life, politics or family. A city surrounded by hostile, alien forces;

a sprawling capital inside a country with dangerous frontiers. In a society where family was everything—protection against invaders, security against attack, business powerhouses; but Harry lived the life of an orphan. From where he drew his identity was difficult to judge: from the family chronicle, his university, his missions, sales conferences, the company he kept. What suited Harry's personality, his business, his career was detachment; it gave him freedom from respectability which was the only freedom ever worth buying. It allowed him to sell killing machines without feeling any guilt.

4

What did Harry Purcell intend to do with the boxes of bone fragments he had collected?

When Tuttle asked him that question, Harry's explanation only increased his curiosity—it was difficult to believe the bone fragments which had come from the north of Thailand had been part of Harry Purcell's research project on hilltribe rituals and magic.

"The bones had nothing to do with his research," said Snow, in the early 80s. "I once tried to do a story on Purcell. But he just smiled that shit-eating grin, lit a cigar, and said nothing. Hey, man, this is not giving me a story. You think Harry Purcell gave a rat's ass?"

"Okay then, why did Harry keep boxes of bones?"

"You are an idiot. Harry's family had zillions of military connections, and intelligence community friends. How else do you sell submarines in Latin America and Southeast Asia?" asked Snow.

"Harry sold the bones?"

"You think he gave them away? Come on, man, get real."

Robert Tuttle remembered the huge grounds, the pond, the rare singing birds, the tree house, the large main teak house, and smaller houses which dotted Harry's compound. Servants slipping in and out of sight with trays of food and drink for the guests. Harry dressed like a Spartan and lived like a king. No university professor on a research grant could have covered the bill for the life style. The explanation, again, was not a secret—Harry Purcell had private income, he came from the right background in England which produced huge amounts of cash to support a small estate in the center of Bangkok. Harry had a strange pride in the history of his family's accomplishments in the history of armed conflict.

"Fucking merchants of death," said Snow. "I think he drinks human blood. He takes girls from HQ, slaughters them by the lake, drinks their blood, and buries them. Later he digs up the bones, and keeps them in boxes. That's what I think. Harry's really a thousand fucking years old and has never been married. A thousand years of leasing. The Purcell family motto is—if it flies, floats or fucks—rent it. What a story Harry would make, if I could get some shit on him, I'd be rich, man," said Snow.

"You think Harry ever feels guilty about selling arms?" asked Tuttle.

"Bullshit. Harry Purcell is incapable of guilt. He told Crosby in HQ that his entire family had dispensed with morality over four hundred years ago. That it was bad for business," said Snow. "You heard him on Nobel?"

"As in the prize?"

"The same guy, man. Harry's got this thing about Alfred Nobel setting up prizes! Harry said Nobel's prize winners acted as high-class pimps for old Alfred's bad conscience. Old Alfred fucking lost it when he invented dynamite. Nightmares, crying jags, the whole enchilada and floor show. The guy took it personal that his invention blew up grandstands of people. Harry claims his grandfather once met Alfred and said Nobel wimped out. His clothes stank of black powder. Greasy hair. Dirty fingernails."

"Harry told me about the pimping bit. But I missed the part about Alfred Nobel," said Tuttle. "It's okay, Snow. You probably dreamt it in some drug-induced state. Acid flashbacks cause this kind of faulty recall."

Snow looked up, his head jerking with surprise.

"Get out of here. Did Harry ever tell you about the time his girlfriend went down on a politician from Costa Rica so Harry could get a Cobra helicopter contract signed?"

"Costa Rica doesn't have an Army," said Tuttle.

Snow smiled. "Harry thought she might change their mind."

Tuttle shook his head. He didn't buy it.

"Have I ever lied to you? Well, not often. Yesterday and tomorrow but not now. The story is, according to Harry, they were at a five star restaurant," Snow continued. "She crawled under the table, unzipped the politician's pants, and blew him. She hummed *God Save the Queen*. Harry said she might have been a Purcell in a prior life."

"Costa Rica still doesn't have an Army," said Tuttle.

Now it was Snow's turn to flash a quick smile.

"Maybe not, man, but they've got traffic cops diving speeders in fucking Cobras."

"He's got style," said Tuttle.

"And enough money to change his style whenever he wants."

5

In the summer of '79, Harry said that the Vietnamese claimed not to know where the bones were buried. He stood at a jungle clearing over the Laotian border with a map and compass. An unlit cigar hung from Harry's mouth as he squinted at the jungle fifty meters ahead. A colonel was reading the map which Harry held out. It had been marked by a villager, who claimed to have witnessed the crash of an American helicopter during the war. It was one o'clock and the sun bore straight down. The colonel sweated, his face wet and puffy; the frustration had been building for a couple of hours. There was no evidence of a crash site. Finally the colonel exploded.

"Charlie, he knows," said the American air force colonel, running his hand through his short cropped hair. "The sly little slope motherfuckers know the story, Harry."

Harry Purcell shrugged.

"You know something, Colonel? I'm a half sly little slope motherfucker myself. On my mother's side. She was one hundred percent motherfucking slope. She came from a long line of slopes," said Harry Purcell, not breaking eye contact with the colonel.

The colonel looked away, facing the sun as his face burned with embarrassment.

"I didn't mean it the way it sounded," said the colonel. "We're under heavy fucking pressure to resolve all the POWs." He had that look of Christopher Walken as he pressed the revolver against his temple and squeezed the trigger.

One simple image was the foundation for an entire industry of bone recovery. For Harry it wasn't the money; he was establishing a line of chits for the family business. An English academic with Harry's credentials, education, language skills was tailor-made for the assignment of bringing the bones home, or locating suspected villages, burial grounds in Laos where American pilots had been shot down in the secret war. The Pentagon loved Harry Purcell. They trusted him because of the Purcell family. And above all, Harry had about the most perfect cover you could ever hope for in a bone yard. The American assignment turned into an obsession with Harry, and one bone led to another bone, and one day Harry's mind flipped back through the annals of the family arsenal business. On that day his thoughts turned to the bones left in the war between Cortez's Spanish invaders and Montezuma's Aztec civilization in Temixtitan. The Cortez deal had been the first war outside of Europe for the Purcells. The founding fathers of the business had armed troops who found the ultimate bone hunter's bonanza—a forty-tower Aztec temple built in the middle of a salt lake in which there were 136,000 unclaimed skulls. . . . And here was history repeating itself in Southeast Asia.

He thought about bones.

Without bones, the hilltribes' conversations with their dead would be eternally interrupted, and as one village headman had told him, "The bone spirits of my ancestors are my audience for despair. Everyone needs an audience, Harry."

His job was to find and return the audience of bones left behind in the war. Bones were the residue left from the family trade in arms. Collecting them appealed to Harry Purcell.

He knew the textbook stuff about how the spirit of the bone remained as a constant household force for multiple life-times. Bones contained the memory of family, tribe, and they belonged with the family, because without them, the family and tribe had no way of establishing belonging. No bones; no audience for the blues. Harry became not just a general in the secret Vietnam bone war but a commander-in-chief. This was why Harry Purcell brought back boxes of bones from Laos. He not only spoke their language, he spoke to their beliefs.

6

As Crosby's cab sped past the burning police kiosk at Asoke, smoke and flames belched into the air. The taxi driver hit the gas, complaining that Crosby wasn't paying him enough to get himself killed. The car accelerated through the dark intersection—the traffic lights had been smashed out. Crosby gave the driver a fifty-baht tip, slammed the door, and told himself it would likely be a boring night on the Soi. He headed straight to the Crazy Eight Bar—a single-shop-house bar with a dozen girls—three bars inside the Asoke Road entrance to Soi Cowboy. Crosby leaned forward on his elbows and smoked a cigarette, looking over the crowd. He wore a faded T-shirt which had printed on the back: "If your wife drives you to drink, have her drop you off at the Barrel Bar." Crosby was a T-shirt freak and had personally started a fad in Bangkok. There was snob appeal in wearing old T-shirts from Patpong and Soi Cowboy bars that had gone out of business years before.

An old Bangkok hand would come up and say, "Yeah, I remember the Barrel. Number 15 was the best girl in the place. She married a cab driver from Ohio. A grifter. Who gave birth to three or four little grifters."

No one came up to Crosby at the bar. The Crazy Eight Bar—like most of the Soi—was dead quiet. The old hands had holed up in their apartments waiting for more reports of the killings. On the bar TV, Channel 5 ran the military version of the newspeak. The news left out a few minor details such as the massacre of civilians, the slaughter of young people around Sanam Luang. The commentator said the Army had discovered that the demonstrators had been infiltrated by communists and vandals, and the Army had intervened to save the country.

"We had to burn the village to save it," screamed Ross from across the room. "They stole that line from the US Government."

Then an Army officer stared into the camera and blamed the loss of life on the "Third Hand."

"I don't mind all the fucking lies," said Ross. "But this bullshit about a Third Hand crosses over the line. Why not say, the country is under siege by men armed with two huge swinging dicks?"

Crosby didn't have an answer. He had arrived in Bangkok three days earlier and had been told by Ross that Tuttle had gone upcountry to fuck young girls. It was an explanation which suited Crosby's idea of why anyone in their right mind would travel upcountry. Someone turned off the TV and tuned in 108.3 on the radio. The modulated DJ voice hyped on fear, booze, and pills was shouting.

"The radio station is surrounded by tanks. I'm counting the bullet holes in the ceiling. But, freaky, I've lost track at twenty-seven. Listen to this." He moved the microphone away and there was the hard whip crack of automatic gunfire. "Hey, those Army guys are some crazy guys. They don't like the show. So they're trying to close us down. They've threatened us; told us to go home. Someone threw a rock up the staircase with a note attached. It says go off the air or we will come in and kill you. Right. Come on up, fellahs. We've got Navy, mean-ass guards watching the stairs. These are armed, mean motherfuckers and they don't like what the Army is doing. The Navy is keeping us on the air. They want you to know the truth. We have tanks and armored personnel carriers surrounding our building. Soldiers in the streets want to close us down. We say no. We're staying here, Bangkok. We are staying here for you. Phone us at the hot line. Tell us what you've heard, what you've seen. The phone lines are lighting up. We had a call that trucks filled with bodies are heading north out of the city. Keep the news coming in. We aren't going off the air until it's over and it ain't over yet. We'd like to dedicate this next song to the officer downstairs who ordered us to surrender. *Power to the People.*"

The song *Power to the People* blared across the bar, until someone reached over and turned it down. Ross stood throwing darts several feet away. He was unsteady on his feet, balancing with one arm over the shoulder of Noi, who kept him pointed in the right direction. His chin pointed forward as he threw a dart.

"You're in a bad mood, Ross," said Crosby.

"Yes, I am. I wanted to fuck Daeng," said Ross. "But she quit. She's a nineteen-year-old whore from Nakon Bumfuck, or maybe Nan. I forget. And I heard she's demonstrating for democracy. She can't even pronounce the word—democracy—but she went to Sanam Luang."

"Tuttle's looking for her," said Crosby.

"He can't have her. I don't care if he is my client. I found Daeng first. I have first right of refusal."

Crosby decided to bring up Snow.

"Snow's sleeping with her at the Royal Hotel."

Ross turned pale.

"Snow is screwing my Daeng?"

"But she fled the scene."

"Let me get this straight. Snow and Tuttle both want Daeng?"

"Apparently," said Crosby. "But she's disappeared." He paused and watched Ross grow silent. "Ross, what is it about this girl? There are a thousand Daengs, Nois, Leks. Why is everyone looking for this one?"

Ross clenched his jaw, his lips curled into a sneer as if this were about the most stupid question anyone had ever asked.

"You wouldn't ask such a question if you knew Daeng. She's cursed. She bears the scar from a violent dog attack." Ross's voice lowered to a whisper. "And sometimes in the middle of the night she hears voices that no one else hears, in languages she doesn't understand. And she loves men."

"In London, you never find a woman who loves men. You never tell an English girl that you spent the last twenty-five years of your life living in Bangkok," said Crosby.

"Why would you want to tell them anything? Why not just fuck them?" asked Ross.

"You ever hear of date rape?"

"That's an Arab thing. Yeah, I've read about it."

"Not fruit rape. Date rape. Going out on a date with a woman and you fuck her."

"Oh, dates," said Ross, throwing another dart.

"Women in England bloody well crucified me each time I mentioned Bangkok. As if living in Bangkok is a criminal offence against their sex."

"They are men-haters. Thai women like men. Daeng likes men. She adored her father."

"Ross, you'd have trouble going back."

"Trouble's my middle name. I had a law partner who used to say that. He's dead, so maybe he was right. Trouble was his middle name."

"In London, my line was I had spent the last twenty-five years in Hong Kong. Skyscrapers, banks, money, and the Star Ferry. They liked that image. No woman in London has ever heard a sentence which contained both the words Hong Kong and sex."

"So did you or didn't you get laid in the four months in London?" asked Ross, looking away from the dart board.

Crosby slowly shook his head. It was a gesture that spoke volumes of what he had gone through in the past four months, and even Ross was moved for a moment. Then he threw his darts and the moment passed. Such was the length of time in which compassion was measured in Bangkok. He walked up to the dart board, counted his score, and pulled out the darts.

"I bet you weren't the only one . . . I mean who wasn't getting laid," said Ross, trying to comfort Crosby. Even though Crosby flogged T-shirts and operated a fly-by-night date-matching service, Ross kind of liked him because he was a good drinker. Crosby could hold his booze and therefore was more deserving of compassion than someone who didn't drink or passed out.

"I'm afraid it's become a way of life for most men," said Crosby. He ordered Ross a drink.

"Why don't they just leave?" asked Ross.

He watched Ross down the free drink in two gulps.

"They wouldn't know where to go," explained Crosby. "After a week without sex it gets easier. Your energy goes into other things.

By the time you hit the four month corner, you don't even think about getting laid. It never enters your mind."

Ross leaned with both hands on the bar and stared for a long time at Crosby. "Let me tell you what I think about this theory." He belched, cleared his throat, and roared at the girl behind the bar for another Old Granddad.

"About this theory," said Crosby, reminding Ross of the lost train of thought.

"You guys had an empire. A great empire. The sun never set on the British Empire. But you never got seriously into getting laid. The English never missed fucking; because they never knew what they were missing. All that time in places like Eton and Harrow. Boys buggering boys. If you had gone to co-ed schools like normal people you would have made Thailand a colony two hundred years ago. Only someone who had gone to an all-boys school would have taken Malaysia and left Thailand. Even the French had the good sense to take Vietnam. They knew the country was full of women. But you guys took Malaysia. Why? Because you wanted rubber plantations instead of getting laid. You wanted to make money and to hell with fun. Anyway, that's my theory."

Ross's first dart missed the board and stuck in the wall.

"Ross, you should have your oil checked. Your motor's running a little hot tonight."

"Did you hear the rumor the Navy was staging a coup against the Army?" asked Ross.

"I heard the Army closed the port and that someone bombed Channel 7 and that there was a curfew and that UFOs were hovering above HQ," said Crosby.

"Did you hear the Army killed a *farang?*"

This caught Crosby's attention, and he swung around on his stool. "Yeah, anyone we know?"

"Someone who was around Banglamphu. The government says he was a tourist. Radio 108.3 said he was a monk."

"Where did you hear this?" asked Crosby, spinning around and slipping off the bar stool.

"It's just another unconfirmed rumor. Bangkok's swimming in rumors. Soon the streets will be teeming with *Shitemper Sewertums*.

A very rare fish rumored to be released by the Third Hand to frighten people to stay inside and not fuck women on Soi Cowboy. But what am I talking about? My hilltribe darling is not working. She's out demonstrating for democracy."

"Did I tell you that Denny Addison has done a film about my secretary? A girl named Toom. She lived in England about ten years. Addison thinks this film is even better than the other one. I can't remember the name," said Crosby.

"*The Unexpected Answer*," said Ross.

"Yeah, that's it. Quite a nice piece on Bangkok," said Crosby.

"You think Addison banged that *katoey*?" asked Ross. "Or maybe he banged your secretary?"

"The only people getting banged, Ross, are those poor bastards at Sanam Luang." Crosby made his right hand into the shape of a gun, put it to his head, and dropped his thumb.

Ross looked thoughtfully into the mirror, watching a go-go dancer shuffle her feet on the stage. She wore a pair of scuffed high-heels. "Why would Tuttle look for Daeng?"

Crosby shrugged. "I don't know. But when you come up with the answer it might be worth putting on a T-shirt."

There was a sense of doom; a feeling this search would never reveal a reason for such an action. To discern the motive of a man looking for a bar girl in the streets of Bangkok as soldiers were shooting people in the street had as much chance of succeeding as visualizing the color of the wind.

"Just one more thing, Crosby. I hope he finds her. I like a girl who hears distant voices she can't understand. I have to drink a great deal to reach that stage myself."

7

The tension between the Army and crowds of demonstrators had been building for weeks. Snow had a feeling that something was about to break in Bangkok while hanging out in a shopping center parking lot in California. He prided himself on never missing a coup, a blood-letting, or being one of the first into the palace to see Mrs. Marcos' shoes.

Snow had been sitting with his legs folded on the molded plastic chair. On a clear, blue California morning, he was reading a letter from Robert Tuttle and several of Trink's Nite Owl columns from the Saturday *Bangkok Post*; he stuffed Tuttle's letter inside a copy of *TV Guide* ringed with watermarks from his favorite coffee cup. At that precise moment, a biker had rammed into his parked Winnebago trailer, shaking the breakfast table and knocking a plate off an overhead rack. The plate shattered in the kitchen sink. Jennifer had been standing two feet away cooking pancakes in an electric skillet and watching a *Star Trek* rerun on television.

Snow had pulled back the curtain, put on his glasses, and peered out the trailer window.

"A fucking biker just smashed into our Winnebago. You got that? Slam, banged right into us. And he's not even fleeing the scene. I hate fucking bikers. Piano wire. Drape piano wire across every intersection in the world and when the lights switch from red to green, you yank on the piano wire until it is taut and invisible and wait for the heads to roll, man."

"Ugly. Violence breeds violence," Jennifer had said, flipping over a pancake.

91

He had continued standing at the window and burning up inside with anger. "Would you look at this. The asshole's giving me the finger. He looks like a white trash skuller."

"What is a skuller?" she had asked, another pancake in mid-air.

The biker had drummed his hairy fists against the Winnebago. It was as if the Hunchback of Notre-Dame had gone to hell and back on too much speed and had mistaken the Winnebago for a massive bell. Snow had thought that this was the new America—a prototype post-modern police state with 200 million sheriffs and 50 million fugitives. One of the fugitives was at his door. Snow let the curtain drop over the window.

"I'm buying a gun tomorrow. A .357 magnum. If I had a gun, I'd shoot this fucker. I'd kill this louse, scumbag, skull, shithead."

"Maybe it was an accident. And he's letting off some steam," Jennifer had said.

"And JFK was killed in a hunting accident in Dallas. This biker is a dangerous criminal. He should be boiled, peeled and sold as dog food," Snow had replied.

There had been complete silence except for the crackling sound of oil bubbling in the electric skillet. The biker had stopped banging his huge fists on the side of the trailer. They were parked in the corner of a huge LA shopping mall complex. Lawlessness was making Snow crazy with loathing and fear. Sure, he had told himself, there were assholes in Bangkok, he had run into them at HQ, he had walked the Alley of Revenge, but he had never thought about carrying a gun. In Southern California gun ownership was a difficult habit to kick; it was up there with other addictive habits like smoking, alcohol, watching TV, or shopping. The usual suspects invited to participate in TV encounter group therapy. Snow had let the curtain drop back and watched Jennifer working over the electric skillet. The full reality of American living had flooded through his consciousness at that moment. First his home had suffered a vicious, unprovoked attack by a demented biker. And as a victim of crime, he had received no emotional support from his woman. Wait a minute, he had said to himself. Let's have a close look at the woman cooking my breakfast. She is forty-one years old, gray strands of hair are swept back from her face, and blue veins rise like canals on the back of her legs. Camping out for the night at HQ Crosby had once said, *"Fucking a white woman is a step away from homosexuality."* Snow had flinched and felt a shiver run down his spinal column. That chill had returned as he had watched Jennifer cooking breakfast.

"I can't believe this, our home has been assaulted by a biker and you keep on cooking pancakes like nothing ever happened," Snow had said, his eyes looking at her blue veins. "Aren't you going to say anything?"

He couldn't say anything but he was thinking about something else. What haunted Snow was one of his own axioms he had put in circulation at HQ—a man can only be in touch with his reality when he sleeps with someone his own age. His one-liner had ended up on a T-shirt sold by the now defunct "Y-Not Bar." He had remembered that Crosby had half-a-dozen of that particular T-shirt in his collection, and each year doubled the price he would take for selling one to Snow. Crosby had refused to acknowledge that Snow's claim of ownership of the one-liner entitled him to a big discount. Crosby had also stolen Snow's all-time favorite—"Life is short time"—and run it on the front of the Pussycat Bar T-shirt. This was after Crosby had promised not to steal it and Snow had believed him and told him anyway. Snow hadn't spoken to Crosby for six weeks after that theft was revealed one night in HQ when one of the Tommys wore it to work.

In Bangkok many hardcore *farangs*—the lifers—had a gross, nightmarish fear they would be forced at gunpoint to jump the bones of a woman their own age. They had structured their lives in such a way as to insulate them from the experience of two sets of old bones and flabby flesh struggling under the sheets to copulate. The "Y-Not Bar" T-shirt had captured this fear of copulating with old meat.

"Not until you tell me what a skuller is." She was toughing it out and he had not liked the pressure.

"I don't fucking believe this," Snow had said.

How did he explain skull bars in Patpong and skullers who inhabited them? He couldn't just come out and say they were blow-job bars. He knew she would want full details, a moral audit, the kind of accounting which he would fail. Why did any *farang* go to a skull bar and watch teenage peasant girls giving blow jobs to old men wearing T-shirts and their trousers around their ankles? No way was he in the mood for that question after what the Hell's Angel had already started. So he had lied.

"A skuller is a kind of guy who runs a Harley into a parked Winnebago and then flips you the bird and pounds his ham-sized fists against the side of your home."

"I never heard that before," she had said. "Does that expression come from Bangkok?"

"Sort of," Snow had said sheepishly.

"Do they have Hell's Angels in Bangkok?" Jennifer had asked, turning over the last pancake. *Star Trek* had faded to the credits and Jennifer began to load one plate with pancakes.

"In Bangkok, we have Angels from Hell," Snow had said, picking up the broken pieces of plate from the sink.

"You never say 'we' when you talk about LA. Only about Bangkok. Then it's 'we' do or have or whatever. The way you talk about Bangkok, I can't understand why you aren't back there now." She had set the plate on the table and poured thick maple syrup over the steaming stack and begun to eat.

"Hey, man. Where are my pancakes?"

Snow had watched her eat. She ate slowly as if the fork travelled from some time warp distortion caused by the mad biker's collision into the Winnebago.

"If you cooked your own pancakes, then you'd understand how they are made," she had replied.

"I don't care if they come from outer space. I just want to eat a pancake and the process is irrelevant. So cut it out, and give me some."

She looked down at her plate, failing to show any indication that she acknowledged Snow's plea for food. I can't believe this high-miler is ignoring me, he had thought. High-milers like old cars had been around all the tracks and all the circuits enough times that the odometer had started over again. He thought of another T-shirt one-liner—You don't need speed bumps for high-milers because you can never get them going that fast. Maybe he could sell it to one of the bars. The commercial opportunity shot through his mind quickly, and he was back in LA, no pancakes, in the presence of a round-eye causing him anguish. In Bangkok no one would talk to her, he told himself. *Farangs* would scatter when she entered the room because she would demand attention, conversation, and exchange of views. Jennifer was more than a high-miler, she was a high-maintenance high-miler, he told himself.

Snow had gotten up from the table, opened the door and walked across the parking lot to an International House of Pancakes, parked himself in a booth and ordered a pancake breakfast special. About a minute after the waitress had set down his breakfast and he had picked up his knife and fork, the biker from hell had walked out of the bathroom and come straight at his table. He was early 40s, big shoulders, naked hairy arms, greasy hair, gold-capped teeth, and salt and pepper beard. He had bacon bits rimmed around his moustache as if he had been feeding out of bowl like some wild animal. The first thing the biker had done was to slap Snow across the face. The blow had knocked off his glasses, and rolled him back in the booth. Snow, caught white knuckled, clutching his cutlery, had realized the opportunity to sink the fork into the biker's kneecap and with his other fist had jabbed the knife into the biker's thigh. The biker had the pained, embarrassed look of a dog startled while taking a shit, and then his eyes had rolled up into his head, and he had collapsed with a loud scream, striking his forehead on the edge of Snow's table. Blood had poured from the biker's head and multiple leg wounds.

"Excuse me. This man who appears to be a messy eater just had a seizure. You better call for an ambulance," he had called to the waitress, as the biker lay on the floor, his eyes rolling into the back of his head as if he were about to pass out. Snow had leaned over and picked up his glasses, then had a final look at the second pancake breakfast he was destined not to eat and accepted this as an omen.

He had walked back to the Winnebago, kicked over the motor-cycle of the biker and stomped on the gas tank, putting a foot-sized dent in it. He had opened the Winnebago door, blood dripping from his hands, had gone directly to the sink, rolled up his shirt, rinsed his hands, found his passport and money.

"Where you going?" asked Jennifer. "My God, you're bleeding."

He had looked up from his suitcase.

"Bangkok. And it's not my blood."

"Isn't there trouble there?"

"There's trouble everywhere."

"It's because of the pancakes. Honey, I'm sorry."

Snow didn't answer.

"Are you serious?"

The sound of an ambulance siren wailed in the distance.

"I'm outta here," Snow had said, swinging open the screen-door.

"You can't just leave. When are you coming back?" she had asked, as he shut his case.

"Don't know."

8

Crosby had occupied a window seat in the First Class section of a British Airways flight from London to Bangkok. Sitting next to him was the Managing Director of a textile company listed on the stock exchange; someone who was a member of all the important clubs, and knew all the right people in London and Bangkok. Someone that Crosby had decided must have connections with the T-shirt business. He had been raised to believe that you must obtain the confidence of someone you want to pitch a business deal to. When the air hostess asked for his selection for breakfast, Crosby chose eggs Benedict. The eggs Benedict arrived in perfect condition. Through the light Hollandaise sauce the orange yolks looked as if they were covered by a thin membrane—the hazy film which covered the eye of a blind man. Crosby made a point of voicing this thought to his seat mate.

"I'm an eye surgeon. In my practice, patients from all over the world pass through my surgery," said Crosby, lying through his teeth.

"I'm in charge of our undergarment and foundation export division," his seat mate had replied, his hand involuntarily adjusting his power-red necktie.

"Do you make T-shirts?" Crosby had asked.

The man had nodded.

"Now we are on to something," Crosby had said with a wicked smile. "Panties, bras, T-shirts, and a blindman's eyes."

His seat mate had winced and cleared his throat. "I'm afraid I don't understand."

"I have perfected a certain specialized microsurgery technique," Crosby had whispered. "It has made me controversial. And I have not always been successful. I'm commonly written up in journals. By the time my patients reach me they have tried everyone and every other process. They are desperate. Their condition is hopeless. They have become resigned to a life of blindness. Maybe a pinpoint of light. My colleagues are divided over my techniques. People may make fun of your line of work. Selling panties and bras. But believe me, my friend, such is a minor humiliation compared to being called a medical charlatan, an eye-hole butcher, and Dr. Laughing Gas. To see your name attacked in print is terribly upsetting. To watch defensively as people go on TV talk shows and tell jokes about you. It's the fashion of the time, to cut down anyone who's successful. And when you are on the cutting edge of new laser hydro-gas-plasma technology, they come out with knives drawn."

"Laser hydro-gas-plasma?" his seat mate had nodded, not wishing to acknowledge that he had no awareness of the controversy.

"Yes, quite a mouthful. But it's actually simple. It is a combination of ancient Chinese techniques with the best of Japanese and American research and development, some of which has been earmarked for top-secret military and space projects."

Crosby had insisted that the eggs should be delivered sunny side up, saying that anything less would deeply distress him. When the eggs arrived as they had been ordered, he had made out his case as an eye surgeon. An eye surgeon who has been sent to Thailand to teach the Thais how to perform a delicate surgical procedure on rich people. Crosby had spoken loudly enough to attract the attention of other passengers in First Class and the attendants. He had described the operation in great detail, slowly bringing up his knife as one specialized instrument and his fork as another. He had practiced using a knife and fork as the surgical instruments in many London restaurants. At the crucial moment, he allowed both knife and fork to slip, slashing through the runny yolk, showering the aisle and several people with flecks of yolk. A small knot of air stewards and passengers who had been watching jumped as if hit with a sting ray. One or more people ripped out their sick bags and vomited.

"Why did you do that?" asked the Senior Steward.

"I was a little nervous," Crosby had replied. "First Class stage fright."

"You have disturbed everyone," the Senior Steward had said.

"You think I might have another gin and tonic before you write your report?"

The Senior Steward had stormed away, murmuring that Crosby was mad.

"You see the kind of reaction people have to my technique."

"You could hardly call that technique."

"I lacked the right tools," Crosby had said.

"Why did you do that?" his seat mate had asked.

Crosby had grinned.

"Because I have a business proposition for you."

"What kind of business?" His seat mate had pulled back.

"The T-shirt imagination business. I can get people to buy just about anything. Take a look around. How many people do you know who could convince First Class to believe this yellow stuff is the same as the human eye? First Class passengers vomiting in air bags because my knife cut into an egg yolk. Think of the effect on the tourist class. They would be jumping out of the plane. I can sell thousands of T-shirts because I can make them look at the shirt."

His seat mate had taken a small silver case from his pocket, opened it with his thumb nail and removed an engraved name card.

"Next week, make an appointment with my secretary and we can discuss the T-shirt business."

Crosby had glanced at his watch.

Next week seemed so far off in the T-shirt business. But he would wait. He had a notebook going back ten years with Snow's one-liners. His time was about to come. And he really wished he could find a way to get another gin and tonic. He had reached up and pressed the call button and watched the flashing red light. It reminded him of Patpong, and that made him happy; gambling, whores, gin and tonic, and T-shirts were the ingredients required to lead a full, productive life. Crosby was thankful that early in life he had been granted a deep understanding of the great mystery of the universe—it was a vast cosmic T-shirt in search of a slogan.

He wondered how long it would take to restore order in First Class, with people going back to normal activities and conversation. He had created chaos. On a long-haul flight with all the essential ingredients on the ground there was no alternative but to make everyone else as miserable as he felt. There was great satisfaction in a scheme which infused people with fear and loathing and allowed him to close a business deal at the same time. During the several months he had been living in England, Crosby had cracked up and made scenes in public places: the tube station, bank and hotel lobbies, restaurants, and the cinema. If he had been a foreigner, the authorities would have likely deported him. Instead, he had deported himself. A feminist with a powerful right hook had punched him in the mouth in the Oxford Circus tube station during the morning rush hour. He had been wearing a Pussy Alive T-shirt—Fucking a white woman is a step away from homosexuality. The punch in his face was as close as Crosby had come to a sexual encounter in London. Having discovered the first mystery of the universe, he had discovered the second mystery of the universe while in England—the essential ingredients of life were available in only one place on the planet—Bangkok. He was returning to Bangkok to humanize himself. The West succeeded in making animals out of normal people, Crosby thought. He had become a sulking monster. All of a sudden on the flight back, he had felt things were about to return to normal. He could relax, breathe . . . and just as he closed his eyes the Senior Steward returned and accidentally on purpose spilled a gin and tonic over Crosby's head. The passengers in First Class applauded and the Senior Steward took a modest bow.

9

Harry Purcell had built himself a powerful image at HQ. Smoking his Havana cigars and dressed from head to toe in black silk, he moved silently. He appeared as if he had come like a mist through the floor. But Harry was no ghost. He was a polyglot: his language fluency included English, Chinese, French, German, Spanish, Thai, Lao—and enough Vietnamese to discuss weapon system operations. At school he had received high marks for his knowledge of weapons and dead languages—Latin and Greek. His Eurasian features gave him a dark, mysterious, and from the profile, alien appearance of an abductor from a UFO hovering above an operating table. He easily had passed as Greek, Italian, Jewish, Turkish—and had the passports to support the nationalities; his face and solid, short body blended a dozen cultures. Purcell's face was difficult to place—it was a face which lacked a certain identity and it was impossible to forget. Harry wore his white hair in a long mane which tumbled over his collar, and his eyebrows were bushy and white like two-hundred-year-old bird's nest bleached in the sun. He had a studied, self-possessed ironic expression as if he were in the audience of a local production of *The Tempest*. Even this was an inadequate description of the feelings Harry Purcell invoked. The way he smiled, rolling his Havana between his fingers as someone else talked. There was the hint of a man who knew the location of a secret passage and as soon as the collapse started, panic in the streets, he would slowly rise from the table and disappear through the passage and exit into a safe haven with huge bank accounts, expensive houses, cars, cigars, wine, and women.

Tuttle found Purcell sitting on the veranda of his house, drinking a cup of coffee and reading the newspaper. He was turning the page when he caught sight of Tuttle, who looked tired, haggard. Tuttle had been back in Bangkok two nights and so far had not found Daeng.

"Papa Tuttle," Purcell said.

"Don't you start." Tuttle sat down at the table opposite Purcell and a maid appeared a moment later with another cup of coffee. Was it possible that Purcell never slept? He looked as if he had been refreshed by eight hours of sleep, sitting relaxed, reading his newspaper.

"Your son-in-law is making quite a mark on the radio."

"He's not my son-in-law. Asanee's only living with him."

Purcell paused, looking at Tuttle's wrinkled clothes with the splattered blood.

"Had a rough night by the look of your clothes," said Purcell.

"What's going on in Bangkok? Can you explain it? Why, Harry, why is the Army doing this?"

Purcell carefully folded the newspaper and laid it on the table. He stretched his arms and cupped his hands behind his head of white hair. "Once my father was with a customer. I was about ten at the time. And the customer who was French asked my father if East and West would ever meet. My father pointed at me and smiled. 'That meeting's being held inside Harry's head.' After the customer left, my father put his arm around my shoulders and said, 'Harry, that man just spent ten million dollars for weapons and he knows even less about life than you do. So if you put your mind to it, by the time you reach sixteen I want a full report on my desk and in that report you write down what's been happening in this meeting between East and West going on between your ears.'"

A Thai girl came out onto the veranda and wrapped her arms around Harry Purcell's neck. He looked up and kissed her gently on the cheek. She wore a red silk robe with the initials HP stitched above the pocket. Tuttle recognized Aow as one of his English language students; she was nineteen, twenty years old. She had long smooth, tapered fingers—not the hands of someone who had been working in a factory or the fields.

"My personal barber," said Harry Purcell. "Say hello to Khun Robert, Aow."

She *waied* him. "Khun Robert is my teacher."

"Is that so?" asked Harry Purcell, smiling.

A moment later Aow disappeared off the veranda and back into the house. From the veranda, Tuttle picked out the fast-paced tempo of Denny Addison's voice on Radio 108.3 but the words were lost as Harry spoke.

"Women are such a dangerous species," said Purcell. "It takes years before you know whether a woman is a cupcake. Whether she will turn out to be good or evil. You have no way of knowing."

"Did you give the report to your father on your sixteenth birthday?" asked Tuttle, glancing through the window and watching Aow dancing to Denny Addison's selection of music for Radio 108.3 listeners—Pink Floyd's *The Wall*.

"Of course. I was at Cambridge. I was the youngest undergraduate in more than one hundred years to be admitted in my college. But my father had his report. But what you really want to ask is about the blood on your clothes and why people are getting themselves killed in Bangkok. And why families like the Purcells have made a business of arming them. Demographics explains a great deal, Robert. Take one square kilometer of England. What do you find inside? Nine adults, three dogs, six children, a couple of pubs and a church. Now take one square kilometer of Asia. You find three thousand families, eight hundred dogs, two hundred monks, and four hundred generals. Everyone is bunched up; squeezed together; stepping on each other's feet. You can't move without someone noticing. You can't raise a concern without causing someone offense. And the person you offend may have power. Remember the four hundred generals part of the equation. The social arrangements are compromised to make certain you don't cause offense. So you don't complain; you don't criticize; you learn not to see problems. The most efficient way of living is to move with great caution; if you step forward from the spot where you stand, always remember that people are watching you. Never move quickly forward or backward without honoring the cardinal rule of the East—yield to those more powerful than you. Spontaneous behavior is dangerous. You must take your time, one step at a time so those in power don't become anxious. You learn to test the water slowly, putting in one toe at a time. It's better to lose a toe than a foot. And it's better to lose a foot than a leg. You master the art of moving without causing offense. One small, measured step, and you stop and count your toes every step along the way. That's how you survive with all those people living on top of each other in one square kilometer of Asia. If you try to run through the territory like it's a Western foot race, then you're in trouble.

"Now we are talking about the how and the why to explain the blood stains on your clothes. Why did the generals order their troops to open fire on demonstrators? It's totally obvious to an Asian. Of course the Army would give an order to shoot to kill. The demonstrators refused to yield to the generals. This isn't America. The demonstrators broke the unwritten covenant. Generals never allow this to happen if they can prevent it. Because if they did, then the generals would lose all of value that they possess—the power to make the others fear and obey them. The demonstrators own cars, mobile phones, condos and this deceived them into thinking they had the power to march in the street and that they had the power to change the Army. So the Army is teaching them a lesson about power and fear. Taking a foot, a leg, and the rest.

"The Purcell family has supplied weapons to five hundred years of generals. We know how they think, react, and what it takes to keep them satisfied. So I wrote my father a report when I was sixteen. It was very short. I wrote that the line where West meets East has never been identified. The exploration has been a trip wire for the unguarded and unwise and I was not about to join their ranks. But I had some thoughts about the family enterprise and terms of credit policy which applied to Asia, Africa, Europe, South America. The mentality of those who desire to retain power is to be careful to watch, observe, notice those who would steal it. They are paranoid about usurpers. Those who succeed in the power game have shown their willingness to force others to yield to them and on their terms. The education system is constructed to teach the people to fear the generals; that language and culture are sacred gifts passed from generation to generation through the blood of the father to the son, the mother to the daughter. Proving that twelve years of school is more damaging to the average person than twelve years of prison. In Asia, the uprisings are blood feuds about the meaning of history and continuity of power. Whatever the price or cost of crushing a challenger is nothing compared with the loss of power and being subject to yield to another. The one with power has the sacred gift. He channels the blood. Generals who combine deceit and ruthlessness usually win. In the gun-running business, this was, I felt, the basis of granting credit: a general with a vast intelligence agency and many spies in the market place, and who never bothered about the blood he let, you gave credit. The others paid cash up front."

"What was your father's reaction to all this?"

"He put me on the board of directors as my seventeenth birthday present," said Harry Purcell, sipping his coffee and grinning over his cup. "Now why did you come here?"

"I'm looking for someone."

"We're all looking for someone, Robert. Most of the time it's ourselves."

10

"This is your favorite DJ and film freak Denny Addison broadcast-ing live at Radio Bangkok 108.3 where we are bringing you music and passing on the news we have gathered from the front lines around Banglamphu. We have more reports of the Army opening fire at Wat Bovornwet. The Army has been spotted sweeping through the area around Democracy Monument. Thousands of protesters have been arrested by the Army in the Ratchadamnoen area. We're hearing reports of soldiers hitting people who are laying flat on the ground. We're talking rifle butts in the head. Soldiers are beating protesters with rifles, making them strip to the waist, and then load-ing them into trucks. Silom and Sathorn Roads are deserted. The buses have stopped running. Robinson, Central Department Store, and Foodland have called it a day and sent their employees home. There are guards out front to stop vandals. One of the generals was just on the TV. Get this, he says he's sad about what is happening and the Army is using restraint and patience. But these rioters—that's what the demonstrators are now called by the Army—have been called communists. The Army has announced a communist alert. So what are we talking about? Treason? Thailand is under threat of a communist takeover? Get serious. Whatever drugs these guys are using, I want a double order delivered to the sixth floor where we are broadcasting live. We are talking some very freaky images rolling around the city. Communists in Thailand? Have the generals been living in a time-warp or what? The Cold War's over, fellahs. Don't you read newspapers? Do they sit in a war room and say,

'Hey, man, we got about 100,000 Marxist radicals occupying Sanam Luang. These commies showed up in their BMWs. So maybe we should blast them.' Wow, let's round up the usual suspects. Never mind that there is no more Soviet Union. Or there is no Berlin Wall. You never know, these rioters might bring back the 1950s. Give it up. If the generals are looking to sell the world that there are rioting communists in Bangkok they're gonna have a rough time finding an audience. Final word before we play some more music. We have reports of 20,000 people around Ramkhamhaeng University. More people are pouring into the area and there are ugly rumors circulating around town that the Army will be moving in after them. Now there's an idea. If soldiers are at Ramkhamhaeng, they might want to check out some courses on history, current events, and logic. Now to ease your mind let's play some music. Radio Bangkok 108.3 brings you the Everly Brothers' *Bye Bye Love.*"

PART 3
THE INTIMATE FRIEND

1

THE INTIMATE FRIEND

A Short Story
by
Robert Tuttle

The jeep driver cut the engine, then switched off the head lamps. In darkness, the Army jeep coasted along on the quiet, narrow soi with cars parked on both sides. Squeezed in the back of the jeep were three soldiers in combat dress, clutching their M-16s. On the passenger's side, an officer held a pair of special night vision binoculars, scanning the windows of some shacks about twenty meters away. The officer dropped his hand and the jeep pulled to an abrupt stop beside the curb. No one inside spoke. The officer had ordered his men to maintain strict silence before they had turned into the soi. His men always followed orders. They were taught to respect command. Loyalty to an officer was the highest loyalty a soldier could hope to offer in a combat zone. Bangkok was at war. Communists, troublemakers, rioters, and the Third Hand were out in force to disrupt the country for their own malevolent purposes. Their officer was taking them on a mission. They would never question the mission or their officer's orders. They sat, waiting further orders, as the officer continued watching through the binoculars.

After several minutes, a Thai male aged thirty-four emerged from one of the shacks. He was well-dressed, wearing a white shirt, a tie, black trousers and polished shoes. His BMW was parked four meters in front of the jeep. Leaning in the door of the shack stood a young woman, her head cocked to the side, combing her hair. She looked wistful dressed in a white silk night gown. She could have been no more than twenty-two. She licked her red lips, the back light revealing her breasts, hips and legs through the white silk.

"You come back tomorrow?" she called after him.

He smiled, turned around in the street, hands in his pockets.

"Wednesday. I come back."

The officer nodded to the soldier directly behind him, and pointed at the man in the street. The soldier stood up in the back of the jeep, braced himself for a clean shot and fired. An M-16 round ripped through the man's head as he fished for his car keys. Skull and brains spattered the BMW windscreen, and he dropped in the street. Wednesday, I come back were his final words on earth; words which promised a time and place commitment and assumed a future he could not keep.

The officer gave another hand signal, this time to the driver, who switched on the engine and sped away from the curb. The officer did not order the driver to stop for an examination of the body in the street. This "communist" had stolen property; he had slept with the officer's minor wife. He had thought long but the decision was not that hard to kill the intruder. To have killed the woman would have been another, more difficult option but the thought crossed his mind. He thought of himself ordering one of his men to shoot her, and looking at the surprise on her face as the blood poured from the wound. She had taken his face, he would take her life. Then he told himself to have a cool heart. There was always another time and place. The body in the street would be a warning. There would always be a next time, he thought. She would not forget this night.

The young woman ran barefoot into the road screaming, "No, no," her thin naked legs flying from under the white silk night gown. The officer had given her the gown as a present. She ran into the street wearing the gift gown and dropped down on her knees, touching the dead man's face. She felt his warm blood between her toes. The officer had always liked this white silk gown on her. As she wept, kissing the dead man's face, she rocked back and forth, cursing the Army, the fighting, the killing.

The dead man's forehead was blown out. The bullet had left a large, ugly mallet of gunk—a stew of bone, brain, and blood. She rolled him over, reached inside his back pocket, removing his wallet, then his ring, and watch. She wiped her eyes and ran back into her shack. There was blood on the white silk which left a stain.

When the officer asked her about the stain she said, bowing her head, that it was from her period. And the corners of his lips turned into a smile, as he remembered the snap of the man's head in the street, and the whisper of the word Wednesday.

She asked, "Did you kill anyone during the troubles?"

He didn't answer her, letting the question fill the silence between them for several seconds. He watched the light dancing in her eyes and wondered what the dead man had seen when he stared into her eyes.

"Only a communist," he finally said.

"What is a communist?" she asked, lips pursed with irony.

He had prepared himself for this question. He knew her attitude wasn't political; she had merely wished to test him. He had practiced what his response would be and was happy to repeat the answer he had memorized.

"A communist is a man who takes another man's property without paying compensation. He violates another man's property. He doesn't believe in private property. He believes all property is public; owned by everyone. This is foolish. We cannot tolerate such acts. I am certain you agree."

"A capitalist invests in his property," she said. "The better the property, the more the investment costs. And he must maintain his property or someone else may take it."

He handed her a gold necklace and she smiled, cupping her hands and raising them to her forehead in a perfectly executed *wai*.

"I'm a good capitalist," he said. "Tonight I want you to wear the white silk gown I gave you."

She looked him straight in the eye. "I cannot. A large rat chewed a hole in the gown. I had to throw it away."

"How do you know it was a rat?"

"I saw its body caught in the trap. It was dead."

The officer liked her answer.

She didn't tell him about her nightmares from the previous nights. It wasn't about a rat but her dead lover. In the nightmare she tried to wash the blood off her feet. But no matter how much soap and water she used, the blood was never washed away. She no longer remembered her dead lover's face. She closed her eyes and tried. But this memory of blood gushed from a hidden source and flooded her dreams a deep shade of red. Red had been the color of the communist flag.

2

"YOU are tuned in to Radio Bangkok 108.3. This is Denny Addison bringing you the latest news update in Bangkok. About ten minutes ago the Army tried to storm the staircase to our building. We're on the sixth floor. The Navy personnel are outside the studio. We heard the soldiers rolling down the stairs. We have blood all over the place. It's weird inside this building, and particularly in this studio. It's like being a fish in a tank. We are surrounded by tanks and soldiers trying to blow us away. It's wild, man. You remain our lifeline to the outside world. If they blow us away, let the people on the outside know that we gave our best. That we did everything to stay on the air. And we aren't gonna stop for a minute bringing the latest updates on troop movements, the shootings, and the other chaos flying around the City of Angels. Remember one thing. Don't believe anything you hear on the government channels. Let's put it to a democratic vote. All those who believe what the Army is telling you raise your hand." The DJ pushed the button for the laugh track. Several seconds of sustained laughter ripped through the airwaves. "Seriously folks, the Army may be a little confused about the truth of what they are doing. What's on TV are lies and more lies. A lot of people are getting shot. Is the Army giving you the straight goods? Or showing you any pictures of the killing going on? No way, man. Check out the BBC and NHK. They have enough bodies and beatings on film to make a TV series. The whole world is watching the boys downstairs. The world knows who is being naughty and nice. They have your picture on film. We've got more reports of dead bodies loaded into Army trucks. We had a call from a banker. A banker saw the bodies. You know what? It was too much for him. He's joined the demonstration. Hey, fellahs, where are you taking the dead? Here is another tune for the Army officers who keep ordering soldiers to break through to the sixth floor and silence us. They have threatened to kill us dead. So we send them this song with love. *We Shall Overcome.*"

Reports and rumors careened around Bangkok like a drunk whore, slurring her words, forgetting where she'd been and where she was going next. Shoppers at Villa had pocket radios tuned to 108.3. Grabbing food hand over fist and listening through headsets plugged into their ears. The DJs whipped up their fear and paranoia.

"Okay, we had a call. The callers says a general has been killed by his troops. Unconfirmed but there it is. Who knows who is killing outside or inside? Another rumor has the head general buying tickets for a flight to Sweden. Just in case things turn ugly for the Army," said Denny Addison.

Still other rumors circulated in the street; neighbor to neighbor, friend to friend, and in the work place. Some rumors had one faction of generals in control, staying for the duration and murdering anyone who resisted. *Farangs* and Thais had the rare experience of finding themselves equally at risk, on the outside, and facing a common enemy. In the panic people were on the run, hiding, pacing around, sneaking out for food. Life was on the skids greased with anger, fear, loathing, and confusion. Middle-aged white women, lipstick smeared from shaky, hurried hands, wearing crumpled sun dresses, rushed around the supermarkets stuffing wire baskets to overflowing with bread, tinned hams, packaged pasta, breakfast cereal, Coca-Cola by the case. These food wagons lined up for hours at check-out counters. The foreigners hugging their bags of food became insane with fear. Food fears, gun-shot fears, robbery, rape, vandalism fears wormed their way into the hearts and minds of everyone.

"Someone threw a brick through a window at Villa," said one of the women in the line for the cash register.

"My maid refuses to leave the house. I have to do the shopping," said another expat woman.

"At least you have a maid. Mine is at the demonstrations," said yet another.

"They've closed the international school. They are cutting the electricity at seven tonight."

"My husband says the Army has orders not to shoot white people."

Gossip and rumors infected everyone in the city. The sudden realization of danger made people insane. Someone started a rumor that it was snowing in Chiang Mai. Some people believed it. The rumor disease swelled the size of the demonstrations; the crowds pressed into the streets hunting down shreds of half-truths, lies, distortions. Maids, students, yuppies, whores, hawkers, office workers, store clerks, hangers-on, media people, the old and the young, all bound by the bond of mutual curiosity, marched into the street all night long.

"Democracy," the students shouted. This wasn't part of the sacred gift which was transmitted in the blood from generation to generation.

Bang, bang. That was the reply of the troops, exchanging bullets for words. Some respectable people were shot in the head.

The reign of confusion and terror swallowed all conversation, thoughts, and dreams. Except at HQ where the girls still went short time for three reds, and this fact contributed to the twisted rumor that Thai girls were seen plotting with three reds—so the confirmation bounced to the Army side that communists were seen at a place the *farang* called HQ. History hadn't ended after all—it had holed up at HQ. The old enemies of Thailand were in the Alley of Revenge, looking to aid and abet all invaders, and the generals told themselves that the Army had to do what had to be done.

Crowds clashed in deadly confrontations with soldiers who were following orders. Hit and run missions. Some demonstrators peered around a corner and an Army patrol opened fire. Thousands of rounds were fired into the air.

"Radio Bangkok 108.3. We've got a contest for the best rumor. What are you hearing? What are you seeing? What in the hell is really going on out there? The numbnuts downstairs are still shooting at us. That ain't a rumor. Listen for yourself."

Bang, bang.

"Heard enough? We got a general escaping in a hot air balloon. What else you got, Bangkok? We just had a nice gentleman from the

116

Army phone and say they were going to machine-gun my family. We already thought of the family death threat angle, fellah. We are one step ahead of you. The family is in hiding. Save your severed dog's head and shot-gun attacks for another day. We are staying put. More rumors out there? Anyone seen that general hanging out of a weather balloon?"

The mysterious Third Hand was sighted lurking in the shadows by an Army patrol, before the hand running on all five fingers disappeared down a narrow soi. *Maw pii* or witch doctors had visions of flocks of black swans circling above the city. There was a rumor of the Army splitting into factions, and the prime minister splitting with his supreme commander. Rumors of summary executions were high on the popularity list. More gunfire was heard around Democracy Monument. Reports of troop movements from Nakhon Ratchasima and Chiang Mai heading to Bangkok from upcountry passed from one fax machine to another. A detachment of marines were rumored to have protected a group of demonstrators from the Army. But the killing machine operated through the night, throughout the city—that was no rumor. Small groups of protesters hid themselves in doorways, trying to make themselves small. Troops were under orders to follow the demonstrators through the dark streets with full magazines loaded in their M-16s.

Another fax: "Soldiers are reported arriving from the north and south and the west. Moderate factions of the Army are marching on Bangkok. The telephone lines will be cut in three hours. Then the electricity."

No one knew what would happen next. *Farang*s and Thai alike switched between 108.3 and the BBC, VOA, and ABC—avoiding the government stations which called the demonstrators troublemakers—the foreign journalists broadcast from the front lines, witnessing the killings, the beating, and telling the world that the city was waiting for the gunfire to draw closer . . .

Tales of black magic rituals filtered out. The organizers had an old traditional formula for their revenge, working under a dim fluorescent light bulb hung inside a fruit vendor's cart. An ingredient in a Thai black magic spell called *kradook phi tai-hong*—the bone fragment of a person who had died in an accident or violently.

The bones were produced from an old bag and laid out on the table. Next a peasant with bowed legs and Khmer writing tattooed in blue ink on his chest returned with pieces of a brick from an abandoned temple, a broken monk's bowl, and a broken pestle. One person untied the ropes holding a makeshift coffin on an ice cream cart. With some help from the tattooed man, they lugged the coffin off the cart and set it on the ground. They placed the ingredients inside, with a picture of the generals taped to the side. An old woman with cobweb hair spit in the pan as she stood before an open fire. The spit bubbled and hissed in the pan. A young girl in a school uniform stifled a scream. The old witch never missed a beat, and her croaky voice raised in a sing-song chant broke the silence. She used a wooden stick to stir a pan of chili and salt. She was cooking the food the spirits order before taking the requested revenge. The chef was a widow. She rotated the cooking duties with a widower who sweated over the fire.

A small crowd—mostly upcountry peasants from squatters' slums—watched the black-magic brew taking form; the air smelled of garlic and chili, the stringent smell of revenge. No one talked much in the darkness. Faces lit from the smoky fire. Lookouts watched for Army patrols. The old man turned the widow's stick inside the pan. The chanting swept from the old man to the old woman and into the small crowd. As they stirred, the widow and widower enlisted the gods in the cursing ceremony to deposit nails, dirty socks, and broken glass inside the stomach of the cursed person.

"Smells about right," said Montezuma, moving from the shadows, and looking over the widow's stooped shoulder. "Never under-estimate the power of witchcraft. Generals fear spells, curses, pots boiling with the sickly smell of sweet revenge."

Cortez materialized next to the fruit cart.

"Show time," said Cortez, but without much conviction. He was looking for Daeng and had talked with her at the Royal Hotel. She was supposedly waiting for him; but Daeng didn't seem all that reliable. Would she bolt? Or would she stay until he could help her? Cortez had so many questions and at the same time had to humor, and play along with Montezuma who would have struck Daeng dead if he'd had any idea she existed.

"Ah, revenge," said Montezuma. "The mere thought makes me flutter with that old-time anticipation."

"Time to gather some skulls, old chum."

"Not before we have our dinner," said Montezuma.

That was an Indian for you, thought Cortez. Dead four hundred fifty odd years and still he was a sucker for chili peppers sauted in an old witch's spit. Montezuma read Cortez's mind, and flashed a Jack Nicholson smile. "Of course, I would haven't touched the spit without the chili."

"Radio Bangkok 108.3 broadcasting live. We just had a caller who wins a prize for the best rumor of the hour. This caller claims to have seen ghosts in the region of the Royal Hotel. One ghost is *farang* and his friend is some kind of American Indian. They weren't speaking English. But they were rocking and rolling. Like the Blues Brothers. The Army has turned into a killing machine; and now this. Spirits of the dead coming back, shaking their heads—if ghosts have heads—and wondering why young people are being machine-gunned in the streets. I guess it would take a ghost to answer that one."

3

CORTEZ'S TEMPLE
by
Harry Purcell

William Hawkins Morris Purcell—fondly referred to by other family members as "Hawks" or the "Original Hawk"—in 1519 reported that Cortez experienced a weak stomach, blood in his stool, and a huge moral chip on his shoulder, a flair for command, and a king and Pope riding on his back. Cortez feigned a major hang-up with the Aztec universal practice of sodomy. That was Cortez's cover story; but as Hawks reported at the time, people write a lot of shit. They knowingly falsify reports to please those in power. Hawks' account is vague on a number of central issues. For example, it is difficult to know exactly how much Cortez personally saw or how much he relied upon the lies in reports written by others who feared offending the orthodox views of those in Spain and Rome. Cortez was an able field commander. The weapons the family had sold him and which were under his command did the job. Thus there was never any issue of insufficient fire power or malfunctioning weapon systems. The hard lesson that Hawks passed down from generation to generation in the Purcell family was largely formed from his association with Cortez and was that generals were limited people. Power had not just corrupted them but limited them in the size and complexity of the world they sought to control. This limitation was their strength and weakness. Strength—they rarely suffered from over-thinking a problem or from indecision. Weakness—they rarely understood the limits of power. Cortez was a military type and mindset, his sixteenth-century Spanish brain was further disturbed by the great wash of daily masses and belief in God. Perhaps the temple with forty towers was not part of a temple after all—or at least not the kind of temple Cortez had any frame of reference for.

If Hawks were alive today, he might see the Aztec temples were more likely prototype Patpong skull bars. The Spanish were just another bunch of soldiers on R & R, looking for sex, drugs, and rock 'n roll. What skull theory linked the three or four skull bars in Patpong to the Aztec skull temples? Before the big "A," the Patpong skull bars filled up every night with shipwrecked sailors and off-duty soldiers drawn from the four corners of the earth. Bar girls slithered inside dark rooms, requesting money in return for supplying their head to these fighting men who were facing an uncertain future, thinking that taking a head in this way might be their last chance, it made them forget the war, and closed the open ring of passion before returning to combat.

A bar girl feels *kai nah*—selling the face—outside the temple of skulls. She has sold her face for a few hundred baht. But this reduces the transaction to a turn of phrase. The skull bone behind the face has a history of possessing an independent spirit; one that survived after the spirit of the flesh had been swallowed back into the earth. The skull behind the face was not sold; the skull remained for the cremation fire, the journey down the Mekong or Nan River where bone spirits travelled for the release.

Some said that a bar girl who worked in a skull bar suffered deeply. Others said she was a hostage to a condition of life, a way of being, which she did not want, understand, or choose but remained helpless to resist. The skull profile—she was either too old, uneducated, or afraid to dance. Dancers and skullers were two different kinds of women. Dancers worked off the premises and made big money; skullers worked on the premises for small change. Two classes of sexual workers. They represented two modern classes of human sacrifice and the modern patrons fell into two classes of customers as well: those who liked their head hunting ritual in private and those who liked a head in their lap as they drank their beer in public. The temple skulls talked on Patpong Road. In Temixtitan the polished skulls were silent.

Where, when and with whom a soldier had sex was a military decision. A question of support and comfort for the troops who had been combat trained. Men who had been ordered to use weapons of destruction. When such men were sent to temples they were confronted with skulls. In Hawks' time, the skulls had no flesh. In modern times the flesh remains intact. This has been called an improvement, an advance of civilization. Bone head logic.

Cortez, for example, had seen the skulls collected in the Aztec temples as evidence that the Aztecs had gone terribly wrong in the gods they worshipped—soldiers in a skull bar had evidence of rituals of worship they did not question as right or wrong. Each ritual skull user—Aztec, Spaniard, or Patpong patron—found a release system. Who is to say that in the battle of skulls, Montezuma's temple skulls were wrong? His temples were offering to powerful gods who communicated through omens. A sacrifice is a human being's way of controlling his fear of gods which no weapon system can destroy. Generals have their fears. The politicians have other fears. The root fear is that forces beyond their control can and will cause their mysterious defeat. It is containing his fear that gives the alpha male his edge over the pack. What has changed is how the human sacrifice is carried out. In skull bars, and in blood on the street. For it is in sex and blood that generals believe that fear is transmitted.

As Hawks said in his chronicle there is no cause for Everything and All that Stuff. But what there is, however, out there waiting, is a business opportunity to allow the arms merchant to take over the role of the gods.

4

That same night a soldier threw a stone with a note demanding surrender up the stairwell at Radio Bangkok 108.3, Cortez had slipped away from Montezuma and materialized in Patpong. He had been reading about Hawks over Harry Purcell's shoulder on several occasions. Checking out the skulls in modern temples was something Cortez could never resist; he would go so far as to say that it was a weakness. With the Thai Army shooting into the crowds, the skull bars were vacant and as black as combat boots. The girls squatted on their haunches, and Cortez's ghost radar picked up their pubic hairs stirring feathery balls of dirt, ash, cockroach shit, dead skin, hairs, scattering them across the floor. Three or four whores huddled near the door like pets waiting for the owner to come home and feed them. The girls were all wet eyes and tongues like they had just been chased at gunpoint out of a shower. One scratched her ass with a nail file. Another one hugged a bottle of Mekong between her bare tits and blew on the top, making a little tune. Disco music blared like a foghorn from a speaker hooked by wood, nails, and rods like a monster's nest to the ceiling. The square speaker had a brown fungus spreading on the cloth front, and small puffs of dust exploded when the bass part kicked in. Cortez surveyed the rest of the bar. Not a single customer was seated at the bar and the sofa was empty; naked youngsters waiting for money to swing through the door and all they had got was a ghost.

You could have any whore you wanted for a song.

And five hundred baht.

Cortez had vomited on his boots when he had seen the Aztec equivalent of skull bars four hundred plus years before. Cortez had written to Charles V that the Aztecs—not some but all of them—practiced sodomy. Cortez, a man who never missed a mass, or a message to the Pope, had been horrified these fucked-up Aztecs had skulls in the temples and sodomy in the archways of the towers. When Cortez arrived in Patpong, and walked up the flight of stairs, he was a ghost so he couldn't barf and he had no feet on which to put boots. He didn't see much in the bar except a lot of fear and boredom. The usual wartime companions. He was no longer disturbed—nor did he take it personally—that some people who sensed a ghost giggled and ducked out the back door. A couple of girls squatted on a small stage eating rice and grasshoppers fried in hot oil. The air-conditioner was turned off. The stale air was smoky from cigarettes. What would Charles V and the Pope have made of Patpong? He crossed himself and walked across the room.

One of the girls was curled up on a sofa while another girl dry humped her. Their long, black hair covered their faces. He had a wild hope that Daeng might be among them. But she was nowhere to be found in the skull bars or on Patpong. She was miles away waiting to be rescued by Robert Tuttle who could not find her. Frustrated by this failure of connection—since Cortez's own fate rested on the success of this rescue operation—Cortez, a curl of cigar smoke, blew downstairs and into the street. He was resigned to watching the Army killing civilians in the streets of Bangkok. That, at least, made sense. Cracking heads was a black and white, and good and wrong business. He wondered if the Army had been supplied by the Purcells, whether they had the helicopters he had once been promised. Back on the street he watched a couple of *farang* buy condoms in a drugstore. The ribbed, lubricated kind which came in flavors like strawberry, coffee, cherry, and nutmeg. Then he headed down Patpong Road where the merchants sold pirated tapes, videos, shirts, belts, and pimps held up signs offering sexual menus involving boys and girls. He was late for an appointment with Montezuma. The humid heat reminded him of Latin America. The more he thought about it, the more worried he became that Daeng would be one more in a long line of missed opportunities. He had gone to the skull bar, thinking it was a kind of local temple where the gods accepted offerings. After all that time—about five hundred years—he had been preparing himself for the temples at the front lines—he was, after all, from the Old World—and in Patpong he found temples where human sacrifices retained the flesh around their skulls, where their lips still puckered, and their tongues were still wet.

Cortez was racked with questions. What had he witnessed? A few naked girls dry humping on a sofa. What would he report to Montezuma? And would Montezuma ever trust any report delivered from such a temple? Patpong—a temple with forty towers—all filled with live, working skulls. That would freak out Montezuma.

Cortez decided to make something up. Reality lacked the basic elements of believability.

He had watched a girl playing with herself in front of a mirror.

It occurred to him what he would say.

The Army had used chemical warfare. The women in the skull bars were horribly disfigured, skin the color of steamed rice peeled off their naked bodies, and they whispered for medicine and death.

That's what he would tell Montezuma, and he would like that explanation.

Montezuma often spoke of the trenches during World War I. The Purcells had made a small fortune selling tons of mustard gas to the Germans, English and French. Cortez had climbed the stairs to a skull bar and found whores with lungs filled with dust spores, twisting and rolling around in agony. Whores suffering from chemical wounds, that's what he'd say.

5

May 18th, 1992—Fax
London

Dear Robert,

B angkok is the lead story on the BBC evening news. But you are
there—on the front lines, so to speak. I won't bore you with
the facts from England as you already are painfully aware (though
Graham Greene once said the closer you are to the fighting the
less you know) that the Thai Army opened fire and killed many
demonstrators in Bangkok. Burma in '88, China '89, and now
Thailand '92. These appalling images of brutality rolling over the
Asian landscape make for a most disturbing reminder of excess and
cruelty. I hope that your daughter, Asanee, was sensible enough to
stay away from the free-fire zone. It must be extremely difficult for
you, her, and your friends. My thoughts go with you. . . .

Now on to Harry's gift of bones!

I received the bone fragment you sent some weeks ago. And as
you requested, I gave it to a friend who works for Scotland Yard,
and a Carbon 14 dating test was performed and this morning I
received the report. The bone is probably the femur of a male, Asian,
who weighed around one hundred twenty pounds, aged between
60 and 65 years old, and he suffered from the following disabling
diseases: malaria, typhoid and rheumatism. The bone fragment is
three hundred years old, give or take fifty years. Not much else
can be divined (with any degree of certainty) from a shard of bone.

Harry says it is from one of his Chinese relatives, a General Xue. The lab report can't give a rank in the Army, the Chinese part does fit. Beyond this point of reason, I am afraid the descent into the realm of mystics is precipitous. The Orient has kept alive the flame of voodoo, ghosts, and wandering souls more than does present-day London, which is preoccupied with sales at Selfridges.

It is strange Harry would have given you this. The Chinese revere their dead relatives and would hardly part with the bones. But Harry is only half-Chinese and his upbringing is likely to have disrupted many of the traditional Chinese beliefs. But it is not only the Chinese who have held these beliefs.

There have been bone cults as far back as the Stone Age. Ancient man gathered the bones of animals killed on a hunt with some hope of reviving the spirit of the slain animal. In South America peyote gatherers planted deer bones with peyote root; transporting the spirit of the deer to the power of the peyote. One might be cynical and say so what! They were stoned. People under the influence of drugs are likely to do and believe whatever pops into their head. In any event, only much later did Stone Age man go the next step and believe that man's bones had an immortal soul.

If you go back and read Herodotus, he records a tribe living along the Black Sea who disposed of shipwrecked sailors in an artful manner: "As for the enemies they overcome, each man cuts off his enemy's head and carries it away to his house where he impales it on a tall pole and sets it standing high above the dwelling, above the smoke-vent for the most part. These heads, they say, are set aloft to guard the whole house."

What you are suggesting, I think, has been thought and written about before (at least in the academic journals). In the West, not all bones were equal. The skull has since ancient times been thought of as the dwelling place of the soul, and the brain the bone marrow of the skull which produces semen. It is an old myth and like most myths never quite died out completely. My point is that when you cremate the bones, all the bones are treated as a unified entity; the spirit resides throughout the skeleton. Our obsession with the skull has defined our cultural destiny. Without it, for example, how does a Western culture produce a Descartes? The short answer is that most of our religious and philosophical ideas are recycled bone cult notions updated and perpetuated as modern, progressive faiths.

On to a personal matter which concerns Snow.

I had a disturbing letter from him last month. He has had flashbacks to his days as a hostage in the north of Thailand and is taking medication. He has what he calls a "high-miler" round-eyed American girl friend and they have travelled the west coast of California in a Winnebago, camping out in shopping centers at night. He suffers like a dog which has been beaten and cowers in the corner, shaking and whining. Snow appears to be lost in action. A POW who has returned to America but no one has taken the effort to discover him in their midst. I wrote Snow to the same effect so don't think that I'm speaking behind his back. I have the feeling he will return to Bangkok not because I profess to be a "seer." Such a return is not uncommon for a hostage who desires to relive his experience, in order to come to terms with it, and bury the devils which haunt him. If I'm right, then he may be walking as I write into a killing field in the streets of Bangkok.

Ever since my promotion to Harry Purcell's Chair at the University I have had this uneasy feeling. Harry loved working in the field. Perhaps it was in the Purcell blood, running guns for countless generations is bound to make one different. He was restless in London like an inmate in a cell, waiting for a chance to escape over the wall. Unlike Harry, I feel that there is something reassuring about the solitary confinement a university cell provides—beyond the ordinary prison. Harry believed it was a gross felony to have government, foundations, corporations and others pay us to think for them, to solicit our views and ideas, and to write them down on paper for them to read. Ironically, this came from a man whose family fortune was based on selling instruments of death and destruction; living on such funds never caused Harry the slightest moral problem or doubt.

Harry wrote one brilliant monograph: *Magic Hilltribe Rituals.* No one can still accept Harry's reason for resigning from the university. Myself, I accept his words at face value. He gave one of those boyish Harry smiles and said, "I am finishing the family chronicle."

He was always secretive about this chronicle which somehow involved his family. Perhaps he confided in you about these matters.

I am afraid he never took me into his confidence on personal matters. He was, I gather, an intimate friend of yours.

There are those who say that Harry Purcell was not politically correct, that he was out of step, out of date with modern developments. From your years of teaching, I don't have to tell you about the nasty daggers looking for backs to stab in any university. Harry may have appeared eccentric, but as one who now occupies his Chair, I must say he discarded a great deal of conventional scholarship as disconnected with reality, as useless. This hurt the pride of colleagues and others who thought Harry had dismissed their lifetime of work. Harry liked the Goethe quote, "Few people have the imagination for reality." One of his common-room critics once replied, "Even fewer people have imagination for the act of mass extermination."

Yours,

Richard Breach

6

May 19th, 1992—Fax
Bangkok, Thailand

Dear Richard,

The killing is not over in Bangkok. I saw enough last night to convince me that your fax yesterday raised the right question: What can we say or truly know about what goes on inside the skull? Harry Purcell's family chronicle was a half-millennium burden he thought he could carry; but I am not convinced that he can handle the full weight of what has passed into his hands. As for my friendship with Harry, I think of a famous painting with two people with bags over their heads looking at each other. The image sticks in my mind as the kind of intimate friendship I have with Harry.

I returned from a kayak trip on the Nan River to discover the killings first hand. Snow is in Bangkok reporting on the street battles, and Crosby is selling T-shirts at HQ. Thus the world of Bangkok is much as you remember it.

In a small village on the Nan River, I made a complete fool out of myself. I delivered the headman a handful of what I told him were floating stones, so he treated me—and he had every right to—like a simpleton. If I couldn't tell a stone from a bone, surely I wasn't to be expected to know the location of the invisible spirit.

Spirit, mind, and brain are another magical trinity for which there can never be a rational, materialistic answer. If there is a consciousness, now, from moment to moment, when the brain ceases to function, does this consciousness continue in some form or does it stop altogether like a machine unplugged from its energy source?

When I saw Thais dying before my very eyes last night, I asked myself what became of this thing called consciousness, the invisible self. Since the Buddhists call the self an illusion, what is the non-self? And is it this non-self that Buddhists believe is reincarnated lifetime after lifetime until enlightenment occurs? Is non-consciousness, like the unborn and the non-self, the state called enlightenment?

As for Harry Purcell's views on living, it probably would come as no shock to you that he has built a super-computer, virtual reality system in his house. He closets himself away in a simulator, where he tests weapon systems in famous battles of the past. I told him this is the Purcell equivalent to a busman's holiday, and he smiled. He hints at things in a Harry kind of way, but never goes into detail. A confession: my motive for sending the bone fragment. Snow once said years ago that Harry was a vampire. He probably drank the blood of young girls and had lived a thousand years. I had this strange feeling there was something not right about this bone. I am grateful your expert has proved my instincts to be wrong.

Yours,

Robert Tuttle

PS Radio Bangkok 108.3 just reported a rumor that the Army was going to cut all electricity to the city. So I hope I can get this faxed to you before we go off the grid.

7

In Bangkok in the week before the killing started, there had been a lull when the Army and the pro-democracy movement had reached a kind of compromise. Hope of a peaceful resolution hovered like a fog of hope in the polluted city air. It was enough of a breather for Robert Tuttle to take his kayak up to Nan Province; the night before he left Bangkok, Tuttle had checked into HQ. An hour later, Harry walked in carrying a battered briefcase. He had a portable library of family notebooks, old letters, ledgers, articles, books, and clippings about head hunting and cannibalism. Harry unpacked part of the contents and set up camp in an HQ booth with Tuttle looking on. As the prostitutes watched, they gave Purcell's booth a wide berth, shaking their heads over the strange behavior of a half-*farang*.

Tuttle had seen the inevitable changes in Harry's physical appearance over the years. His hair was pure white and shoulder length; his eyebrows coiled like a witch's collection of amputated spider legs. His gold capped teeth sparkled as he smiled, concealing some secret family atrocity. The fingernails on his little fingers—both right and left hand—had been left to grow three inches in length and he painted them firehouse-engine red. He could have passed for someone five hundred years old, or how men would appear five hundred years in the future—of indeterminate race, age, and nationality. His physical appearance spooked some of the HQ girls who made a point of steering clear of his booth.

He spent little time in England, and more time on the road—as an ex-full professor he had what he called "scope." Harry had been working day and night on a short history of head hunting and cannibalism. It was a personal project to amuse himself and shock his friends. As Tuttle's Singha Gold arrived at the table, Harry Purcell spoke.

"The Tibetans drank from the skulls of their ancestors. Think of that. Tuttle raises his cup which just happens to be the skull of his grandfather and takes a long drink of Singha Gold. The Teutons in ancient times used the skulls of their enemies as drinking cups."

"After they were dead," said Tuttle.

"Most of the time," said Harry Purcell. "For thousands of years Asians and Europeans and Africans drank from skulls. As a linguist you will like this," said Harry, pulling out one of his photocopied books. "La Barre has the Italians using *coppa* which means cup and skull. There was no distinction between the two. In Sanskrit the skull and cup become *kapala*. In Germanic languages *kopf*; Scandinavian *skoal*; the Scots *skull* and the French *tête*. From the Chalcolithic to early Bronze Age, Europeans had a common language: *skull* meant *cup*, and *cup* meant *skull*. The only difference was—whose skull are you drinking your beer from? Your grandfather or the warrior you killed in battle? When you raised your cup in a toast, you raised the skull of another human being to wish the good health of others."

As Harry finished his drinking story, Crosby appeared in a T-shirt with the words printed on three separate lines:

No Experience

No Family Connections

No Chance

He joined them in the booth, sitting next to Purcell, brushing some of Harry's computer print-outs to the side.

"Sorry to interrupt your lecture, Professor, but I prefer to drink my beer straight from the bottle," said Crosby. "With most of the skulls I see, one would be hard pressed to get half a pint inside one."

"*Skoal*," said Tuttle raising his glass. "Harry was making a point . . ."

"You should think about cutting the first two lines from your T-shirt, Crosby," said Harry.

Crosby looked down at his shirt. "There was once a Last Chance Bar."

"It went out of business," said Tuttle. "It burnt down."

"Someone threw a bomb. Personal conflict, the press called it."

"Personal conflicts were far more interesting in earlier times. Cortez found 136,000 skulls in an Aztec temple," said Harry Purcell. "Imagine you sail in a wooden ship from Europe with its history of skulls as drinking cups centuries behind you, then pull open the temple door and find 136,000 skulls."

"The ultimate coffee shop, Cortez must have said to himself," said Crosby. "Or he thought he had cornered the cup and saucer market in Spain for the next century."

"In the sixteenth century, the Spanish had stopped drinking from skulls," said Harry.

"Thanks, Harry," said Crosby.

Tuttle watched a girl curl herself around Crosby. She hugged Crosby and flashed a wink at Tuttle, pursing her lips into the kiss phase. He wondered if there was any other place on earth like HQ. As the conversation moved between redesigning Crosby's T-shirts and the ancient practices of taking and using skulls, Gow whispered in Crosby's ear. Gow appealed to those hardcores who insisted on a woman with a dancer's body and a drinker's face.

"We go now," Gow said. "Short time, okay?"

"I'm making business," said Crosby.

Harry's Zippo lighter shot a large bolt of flame into the air; he moved it forward, touching the end of a Havana cigar. He puffed on the cigar, sending a thick cloud of smoke across the table.

Gow leaned forward, coughed and whispered in Tuttle's ear.

"That *farang* is devil. Why you do business with devil?" she asked. The smoke made her eyes tear.

"Sweetheart, if the devil has a purple you would gladly do the devil's business," said Crosby, who had overheard her comment on Harry.

She raised her fist to strike Crosby. Harry caught her wrist mid-flight, brought her wrist down level with his face and kissed her hand as if she were a princess. She struggled against him and pulled her hand away, jumped from Crosby's lap, and fled in terror to the next booth, screaming to several HQers that the devil had kissed her and that nothing could purify her. In her mind only a demon sent from hell would kiss the hand of a whore in such a fashion—this hellish mocking kiss reserved for those whose worth was measured in gold rather than purple.

When Tuttle turned around, he caught a brief glimpse of the other girls huddled with Gow. If he had looked closely, he would have seen a new face in the booth. She was young—nineteen, twenty. Her head craned around to catch a look at Harry Purcell. There was a half-moon scar on her face, casting an arc of shadow where the face should have been smooth.

"He's not the devil," Daeng said to the other girls.

"Women," said Harry. He was thinking, "To command a she-devil with a kiss is a kind of victory." But what he said to those around the table was a different story. "I had a relative on my mother's side. General Xue grew a moustache so long it hung down to his chin. Before the general went on a long campaign, he had one of his mistresses braid ivory beads into the ends of his moustache. The ivory came from rare white elephants specially raised by the general for their tusks. A craftsman, really an artist, made the round ivory balls bearing the likeness of General Xue. Special care was taken to drill holes through the ivory for the general's facial hair to pass through. He wore seven ivory skulls on each side of his moustache. He wore them into battle. He wore them into the brothels. General Xue would take a woman, and afterwards, he would give her one of the ivory skulls. When he returned home from a campaign, one could count the number of women he had taken by the number of missing ivory pieces. He often returned from one of his fourteen ivory campaigns, and inspected his white elephants for the growth of their tusks. Not until another tusk could be harvested and carved would he contemplate another campaign. He was a great warrior and lover. Once a man confused the ivory for pearls."

"Pearls before swine," said Crosby.

"General Xue once had a European executed for that very remark," said Harry, looking thoughtfully at his teeth marks in the base of the cigar. "Beheaded."

It was the kind of Harry Purcell story which had often led Snow to say that Harry was full of shit. Harry saw from the way Tuttle and Crosby exchanged looks that they shared Snow's opinion.

"Tuttle, tomorrow, come around to my house. I have a piece of the general I'd like you to have."

This sent a shiver up Tuttle's spine.

"What piece?" asked Tuttle.

"A piece of the general's femur bone." Harry's eyes sparkled, laugh lines stretching to his hairline. He liked this shock value. It was a family trait. His mother's father had once told a journalist that a Japanese sniper had shot off his cock during World War II, and that he had a silver penis implanted to replace the missing cock. He showed a photograph of Harry's mother to the journalist, and said, "This is my daughter from the silver cock."

Tuttle sat across from him wearing an expression of disbelief and terror not unlike what Harry imagined had been the expression on the journalist's face. But the face which interested him most was that of Cortez. What had been the expression on Cortez's face as he entered that temple and found himself in the midst of a mass carnage beyond anything he had seen on a battlefield? What was the look in Cortez's eyes? Horror? Surprise? Did he stumble back, gasping for air? Or did Cortez have difficulty at first understanding the objects before him? He must have wondered about an explanation such as a natural disaster, divine punishment, or a devil living among the people of an uncivilized land.

"Cortez should have smoked a Havana before he went through the temple door," said Harry.

"He could have defeated the Aztecs with one of those things," said Crosby.

"Harry, does it matter what went on inside Cortez's mind?" asked Tuttle.

For a long time Purcell said nothing. "Understanding the workings of a general's mind is research and development for our business," he said as a new round of drinks arrived.

"What if nothing went through Cortez's thoughts? His brain blanked, cut out," said Tuttle.

Harry liked that possibility as Tuttle believed that he would.

"Hawks would have disagreed. Cortez's mind was to think like a military man—so he would not have blanked out. He was a good businessman as well. We fucked him on a helicopter deal. He threatened us. We threatened him. But that's business. His soldier's mentality would be to ask the question of how long such a slaughter had been going on? But the real question is what would you think, or I think, or what would Crosby think?"

"136,000 less *farangs*, assuming Indians are *farang*, to buy T-shirts in Bangkok," said Crosby.

"A practical, Crosby-like answer," said Harry.

"No matter how many skulls you collect, store, no matter how many temples you build to house the skulls, you can't escape your destiny which is the same as for any other animal on earth—sooner or later, your skull goes on the shelf," said Tuttle.

"The realist's answer," said Harry Purcell. "The more man tries to deny he is an animal the more animal-like his behavior becomes. What other animal would build a temple and fill it with skulls of its own kind inside?" asked Harry, as Snow pulled up in his Hawaiian shirt, his glasses down on the end of his nose. He saw the young girl with the scar in the booth behind and made a mental note. You had to be careful with a booth of hardcores. It was better to keep one's personally acquired HQ intelligence information about new girls to oneself; until the girl was checked out. Then the information would go public.

"Ninety-nine beer mugs on the wall," said Snow, shoving in next to Tuttle, picking up the thread of Purcell's conversation as a perfect cover and pouncing on a distraction technique Tuttle had taught him years ago. "While you wandos are talking about that super wando of them all—Cortez—and the meaning of skulls, you missed a ringer who just walked in. She's over by the jukebox, looking a little scared. Today's rent day, so the hunting for ringers should be excellent."

Crosby looked through the crowd and spotted the girl in a slinky black dress, looking like a baby black widow spider spinning a web. "She's not a ringer. She's a semi-regular. Six months ago she might have been a ringer. But she crossed that line. I had her last week. Before she learns to say 'ringer' in English, she'll be inducted into the HQ genito-urinary hall of fame. And from that point she's . . ."

"A shark who can smell blood-money in the water ten miles away," said Harry without looking up from an article.

"Exactly," said Crosby. "She ran me a bath and then poured in half a bottle of Listerine. I questioned her about it. And she said

Listerine killed germs. AIDS was a germ. Now comes the logical part. If she gave me a good soaking, scrubbed down the vital parts before we screwed, then in her mind I was AIDS and germ free. And you took her as a ringer?"

From the jukebox came the song, "Moonlight and love songs never out of date . . . woman needs man, and man must have his mate, that, no one can deny. You must remember this. . . ."

"Listerine. God, you mean the shit that you're supposed to gargle with?" asked Snow.

"She buys the stuff by the case from some bloke who works the port at Klong Toey. It's imported in containers. A few cases go missing. She tells me that she gets her Listerine at a very nice discount, too."

"But I really thought . . . I wanted . . . Listerine? I'm losing my ringer's sixth sense. For godsakes, I could be in a state of advanced senility and not know it. All those drugs I took in the 60s. My mind could be a blank. Soon I will forget Crosby's name. The purpose of Listerine. How to give directions to HQ to a cab driver. I will forget where I live. The girls will see that I've lost it, I'm cut adrift. A mere leaf in the storm. They will ask me how much money I have in my bank account, and I will tell them. I will live alone and not know what the story is. Where I parked my Winnebago. Or why a dog licks its balls."

"Why does a dog lick its balls?" asked Harry Purcell.

"Because it can," said Snow.

"Because it's not afraid to try," said Harry.

"You're sick, man," said Snow.

Tuttle watched the Listerine girl, she was nineteen or so, black tight-fitting dress, with a matching handbag and fake pearl necklace. She might have been a ringer. Crosby might have been pulling Snow's chain simply to have a bit of fun knowing Snow's obsession with AIDS, germs and bathing before and after sex.

"Ringers are becoming as rare at HQ as *Shitemper Sewertums*," said Tuttle.

"What in the hell kind of girl is that?" asked Crosby.

"One with scales, the mouth of a grouper, a head the size of a bulldog and a powerful tail," said Tuttle.

"I've not had her," said Crosby.

"But you had her younger sister," said Snow. "Noi *Shitemper Sewertums.*"

About then Daeng had dropped a baht coin into the jukebox and pressed number 108—*Say you, Say me.*

8

"Bangkok's Radio 108.3 has received another entry for the best rumor of the mass murder award. We have a report of chemical warfare on Patpong. It is unconfirmed. And that makes it, a rumor. The problem with this rumor is that it gives the pinhead generals ideas. That's a novel thought. A general with an idea other than killing people and asking questions later. We are still here broadcasting. Stay off the streets unless you wanna become target practice for the trigger happy. I'm telling a lot of jokes but I haven't had any sleep for forty-eight hours, and nothing I'm seeing in the street below is funny."

Tuttle was listening to a portable radio on the back of a motorcycle taxi. He had given the nineteen-year-old kid five hundred baht to take him to the front lines. The streets were empty, silent; nothing moving in the night. In the distance they heard gunfire. The kid knew his stuff, winding in and out of sois, avoiding Army patrols, and finally letting Tuttle off near Khao San Road. He joined a crowd coming out of a *wat*, when the Army opened fire. About a dozen people in front of him fell to the ground. He saw blood flecks on his forearm from someone beside him. The body didn't move. Gunfire raked the perimeter. People moaned, groaned; some were crying. He heard trucks pulling up as he rolled around, crawled into a doorway and watched

The radio plugged in his ear, he listened to the familiar voice of Radio 108.3. "You just heard Simon and Garfunkel's *The Only Living Boy in New York*. We just had a report out of the Royal Hotel that the Army has stormed the place. Repeat the Army has stormed the

Royal Hotel and we have unconfirmed rumors of indiscriminate executions going on in the lobby right now. We have a journalist George Snow on the line who is at the Royal Hotel. What's happening? We can hear the gunfire."

"The Army invaded the Royal Hotel five minutes ago."

"The Army cut our water and electricity ten minutes ago," said the DJ. "We're working off a generator."

"All I can say, I saw one girl who took a round in the leg. She's down. Outside the window, they are loading people into trucks."

"Dead people?" asked the DJ on the other end.

"Some aren't moving. I presume they're dead," said Snow.

"Presume all you want. There is serious killing going on."

"Now I'm hearing more intense gunfire outside. Hundreds of troops are firing into the air."

"They're not firing into the crowd?"

"These guys are firing in every direction you can think," said Snow. "Gotta run, someone's shooting on my floor."

Click. There was a moment of silence.

"That was George Snow, a journalist, who reported to us live from the Royal Hotel. Snow has eye-witness accounts of multiple casualties and Army trucks taking away the living and the dead."

Tuttle had risen from the booth at HQ, walked past the jukebox, out the back, through the kitchen and piss-holes near the alley. He had kept right on walking. He had made up his mind to return to the street. One or two cars had passed on Sukhumvit Road. He had bought five baht's worth of watermelon from a street vendor. He had been putting off seeing Dee. They had not parted on the best terms. He worried that she had been pinned down in her apartment with all the shooting going on in her neighborhood. Soldiers raking Sanam Luang with gunfire were reported to have spilled over to her soi. Dee—which means "good" in Thai—was waiting for him. She had once told him that in between his visits to her apartment her life stopped. Nothing happened. It was like white silence. Waiting for her man to return. It's what all Thai girls did until their boyfriends returned.

He couldn't say why he was doing this; it made no sense, but nothing that was going on in Bangkok made any sense. She would more than likely hurl another stone at his head and he'd end up like Montezuma. There was insanity in the air. Like a fever or a dose of crabs, it jumped from person to person, infecting one, then the next, sending them out against men with M-16s with orders to shoot any motherfucker who was out there. Tuttle was not immune to this fear. Daeng could be anywhere; at least, he knew where to find Dee, and, at that moment, she might need him.

Not long after he was in the back sois near the Royal Hotel. He cursed this fever of killing sweeping the city. He watched as some bodies were dragged away and thrown into trucks. On the Nan River the floating stones had been bones; on the streets of Bangkok the dead were fresh and warm. He looked at the sky and watched the tracers overhead. A light show of shooting stars in the middle of the night. He strained looking at the horizon and swore—for a split second—that he saw a ghost.

When he reached Dee's room, she was sitting on the wooden floor watching TV. She wore a T-shirt which had printed on the back, "If play for money and work for fun, come play at the Rose Bar." Tuttle put his arm around her shoulders and kissed her on the cheek. She had been a twenty-eight-year old hardcore who had worked in Patpong for twelve years until Tuttle set her up in the room and got her a job in a restaurant. Her face softened as she kissed him back.

"I know you come back," she said. "I wait you."

"You don't hate me?"

She shrugged. "Of course, I hate you. But I love you, too."

"You eat today?"

She shook her head and her smile vanished. "TV says don't go outside. Bad people are in the street." She wrinkled her nose, leaned back on her hands, her long, tapered legs, crossed at the ankles, were stretched out on the floor. It never occurred to her once to ask him about his trip to the Nan River. Where he had been or what he had seen. In terms of time, it might have been as if he had gone outside to buy the fruit he had in his hand. Her sense of time was the eternal now.

He handed her the watermelon he had bought outside HQ and which he had squashed while lying flat on the ground as the soldiers killed the people in front.

"Eat this," he said.

She opened the plastic bag, dumping the watermelon slices the shape and texture of red brillo pads into a small, white bowl. The watermelon didn't look like food. They stared at the contents of the bowl for about a minute before Dee reached in and offered him a broken, runny shard. He shook his head. The shooting outside was getting mixed up with the shooting on the TV. Tuttle reached forward on his knees and switched off the TV.

"You can't believe what's on TV," he said.

She shrugged her shoulders. *"Farang* don't tell lies?"

She had worked the bars long enough to know no race or nationality had a monopoly on the hustle, the quick scam, the twisted and distorted promises made in the heat of the night. This was part of her attraction. And despite the fact she had worked the bars, most of the time she had worked as a cashier. In status terms this made her less of a whore than the dancers. Dee simply hated dancing. She liked to watch. Patpong cashiers never had much chance to learn English. Dee was no exception. Tuttle always spoke Thai to her; the language of the relationship evolved as that of Thai. Snow had once hit the mark when he said, "Man, you gotta speak only Thai to the girls. Speaking English in bed with a woman only brings on flashbacks of a bad trip."

Later in the evening, as the gunfire died out and Tuttle had gone to sleep he felt a flame near his face. His eyes opened and Dee was sitting near him on the bed, holding a yellow candle, the kind the Thais use in the ceremony before the house Buddha. He looked up at Dee. She had melted the end of the candle into a beach stone from Koh Samui. Candle light washed over her face, and her large, wide-open eyes.

"You afraid?" Tuttle asked her, thinking the blood she had found on his clothes had frightened her.

She didn't move her body. Her eyes in that yellow light were intense with purpose. "I'm a tiger," she said. "You have English in your mouth. English is like food and you must feed me. I want it. Each day I want English. I'm very hungry. You forget to feed me English, I bite your nose, then your cock. Like a wild tiger. I don't live in the jungle. If this tiger stay in the jungle, then I say never mind. English isn't important. But I live in the city. I must have English. You understand me? If you don't feed me, then I pay *farang*

143

teach me English. I think other *farang* teach me English. I think better if you help me. But up to you. Tiger wait one, two more weeks. Then attack."

Then she blew out the candle.

Tuttle reached over to the radio on the floor and switched on Radio Bangkok 108.3. "We are still with you, Bangkok. Are you with us?" The DJ's voice was hoarse, the confidence drained. "I just had a call from a neighbor of mine. His fourteen-year-old son took an M-16 round in the head. The kid was an A student. He played sports at school. He had friends. He was idealistic. What fourteen-year-old isn't? The kid wanted to be a doctor because he thought it would help his country. I'd like to think I was one of Tom's friends. Once he came to our house with his father and asked if I could help sponsor him for a scholarship. One of those exchange student things. I said, hey, man, of course, I can. Tom was supposed to go away to school next autumn. Only he ain't going nowhere. He's dead. A life blown away. For what?" The DJ's voice quivered, then broke and he started to sob on the air. "Here's a song for you." The DJ put on Tracy Chapman's *Baby Can I Hold You?* "Words don't come easily, like I love you, I love you. You can say baby, baby can I hold you tonight, baby if I hold you forever. . . ."

9

Harry Purcell had traced the history of weapon transactions through his family's holding companies from the Spanish conquest of South America and the Japanese conquest of China and Southeast Asia. His father, Charles Purcell, had been chairman of the board during World War II. The Purcell family made a great deal of money selling arms during that war. Charles Purcell had taken a personal interest in Asia. It had been Charles Purcell who had married a Chinese general's daughter—the one who once claimed to have an implanted silver cock. Harry Purcell was the only son of their marriage. A week after his mother died the household remained in a state of mourning. Monks had come and burnt paper money. He had attended the cremation of his mother and was given the urn of her ashes. He was still a boy.

Charles had been given the Purcell chronicle by his own father and, as was the family tradition since Hawks, had added his own observations about the Japanese during the war.

"War and sex can never be separated," Harry's father had told him. "These are the real facts of life. Sex education starts with an understanding of conquest. Men in the field. Men in battle."

"Supply and demand," said Harry who was a young boy when he stood at his father's desk. It was after dinner and a single light cast his father into the shadows.

"Both are big business. The fear business. The intimidation business. Fortunes rest on this connection. Each generation of Purcells has handed down the facts of life to the next. It is your time, Harry. In this envelope is a report which explains everything in clear language that a bright lad like you can understand. If you have any questions, then we can discuss them. Do you have any questions now?"

Harry thought for a couple of minutes as his father rolled a Havana cigar between his fingers. "Did mother's father in China have a silver cock?"

His father lit the cigar, the expression on his face not changing. "A golden cock, Harry. Pure gold." The cigar smoke crossed the horizon of light like a haze, a fog from another world. He remembered a kind of melancholy laughter from the darkness where his father sat.

10

CORTEZ'S TEMPLE
by
Harry Purcell

The Imperial Japanese Army deployed Mobile Skull Temples on the front lines—mainly China and Southeast Asia—before and during the Second World War. Japanese military researchers had closely studied the exploits of the Spanish in the sixteenth century, and as with so many good concepts, the Japanese appropriated the theory to their own use and culture. When groups of Japanese soldiers—they never came alone—walked into one of these Mobile Skull Temples, they found what Cortez had been looking at all along (but edited out from his dispatches for the king and Pope)—female skulls with beautiful, young female faces attached to female bodies. The entire female package had been placed inside the temple for the soldiers' own private, personal sexual rituals. Rituals which had their own independent morality.

Cortez let himself go once as he described the Aztec women's choice of dress which placed them in one of two categories: Aztec ladies came either topless or bottomless. Sixteenth-century tits and ass descriptions left a lot to be desired. What did Charles V and the Pope make of that? Soldiers (and their commanders) who notice and record their observations on how local women are not dressed, what is left exposed, are soldiers (and commanders) commenting on more than local fashion, leisure wear. In the Japanese-occupied lands—including China, the local women appeared to come as a perk, a bonus, a payment in kind. Women in Mobile Skull Temples were supplied like ammo, rations, tents, transport, uniforms, boots, and rifles; they were part of what was issued to soldiers who served in the occupying Imperial Japanese Army. But if soldiers (or their commanders) took too much account of local women exposing their breasts and asses outside the Mobile Skull Temple, then the effectiveness of the fighting and occupying forces could be at serious risk from a military point of view.

The Mobile Skull Temples with their comfort women cleared the soldier's mind so he could concentrate on the pressing questions of occupying China: What is that coming down the road? Is it an enemy? Do we shoot it? If we kill it, can we eat it? If we let it live, can we fuck it?

MSTs were as popular as raw fish and sprang up like a new religion across China and Korea. Temples had been organized by the Japanese along the lines of Taoist thought—sex happens. But not without an abundant supply of local sex goddesses; Korean, Chinese, and Malay women—hundreds of thousands—were recruited and these forced-labor goddesses were called comfort girls. The Japanese Co-prosperity Zone was dotted with Mobile Skull Temples, serving the line troops like a vast sexual mess hall.

Comfort girls—a strangely accurate description of their function. Comforting a man facing the fear of a violent death; comforting a man who starts to worry he has no future; comforting a man so he will follow the commands of his officers. Sex was comfort. Sex gave courage. Sex gave confidence and inspired commitment to the unit. The mission was comfort and not passion or lust. Women could be conscripted to supply comfort. They were compelled to perform sex for dozens of men. The comfort women were more than sexual objects—they were a lesson in fear. The ordinary soldier for a brief moment over the body of a woman who was made to submit to him had the most precious gift—the gift of command. He forced the woman to submit as he commanded. To command the she-devil allowed the front-line soldier to have a taste of power. He came to know the duty to his commander through his refuge in the body of a comfort woman. And there was more—these woman had an ability to withstand the pain and this was a further lesson—this time, not one of command, but in the endurance of fear and bravery face to face with the enemy.

The women were sent into sexual battle, sending a powerful message to the men—are you less able to serve your commanders than these throw-away women—these worthless beings whose only function is sex and comfort to the soldiers guarding the Co-prosperity Zone? Comfort from what evil forces lurking inside the Zone? If the Zone lacked Japanese female sexual partners, why not import them? Was it the usual loss of morals arising from an absence of the normal influences of home, friends, and family? The long periods among a hostile Zone population? Or was the comfort of strangers a welcome diversion from the killing of the locals? The Zone soldiers of the Japanese Imperial Army never appeared to experience discomfort in taking these women. There is no recorded case of one Japanese Imperial Army soldier or officer objecting to the comfort-woman system or forming a one-man rescue effort for a single comfort woman. They all participated; none complained. Why such uniformity in matters of sex?

Command.

Sex on demand.

Sex which is commanded.

Comfort on command.

Passion was for civilians.

An Army which celebrates victory rather than defeat is based on rigid, unquestioning command. There are no politicians who raise issues of detail. An Army which does not provide sex and comfort cannot command its forces to victory. This is a fact of life. And of war. Sex and battle plans require commanders who are hungry with passion. Reason and logic have no place in command or passion. A soldier's mind is simple: Can we fuck it? Once they crossed the threshold and were inside the MST the questions of will it kill and eat me or can I kill and eat it did not arise. It is not likely you would find one who will ask: Can we rescue this creature so it may have life uninterrupted by pain?

Recruitment procedures in the Zone mandated the presence not of "women" but of young girls. They were not whores—comfort is not found in the arms of whores who choose to make themselves available. Any more than a soldier has a choice to shoot to kill. The illusion of supplying innocence was the key to the MST success inside the Zone; it kept the soldiers from questioning their superiors—fucking a comfort girl was following another order without risk of destruction. Soldiers were kept from going mad, from deserting into the Zone and finding their own girls. The generals understood that the function of gods was the provision of comfort. All religions offered gods who promised release from fear, anxiety, and tension from the human Zone.

Why did a village girl become a comfort girl? Because she could not say "no." Whispering this word was forbidden. She had no choice. As many soldiers as wanted her had her—four, five, a dozen, a division—comforting each man who pushed himself erect inside her, making him feel as if she were there only for him. The comfort goddess was the religion of the battlefield. And no religion has ever been defeated (except by force of arms) which offered the congregation unlimited, free sex. The Japanese Imperial Army might have stayed forever in the Zone. The soldiers were born again each time they walked into a temple. No one deserted; no one complained; and everyone felt saved. No shelves were crudely lined with thousands of naked skulls. They entered the temple that Cortez had sought but had not found. And they proved beyond any shadow of a doubt that one person's comfort can translate into another's pain.

With a few modifications, the Japanese adapted the comfort-girl religion to peace time and discovered it worked even better than in war. The new Zone emerged in the post-war period. The Japanese Imperial Army had been privatized as business enterprises, and the new soldiers—the business executives—found themselves in the private, Japanese-only salons and clubs. The comfort girls never vanished from the scene; their numbers increased, they wore numbers, and had the illusion of a life beyond the temple walls. Ah, but you say, these girls are exceptionally well paid for their services, the ones who work today have a choice and can leave anytime; they can quit the club and work in a factory, become a maid, return to the rice fields—these girls, some will argue, can say "no." The modern comfort girl has a choice. She is not a conscript into the temple; she is a volunteer. Any member of the religion of free will would be programed with similar thoughts to agree with your position. A whore decides her own fate; a comfort girl has her fate decided for her by others.

Free will versus determinism. Where in the history of war and sex has such a false division ever been more wrongly placed? And what difference does "peace" bring to women without hope and chance among those who occupy their lands?

The fact remains, nowhere is there a report of a rescue of a single woman working inside these temples. The guns have been silenced but the lessons from the battlefield travels through time. These are the facts of life. The exact description of the mating ritual from battlefield to marketplace. Know your commanders, their fears, their weapon requirements . . . and remember that bullets and temples are the same thing looked at in another way, and from another perspective.

11

When the crematorium-like gray fog began to clear in the pre-dawn morning over Bangkok, a detachment of Thai soldiers found Weird Bob's body hunched against the shell of a burnt-out Honda which had been overturned on a back soi. The barbed-wire barricade was five hundred meters in the opposite direction. Nervously clutching their rifles, two soldiers checked out the body as ordered. They cautiously approached the slumped over figure.

"*Farang bpen kii mao?*" asked one of the soldiers. Was this tall *farang* with an Army like haircut drunk? Wishful thinking.

"*Mai chai, farang lap,*" replied the other. Was he asleep? More of the same.

What was the condition of the *farang* in the soi? Was Weird Bob drunk in the street or sleeping in the street during the middle of a bloody revolution?

His large head was tilted to one side, he had a hanged man's neck, and his eyes were wide open. One of the soldiers leaned down and shook Weird Bob's shoulder, and the body keeled over on the pavement. The rug on his head had dislodged and covered his eyes, giving the strange impression that hair was growing from the center of his head to the tip of his nose. When the soldiers turned him over, underneath the body they found a dented electric fan with a red ribbon. Nothing that couldn't be repaired. As a soldier was about to claim the fan as booty, and another Weird Bob's rug, several young demonstrators came down the soi and threw rocks at the soldiers. The reaction was immediate. Two soldiers aimed and fired over the heads of the youths, who shouted insults—*hia*—cunt—*jai sut*—animal heart and threw more rocks. One of the soldiers knelt and fired a burst. One of the young men was winding up, his arm raised over his head like a quarterback but holding a rock. The M-16 rounds pierced the chest of the demonstrator in a neat, tight pattern. The soldiers turned back to Weird Bob's body and panic set in. Everyone would say—the foreign press were everywhere—that the Thai Army had killed the *farang*. That would be a black eye, bad for the international image. Weird Bob suddenly looked like in death what he had never seemed in life—an extremely important person: what counts is presentation—the *farang* in his expensive suit and tie. In Thailand the white shirt, suit and tie was a badge of authority, class, and power. *Kreeng jai*—a little fear in the heart—was based on lower ranks bowing to the higher ranks. There would be an outcry. Foreigners would blame the Thai Army; the soldiers felt fear that they would be blamed for having killed him. Then a higher ranking officer arrived. This officer, a colonel, surveyed the street and called for reinforcements to secure a forward position. Two armored personnel carriers arrived and pushed forward, scattering more demonstrators. A moment later, soldiers loaded Weird Bob's body into the back of a van; Weird Bob ended on top of a pile of other dead bodies which had been collected.

Weird Bob had been strolling down the street at the time of his death, carrying a new electric fan with transparent green plastic blades and a red bow tied to the grille. Several months before, he had read about a tall man contest in the newspapers and arrived at the hotel in time to win and eat at a free buffet.

"You gotta read the party column of the newspaper and get a press card. Then you can eat free in Bangkok."

It was the only thing Weird Bob had ever won in his life. When pulled by the rumors of Radio Bangkok 108.3 into the streets, he naturally—to his way of thinking—went with his electric fan, his lucky charm, which fate had awarded him for being tall.

Weird Bob wore thick glasses that rode down on his nose, his balding scalp thatched with strands of brownish hair, his pear-shaped body stuffed in baggy clothes. He had been standing near the curb showing *farangs* his first-prize fan. What they noticed however was that Weird Bob's pants defeated gravity, sliding down his hips but never falling down to his ankles. His belly hung heavily over the top and his chest was sunken. It was Snow who said that Weird Bobby could walk into any Patpong bar dressed like a vagrant, carrying his new fan with the red bow, and walk out five minutes later with a beautiful teenager. And Crosby was the one who said Bangkok was the only place on earth where freaks like Weird Bob who finished last anywhere else in the world finished first for an entry fee of five hundred baht. Everyone with a purple stepped across the finish line a winner. It was the only place on the face of the earth where charm, good looks, intelligence, breeding, and wisdom amounted to such an insignificant advantage. Given the time and money needed to acquire such attributes, Weird Bob was living testimony to the fundamental error that such resume entries carried any real value on the sexual front lines of Bangkok.

Montezuma stood with his arms folded not far from the barricade, smoking a cigarette (a habit he had developed about one hundred fifty years ago) and staring at Weird Bob's body.

"Where will they take the bodies? In which temple do they keep the skulls?" asked Montezuma, measuring the heads of the dead like a film director framing a scene.

Cortez laughed. "What is that Aztec humor? They are going to burn the bodies."

Montezuma sighed heavily. "It reminds me of the old days, when we would burn the guts and hearts. Those were the good old days. What beautiful idols we made. The idols I'm convinced liked the smoke. Burning bodies makes a good sacrifice. I like these people," said Montezuma. "They do their gods well."

This disgusted Cortez, and made him wonder why he spent so much time hanging around Montezuma who after four hundred and fifty years of being had shown such a dismal learning curve. Until he remembered he had no choice in the matter. In the Temple of Death, Montezuma and Cortez had found themselves bound together. The sentence of doom had been sealed with Montezuma's death. Frankly, Montezuma had got on his nerves from day one. Cortez plotted his release from their bond. He looked over at Montezuma who pulsated between something vaguely human in form and a formless lime-green mist—one with a lit cigarette hanging out of the sickening green cloud. It looked like the cigarette smoked itself. There was an explanation for Montezuma's condition (it affected Cortez less). They had smoked through a virus in Harry Purcell's computer when he was connected to the Internet system. He downloaded a video computer game—his software didn't alert him that his little prize from the Balkans had ghosts and a virus. It had been Montezuma's idea to lodge in the video game called Montezuma's Revenge—Harry was a sucker for any game naming the Aztec or Cortez. The irony was the programer's virus had lodged in Montezuma and turned him into slime without any warning.

Cortez asked himself the difficult question: How could anyone who had been dead three hundred years take up such a disgusting human habit as smoking?

"They will burn the bodies. The reason is simple. Politics. A command has a choice. Count or destroy the evidence," said Cortez. "Otherwise the evidence will destroy them. In this century it is a crime to sacrifice human beings. Belief in idols is no defence. The way you Aztecs carried on, the whole lot of you would have been tried on charges of crimes against humanity."

"It was religious freedom," said Montezuma. "There's nothing quite as wonderful as a human sacrifice. If I had a pulse, it would be throbbing just thinking about it."

Cortez ignored his friend as he watched the Thai colonel close the rear door of the van and wave the driver on, who then sped away from the scene.

"That would take a miracle," said Cortez after a thoughtful pause. "You having a pulse."

"A pulse with blood that flown at a different rate. In our day, we cut out thousands of hearts, ripped them hot and steaming from the chest, and built idols from human blood. We believed in miracles. Blood excited us. It made us alive. Blood filled us with hope and joy and pleasure. Blood is sacred. If only you could get past this Catholic barricade, Cortez. You are so limited." Montezuma turned and began to wander away in the direction of the demonstrators.

"Where are you going now?" Cortez called after him.

"To a skull bar in Patpong. I'd ask you along. But I know how you feel about these things as a Catholic. I read your dispatches. And I know—and you know—and you know that I know that you know—what you really did with some of our Aztec women in

Temixtitan. You didn't divulge everything to Charles V or the Pope about those activities. True or false?"

This shut Cortez up, as it always had. It reminded him why he followed Montezuma—to keep him away from Charles V and the Pope.

"Wait," shouted Cortez.

Montezuma wasn't surprised. "Come on, I'll buy you a girl."

Cortez caught up with Montezuma. "No, it's nearly time for us to go to work. We have a job, Monty. You think we materialized in Bangkok to have fun? You know the ground rules. Fun in Bangkok is strictly for the living." The time had arrived to tell Montezuma his story about the chemical attack on the Patpong skull bar but he lost his courage.

"Watch the skull collection but don't interfere with the skull selection," recited Montezuma as if it were a mantra.

"Full marks for the Aztec," said Cortez.

"You coming or not?"

Cortez sighed the eternal sigh of a ghost with a troubled conscience. "You will be disappointed."

"Skulls have never disappointed this Aztec." In a flash of slime-green fog the Aztec vanished.

PART 4
THE LOVERS

1

Montezuma refused to budge; he issued a command, ordering Cortez to attend a sex show in Patpong. It wasn't a question of permission. Cortez had to obey the order of his victim. This was the worst part of being dead, thought Cortez. Though he admired the Aztec, who in his opinion had a perfect instinct and timing for a night of temple hopping as the gunfire echoed on the streets. Cortez tried to hold himself together, now was not the time or place to go unglued; he fought off the memory of the eerily decaying place he had visited earlier. How he had ever defeated this Indian in life was one of death's great mysteries. Inside the upstairs bar Montezuma had chosen as an interesting temple tower, they sat in darkness as a Harley Davidson motorcycle descended from a hole in the ceiling. A man in his twenties stripped naked from the waist wore a black leather vest studded with silver decorations—stars, buttons, Nazi crosses—and a black military hat with a plastic bill; the hat was pulled forward until it rested above his eyebrows, making him look like he was tilting off balance and about to fall off the bike. Under the rider, with her legs splayed apart, arching her back, displaying her small, dark, wet patch of land, was a young naked girl with a flat belly. Her expressionless, dull eyes stared at the ceiling and her small mouth shaped in the letter "O" sparkled with glittering flecks in her red lipstick. She moved her hips as the Nazi driver pumped and grinded pelvic bone to pelvic bone on the back of the motorcycle. While he fucked, he stared off into the distance. Like this was just another job. Another mountain to climb, another performance, thinking about scoring some drugs.

"You think they are temple lovers?" asked Montezuma.

"Is this a trick question?" said Cortez.

"Ah, to be alive. Every Tom, Dick, and Harry sitting around the bar as if their biology would last forever," replied Montezuma with a chuckle. He leaned over an old slightly torn Greenwich Village catalogue of sex aids: hundreds of different vibrators—some electric (batteries not included)—in many shapes, sizes, and colors, penis rings, handcuffs, nipple clips, bondage ropes, plastic blow-up dolls, porno films, and 900 numbers (credit cards: Visa, Diners, American Express, and Mastercard only). Montezuma flipped the page with a long sigh of regret. There was a full-color lay-out of a long-legged blond, lying on her side, her legs scissored. The camera angle was from the back, and she was frozen in the act of inserting black beads into her anus. He sighed again, wrinkling his nose.

"If we had this advanced digital insertion equipment in Temixtitan, we might have spent our time ordering out of the catalogue and less time making human sacrifices. Yes, we could have been corrupted. Leaving aside blood and skulls for the new age. Century after century, I've seen the technology improve. And I can't help ask myself, 'Why, Montezuma, did you live in an age when all we had to make our idols were dried out vegetables?'"

"You said the same thing about the typewriter and telegraph," said Cortez. "You seriously believe that the absence of electronics and plastic vibrators was the cause of your Aztec perversions? The reason you made temple idols from seeds and vegetables? What you did to your victims before you slaughtered them . . ." Cortez stopped cold; there was only so far a general could go in criticizing a commanding officer.

"Afraid to say it?" asked Montezuma. "I order you to finish this thought. The one you fear is not listening." Cortez looked around the bar, having a quick once over to see if the Pope, who rarely materialized in Patpong skull bars, had paid a temple visit to check up on him.

"Say what?" Cortez was on the defensive.

"We had sex with the victims. Not all of them, of course. But we fucked as many as seemed comfortable. It was a way of comforting them. Sex is perfect for comfort. It's not half bad for lust," he chuckled. "Ah, if we had the telegraph it would have been a different story."

"But we would have had the telegraph, too," said Cortez.

Montezuma stared up at the stage, ignoring Cortez. "You simply got lucky and caught us with our pants down, seeking comfort."

"I knew it," said Cortez, as the live sex show started. On the stage, a naked girl with tattoos spread her legs, raised her pelvis, inserted a dart in her vagina. She aimed and suddenly launched the dart from her vagina, popping a balloon near the head of Snow, who managed to duck just in time to save the loss of an eye. He had taken a break from the frontline for some R & R.

"A Scud-tart attack," shouted Snow. "Duck. Who knows if you can get AIDS from a paper dart? Do you want to be the test case?"

Crosby picked up the dart and tried to examine it in the near darkness. "Rocks fall, bikes disappear into the ceiling, darts fly on Patpong Road as civilians flee the scene under a fresh attack by demon whores. The Army will be sent in to finish off the tarts."

"'The lawless dart-shooting hussies deserved a bullet,' the general said. Yeah, I can see that playing on the wires," said Snow. "Which reminds me, I've got to get back to the Royal. Catch you at HQ later."

"You Aztecs. . . ," said Cortez as Snow walked through Montezuma without having the slightest idea he had gone through a ghost.

"Don't 'you Aztecs' me. It's racist," said Montezuma, who hated being walked through. "We had to make do with whatever sex devices we could grow. Who ever heard of a 'machine'? In sixteenth-century Spain are you going to tell me that you had 'machines'?"

"Sodomy is a sin," said Cortez. "Every God-fearing person knows that. Eye Wave Machines which assist sodomy are the most sin-ful."

"Fearing God earned you me as your after-life commanding officer," said Montezuma.

Cortez went from slime-green to pale white like the scales on a decayed fish. He hated this reaction every time the Indian scored a direct hit on him inside a foreign temple.

Montezuma didn't let up either. "If I had a porno flick, it would display my favorite Sound Wave number—900. Dial 1-900-666-Help. What a world they the living live in—Eye Wave Machines which display numbers to punch into Sound Wave Machines. You remember the ad on the Smart Eye Machine—of course you do—for the best blow-jobs in town dial . . ."

"Stop," shouted Cortez. "You're technologically illiterate. The Eye Wave Machine is a TV. It's what Americans use to sell cars and the Smart Eye Machine is what Americans use to guide bombs through windows. It has nothing to do with oral sex." Even after being dead nearly five hundred years, Cortez could not bring himself to use the expression: "blow-job."

"People in this time can have home delivery sex and remote control human sacrifices."

Cortez watched as another dart passed through his hand and punctured a balloon held by a bar girl who bounced up and down on the lap of a tourist.

"Dial 1-900-666-Kill," said Cortez.

"I don't know that one." Montezuma looked confused.

Cortez liked catching him out like the day when they were both alive and Cortez had cried, "Look!" And as Montezuma turned to look, a stone had smashed into the side of Montezuma's head.

"If you had been running the Sound Wave Machines in the temple, that's the number you would have used. A dial-a-victim hotline."

Montezuma smiled. He was not in the least offended. "That would have been a nice touch. Look around. These people don't know how lucky they are. They don't have live Spaniards invading their temples. They have tourists paying for sex. While the local soldiers make the usual streetside human sacrifices. Boys will be boys, and rituals without blood are useless exercises," sighed Montezuma. "Another two, three hundred years, just think what technology will do for sex. Smart beds, smart mirrors, smart wallpaper, and smart carpets—they will read a person's mood, sexual desires, reserves of energy and deliver the right machines, toys, and tapes. About then I might decide on risking another rebirth."

Such talk always unsettled Cortez who as a Catholic still clung to the thought that rebirth was nonsense even though almost everyone he had ever known had been reborn multiple times since 1519. Still it was an article of faith which died hard even for the dead. But he be grudgingly understood the ground rules of karmic twinning which applied to the dead. If Montezuma were reborn, then he would have to go back as well. The trade-off was that Cortez was entitled to believe after his rebirth that he was unborn.

"Why don't we go back to Sanam Luang or the Royal Hotel and watch the killings? We are probably missing out on some real fun looting, beatings, roadside executions." He knew how to get Montezuma's attention.

"Executions? We saw a few in our time. We weren't half bad at it," admitted Montezuma.

"The soldiers were doing such a wonderful job of slaughtering. And you are right, it does bring back memories of the old days. And you know how fresh human blood cheers you up."

"It's what we Aztecs used to live for. But now that I'm dead, fresh human blood? I've gotta confess, Cortez, somehow the old magic is gone. It has lost some of the old thrill," said Montezuma wistfully.

2

"Radio Bangkok 108.3 update on the insanity. News flash. We are live—mostly live—coming to you from our broadcasting headquarters on the sixth floor. Another invasion to take us off the air has been repelled. About ten minutes ago the Army just tried using the elevator to the sixth floor. Now there was an original idea. By our count five soldiers marched into the elevator and pushed the sixth floor button. Did you guys volunteer for duty? Fat chance. You were ordered into the elevator. When the grunts hit the sixth floor the elevator door opened. And guess who was waiting for them? The Navy. The brave men who have risked their own lives to keep us on the air. We owe our lives to the Navy. They've pitched in and helped because they believe what is going on in the streets is wrong. It can't be allowed. And they know that keeping one non-Army radio station is one way of getting the truth out. So back to the elevator incident. The doors opened and four of the Navy's finest were waiting. They knelt on the floor, they had their rifles against their shoulders, watching as the elevator light bounced from the first, to the second, third, fourth, and fifth floors. As the doors parted and the soldiers saw who was waiting for them and what was pointed at them, guess what the soldiers did? They slammed their fist against the close door button. It was save your ass time. It takes one kind of courage to shoot civilians in the street and another to come out of an elevator with the Navy aiming at them. So they stared down the barrel of those Navy rifles for one second before fleeing the scene. It reminds me of a ten-wheel truck driver hitting a bicycle on the highway; the driver steps on the gas, he's outta

163

there in a flash. The Navy guys loaded a bullet in the chamber. This made some noise. Enough noise to make the Army hit team duck and push the eject button. They let their fingers do their walking. A message for the soldiers downstairs. We want to let you know the Navy has got much, much ammo left. They are watching the staircase and the elevator. We think the Army is back on the ground floor tying another note to a rock demanding that we surrender or they will really come and get us this time. Hey, fellahs, for the record, surrender has two 'r's' not one 'r'. Give up the fight and go back to school. This one is for the boys who can't spell and whose recent visit was unexpectedly interrupted. For the trigger-happy boys downstairs, take a hike, keep out of our face. Up next is a song by Tracy Chapman and it's called *Behind the Wall*. We dedicate it to the boys in the elevator who got cold feet."

3

THE LOVERS

A Denny Addison Documentary Film
Running time: 64 minutes
Black and White

Toom stretches out on a rumpled bed. She wears a black lace bra and black bikini panties. On the nightstand is a telephone. In the corner the TV is turned on; on the screen Asian models in swimming suits and high-heels walk down a catwalk to jazzy music.

"How long did you live in England?" asks Addison's voice off camera.

Toom, watching the TV set, replies, "Ten years."

"Were you ever scared? You know, afraid?"

Toom glances away from the TV and into the camera, nodding her head.

"You want to tell me about it?"

"Harvey took me to church for Christmas Mass."

"That's freaky," says Addison. "And you found that was scary?"

Toom watches a model turn on the catwalk, her movement brushing away the silky top and revealing a large breast with a pink nipple. "I never go to church before. I just follow what Harvey does. He picks up a book and sings. I pick up a book and sing. He kneels down. I kneel down, too. He not tell me about the wafer. You see at this church everyone goes to the front where the priest is handing out this wafer. I never know this word before. Wafer.

I take it from the priest. It is small, flat. Round like candy. I don't know what to do. I don't see what Harvey does. So I stick it inside my pocket and go back to my seat. No one tell me this wafer is the body of Christ. I think it is candy. How do I know how church people think? I'm not hungry so I want to keep. After church we go outside. Harvey is talking with some friends. And I go to get in the car. This old man he runs after me. 'Miss, miss,' he shouts in an angry voice. I think, my God, what I do wrong? He grab my arm and shake me. 'I saw what you did,' he says. 'This is a very big sin.' I say, 'What sin is this?' And he says to me, 'I saw you put the body of Christ in your pocket.' So I say, 'Sir, you must be mistaken, sir. I ate it.' I knew from the way his face looked that he was angry and I must've done something wrong. I didn't know! I think he wants to search my pockets and see if I'm lying. I stand there listening to him tell me I will go to hell and burn because I have the body of Christ in my pocket. My God, I was scared. I think this body is in my pocket and I think it's candy. I'm going crazy, I think. Finally, Harvey he comes to the car. He tells the man that Toom would never steal the body of Christ. He defend me and this old man lose his face. Because what can he do? He has no proof. I tell Harvey, 'I swear, I eat it. It taste very good, too.' Then I think maybe you're not supposed to say the body of Christ taste good. And I think this is a big mistake. But the old man went away."

"What happened to the wafer?" Addison's disembodied voice asks.

Toom's sensual body shifts on the bed, as she swings her thin legs over the side. She opens her handbag and removes a cigarette. She lights the cigarette, crosses her legs, raises her chin and lets the smoke curl from her nose.

"First, can I tell you something?"

There is a long silence. Her large pouting lips suck on a cigarette.

"I never have sexual intercourse with Harvey. He was my first boyfriend. I go with him five years. And I learn English from him. Every day we talk, talk. Harvey's from England and I think maybe he's gay. He goes to a private boys' school. So I think he likes boys. I phoned his wife—they are separated—and I ask her, 'You think that Harvey is gay?' She tell me, 'No, Harvey's very good in bed.'

I'm surprised to hear her say this. I say, 'Are you sure? You not joke me because I'm from Thailand?' And she says, 'No, I tell you the truth about Harvey. He likes intimate very much. He always want the intimate.' Then I think to myself if he's good in bed, then why not stay together? Why does Harvey only want the oral sex with me? Sometimes, three times a day. The first time, I choke, and throw up. But after that, I don't have a problem. In the morning, after lunch, then at night. I throw up the first time, after that, I quite like it."

Toom smiles, flutters her eyes, looking away from the camera. "Harvey taught you English. What kind of English lessons?" asks Addison.

"I know I'm an abnormal girl. But I like to talk sex fantasy. Harvey phone me and talk sexy. Maybe we talk one hour. Harvey asks me many questions. He say, 'Toom, what are you wearing?' And I say to Harvey, 'Toom is hot. She wear very hot clothes for you.' And Harvey say, 'Toom, do you wear underpants? What color is your bra?' And I say, 'Harvey, my bra is black, and I'm taking it off now. I touch my nipples. I pinch them. They are hard, Harvey. Tomorrow, you take your little Toom shopping. Can you?' He say, 'Yes, I can take Toom, but can Toom take Harvey in her mouth?' And I say, 'Toom can take.'"

"Toom, what happened to the wafer?" asks Addison off camera.

Toom giggles, sucks hard on her cigarette, holding the smoke in for several seconds and then blows it out in rings.

"We drive away from church. Harvey like blow-jobs in the car. He tell me every man like that. I say, 'Oh really?' He says, 'It's true, Harvey doesn't tell a lie.' So we are driving in London, and I reach over and touch him. Like this, with my hand. Then I unzip him and go down. We are at a red light. A man in a truck see us do like that. Harvey say, 'Never mind, the light change we go like hell.' After Harvey come, I take the wafer from my pocket and show him just one second and then put in my mouth. His eyes are very big. 'You lied to that old man,' he said. 'If he knew what you do, then he would make big trouble.' The wafer is between my tongue and roof of my mouth. It is too late to take it out. I try but it's all sticky on my fingers. I lick off my fingers. Two seconds, it's gone. Dissolve. That's the word in English. I don't know why I did this. And I said to Harvey, 'I'm very afraid of that old man. I think he crazy. He say this candy is body of Christ. I know cannot be. It looks like mint. But I don't want to say. It taste like nothing.'

"Harvey didn't say anything for ten minutes. Maybe longer. Then at a traffic light, Harvey started laughing. He squeeze my leg here with his hand. I know he's not angry anymore. But I ask him, 'Harvey why you laugh like this? You have joke? Tell me.' And Harvey says, 'That old man was trying to make a citizen's arrest. In the name of God, stop, you, and hand over the wafer. What does Toom do? She pleads ignorance and innocence. He knows you are lying but there is nothing he can do. I think you are telling the truth. You did take the wafer. If God has a sense of humor, then we both go to heaven. Otherwise, we burn forever.' Then he started asking me if I had on underwear, and if I were getting wet down there. But I never go back to that church again. Once was enough. I think that old man will be there, watching for me. I don't know. But Harvey's a little crazy. Maybe he tell the old man what I did, and he call police and they kick me out of England for eating the wafer. I tell you the truth, now I think maybe the English throw me out then. Because I never have intimate with my first boyfriend. Harvey only want blow-job. And the English he teach me is good for what? Making crazy movie like this?"

4

The sky ached with clouds, rolling overhead like gray smoke pouring from the barrel of an old gun. This vast dull ceiling pressed down to the streets. It was a sky painted with a gruesome natural brush stroke streaking out of the violence of a forest fire or an earthquake. Robert Tuttle took a motorcycle taxi home from Harry Purcell's house. The motorcycle driver said, over his shoulder, as he drove down the nearly deserted streets, that two of his friends had been killed on the street the night before. He didn't know what happened to the bodies. But he saw the blood. He knew they were dead. He ran and ran and thought he was going to die, too. He said that he felt very sad for his country, and wanted to know if Tuttle could help. He refused to accept Tuttle's money. Tuttle stuffed five hundred baht in his shirt pocket and walked away. As Tuttle entered his compound gate, his maid and several other women in the compound ran up to him, crying and wringing their hands.

"We think you dead," said one of the women, looking at his face, hands, and bloodied clothes.

"I'm okay."

"We so scared for you, Khun Robert. You not come home last night. We think soldiers shoot you dead," said his maid. Her eyes ran red like blood rain.

"I stayed overnight with a friend," he said. "Really, I'm not hurt."

"We sure Army kill you," said the maid. The other people in the compound—all part of an extended family—assumed Tuttle had been killed or arrested. He arrived like a ghost from the grave to find them in a state of grief for his passing.

In his sitting room fresh incense sticks burnt in a forest of burntout sticks. He looked at the Buddhist altar which he had long ago fixed to the wall. Fresh orchids in slender vases were positioned on either side of the Buddha, and in front of the flowers, yellow altar candles melted wax into tiny bronze bowls. Dead flowers covered the base of the altar, and a small clearing had been made for a photograph of Tuttle. He found his picture tilted against the Buddha image. He couldn't help feeling moved by the deep emotion behind the ritual his neighbors had performed. These people had really cared. They did all they could to pray for his return, and if he didn't return, then for the release of his soul. He turned and looked at the dozen people in his compound who had gathered, standing a couple of feet away. He didn't know what to say; words wouldn't come for several seconds.

"We very happy to see you," said the man everyone called Old Uncle. Old Uncle stood barefoot, wearing a pair of cotton shorts and a singlet.

"*Duang dow dee*," Tuttle said. My destiny is good.

They understood and believed him. Old Uncle addressed the others. "Khun Robert not like other *farang*. He special. Very special. We afraid for you. That you shot."

Tuttle thought about Dee and her candle as she hovered above him with wide open eyes. "I'm a tiger. You must feed me English. Or I kill you." While his neighbors had not slept the entire night worrying about his safety, he had been with a Thai girl who had once sold her body. He wasn't special, he thought. He was no different from other *farang*s. He had taken a Thai woman on his own terms. What moral grounds separated him from the generals, forcing Dee to yield to his own force and power of will and money? He couldn't find a satisfactory answer; because deep inside he knew there wasn't one. It was disturbing to stand before this admiring group—the people who worried about him, looked up to him, had lit candles for his return—and admit to himself how far short he felt from their expectations and from his own.

After his neighbors left, he stood under the shower trying to wash off the blood and guilt. Changing into fresh clothes, he went into his office and played back messages on his answering machine.

"Daddy, why aren't you home? Are you all right? Please don't go out and when you come back phone me." During Asanee's message he could hear the background clutter of voices in the control room of the radio station.

"Robert, this is Vivien from New York. We are concerned about you. Bangkok is on the front page of the *New York Times*. It's top of the evening news on ABC, CBS, and NBC. Your publisher has had an inquiry from ABC for an interview with you about the violence. They would pay a fee. What do you think?" Vivien was his literary agent in New York, and she was trying to send him an easy piece of work, he thought. After his homecoming he was in no state of mind to comment over the airwaves about what was happening in Bangkok.

"Hey, man, just checking out to see if you're still looking for Daeng. I've got nothing to report on her alive or dead. HQ at midnight. Don't wimp out." Snow's messages were always short, and to the point.

"We know your daughter is helping the terrorists at 108.3. You must tell her to stop before she gets hurt. Do you understand what I say? If you do not stop her, we will. That's a promise, *farang*." There were several more threatening messages recorded in Thai on the answering machine.

He sat back in his chair. He needed to think. Too much was happening all at the same time. Too many loose ends which would never match up—threats mingled with opportunities. One of the main messages of life was to have the courage to run the risk of the threats to seize the right chance to do right. He left the radio and TV switched off; the news overload from Addison's crazy voice was more than he wished to endure. He thought about Asanee and wondered how much longer she could hold out. At first, he had thought that Addison was making up half of what he reported and passing on unconfirmed rumors because he lacked the imagination to invent any himself. The threatening messages confirmed someone was having trouble closing down the station. But it still left open a lot of unanswered questions. Who had made the threats? Why hadn't the Army closed down the radio station? Addison's version still remained untested by an independent observer.

Tuttle's English language school had been closed. The teachers had been sent home; the students never returned after the first shots were fired. It was too dangerous to learn English. Studying English was the promise of a better future. At the moment no one thought about the future. They thought about staying inside, and alive in the present. He sat in his chair, peeling an orange. Using a thumb nail, he opened the skin and slowly wound the peel back as one, long orange band. The scent of the orange overcame the smell of the incense. From the ashes, it was evident there had been a kind of vigil. Several dozen incense sticks had been reduced to gray, twisted ash in the copper bowl filled with uncooked rice. He slowly chewed the first slice of orange. What could he do? he wondered. The orange was sour on his tongue. What should he do? He spit out one seed, and then another. What gesture of doing right made sense when so many were inflicted with the passions which led to temporary madness?

The image he saw was a canister with the markings—"Hand Grenade MKII Cont. M41A1." The old woman with her claw-like hands, begging him to help find her daughter. The headman grinning that the daughter was beautiful. The daughter who had sent the money for the old woman's pride and joy—the electric water pump for the well. Daeng. The twelve-year-old girl's picture in a canister. He had tried but not hard enough. He had given up. The right thing, the decent thing was always the small gesture. The altar heaped with the ashes watched over by his neighbors on the night incense sticks burnt in homage for his return—this was the right thing, the small gesture, the not giving up. He finished his orange, pushed back his chair. He knew the eyes of the compound would be on him as he left again.

"I have to help," he said to his maid.

Old Uncle and some other neighbors ran after him as he reached the gate. "Where you go?"

"Don't worry, Old Uncle. I will come back soon," he said. How could he say he needed to redeem himself for all the ashes they had burnt in his honor, and that he couldn't come home until he had made that journey.

5

The place he went for information about Daeng was a girl who was more than just an old friend. They had been lovers many years before. She had a child that she never told him about. He found himself walking into Bunny's Bar on Soi Cowboy, a strip of go-go bars, which closed at two in the morning. It was here at Bunny's he had discovered he had a daughter. Asanee. In the years since that discovery, it seemed impossible not having her in his life. Bunny was sitting at the bar, nursing a black eye and a Bloody Mary. She had descended to a bar girl who now had a drinker's sagging body and falling face. She had gained twenty pounds since he had last seen her. It wasn't even ten in the morning and she was on the booze. A go-go bar by morning light had the shock value of a strange bed partner staring eye-ball-to-eye-ball at you the morning afterwards.

"Tut, I'm happy you come," she said, not having seen him for months; it was as if she had seen him the night before. "This is terrible, terrible. Killing for what?"

"What happened to the eye?" He sat on the stool next to her, reached over the bar and poured himself a soda.

"Don't want to talk about it," she said.

"A customer?"

She shook her head.

"The Army?"

Not likely. She shook her head again. "I told you I don't need to talk about this."

"Which means the husband."

"He's a bastard. I say to him. 'No good staying open. No business.' And he say, 'Customer come. Don't close the bar.' I say, 'What you gonna do to me?'"

"Where is he?" asked Tuttle.

"Upstairs sleeping. He drink too much. It make him mean. Man drink all the time get mean like a dog kicked on the street everyday. Why don't Army shoot man like him? Shooting these kids makes me angry." Her fleshy, soft face turned red as tears filled her eyes. She bit her lip and slowly shook her head, looking into her Bloody Mary. "What did you come here for, Tut? It sure wasn't to see me."

"Asanee's safe. I thought you'd want to know that," he said.

She looked up at him, her lips tight. "He shouldn't have hit me like that Tut," she said, as if news about her daughter's safety didn't matter much one way or another. Asanee had become her father's daughter; his problem, his worry, his responsibility.

"I know that. You're the only one who can fix it. Divorce him," said Tuttle.

"Easy for you to say," Bunny said, raising her Bloody Mary to her lips. She swallowed real slowly, letting it flush her throat of the lump she felt would never go away. "Life ain't organized for women. You know that. We grow old. And look at you, Tut. Even when you're seventy you'll have some twenty-year old to take a long bath with. I got a man. He's not the best. Yeah, he hits me now and again and he drinks too much. But he's my husband. You think there's another one out there waiting to take his place? If so, send him in. The interview starts in five minutes."

Personal misery extinguished all other misery. It didn't much matter about the killings once she started talking about the wreckage of her own life. The images on the TV were abstract. Sure they made people cry a little while but the pain didn't last much beyond the tears. Real pain was one's own personal hell. The suffering of a life which never was going to right itself.

"I need your help, Bunny," said Tuttle.

She lit a cigarette. "Here it comes. The reason why you came around. Not some bullshit that Asanee is okay."

She had him cold. She always had that ability.

"You're right. Can you help me?"

"Depends on what you need."

"I was upcountry on the Nan River. I spent some time in a village. There's a villager worried about her daughter. Named Daeng. She's nineteen. Has a small half-moon shaped scar on her right cheek. Her mother said Daeng's working the bars on Soi Cowboy. I know that's not much to go on. She could be anywhere. I don't know where to start. Where to look. But I told her mother I'd try and find her," said Tuttle.

"So you can screw her?"

Bunny regretted it as soon as the accusation hit Tuttle. She saw him flinch and go all sad.

"Okay, Tut. I'm a little fucked up this morning. Never mind. You're not angry with me? You want to give me another black eye? Can. I would deserve it. Sure."

"Bunny, I'm not angry. Can you help me?"

"Girls come and go all the time." She gave a long, frustrated sigh. Tuttle rarely got angry, she remembered that. He was mister *jai yen*. The cool-hearted man, climbing over the walls for a sweet woman's dreams just long enough to make certain that he'd be remembered before slipping away. It had happened to Bunny with him all those years ago when she still had dreams. "I can't keep track of who comes and goes in my own bar, Tut. None of my girls are from Nan," she said, running her finger through her graying hair. Yeah, this was the man who had touched down during that moment of youth. She smiled. "It's good to see you, Tut. Did I tell you that?"

"It's good to see you, too, Bunny."

Tuttle made the rounds of several more bars. He came up empty until he met up with a bar girl in plastic sandals with a T-shirt reading—The Bullet is the Target—Crazy Eight Bar. She was buying a bag of fried grasshoppers. Tuttle gave the vendor a twenty-baht note before the bar girl could react.

"You good man," said the bar girl, smiling and offering the bag. She brushed back her short hair, and looked Tuttle over. Then gave him a crooked-tooth smile.

Tuttle pulled one of the perfectly preserved grasshoppers out of the bag. Fifty or more tiny bodies had been poured into the bag. Likely the grasshoppers had been killed with lethal insecticides then cooked in rancid oil; but there were upcountry girls who shrugged off the health risk and couldn't get enough of them. He ate the head first, then slipped the slender body into his mouth. It made a crunching noise like granola.

"*Geng*," she said, admiringly. Skilfully done.

Then after a couple of minutes she told him that her boss hired girls from that region of Thailand. This was her first week on the job. "Boss in a bad mood," she said, as she walked back to her bar with Tuttle.

Crazy Hank, the owner of Crazy Eight Bar, wasn't in a bad mood; he was in a hysterical rage. His fat gut exploded over his belt, swelling and bloating the graphics on his T-shirt. Below the words—The Bullet is the Target—Crazy Eight Bar—was the picture of a standing naked girl, her buns facing out, looking over her shoulder, and a bulls-eye target around her ass. On Crazy Hank, the legs of the girl stretched over his huge bulge, making the girl on the T-shirt look like she had double-jointed legs. He bellowed at the girl behind the bar, who was cleaning up broken glass with a broom.

"I'm docking your pay for that glass," he shouted.

The girl with the bag of grasshoppers fled to a corner and tried to make herself small. Tuttle walked over to the bronze bell hanging over the bar, and rang it. Crazy Hank spun around on his stool.

"You know what that means?" asked Crazy Hank. "You buy drinks for everyone in the bar."

The bar was empty except for Crazy Hank, the grasshopper eater, the girl sweeping the glass, and two other girls squatting on the floor and eating sticky rice and fish paste with chili sauce.

Tuttle put a purple on the bar, not taking his eyes off Crazy Hank who was expecting this guy to start an argument.

"This round is on me," said Tuttle.

Crazy Hank made a crumby, gurgling sound—half smoker's cough and half nervous tic—when someone caught him wrong-footed.

"Make mine a double Jack Daniel's," said Crazy Hank, who looked to be in his early 60s. He was from Indiana. Drinking double Jack Daniel's until he became abusive, violent and stupid with mindless rage had resulted in Hank Galan's nickname—Crazy Hank.

"Make mine a double orange juice," said Tuttle.

The girls ordered beer and Mekong whiskey.

"Before I started this line of business. I was in the snake business. I exported big snakes. The biggest mistake of my life was to believe that running a bar with these girls was more profitable than selling snakes. Now the fucking Army's shooting up the town."

"So I hear," said Tuttle.

"You know what that's gonna do to the tourist business? It's flushing it down the goddamn toilet. Who in their right mind is gonna come to Bangkok this year? At least with snakes, it was all export. The Army can shoot the hell out of people on the street, and it don't for a minute affect the snake trade. Snakes don't break your glasses. Snakes don't quit and disappear on you. Snakes don't come down with VD. Snakes don't bite your balls. You know what I'm saying?"

Tuttle had the basic idea that Crazy Hank was disappointed in his career move. In the corner of the bar, near the door, where his friend ate grasshoppers, was a bulletin board of polaroid photos of girls with their nicknames written below. There were four rows and each row had six photos. Tuttle scanned each row, looking for a photo of girl with a small half-moon scar on her right cheek with the name of Daeng.

The double Jack Daniel's had softened up Crazy Hank.

"You looking for a girl?" asked Crazy Hank. "I can tell you now, most of them aren't showing up. I've got ten, twelve living upstairs. They're still sleeping. And snakes don't sleep all night neither."

Tuttle described Daeng. Afterwards, Crazy Hank leaned over the bar, and pulled out a shoe box containing about a hundred polaroid photos which were in no apparent order. "These girls once worked here. But have fucked off. To where? Your guess would be as good as mine." He shoved the box across the bar.

After twenty minutes, Tuttle found a photograph of a girl with a half-moon scar. "You remember her?"

Crazy Hank didn't remember. But one of the girls who was drinking Mekong looked over Tuttle's shoulder.

"That's Daeng."

"Daeng from Nan province?"

The girl nodded, sipped her Mekong dry and put the glass on the bar.

"One thing to remember, Hank. Snakes don't have much of a memory," said Tuttle.

Tuttle leaned forward, reached up, and rang the bell again. Peels of laughter rang out. The girls liked any excuse for a party, some excitement in the middle of all their boredom.

"Yeah, I remember her. She was a good earner. Strange but good. Fucked off a few months ago. I ain't seen her since."

"She work HQ," said the girl who had spontaneously remembered Daeng.

A bar girl had remembered—the girls had developed a memory for faces and names. There was little slippage among the girls. But not Crazy Hank. And not Tuttle. How could that be? Why had Crazy Hank and Tuttle mortgaged their memories? Tuttle had more questions than he cared to find answers for. The reality was plain, and not one Tuttle could ignore. Daeng was not a stranger; she had been working the crowd at HQ. She had been at HQ night after night, for all those weeks before Tuttle had gone upcountry. It stood to reason he had seen her but at the same time he had not seen her. Nothing was more disturbing, unsettling. Looking for someone that he had seen and never recognized. He had done much the same when he had bought his own daughter out of Bunny's bar on Soi Cowboy years before. He had learned nothing, he thought. History was about to repeat itself. If only Daeng had gone to another bar. He could search with noble aims of paying back the kindness of Old Uncle and the others in his compound. It was no longer that simple, the motive no longer so pure.

The full weight of responsibility for Daeng's whereabouts doubled up on him like Crazy Hank's double Jack Daniel's which pushed him over the edge. Hardcore HQ regulars were woman blinded; it was like a whiteout in a snow storm, up and down no longer had definition. There was a big difference—one would recover the ability to see the landscape separated from the sky once the snow storm blew itself out. In HQ, the sexual storm winds never stopped blowing, leaving the HQ hardcore blinded and without memory. If he could find this Daeng, another throw-away prostitute, someone who came and went without a flicker of recognition, Tuttle knew he had a chance of recovering the kind of vision necessary to witness humanity. Without that vision, he saw people no differently than the generals. This was the broken continuity he had gone upcountry to discover. Daeng was one more HQ girl who yielded. Those who yield are faceless, meaningless, and without purpose, Harry Purcell had said. But Tuttle didn't want to see Daeng through Purcell's eyes. He wanted to start seeing people again; not in Denny Addison documentaries which were entertainments for those permanently damaged by sexual whiteouts. Daeng would pull him back; let him recover the person his neighbors had prayed would return or be released from the wheel. Daeng was the reason he had gone to the Nan River. He had been looking for what he hadn't seen before his own eyes.

"Why did Daeng quit?" asked Tuttle.

The girl slumped over the bar, her head propped on her hand. She shrugged, as if there needed to be a reason. "She bored. Daeng not like other girl. Not drink. Not smoke. She save, save money customers give her. She tell me that she want to buy water pump for her mother. Daeng has very good heart. She have a hard life. Father die. Dog eat her face. She talk to ghosts." She giggled a fearful laugh. "She have good heart. Buy water pump very good."

Having finished his second double Jack Daniel's, Crazy Hank exploded. "Water pump! Fuck, that's a new scam. It's usually a TV, VCR, or a motorcycle for their boyfriend. Or a gold chain to show off in front of their friends. Most of them gamble the money away as fast as they make it."

Tuttle put another two purples on the bar counter.

"Her mother showed me the water pump, Hank," said Tuttle, rising from the stool. "I saw it."

Crazy Hank ignored the information. Hard facts had a way of being wired into the hardcore circuit board of gossip, double-crosses, and double Jack Daniel's.

"Another thing about snakes. They never bullshit you," said Crazy Hank, belching as Tuttle walked out of the bar. He was in a hurry like a man who had decided he was lost and now had the chance to find and recover himself.

6

At Radio Bangkok 108.3 the DJs, staff and Navy personnel had gone cranky, pale, silent; some had the shakes from the lack of sleep, nerves and tempers were frayed. Asanee sat with her head down next to the phone which had been ringing without her or anyone else answering it. Somewhere in her dream she saw herself naked standing under a waterfall. The falling water made a ringing, comforting sound. One of her eyes opened and she stared straight into Denny Addison's hand-held camera. He had been filming Asanee for more than twenty minutes.

"Denny, what are you doing?"

"You were sleeping."

"I hate it when you do that. Why do you film me when I'm sleeping?"

"That's cool. Look up."

She raised her head. She picked up the phone. "Hello, Radio Bangkok 108.3. No, we have no intention of surrendering." She slammed the phone receiver down.

"What's that on your cheek?" asked Addison.

Asanee opened her compact mirror and examined a small, reddish triangular shaped impression. She snapped the compact shut and smiled. Around her neck on a two-baht gold chain was an amulet. Once or twice before, she had been tangled up and the amulet pressed against her flesh, leaving a reddish calling card. A fortune teller once told her this was a sign of good luck, strength, a destiny aimed in a straight shot toward the right target in this life. She believed and didn't believe this explanation.

"It's from this," she said, holding the amulet out on the chain to the camera.

"What is this?" asked Addison.

"You know what it is," she replied.

"But not on film."

"It's an amulet. My father bought the chain but the amulet is from my mother's mother."

The camera zoomed in on the amulet. On a gold chain, the amulet was a white Buddha entombed inside a gold heart-shaped locket covered by a glass dome.

"And why do you wear it?" asked Addison.

The camera remained on the amulet.

"It brings good luck. It keeps away evil and misfortune," answered Asanee, as the camera pulled back to reveal her face.

"Bizarre," said Addison. "And you believe this?"

Addison had been filming Asanee while she slept, and she started to resent his cross-examination, his condescending tone, and the way he walked around pointing the camera in her face.

"Of course I believe or I wouldn't wear it."

"Now you're angry. I like that. What makes you feel this way? Okay, forget that. Tell me the history of the amulet."

"It's a family heirloom. My mother received it from her mother, and my mother gave it to me. The Buddha image is carved from the tooth of her mother's grandfather." She fingered the amulet, toying with the glass dome, catching the overhead light and showering the rays across the walls of the control room.

"As long as you wear it, then you're not afraid of the soldiers downstairs trying to kill us?" asked Addison.

"I'm not afraid," she said.

"Does your father wear an amulet?"

She nodded. "Always."

Addison paused, but kept the video camera rolling.

"Have you talked to your dad today?"

Asanee blinked into the camera.

"He's looking for a girl," said Asanee. But it came out in a way she hadn't intended.

"Wow, the streets are filled with tanks and soldiers and Robert Tuttle is searching for a girl! Now that is totally bizarre."

"No, no, no. Not that way. He promised her mother he would look for her. When he was in a village in Nan, a villager was worried about her daughter. She asked my father to help."

"What does this girl do?" asked Addison.

Asanee didn't want to answer.

"Is she a secretary? Work in a bank or for the government?"

"Daeng worked in a bar," said Asanee, her expression going grim.

"Daeng. That means 'Red,' Right? Right. Your father is on the streets of Bangkok looking for a 'Red' prostitute because some peasant in the country was worried about her daughter? Amazing," said Addison, laughing.

Then he asked, "Where is he looking?"

"Around the Royal Hotel area."

"Tuttle in the heart of the killing zone. Wow, is this the Robert Tuttle trip? He's going into the line of fire to rescue a prostitute? Or is he just crazy?"

"I'm proud of him," said Asanee.

"Do you think he might have a death wish? Or a Hemingway complex? The great Robert Tuttle defies the jaws of death, avoiding Army patrols to locate a fallen angel from the countryside. Wow, what a great documentary. You think he would let me do a film about this?"

"No," shouted Asanee. She was showing her anger.

"What about Daeng? I'll do Daeng. She'd be much better than Tuttle anyway."

"You are the most selfish man alive," said Asanee. "I can't believe I let myself expose myself in your film. I'm ashamed."

"Hey, at the time, you were into it. Admit it. You're just upset because you're tired. But you have to admit what your father is doing is far over the border of sanity."

"It's up to him," she said.

"Maybe he's wearing an amulet so he figures he's protected. He has magic. So he's not afraid," said Addison.

"Why do you want to argue with only me on camera? Why don't you ever show yourself? That's what my father says. You hide behind the camera and make everyone else look simple, stupid, confused while you play God. That stupid ferris wheel from Mexico doesn't make you a film maker or God."

"Robert Tuttle said I played God?"

She refused to reply and swung around in her chair, her back turned to Addison's camera. He was unfazed and kept the camera rolling.

"Do you think he'll find Daeng the prostitute?"

"I don't know."

"I've turned the camera off. You can turn around," said Addison.

"Good," she replied, refusing to turn around. Asanee stared at the wall, her arms folded around her breasts.

"Is that all you're gonna say? Good?"

The phones were ringing. A couple of floors below there was the sound of gunfire. "I've decided to go and help my father."

"Are you crazy? Don't you hear the shooting? What is this crusade to find one girl in a city of ten million people?"

"Dad was right about one thing about you, Denny. You end every sentence with a question mark like some guy addicted to other people's answers but not having any yourself."

"Wow, your father said that?"

"Another question."

She got up from her chair, as Addison shouldered his camera and followed her out of the control room, into the hallway, and watched her walk toward the bank of elevators. Two Navy marines blocked her way. She stopped, boxed in by the marines, and looked back at Addison filming her.

"Why not show them your grandmother's tooth amulet?"

Asanee burst into tears and tried to walk around the marines. They wouldn't budge. One of the Navy marines with Khmer blue-ink tattoos on his neck told her she couldn't use the elevators. Radio Bangkok 108.3 music was piped into the hallway. The DJ had put on Muddy Water's *Trouble*. She did an about-face, rushed Addison, grabbed his camera before he knew what she had done. She ran three steps and hurled his videocam down the staircase. The ugly crashing noise of plastic, glass, metal exploding on the marble stairs made her laugh and jump up and down with joy.

"*Ting rabut,*" screamed a voice from below. Someone has thrown a bomb. The scream was followed by automatic gunfire and the sound of boots stumbling down the stairs in a frantic escape.

The marines grinned. Some soldiers had been sneaking up the staircase for a surprise attack. Then Asanee had the good fortune to hurl Addison's camera down the same passage, and thinking a bomb had been hurled the attackers were routed.

For the first time since the killings started Asanee felt happy.

Addison, his mouth open, rotated his head.

"Are you crazy?"

"Try and find the answer yourself," Asanee said and stormed back to the radio station.

7

Inside HQ Crosby was surrounded by prostitutes. He had bought them all beer and cigarettes. He had given one of them a handful of baht coins for the jukebox. Crosby had everything he ever wanted in life. A teenage prostitute giggled as she bounced on his knee, shaking as she drank straight from a bottle of Singha Gold. The beer spilled out of her mouth and the suds dribbled down her bare throat. As Crosby dabbed Lek's neck, his hand dipping into her bra, cupping her breasts, Snow sauntered into HQ, having ducked through the back alley entrance. It was midnight. Snow's Hawaiian shirt was wrinkled and untucked. He ordered a glass of cola, then he waited until two of the prostitutes tumbled out and then slid into the booth across from Crosby. The girls piled back in, squeezing Snow's arms and thighs, trying to figure out if he was strong, armed, and rich. He nodded to Lek who offered him a drink from her bottle of beer as Crosby played with her breasts. Snow waved off her offer.

"How's the civil strife business, Snow?" asked Crosby without missing a beat.

Snow shrugged, sipped his drink like a serious artist. "It's been hell. But war's like that. File, file, file. So what's happening in the T-shirt racket?"

"Filing quotes away for future reference," said Crosby, glancing down at his hand, pumping Lek's breast.

Snow sipped the freshly arrived Coke.

"At least that wando, Addison, hasn't been on the air for hours."

"Maybe he's dead."

"Don't get Tuttle's hopes up. But I have to say, I was rooting for the Army to shoot him. The reason you have coups is to shoot people like Addison. Radio station cleansing. It's essential. Looks like the T-shirt business is looking up." Snow turned one of the girls around, smoothed out her T-shirt and read it. All the girls squeezed into the booth were wearing identical T-shirts with the phrase—Ding Dong and Run on Cash. Underneath was a pile of bank notes from a dozen countries: baht, dollars, pounds, and francs.

"I came up with the line myself," said Crosby.

"It's difficult to believe you would have stolen it. Anyway, it's false advertisement. These are all short-time girls," said Snow. "Why not, 'Ding your willy on this Dong'?"

Crosby removed his hand from Lek's breast, took out a piece of paper and wrote down Snow's suggestion.

"It's the beauty of test marketing. You receive feedback," said Crosby. "The Ding Dong Bar has ordered two hundred T-shirts. I started with this dozen." He stared at Lek's rumpled shirt. "You think the Germans would understand what a willy is?"

"Beats me, Crosby. What can I tell you? It's one thing to steal other people's ideas, but you go the whole distance. You mess with their reality."

"How else can you make money?"

"The world's full of hard luck stories," said Snow.

"Did I tell you Immigration is causing me problems? I was in England when my residence card expired. Only bloody three weeks late. You'd think they wouldn't bother. People fleeing the country like rats, and this official wants a hundred thousand baht."

"That's a convoy of T-shirts," said Snow.

"I said, 'I was born here. Where do you expect me to go, Liberia?'"

"Not a good place to get your dong dinged."

"I like that, Snow." Crosby wrote down on his note pad. Ding Dong Bar—a great place to get your dong dinged. He ordered another round of beers for the booth. Six girls leaned over and kissed him on the face, laughing and pulling each other's hair.

"Where you going?" asked Crosby, as Snow pulled out of the booth.

"I've gotta file a story. T-shirt tycoon attacked by six terrorists in Ding Dong combat fatigues."

"War's a grim business," said Crosby.

A couple of minutes later Snow returned with Tuttle. They had nearly collided at the back entrance, as Snow's attention was diverted. Inside one of the open toilets, the door off the hinge, Snow was taking in a glimpse of an HQ girl sliding down her jeans. He was trying to remember if he had taken her when he slammed into Tuttle, knocking his glasses off into his hands.

"Nice catch," said Tuttle.

"Hey, Tut, what's happening, man? Find the fair Daeng?"

"I've been looking for her in all the wrong places," said Tuttle.

"HQ is all the wrong places."

"Seen Crosby?" asked Tuttle.

"That capitalist slut had six Termites attached to his face last time I looked. They were making an awful sucking sound," said Snow. "I think they've discovered his head is made of wood."

They talked next to the wash basin beside the cracked mirror which hung on a nail. Two girls adjusted their make-up, combed their hair, watching Tuttle and Snow in the mirror, trying to figure out if the play action of the *farang* might include them.

"I thought you were at the Royal Hotel for the duration," said Tuttle.

"Things change, man. The Army arrested Chamlong at Paan Fah Bridge. Sanam Luang is empty as doom. The troops are in the hotel. There are rumors the action has moved across town to Ramkhamhaeng. I lost Daeng who was last seen fleeing the Royal Hotel muttering about ghosts," said Snow. "I never have any luck finding stable women. Maybe there are no stable women. It's something to think about after the shooting stops."

"Come on, Snow. I'll buy you a drink," said Tuttle.

The girls in the mirror trailed after them.

"You know the Kok Wua intersection between the Royal and Ratchadamnoen? You should've seen it, man. Burnt-out cars, trucks, oil tankers. Torched buses. Heavy damage. The Public Relations Building torched."

"How many killed?" asked Tuttle.

"Who knows, man? Like in '76. An old Bangkok hand once said, 'The average Thai knows to the last baht how much money he has.' But the generals say it's impossible to count the dead. Commies and terrorists aren't counted as kills. So what you get is chaos. Numbers that aren't numbers. Never try to audit the dead when the Army goes into the street. It's a rule of thumb. And in case you haven't heard, the generals are saying the communists are behind this," replied Snow.

"I heard."

They stopped at Crosby's booth. Two of the girls were massaging his neck. Across the table two more girls were massaging his arms which lay stretched out. His eyes were closed and there was a look of pleasure on his face.

"I hear a rumor you're an illegal immigrant," said Tuttle.

"A *farang* can't immigrate to Thailand," replied Crosby, a slit in one eye opening to find Tuttle. "But my residence card is the subject of a ransom demand."

"I'm looking for a girl from Nan Province. Daeng. She has a half-moon scar about here on her face. You can't miss it," he said, touching his right cheek.

"Nan Province," purred Crosby. "I once had a girlfriend from Santi Suk. Her father was a gangster. The Burmese killed the old man, and the mother sold the daughter into whoredom. She kept her father's bones in a mayonnaise jar with a screw-on lid. That's the way I wish to be buried," announced Crosby.

As Crosby resumed his comatose state with the girls working his every muscle zone, Snow looked agitated. His legs made the butterfly beating movement, his knees knocking together under the table.

"I'm feeling guilty, man," said Snow. "I spotted her one night a couple of weeks ago. You were here. Purcell the gun-runner. Crosby and his T-shirt groupies. But I didn't say anything. Man, if I'd known this girl was so important, I would have delivered her. But I don't think you've missed that much. She's a loon, man," said Snow.

Tuttle who leaned on the table, looked up. "I don't think so."

"Christ, I took her short-time from HQ on the 17th. You were paddling your boat upcountry. I took her back to the Royal. She stayed with me until the Army smashed into the room. She was cool. She stayed in bed, behaved herself. The usual heavy reading material in her bag—comic books. No sweat. I'm on the phone with you. The Army comes through the door. An officer took her in the hallway, asked her some questions, then she came back. But it must have spooked her," said Snow.

"Where is she?" asked Tuttle, pulling up a chair and sitting down. His legs felt weak.

"That's what I'm getting to," said Snow.

"She buggered off," said Crosby.

"Did she say where she was going?"

"Why do you care, man? There must be another Daeng here. Another girl from Nan Province. There is an HQ rule that Daengs always come in pairs," said Snow.

"This is serious," said Tuttle.

"That's why I gave you a serious answer."

"Why did you let her go? You saw what was happening out there," said Tuttle.

This accusation made Snow smile; he wrinkled his nose, and pushed back his glasses, making his lips thin, narrow and shaking his head as if he were looking at a lunatic.

"She left me for a ghost."

"That's a new one," said Crosby, writing on his note pad.

"Ding Dong Bar—come seance your willy," said Snow, which stopped Crosby from writing.

"She could be anywhere, Tut," said Crosby.

"Why do you care?" asked Snow.

Tuttle lifted his head toward the ceiling and wished he knew a simple one-line T-shirt answer to the question. He thought of the old woman and her electric water pump, Old Uncle, his maid and the other Thais who burnt the incense during his absence. He searched all their faces, looking for some mirror where he might find an image he could call his own and which could whisper why this one girl out of the millions was worth caring about.

"Because she matters," said Tuttle.

"Enough said," said Snow. In the days when Snow taught at Tuttle's English school, he remembered that Tuttle put a lot of thought into what mattered in a world where most things did not. "I gotta tell you, she came unhinged. I'm not certain what the Army did to her. Or maybe it was the madness of all that shooting. When she came back to the room, she rabbited on about seeing a ghost. She was strange, man. And her conversation wasn't with your average, nameless ghoul. But the Spanish sixteenth-century thug suited up in uniform—Cortez—and she said Cortez was talking to her in Thai."

Crosby stretched his arms around the girls on either side of him in the booth. "And who goes around filling these girls with stories about Cortez and Aztec skull wars?"

"Purcell!" thundered Snow in a rare outburst which scared a couple of the girls wearing the Ding Dong T-shirts into a clutching embrace.

"She was sitting right there in that booth when Purcell was talking about Cortez and his usual mix of weapons and pillage stories. She probably plugged in," said Crosby.

"Shit, why didn't I think of that? Sometimes, Crosby, you manage to earn yourself five seconds of respect. Which of course you squander in three seconds flat."

This left Tuttle wondering if Harry Purcell had taken Daeng; if Harry Purcell, weaving his stories of Cortez, might be the man she would run to if Cortez's ghost had come to Bangkok for a haunting time.

"You remember what time she left?" asked Tuttle.

"After the buses were torched," said Snow. He closed his eyes tight, set his jaw, mouth half open. "After I talked with you on the phone. Say, early morning. One moment she was there, and the next . . . gone."

8

When Daeng had walked out of Snow's room at the Royal Hotel she had known that she would never see him again. She felt a profound sense of relief that she would not go back. Something had touched her life, turned it around, and she followed the voices which had spoken to her. The officer who pulled her from Snow's room said she would be in danger if she stayed. His commander had told him that soon the Army would come and take everyone away. Unless she left, the Army would throw her into prison. His eyes looked sad as he spoke these words of warning. Daeng thought the officer seemed like a brave, kind man. She thanked him and returned to say goodbye to Snow. She didn't bother to ask him for money. For the first time since she arrived in Bangkok money wasn't on her mind.

In the hallway, she slumped against the wall, thinking about what she should do next. Then she remembered her father's photograph. The one he had taken before he left Thailand to work and die abroad. She had wrapped it in a piece of silk and kept it inside a secret pocket in her handbag. She had taken it out and asked her father's photo, "Father, I must go. Do you mind if I go? I have this hurt." Then she put it back, descended to the lobby, stepped around the bodies. Some were dead, or at least not moving. Others had blood-soaked clothes. Doctors and nurses, blood up to the elbows, worked on the bodies; they had turned the main lobby into an emergency operating room, attaching drips, tearing open the bloodied shirts, and removing bullets. The doctors had worked around the clock until they could no longer stand straight. The nurses worked at their side, giving comfort to the wounded and the dying. Daeng saw that this was the moment when people found out what they were made of and what made them cry and what made them stay or run.

She slipped out a side door. The night sky was lit with fires. A pre-dawn Bangkok morning with fires raging as far as she could see. The smell of fire clung in the air. Thick smoke rose from burning cars and buses. Razor wire—the kind with tiny razors raised at hundreds of angles—had been strung near the brackish canal. Hundreds of sandals and shoes lay in the street. As if the people wearing them had taken flight and flown away, leaving their launching pads in the streets. The death litter of street battle, whirlwinds and eddies of killing debris blew across the field of vision like sagebrush in the old west; a horizon of smoke, paper cartons, stones, broken bottles, pieces of wood, smashed motorbikes, and charcoal-black wreckage twisted from heat.

She turned down a side street and walked no more than a hundred meters before she saw a dead boy wrapped in a Thai flag. He was fourteen, fifteen years old and lifeless in the street like the sandals and shoes among the abandoned rubbish. He was like the boys she remembered who played on the river banks before she came to Bangkok. A *farang* was taking a picture of the dead boy. The *farang* was snapping his camera and crying at the same time. He shook his head, and said over and over, "Why, why, why? Jesus Christ, why?" She didn't know the answer to the why question which made any sense, and walked on, kicking old newspapers drenched in blood. One of the papers stuck to her leg. She pulled it off and saw that her hand was stained with sticky blood. A thin blue wisp of smoke floated out of the sewer, and Cortez materialized, blocking her path.

Cortez told her, "Daeng, you have been chosen."

"Why little Daeng? You know what I do? I sell myself for money. I'm ashamed."

"Tonight you will get out," said Cortez.

"Where are you sending me?"

"Out of the temple."

But she couldn't hear his reply over the gunfire on the street ahead. She saw a man running and a hail of bullets cut through his body. He fell, rolling like a rag doll, trailing a blood spray. By the time the shooting was over, Cortez had vanished into a column of heavy smoke.

9

The waiter brought to Crosby's booth another jumbo glass mug filled with ice cubes and seven small bottles of Kloster. Snow, his Hawaiian shirt untucked, walked over to the jukebox and pushed the buttons. When he came back, the sound of *A Wonderful Life* filled the background.

"My exit song," said Tuttle, and then left.

"Every man needs an exit song at HQ," said Snow. "Tuttle's doomed. He'll find true love in Bangkok before he finds Daeng."

Crosby ignored this. He didn't care about Tuttle's search and rescue mission. HQ had a revolving door for people who were failed searchers and those who were beyond rescue. That never stopped these people from hoping; but theirs was a lesson never learned, Crosby had often thought after several bottles of Kloster.

"I remember Ding, Dong," said Crosby, his mind still fixed on the T-shirt business. But it so happened this was also a song; one which had been a favorite on the HQ jukebox and the title song had been pirated by the bar he was now trying to fleece with the T-shirt deal. "Unfort-unately, it's no longer on the jukebox," sighed Crosby. "Ding, Dong reminds me of the time Noi and I were fucking and we punctured my Lilo."

"Say what? Punctured a kidney?" asked Snow.

"A Lilo," insisted Crosby, pouring his Kloster over ice.

"Man, talk English."

"It's like a mat but it's got air in it."

"You wando. You mean an inflatable mattress."

"We call them Lilos."

"And the blow-up fuck dolls. . . .what do you call them in England? Miss Lilo. I had a screw with Miss Lilo last night, but her ass was low on air."

"No, we call them fuck dolls," said Crosby, drinking from his mug.

"How did Noi puncture the Lilo? With a sonar controlled fart?"

"She was wearing an amulet on a two-baht gold chain. You know how the girls like to flip the amulet around, so the amulet won't press against their tits and they feel the image can't see what they are doing? Well, she had the amulet turned around so it hung down her back. I was giving her a real good one. We were pumping up and down on the Lilo. The edge of the Lilo must have caught on her gold chain. Because there was a loud boom, and then a violent hiss like a tire on a Land Rover blowing at eighty plus on the M1. You ever try to steer a woman on a Lilo losing air like a sonofabitch?"

"Can't say that I have," answered Snow. "But a racetrack driver like you must have brought the vehicle under control."

"I got off her and turned on the light."

"And you're a real gentleman of the old school," said Snow.

"And the girl. She's like a dog leashed to a kennel. She was hooked. She couldn't raise her head more than twelve inches from the deflated Lilo. Her amulet held her down. The gold chain pressed into her neck and her eyes went wild. I think she was damned scared. This bloody amulet was giving her a real working over in her mind. Spirits flying at her. *Pee* swooning down to devour her guts. She had violated something sacred and now the spiritual forces were seeking their revenge in her mind, screaming at her, 'Fucking shape up or next time we'll have you good and proper.'"

"In an English accent? On the deflated Lilo?" asked Snow. "And now the big question, did you or did you not come?"

"I must confess, I don't remember. The burst of the Lilo was a bit of a shock. Nothing like that had happened before. The same with her. She had been screwed on mats, floors, tables, chairs, and no doubt on beds. No big deal. But this was a first for her. She was hardcore. Still she felt special for a few seconds. I didn't want to get carried away. I helped her unhook herself. She was in no proper mood for me to blow up the spare Lilo I kept in the closet. After she was up and about, she started shaking, cupping the amulet between her palms in a *wai*, and touching her forehead with her hands. She was muttering in Pali. Then, in Thai, I heard her make a promise, that if the spirits didn't properly fuck her over, let her off with a warning, spared the pain bit, and gave her and her mother a long life, she would never return to HQ and sell her body again." Crosby made a great show of pouring out the last of his Kloster.

"And, aren't you gonna tell me the obvious. . . ?"

Crosby smiled. "She was back at HQ a week later. She was hardcore. All those promises to the spirits were in the heat of the moment stuff. But afterwards she wouldn't go with me. She wouldn't even acknowledge me. I tried. I promised no more Lilos. We'd go to a proper short-time hotel with a bed. A real bed. None of those water bed jobs where fear of drowning would have crossed her mind. But she refused, clutched her amulet and walked away. She had lost too much face."

Snow nodded to a *farang* who stood leaning against the bar. The *farang*, late 40s, had a chinless face, dirty braided hair, wore cuff-off shorts, plastic sandals, and a Crosby T-shirt with the words "Stop me before I fuck again" printed on the front. "See that guy without the chin, Crosby?"

Crosby picked him out of the crowd, and gave Snow a so-what look.

"I nominated him for the HQ psychopath of the week award."

"It's the new generation," said Crosby. "But his taste in shirts is impeccable."

"The new generation, man! That guy's old enough to be your father. How did you leap-frog from your 20s to sixty- something? You've not even hit 30."

Crosby poured his Kloster over the ice inside his freshly delivered mug. "I'm quite looking forward to hitting 30. When I'm your age, Snow, I will have virtual reality sex every night. HQ home delivery downloaded via a computer Skynet feedback loop."

"And you will be the first wando to pick up a virtual reality dose. Crosby will be immortal as the first man to contract a sexually transmitted computer virus," said Snow.

"The Lilo after her amulet ripped a hole in it made this long bleating hisssss sound—hisssssssssssssss."

"The sound of virtual reality when the amulet bites."

Snow pushed off to cover the mass of people flooding into the Ramkhamhaeng University area of the city.

"Try taking a course in reality while you're at the university," Crosby called after him.

Snow turned. "Crosby, you know no limits. Now you're ripping off the lines from that wando on 108.3. He said that about the Army. Addison. What an asshole."

10

CORTEZ'S TEMPLE
by
Harry Purcell

General Xue braided ivory skulls in his moustache. He gave
them to young virginal girls as amulets. He worked this scam
until he drank a cup of poison and died. An updated definition:
amulet—an object desired for the sacred power with a lure no
human can resist—a promise that the amulet can protect against
personal destruction. A ticket on the Escape of Death ride.

General Xue was ahead of his time. He was part of the trend
of transforming the religious amulet into currency. Money. Cash
became the source of power. This begged the most important
question—the power to do what? The power to acquire, maintain
and support the best, most healthy sexual specimens of the species.
Power is who you can fuck and who can fuck you. Who will accept
the ivory skulls for favors?

Man learned to count before he learned to write (less than
5,000 years ago), and he was fucking himself crazy for hundreds
of thousands of years before some asshole decided a system was
needed. Arrogance arose through the process of counting. Once you
decide that recording one, two, three, four, etc. is important, the step
into the abyss of writing is one footfall behind. Why worry about
what follows one? Could it be that man wished for a destiny better
than a sexual animal which fucked on the road? So who counted

198

first and what did he count? Ahhhhh, there was a question which was worth pursuing. He may have been a warrior who desired to show his power and counting illustrated accumulation, and accumulation equalled wealth and power; to master counting permitted him to number his women, record what was owed him, establish the number of enemies killed, and friends loyal to him. Counting pointed to a particular kind of relationship with people. Then one day, after a massive counting binge, man invented a written word and named his women, his enemies, his friends.

You count your ivory skulls and earmark your women, they become—if you are a true pagan—like any other token of power. Pagans thought of women as a toy, game, charm, livestock, collectable, slave, or inventory. Thousands of years passed. Then someone counted. Someone invented a new method of counting. More time passed and someone said counting alone was no longer working; there were too many things to count and no way to distinguish between them. Then a written word or proto-cuneiform script appeared scratched into the wet clay. This pictographic script was a woman. This word became woman. Soon an object attracted a status.

Skull display was an early stage of collecting the sacred power in temples controlled by priests. In the next incarnation, amulets were manufactured from clay and stone by temple priests. Temples had the authority—the monopoly—to confer the power of the sacred. Temple priests brought the power of their gods to the mintage of coins. Why go along with this transition? The currency of choice changed; more men had a chance to count and use words, competing for the best women with temple coins. Money became a sacred object from the temples; a new kind of amulet to be exchanged with others, and for others. Coins ruled. And bingo, man and woman were no longer animals. What animal could count, use words, or build temples issuing sacred images for an exchange system? Who ever thought the basis of the exchange system—buying into the sacred sex machine—would be forgotten, repressed, suppressed?

Think of the dawn rising, when man can count and there are words in the world, and suddenly amulets no longer have the magic or force around the neck to bestow power on the holder. Examine the earliest coinage from the temples, and line them up side by side with the amulets and see the obvious connection—temples became the first mass assembly lines producing objects which promised to confer the power of God, and the rush was on for every alpha male to grab as much as he could carry away.

And what image did the priests place on the coins? Heads. Not simple skulls. But skulls masked in flesh and garlands of power to protect the possessor. Heads gathering as money. And what was carved into the ivory but a tiny, smooth skull bearing the image of General Xue? Or could it have been the carver's own face? The carver had hand drilled a hole to allow the braided hair to pass through. He had a deep love for these objects which the general dispensed as gifts of face. General Xue would never have fully understood the horror Cortez felt upon his discovery of the temple skulls. But General Xue never made the mistake of thinking that man was that far removed from the animals which he hunted and collected. Or that man had evolved beyond ivory collectors going to battle. Only a Westerner like Cortez would have bothered to count all the way to 136,000 and to record the word—skull.

11

"This is Radio Bangkok 108.3, Denny Addison back on the air. Give us a call. Hey, hey, we're waiting here for you, Bangkok. We are inside this sick, vile, twisted nightmare with you. I'm sticking pins in a voodoo doll I bought a couple of years ago in Bali. Does it work? Are there any generals feeling pain? Like who cares, it makes me feel better. And that's what counts. So what are we doing? Hanging out, drinking, rotating on the air, and meanwhile rough-as-pig-guts-Jackson, the Aussie, who only realized a few minutes ago he didn't unplug his rice cooker, rang his house. His phone has been disconnected. He didn't pay his phone bill. And of all the fires raging in Bangkok, we get a weeping Aussie complaining about his rice cooker burning up. Okay, what's next? We're trying to catch up on our sleep. I lie. We are on a steady diet of Canadian Club. Only it's fake. This pirated stuff could be used to remove paint from steel. It burns all the way down the shaft. But I've gotta say, we have lost all desire to sleep or eat. We just keep driving ahead. It's weirdness. Tangled, twisted visions of hell, booze, shooting, roller-skating images of tall virgins. But you know all this. You're hip. You're cool. And best of all, if you can hear my voice, you are alive. Latest happenings street level in Bangkok. Do you really want to know? The answer is yes. Of course you do. As far as we can tell what is happening is . . . more of the same old bullets and bottle battles. Soldiers shooting demonstrators armed with plastic bottles and bricks. As you may have heard the Public Relations Building has been gutted by fire. Who set the fire? And why burn that building? The Army says terrorists started the fire. We have people calling

201

in saying that guys with crewcuts dressed in civilian clothes with handguns in their belts torched the place. Sounds a little suspicious. Anyway, there isn't a lot of need for a Public Relations Bureau right now. Man, you need more than public relations to explain what has been happening out there. You need major brain surgery to remove the images. Time, time, and major drug therapy will be needed to do the job. But I don't want anyone to get stranged out. Follow the Hunter Thompson chemical diet. We had a report from one listener that she heard on an Army radio station about the fire at the Public Relations Building five hours before the fire broke out. The caller seemed sober. But one can never be sure. Maybe she's plugged into the paranormal. She might know things before they actually happen. That's one explanation. Or is there a remote possibility that the demonstrators didn't start that fire? But someone else likes to play with matches? Also the Revenue Department building was trashed, burned, looted. Rough-as-pig-guts-Jackson who not only doesn't pay his phone bill, does not pay his taxes, and he's one happy Aussie at the moment, figuring the government tax people will never track him down. Come to think of it, where was Jackson when the Revenue Department was torched? And the State Lotto Building has gone up in flames. Figure that one out. Not even communists are against lotteries. Maybe it was a case of mistaken building identity. Finally, yeah, yeah, we've had several further reports from listeners who claim that headhunters with automatic rifles are riding around town picking off motorcyclists. Could this be traffic control in the New World Order? Why take a chance? If you have one of these motorcycle fixations, get professional help, park your bike and walk. The boys with the hunting rifles are shooting first and not asking questions last. Anyone on a motorcycle remember—you have been designated as targets. And the boys are getting a lot of practice. Unless you have a death wish, stay off your bikes. As for you die-hard bikers, who can't resist a ride through the smoke-filled, trashed streets of our city, here is one from us at Radio Bangkok 108.3 to you, good luck, fellahs, you're gonna need some luck and a bullet-proof helmet. The pirated sound track from Peter Fonda's movie *Easy Rider*."

12

Daeng walked around the desk and stared at the old, cast-iron floor fan with the greasy grille. Bits of grime feathered out on the safety guard like tiny gray banners lashed to invisible poles inside a wind tunnel. Around the base of the fan was a series of chains and bicycle locks that were jerry-rigged around a laptop computer. The chains suggested the owner's hysterical fear of robbery; his passionate desire to possess. This half-assed security system didn't impress Daeng. A tuk-tuk driver blinded with drink and riding high on paint thinner could have stolen the goods in five minutes. She looked disapprovingly as she surveyed the dusty room. The ragged wrinkled curtains were drawn. Her eyes narrowed in the near darkness, trying to find any object which wasn't rotting, rusting or falling apart. She reached over and touched the chains.

"You have *kamoy*?"

"Not so far," Cortez said. He had chosen the dump as a safehouse. He had been in a hurry.

"Why you afraid *kamoy* take? Why a ghost afraid?" asked Daeng.

"It's a lover's nest," said Cortez.

"This place is a slum even for a ghost."

It had never ceased to amaze Cortez just how impossibly confused the living were in their views about the dead. They had a funny idea what spiritual element the dead were made of; it was his purpose to explain what eternal, evil storms raged, what military crackdowns happened inside the souls, what computer software barricades separated the living and dead. Thailand was a tropical country. He had hoped he would have more luck here.

Then her eyes worked across his walls. The same look of horror he had seen for hundreds of years. So this is the way a ghost *farang* chooses to decorate his apartment was the thought he read flickering through her brain. There was a thick, padded wall hanging with mythical half-horse, half-man beings and three dancing girls in traditional costume. It reminded Cortez of the good old days. But Daeng thought of it as trashy art sold to *farang* by sidewalk vendors on Sukhumvit. On the opposite wall were two slightly torn pieces of mismatched hilltribe fabric. She looked away, they reminded her of home. None of the usual appliances were evident—no television, VCR, microwave, or automatic toaster. The room had a closed-up feeling, stuffed with too much old, faded wicker furniture. The bookcases were nicked, dusty, lined with yellowing copies of the *Bangkok Post*. The gray lino was cracked and scuffed. Odd nails had been pounded into the walls like stakes. God only knew what objects had once been connected to the wall. The room might have been in a military hospital or a prison. Or a waiting room in a bus station. It was the kind of enclosure where strangers had no second thoughts about spitting on the floor or throwing their gum away with a flick of the thumb.

She looked troubled, and Cortez saw that Daeng's eyes were swelling up into tears for a good crying jag. What he didn't know was why this storm had crossed her face. Daeng hurt when she saw a *farang* ghost living in conditions as impoverished as her own. But after all, she told herself, he had floated as a blue gas out of a sewer. It made her uneasy that death could be this unfair. It made her hurt that her father could be dead and stuck in such a hole. This poverty which she had tried to escape in this life was just as bad on the other side. The edges of her mouth became hard as she was lost in thought for a moment.

"Why you bring here?" she asked him. Outside was such a scary night and to think the night had crept inside with her. There was no place to run to.

Did he dare tell her? Or trust her once she knew the truth? After all he had broken the rules and if Montezuma ever found out there would be hell to pay, so to speak.

"Because you are not forgotten," Cortez said.

"I don't understand," she replied, sitting on the ragged sofa smelling of dampness. Thousands of brown ants crawled along the wicker arm rest.

"You are perfect for my plan. Because your life registers almost no value," said Cortez. "But despite your absence of value, someone wants to save you. This makes you count. Countable. And if he really, actually succeeds and you survive the killings then this is . . . very good for Cortez."

"What about good for Daeng?"

She really had no idea why she had ever left the Royal Hotel. Snow hadn't been a bad sort, the room was okay, and the soldiers had only said she was better off leaving as soon as possible. Suddenly she was angry with herself because Snow hadn't given her any money; but, then, she had forgotten to ask him, and also the officer had said that if she didn't split quickly, other soldiers would soon come and arrest her, beat her up, and throw her in jail. So far she had been so lucky. Not like the dead boy in the street. Why had the *farang* photographer cried over the body, tears streaming down his cheeks, onto his camera? Cortez saw that Daeng's mind had drifted. She was out of her body, drifting, drifting towards the sun and moon. He called her back, hungry to tell her the truth of distances travelled, and memories of high mountains, rivers, and diamonds forgotten. And skulls lined up end to end until they stretched beyond the seas of imagination.

"If you are so cheap maybe you should cut off your hair and go to the *wat*. I don't think you are any good at being a dead person. Why you no have TV?"

That hurt coming from the living because it was basically true. Cortez had never been good at being dead. He wasn't a patch on Montezuma who was so perfect at it that he might have been born dead.

"The apartment's a temporary rental. The previous owner died. I took it with the chains and locks. I thought it added . . . charm."

"You make joke. But maybe you think like old, dead man. Like monk. Not want any fun."

"*Phom khon john*!—I'm poor," he said. This was also basically true since the dead didn't have money.

But his old-fashioned Spanish attempt at joking at his condition failed Cortez miserably. Montezuma was so fast on his feet, always had people cracking up with laughter. He envied the Aztec for this quality. His wish was to relax her, gain her trust, since his mission rested on her having confidence in him. But all he had managed to do was enrage her and make her more suspicious. She was on her feet, walking up and down with clenched fists.

"You must never say that. Not ever. Unless you really poor. That mean you have no money. Not one baht. You understand."

"*Poot len*—I made a joke," he replied.

"You no understand Thai people. *Khon john!* no joke."

"There is a man looking for you. You do not know him. And he doesn't know you. But now he goes into the streets looking for Daeng."

"Why he look for Daeng?"

"Because a living man believes saving one girl who has no value can make a difference. And he's right. Because such a rescue makes a huge difference."

It sounded like a *farang* con to Daeng.

"Do the dead tell lies?"

He thought about Montezuma.

"Yes, pretty much like the living. This man who searches for you wants nothing for his deed."

"Impossible," said Daeng.

Cortez nodded; so far, in all the years he'd been dead, her observation had proved true. "Remote, but possible," he admitted.

"Okay, what's his name?"

"Robert Tuttle."

She stared at the ghost, trying to think if she had ever heard Robert Tuttle's name. His name meant nothing to her. She remembered practically every man's name she had ever gone to bed with—and they were many—she remembered their faces, too. But Robert Tuttle's name and face left her staring into a nameless, faceless void.

"I don't know this *farang*," she said.

"Ah, that is the point. And he does not know you. It's like two lovers with bags over their heads. But who never lose their faith in love."

Cortez omitted to mention his own vested interest in seeing Tuttle's mission succeed. Until he had assisted in the rescue of 240,000 valueless, worthless individuals from the clutches of invasions, rebellions, uprisings, police actions, wars—the list was quite broad—he could never, and would never break his cosmic link with Montezuma. He thanked Leonardo da Vinci many times for not inventing the helicopter which would have only increased this huge casualty list of those his Army had killed. Cortez spent his time searching for that one person—the Daengs—lost in a battle zone who was worthless and yet someone had launched a search to save her simply because it was the decent thing to do. Cortez's record was dismal. Since 1519 he had three near misses. But as of the blood letting in Bangkok, he had not erased even one from the total of 240,000—the number of kills in Montezuma's home town. This in itself had been a fluke, a mix-up, his Army had killed many more than this, but this was the number Montezuma had been given the honor of choosing. Victims of mass murder were allowed to set the number of missions assigned to the mass murderer.

Unlike Cortez, Montezuma retained an after-life sense of humor. "Cortez, you killed much better in life than you ever rescued in life or death."

Cortez often despaired. Montezuma was so right about his shortcomings and incompetence as a dead general. The odds were extremely long he would ever break with Montezuma. How many living people were willing to risk their own life on a battle ground, in house-to-house fighting, against heavily armed troops, to search for and rescue without a scratch a stranger whose life had no intrinsic value? Not that Cortez himself necessarily believed prostitutes lacked value—battlefield temples were filled with them; but they were on the rather arbitrary list of candidates without value—along with lawyers, tax officials, advertising executives, some baseball players, sit-com actors, and most people in the T-shirt business. Bitter experience over more than four hundred years had taught Cortez that hardly anyone ever wanted to rescue people on this list in peacetime let alone in the midst of an armed rebellion. In the end, everyone he had ever tried to help by intervening on the side of the rescuer went missing in action and disappeared without a trace. There were closings and openings in time and space, and

Bangkok had become a ground for the dead to test themselves with the living. Bangkok was an opportunity for Cortez to remove this black eye. Much depended on the co-operation of Daeng (she was already hostile about the decorative state of the apartment), the skill of Tuttle (someone who confused bones with stones), and of course, keeping Montezuma in the dark (otherwise he would scuttle the rescue). Montezuma liked this cat and mouse game. He calculated that at Cortez's current rate of failure, the universe would stop expanding, shrink back to the size of a pin hole and re-bang several dozen more times before Cortez ever came close to erasing the full number allotted to him. This wasn't eternity, but it was a very long time to contemplate.

"Why don't you have a TV? I want to know what is going on."

"My dear, never watch TV. I will give you money if you stay with me and wait for Tuttle." He lied because, being dead, he didn't have money and even if he could find a way of getting some, giving money was not allowed between the living and dead. In any event, from Daeng's expression, it was clear that she didn't believe him.

"I'm going outside," she said.

"You can't," said Cortez. "I will bring Tuttle here. Then he can rescue you."

"I never liked pimps," she said, and walked right through Cortez, opened the door and was back on the street. "And a dead pimp is probably the worst kind of pimp."

Cortez ran after her, but she walked covering her ears with her hands. "I know where Tuttle is. You will like him. He likes you. He wants to save you. It is important that he save you. Please." Cortez pushed the panic button but everything had started to come out wrong.

"Why would he want to save me? He doesn't know me. Save me from what? I'm just a whore. You said so yourself."

Cortez threw up his hands and watched her walk toward an Army patrol. It was pretty much what he expected. He was doomed just like Montezuma had said. "Cortez, you're doomed. Another couple of thousand years and you will learn to accept it."

He shouted after her. "I want to save you from them." But the sound of gunfire muffled his words. She turned around and looked back at the empty street. Thinking she had heard something.

13

Robert Tuttle found thousands milling around the university. Fires had been set in trash cans. Tongues of flame and sparks shot into the night sky. People gathered around the fires, squatting, lying on a mat, huddling in clusters. Barricades had been put up to stop the Army. Some students were listening to Radio Bangkok 108.3, and he heard Denny Addison's voice belching the usual line.

"Hey, there is in the universe, the bizarre, the strange, the weird and then there is what is happening in the streets of Bangkok. But I'm cool, the Army still wants to shoot to kill and not ask questions later, but I've got my babe, my friends, my records and most of all, I've got you out there. People in the streets telling the dictators that democracy is not a four letter word. Actually it has nine letters. Unless you misspell it—then the number of letters varies. Latest rumor is that public relations has been assigned to Pol Pot. You remember him? Pol Pot and his Khmers were that strange 1970s rock 'n roll band which killed their audience. We're talking a group that took in millions."

Tuttle hurried out of earshot of Addison's voice, he had the polaroid photo of Daeng and showed it to people in the crowd. Everyone was courteous but no one knew her or had seen her; she was just another faceless face in a sea of students, workers, peasants, and yuppies.

He approached a rumple-suited Thai in his 20s.

"You see this girl?" asked Tuttle, showing the photo.

The Thai smiled. "We were at Sanam Luang last week. I've been on the street since. I've seen hundreds of thousands of demonstrators. But I don't remember her. You see so many faces, you can't see one face."

The knot in his flash red tie was smudged with food stains. He turned away and held the mobile phone to his ear. There had been one hundred thousand demonstrators at Sanam Luang in early May. It was like a picnic, a festival then. They were called the *mob nom priew.* The yogurt-drinking mob. Or the *mob rot keng.* The car-driving mob. They gave strength to each other. The yuppy mob had thought going to the demonstrations was a great way to spend time with their friends. Most had fled for the safety of their condos after the first bus was set on fire. Only a few remained out on the street. Tuttle watched the young Thai, thinking why was it some people fled the scene while others stayed behind? He had no answer.

Beside a trash can fire, he showed the photo to a student in jeans and T-shirt wearing a black pro-democracy headband to hold back her long black hair.

"You see this girl?"

"You a reporter?" she asked.

He shook his head and saw the obvious disappointment creep into her expression. It wasn't his battle, his turf; he was an outsider, a spectator who had come to watch and she didn't have much time for anyone who was not part of the movement.

"You should leave. Go home, *farang.* The Army will come soon and start killing us," she said with eyes studying the photo of Daeng.

"I'm not afraid," said Tuttle.

"Then you are the only one who's not. Everyone's afraid to die. Soldiers are already here. I hate what the Army does. I hate it very much. They wait before they start killing us. Sure."

She had used the "killing us" tag line twice. It wasn't killing people, or me; one death was a loss from the whole which she counted herself as belonging to—that was what she was sure about.

"I saw people killed last night," he said.

Tears came into her eyes. "I see people die, too."

"Troublemakers are dwindling in number," said an announcer on a portable TV set someone had hooked up to a generator. The small crowd booed.

The woman wiped away her tears and handed back the photo of Daeng. "I didn't see her," she murmured.

"This is my country," said one of the Thais beside the TV. "They have no right to lie to the people. They care about no one but themselves. They are selfish. They want to destroy democracy."

An old, stooped man emerged from the shadows. He was eating rice with his fingers. His pinched, sagging face and wide-open eyes were illuminated for a moment by a burst from the fire in the trash can near where Tuttle stood.

"No one cares a rat's ass about democracy," said the old man, and then he turned and vanished into thin air. This was a trick Montezuma had perfected over centuries.

14

CORTEZ'S TEMPLE
by
Harry Purcell

We are back to the interior of Montezuma's temple watching the Aztecs becoming aroused as they hacked up their victims, showing beyond much reasonable doubt that we have deified what stimulates and arouses: sex, torture, and pain. The founding elements of pagan and Christian religions. The basic selling line for the latest line of weapons. Our family gun business has flourished alongside the religion and political businesses.

A man nailed to a cross corresponds to a pagan man with his heart ripped out and offered to an idol. Cortez had, much to his horror, discovered himself in the Aztec temples, and recoiled into his prayers and masses to ask for forgiveness for the self which had witnessed itself in the mirror.

But Cortez was a man built from Western sensibilities. The West had long possessed the mythology, teaching its people that there is virtue in rooting for the underdog. Christianity was founded on protection of the underdogs. Montezuma's Aztec religion was founded on taking their skulls. The East adapted the Montezuma reaction to those down on their luck. In Asia the underdog had tank-tire tracks over its back, and was kicked into the gutter with a jackboot. To be an underdog in the East was a sign of weakness, failure, lack of support, and at the first sign someone had slipped and fallen, this was not an opportunity for compassion, to offer the helping hand—no—this was the precise time to launch the attack and finish off this animal before it regained its strength and bought weapons from the Purcells and came hunting for you.

General Xue had come down with a fever when he was given a cup of poison to drink. Some say it was a cup offered by one of his junior officers, a man who left General Xue dead and his mouth covered with ivory from the tusks of white elephants. Others say the cup was delivered by the carver who grieved that another white elephant had been ordered slaughtered and the tusks delivered for more ivory beads.

PART 5
MEGALOMANIA

1

MEGALOMANIA

A Denny Addison Documentary Film
Running time: 57 minutes

The camera wobbles along the pavement, angling on the smooth nylon well-turned legs of a smartly dressed Thai woman whose red high-heels click-clack down a cement stairwell, and then move across a parking lot attached to a hotel in Bangkok. The angle is all important, revealing only the woman's long, tapered legs which look like honey poured into nylon stockings. A black seam snakes down the center of the nylons and disappears into the heel of her red patent leather shoes—the kind of sexual killers with the standard issue buckles circling the tiny ankle. The camera follows a line from her shoes to the trouser legs of hotel security guards who appear and disappear from the frame. The camera angle loiters on registration plates on the expensive imported cars in the lot.

"You have some thoughts about Thai society and car license plates," says Addison off camera.

"It's very simple," says the Thai female voice with a slight accent. "You learn about a person's power by studying registration plates on cars. A person's rank is found in the registration plate number. It's like a secret code. A numbered account like in a Swiss bank. I think not many *farang* know how to read the power code. But maybe I'm wrong."

"Can you teach us the code?" asks Addison.

216

The camera focuses on a registration plate with the woman's calf nicely flexed near the edge. "I can tell the man who drives this car is not powerful."

"But it is a Mercedes," says Addison. "He must be loaded. A Mercedes costs five million baht—two hundred thousand dollars."

"I thought you say that. Big mistake. I not criticize you. Many people think the same. The amount he paid for the car makes no difference. Luxury car is very beautiful. You say, this is not an ordinary man. Not ordinary, sure. Not powerful, also sure. The model of a car can fool you. Because you do not know how to read the code."

The Thai woman walks along the concrete parking lot with the camera following her legs.

"Why isn't the owner of the car powerful?"

"Because if he's very powerful then he can lock a number."

"Lock a door. But lock a number, bizarre," says Addison.

"See this registration plate?" asks the woman.

The camera zooms in on the plate.

"This man is powerful for sure," she continues. "There are five numbers on every registration plate and you see all five numbers are in a row. The most powerful man has 1 followed by a single Thai letter and after that 1111. Like that. Five ones in a row is very impressive. This means you must fear him. It is not easy to get all those numbers in a row. It's no accident. He has to pay a lot of money. Or if he gets it free, then he so powerful even the powerful won't touch his money. You remember the new Mercedes with registration plate with numbers all mixed up? That man has money but he has no power. It is very complicated. People think money is power. It is true but not exactly true. This man with new Mercedes he's new Chinese money. He sees the other man in other car with number 7777, and he thinks important Thai man for sure. New Chinese lets old Thai money go first. Even if all the sevens in a row are on a model not as expensive, he has fear. He stays back until the sevens man finishes his turn or he lets him in line. If he cuts the man with all those sevens, he's afraid the sevens man will take down his number and have him cut into seven parts. That part is a joke. Maybe Mr. Sevens have him cut only in half."

"And what do you do when you drive in Bangkok?"

There is laughter from the woman, she shuffles her feet.

"I tell you what I like best. I like to cut the numbers all in a row off in traffic. I don't let them get in front. I don't care if their number is for the big person. It isn't important for me. I am a Thai person. But I'm not afraid. I know not many people think like I do. But not many people know the code. The secret code is impressive for those who are taught to see how much power comes from locked numbers. I don't think the man with registration plate with locked numbers is better than me. I say, he wait like everyone else. Why should I let him in? That's what I think. So far no one cut me in half."

She laughs and the film cuts away to the credits which roll without ever revealing the face or rising above the waist of the power number reporter.

2

Cortez and Montezuma strolled along Ratchadamnoen Avenue at three in the morning. The Avenue had become a killing field. A free-fire zone, with soldiers shooting thousands of rounds into the sky and finally into the crowd, killing people here, there, and everywhere. An overturned city bus with red stripes smoldered, the windscreen riddled by machine-gun fire. They passed a Honda Civic with bullet puncture marks sprayed across one side. A gas tanker exploded, igniting a ball of orange flames which rose into the night sky. Montezuma did what he often enjoyed, he hop scotched among the thousands of abandoned sandals and shoes scattered on the sidewalk and spilling onto the Avenue. The feet belonging to them had long fled in terror. A column of two dozen soldiers beat and kicked a half-dozen demonstrators. Blood gushed from the wounds of some teenagers who lay on the pavement. Soldiers circled around the bodies, kicked heads, legs, stomachs with their boots, bringing down rifle butts in the soft, fleshy parts of the curled bodies. Others poured gasoline on lifeless bodies and loaded them into trucks. On Sanam Luang one of the soldiers looted a body. As they walked another fifty meters a soldier searched the body of a dead demonstrator, taking a gold chain and watch. Not far away another soldier scored a camera. Another a pager. Mobile phones were a dime a dozen. The crack of M-16 rounds mingled with more diffuse sounds of shouting, and crying and moaning among the wounded who were too badly hit to run away. Off to the right some soldiers stuffed bodies into plastic garbage bags, which they tossed in the back of a jeep.

Montezuma stopped behind the soldier who held up a mobile phone as a trophy. The soldier marveled at the instrument, and so did Montezuma, who liked spoils himself and if sound carried between the world of the living and the dead, he would have dialed to the soldier—"Fool, you are overlooking a three-baht gold chain. Two steps ahead, one to the right, then look down." Not that the line was engaged; there was no fiber optic connecting Montezuma to the soldier.

"If we Aztecs had invented these Sound Wave Machines, we would have known about you fucking Spanish the moment you landed on our turf. Sound Wave Machines would have changed our history—your history," said Montezuma, whose attention reverted to the phone. "You might have avoided your burden." This was the euphemism Montezuma used to describe Cortez's cosmic task to assist a good samaritan in the rescue of worthless human beings.

"It is called a mobile phone, Monty. We downloaded ourselves into Harry Purcell's computer through a phone," said Cortez, avoiding the slight. He had acquired a thick skin having endured more than four hundred years of being needled by Montezuma.

"Rapid fire, invisible communication. A miracle. If only the Aztecs had such an object. Do you think that you would have gotten within ten kilometers of Temixtitan?"

Cortez shook his head. Montezuma had trouble putting two and two together when it came to high-tech innovations. All through the Industrial Revolution he had raved about the advances other cultures had made and how the Aztecs would have kicked ass with access to such a tiny piece of such technology. Cortez pulled Montezuma around the corner, as he had done in other times and other places, and showed him a couple of journalists with videocams, silently and secretly filming the soldiers.

"You see what he's doing? He's recording what those soldiers are doing. Think about journalists with their video cameras, mobile telephones, pagers, fax machines, shortwave radios, satellite trans-missions, telecommunication facilities running around your temples at Temixtitan. They would have shown the world the real truth, the real story of Montezuma, the monster, the slaughter of local natives by the village full. Look around. How many have these soldiers killed? Less than a hundred. An afternoon's work for you and the boys. Your Government—and I use that term loosely—killed more than two hundred thousand. Do you think with a few phones and TVs, you would have gotten away with all that murder and expect others to swallow your excuse—this sacrifice for the temple gods nonsense? Forget it. The United Nations would have been on you like flies on shit. CNN would have had close-ups of your priests ripping bloody hearts out of the locals. Panel discussions, Monty, would have followed. Then a clip of one of your princes smearing blood on idols. The Americans would have paid for someone to slam a stone into your skull."

"Bosh. Soldiers are doing their duty. Look at them. Not a mean bone in their bodies. Like my priests they are following orders, doing their duty. Soldiers killing idiots who have volunteered to sacrifice themselves to the god of democracy. In my day, no one came forward to be sacrificed. We never had a single volunteer. We had to chase them down. These people invited the soldiers to shoot them. They got their death wish."

"As seen from the trash can of a sixteenth-century mind," said Cortez. "Democracy is not a god. It's an idea. You are talking sacrifices; what is happening here are executions."

"What's happening here is entertainment. Executions are sacrifices transmitted by the Sound Wave and Eye Wave Machines. People ten thousand miles away are watching it inside juice joints," said Montezuma. "Remember all those lies which you stuffed into your dispatches to Charles V? 'Oh, me and the boys feel so sad, I simply couldn't get our allies to stop butchering and looting the Aztecs.' You never tried! Your men helped themselves! You never fired into the sky. Spaniards killed 240,000 Aztecs; the dead filled the streets and the lake. What would the people in London, New York, Paris, Frankfurt, and Temixtitan watching such a massacre on TV think of the great Cortez? You would be tried as an international war criminal. The verdict? Cortez guilty on all counts of genocide and crimes against humanity. Instead you are tried off camera as a dead war criminal, and sentenced," said Montezuma, chuckling.

"Remember your defense?" continued Montezuma. "'I tried to stop them.' Did that get you very far? Did it? Mercy? There is none. You, the great victor Cortez, understand that what a general can get away with in life doesn't mean shit."

"You were born in the wrong century. You should have done live talk shows this century," said Cortez. "Your talent is wasted on the dead."

Montezuma looked thoughtful. "With the right sponsor, a little affirmative action, I would have been a star."

"Until CNN news panned the fifty-three heads of my men and their horses which you stuck on pikes, facing the sun and planted in your temple yard," said Cortez, who was getting excited. He framed the remembered scene, using his hands like a film director explaining a shot to the director of photography. "Start with a close up of a horse head, then pull back and dolly past the heads of the Spanish soldiers. What a shot that would be."

"Cortez the movie maker," sneered Montezuma. "The frustrated film producer. Still, you have a valid point. On TV you don't see many heads stuck on pikes. It is a forgotten art. And I think it is very entertaining."

"You are not getting the message, Monty," said Cortez. "These Sound Wave and Eye Wave Machines would have stopped village dictators like you . . ."

They were no longer on the streets but in a TV studio and before a live audience of the dead—this was the kind of living-dead contradiction which the Aztec liked most about the afterworld. Montezuma, green mist pouring out of his ears, smiled into the camera.

"And there will always be pirates and raiders like you roaming the earth, Cortez. Think of the TV cameras on the trail, tracking the massive troop movements of the one hundred fifty thousand Indians who hated the Aztecs. You used them—organized them—to loot a quarter million Aztec bodies in a couple of days. I would have you on my talk show. Our program today is entitled: *The Great Killers and Looters of the Past,* and we are pleased to have—not exactly fresh from the grave—Hernan Cortez who is here to promote his new version of that old favorite—*Liberation—The True Story, The Real Story.* I love the new title, Hernan. Tell us what you Spaniards liked better. The killing, or was it the looting?" Montezuma put the invisible microphone in front of Cortez, who stepped forward, running a hand through his beard as he prepared to speak.

"That was war, Monty. In battle people die, sometimes innocent people. But what you did wasn't war; it was religion."

Montezuma held up a copy of *Liberation—The True Story, The Real Story.* "That was the thesis of your old book, *Conquest.* But now you've reinvented the story from a modern perspective, Hernan, can you explain to our viewers how the old conquest and the new liberation concepts are different?"

Looking into the camera, Cortez smiled. "Good question, Monty. Your average audience alive today owns videocams, faxes, VCRs, they are in high-tech heaven and they didn't have to die to go there."

"What I hear you saying is, it is more difficult to run an old-fashioned conquest today," said Montezuma.

"Exactly," said Cortez, playing with his sword.

"But liberation is a politically correct appointment with history. It is not slaughter for slaughter's sake. And this explains the new title. The story you have written is still pretty much the same old biased reportage."

For a moment, Cortez didn't answer. He was steamed.

"You can't get away with burning, destroying, and killing and call it that old-time religion. Making idols out of blood, guts and heart tissue. The Aztec sense of humor, I guess you might call it, Monty. But we lived in the golden age of murder. I wrote down how I saw it; and that was that. Some of your people wrote down their side. Put them side by side, and it's pretty much the same eye-witness account of murder." The camera followed Cortez's eye line to a soi near Democracy Monument in Bangkok against a background of smoke and flames. "But these soldiers, look at them carrying on—killing, kicking, beating, and looting—in the grand tradition, but they won't get away with it. They will end up like me, searching and never finding it . . ."

"And why not?" asked Montezuma. "And tell our audience out there. What is this 'it'?" The studio camera picked up the action going on around Montezuma and Cortez.

"The moderns call 'it' human rights. World opinion says soldiers killing and looting civilians violates their human rights."

"Another temple god?" asked Montezuma.

"Worshipped in the West as a god of non-human sacrifice."

"What perverse god would not welcome sacrifices? The mind recoils," said Montezuma, getting angry. "Think of the ratings,

Hernan. Your new book is filled with sacrifices and is an eternal best seller. So, Hernan, give us the goods. Straight up."

Now they were cooking.

"Tourists who worship the human rights god know the difference between conquest and liberation. They watch the Eye Wave Machine which watches what the soldiers are doing, and they want to barf out their guts, Monty. Just like I nearly vomited when I saw your idols seeped in human blood inside those goddamn forty towers of your hell temple. Tourists would have boycotted Temixtitan."

"We didn't have tourists in 1519," said Montezuma. "Except you and the boys . . . and then you were hardly tourists. Or is this the point of your new-old book?"

"Tourists and travellers take vacations. They travel like they watch TV . . ."

"To be entertained," interrupted Montezuma.

"Obviously. They travel to countries which have not violated their gods of democracy and human rights. When they witness on their screens these images of Bangkok, right on the avenue behind us, and back at the Royal Hotel, they will feel horror, dread, anger, and danger."

"Another genre of entertainment."

"I hate to break the news to you, Montezuma," said Cortez. "But tourists hate that kind of entertainment when they travel. In my book, *Liberation—The True Story, The Real Story,* I reveal how you felt when I ordered my soldiers to throw your idols down the temple stairs."

"Shock, horror, fright. A world-class sin," said Montezuma. "And a big mistake. You wonder why you suffer!"

The applause sign was turned on and a huge wave of silence engulfed Montezuma and Cortez.

"And your reaction? You wanted to punish me and my soldiers."

Montezuma nodded, remembering the moment he had known bloodshed between the Aztecs and the Spaniards was inevitable.

"Well, Monty," said Cortez, playing to the camera. "Most of the world will demand revenge for what we are seeing in the streets of Bangkok tonight. Heads will roll."

"That means more human sacrifices, that's good," said Montezuma, suddenly feeling better. "More blood. I was starting to feel quite depressed. Come on, Cortez, get real. You and your boys didn't exactly arrive in Mexico on a package tour. No one invited you. But I don't want another fight about travel agents, air fares, and the price of five star hotels. My point is, has a Sound Wave Machine changed human nature? Do living people need human sacrifice? Do they enjoy human sacrifice? Of course they do. Only the names of the gods who receive the sacrifice change. The temples of sacrifice, no matter what you call them, will never come down. After these soldiers finish with their slaughter, the Sound Wave and Eye Wave Machines will broadcast whose gods were stronger and more powerful. The Army will say that their gods of order and command won. The protesters will say their gods of human rights won. Machines report that the gods will always require such a sacrifice if they are threatened. Of course, it will happen again. People never change. People require sacrifice to flush them out. They are cleansed. They are saved. They are all brothers. Everyone should forgive and forget. Until the next time."

"I think it will be different," said Cortez. "The machines are changing the people."

"Tell us about your luck with Daeng. How is it going? Will she be the first? Will you break the cherry with Daeng? After a four hundred fifty year dry patch, will Daeng be the first subtracted from 240,000?" Montezuma hit the applause button again for another earthquake of silence.

"You spy, you scum. How long have you known about Daeng?" asked Cortez. For a ghost he showed a great deal of negative emotion.

"We've been cheering for you. Haven't we audience?" Montezuma raised his hands to the darkness. Thunderous applause splashed back from the void. Montezuma turned back to Cortez who remained seated on the podium. "See, what did I tell you? We want you to score one point."

Cortez smiled, and neither trusted nor believed the Aztec chief for a moment. Montezuma started chanting, "Save Daeng, save Daeng." Soon the audience in the void beyond the lights joined Montezuma, chanting, "Save Daeng."

The chanting stopped when Montezuma raised his hand.

"I'm afraid we are outside of time and space for the show. Thank you Hernan Cortez for being with us forever. If you've not read it, the book is *Liberation—The True Story, The Real Story* written by our guest forever, the self-styled Liberistador of Mexico—General Hernan Cortez. The man who had the chance to jump four and a half centuries with the inventions of Leonardo da Vinci. And blew it."

"Can I take off the mike? Or are we still taping?" asked Cortez, turning around.

Montezuma had already gone.

3

Crosby found the form of a man in black silk, a long shock of white hair over his shoulder, shrouded in cigar smoke and leaning on the new jukebox at HQ.

"One day the old jukebox vanished," said Purcell.

"Missing in action," said Crosby.

"It had character. Life. A history."

"It had cockroaches knitting dust balls under the colored plastic panels," said Crosby.

"You miss the point, Crosby. The old jukebox was the temple altar."

Crosby looked at Purcell, thinking he might be the kind who one day showed up with an automatic weapon and sprayed a roomful of people because someone removed a piece of furniture he had attached supernatural purposes to. The best tactic was to get Purcell onto a subject closer to home. "There was a rumor you brokered a tank deal with the Army. And that your father sold guns to Mao on the Long March," said Crosby.

"What this jukebox lacks are the stained-glass church windows," replied Purcell, ignoring Crosby.

Crosby stopped and studied the three arches rising above the control deck, and the three upside-down arches falling below it. The colors ran from blue, to pink, orange, yellow, and pulsating light bulbs flashed in the central arch loop. No question about it; Purcell was that cigar-smoking loner who would come unglued and take a room of people to the next life.

"You miss the old religion of HQ?" asked Crosby.

Purcell nodded. "When you took a girl you assumed she stayed the night," he said. "Now the girls have broken down the old order. It's all short-time comfort and hit 'n run tactics."

"The girls converted to the new religion of money. Something you are familiar with. Money," said Crosby. "In how many African countries did you flog guns?"

"We sold to Africa before there were countries," said Purcell, seeing the bait Crosby had offered. Then he spit out the hook and went back to his state of mourning for the lost religion of HQ when comfort lasted through the night. "I remember the days when a girl would get up and make you breakfast, sweep the floor, make the bed, and then give you a *wai* as you handed her a purple."

"When was this? Before Thailand was divided into provinces?" asked Crosby.

"Have you seen our mutual friend, Mr. Tuttle?" asked Purcell.

"He's off on a search-and-rescue mission. Looking for an HQer named Daeng. Snow had her. But she slipped away. Proving your short-time theory."

"Daeng," he whispered. "Of course."

Harry Purcell's right eyebrow arched only slightly; there was nothing all that unnatural about Tuttle's continuing his mad search for a whore named Daeng. But there was shooting in the streets, and HQ with the rule of two always in operation was guaranteed to have at least one more whore named Daeng.

"And Snow, where is he?"

"Filing battlefield reports for profit and fame," said Crosby. "What are you doing in HQ on a night of indiscriminate shooting into crowds? Coming to the church of the new religion? Saying prayers for old jukeboxes? Or could Harry Purcell be on a routine field check?" Crosby had mixed feelings about Purcell, which accounted for the sudden burst of emotion.

That a half-*farang* named Harry Purcell had earned a double first from Cambridge at age eighteen, spoke many languages and came from an old, powerful, wealthy family gave him shooting flashes of envy. Most of all Purcell made Crosby feel shallow and small. But Purcell had been generous, giving Crosby many T-shirt slogans, and he had once financed a batch of T-shirts for the Big Promise Bar which read—Load and Fire your Big Gun. The fact the police had seized the entire lot of T-shirts and resold them on the Burmese border was hardly Harry's fault. Nor was he responsible for a gloomy, dejected Crosby who had appeared in the newspaper flanked by police officers. Crosby had been photographed sitting at an interrogation table with his handcuffed hands folded together and pointing at a stack of the T-shirts. Two days later Purcell paid a negotiated fine and Crosby was released from jail. But he never repaid the loan to Purcell, or the fine money, and Purcell, to Crosby's undying admiration, never mentioned the loan or fine. It was guys like Snow who would dig him, "Doing any deals for the Big Promise Bar? Or are you holding your fire? There are sightings of Karen jungle fighters wearing your T-shirts, how did that happen?" But never a word or jab from Purcell who had found a far more effective way to punish Crosby with this noble silence.

Along with the new jukebox, Purcell still had not adapted to several other drastic changes in HQ; someone with dark, black visions had decided to redecorate the interior.

"It takes time to adjust to the new HQ," he said.

"Snow calls it post-modern whoredom," said Crosby.

The job looked like it had been awarded to a firm which had specialized in warehouses, heavy leather bars, and boiler shops. The mirrors—which had become mainly fragments—around the top of each booth had vanished; the booths were reupholstered in black vinyl, and new booths had been installed where the girls used to sit at tables in the back. As Purcell looked around the room, a girl's painted face peered around the corner of one of the booths like a puppet on a string and then vanished.

"It's bound to catch on," said Purcell. "Temples and weapons are the mirrors of change."

"Christ, that goes on a T-shirt," said Crosby. "Temples and Weapons—Mirrors of Change."

"HQ has gone covert action."

The HQ girls had quickly adapted to the new surroundings like smart viruses fighting off a designer drug. They used the new booths to burrow into their hosts; as their private, secretive spring traps, waiting with their bodies mainly out of sight, nervous, sensing danger and ready to take a victim. As a sexual battleground, the new arrangement favored the girls.

"HQers as intelligence agents. No one has ever made that charge stick," said Crosby, lighting a cigarette. He passed the lighter across the table as Purcell stuck a Havana into his mouth.

Some HQ girls, Termites, dressed in tight jeans and T-shirts, leaned on the jukebox, eyeing the field, checking out who was in the gallery. They spotted Crosby—marked down one hardcore, then Purcell—marked down a second hardcore. Whispering to each other, they wondered among themselves whether the killing was going to mean another night hanging around without softcore *farang*s with purples willing to spend on them.

A couple of old Tommys slashed the smoke-filled air with their hands and arms, a dolphin-like sound coming from their throats. They hated Purcell's Havana cigars. Sitting together around a table near the TV set, they coughed and tried to watch the news report about street violence. Pictures of troops walking in closed ranks flickered over the screen. The soldiers fired their rifles into the night sky. The Tommys gestured with screaming hands, in a loud silent rage among themselves, with one of the younger Tommys sending hand signs in a screaming arc across the room to the jukebox *pue-an pod*. Some hand signs were like whispers; others—when the soldiers came on the screen—were like fists looking for a jaw or a belly-landing zone.

In the middle of a Tommy conversation about the killings, Montezuma flipped a coin—should he vaporize, dissolve into a mist or spray?—and sprayed himself into HQ through a greasy air vent in the back alley. There was nothing to match a vaporization. He flown along in a thin, narrow column, crossed the central room, avoiding the toilet squalor. He rolled himself onto an empty stool, and allowed a presence to accumulate. A couple of bleary-eyed *farang*s leaned against the bar only inches away talking to a couple of whores. On the ceiling a small brown lizard with lidless eyes languidly snapped small red ants with its lightning tongue. It shuddered, hunched down in a frozen, immobile position as Montezuma came together directly underneath. Montezuma watched Purcell—remembering over the centuries how many of his relatives had been on his talk show.

At the same moment, Purcell felt an icy chill knife through his body, setting his teeth chattering. He knew the meaning of the cold draft. The "Presence" with a capital "P" was well recorded in the family chronicle. The sudden blast of cold happened whenever a Purcell was in a war zone or travelled through a killing zone. The family divided into factions on the cause of this flash of cold and the remedy dispensed to combat the chill: one group held to the guilt theory and the other held to the spirit or ghost theory. Since Purcell was a combination of East and West he believed in both theories simultaneously. He believed that Leonardo da Vinci haunted the Purcell family, given the role they had in his death, and of trying to steal his plans. This was also the source of the family guilt.

"You have the shakes," said Crosby, quite pleased to see Purcell show a human trait and suffering.

His white hair stood on end on his neck and arms.

"I know. You don't feel it?" asked Purcell.

"Feel what?"

"The Presence," said Purcell. Then he quickly backed off. "The girl over there has the most tasteful way of displaying her breasts. The one lap dancing on the Hun."

Crosby craned his neck around the whores in his booth, thinking this might be the night Harry Purcell turned mass-killer under cover of the madness on the streets, his timing would be perfect. He looked disturbed, all shakes and goose flesh, his eyes wide and unblinking.

The girls had the unofficial Termite floor show going at full throttle—silent voices and hysterical fists sculpting fighting words. He spotted her and smiled, the smile of hardcore recognition, which said without saying, "I've had Meow."

"Nice, was she?" asked Purcell.

"Quite a lovely cupcake," said Crosby.

This was the Meow of Denny Addison's documentary called *The Unexpected Answer*. Meow was the *katoey* whore who used a Q-tip to smear drugs on her nipples, taking her short-time tricks back for a fast lick into unconsciousness before she picked them clean of all valuables. Some people were born with severely retarded short-term memories; Crosby had seen the documentary and had fucked Meow and saw no connection between what appeared on the screen and what happened between his legs. HQ was a bar which catered to the derelicts of history, the rootless wanderers who had travelled from the far realms of the earth, the extreme cases who had washed up in the HQ temple—which they had heard on the travellers' grapevine was a place containing women who could heal their fears.

"The Kraut's an elderly man. Meow might shake something loose in his gearbox," said Crosby.

Meow lap danced on the lap of a bald-headed German named Wolfgang Kleist. He was a tank commander at the battle of Stalingrad where 1.1 millions Russians died and 800,000 Germans perished in the snow and ice. Wolfgang—whom everyone called Kleist—had the aged, smooth look of a man who had beaten the odds, and having survived a battle which had destroyed just about everyone he ever knew, felt obliged to drink and screw with the determination of someone who had faced off the Russians and survived. Kleist had a shaved head. Meow was about to repeat the success of about 1.1 million dead Russians who had died defeating the Germans—she intended to defeat Kleist, get paid, and live to tell her friends about it. Kleist sat on the stool with the look of a gnarled tree the winter storm winds had curved earthward, or someone who had spent years crouched inside a tank and once he climbed out could no longer stand straight. He reached out and snared another girl, pulling her onto his other knee.

"Germans worship trees," said Crosby, trying to get Purcell to joke about religion. "It's absolutely true. The pagan ancestors of Bismarck, Hitler, Mozart, and Liszt for centuries fell on their knees and prayed to large oaks. Teutonic pagans flocked to the mountains and hills and danced in the forest. Old Wolfgang is HQ's honorary war criminal and he would never have hurt a fir."

"Wolfgang did his job. And he lost. Tonight I will give Wolfgang a second chance. Argggggh," shouted Purcell, as another chill from Montezuma's Presence slashed through his chest. The Presence was definitely in the room, and guns, war, tanks, any mention of soldiers or weapons would only made the cold run faster, deeper. His face twisted into a mask of pain.

"Are you okay, or do you need a gun?" asked Crosby, swallowing hard.

A waiter arrived with a tray of fresh drinks.

Purcell drank a gin and tonic straight down and ordered two more doubles.

"Gun-running, pickled-pork bellied, cottage-cheese nosed maggot-filled bum licker," said Purcell.

"That's not on the menu, Harry," said Crosby. "Calm down, this too will pass." Long ago he had accepted Purcell as strange; but Harry was over the top, looking more and more dangerous. HQ had its share of hardcores given to fits of temper, screams for no apparent reason, and heavy drinking bouts, but Harry Purcell was heading into new territory. It was rather like being with some of the unpredictable people who hung around on the London Underground to be seated near Harry Purcell at that moment and Crosby couldn't think of a way to scoop up his T-shirts and bolt out the door.

The chill stopped as suddenly as it had started. Montezuma felt slightly hurt that each generation of Purcells had for the last four hundred fifty odd years confused his Presence with either the Italian arms designer Leonardo da Vinci or the Chinaman General Xue. When he had the Purcells on his show, the surprise they registered when they found out who the Presence was made everyone in the audience crack up.

The waiter the hardcores called the New Kid on the Block set down the two double gin and tonics, scooped up Purcell's empty glasses, loaded them on the tray, and disappeared into the crowd. It had been Snow who, fifteen years before, had nicknamed him the New Kid on the Block.

"The New Kid on the Block's got gray hair," said Crosby. "Soon his hair will be white like yours. I didn't mean it as an insult. I mean white shows wisdom. A cool heart."

Purcell said nothing. He drank his gin and tonic and felt so much better for the regular pulse rushing hot down his arms and legs. He loved being hot. He loved hot women, weapons, and the company of old soldiers. The shooting in the streets was small-fry murder compared with the vast slaughter Kleist had witnessed in Stalingrad; it was why Kleist was at HQ, it was simply another night in another city. A flicker of happiness danced in Purcell's eyes. A candle flame of hope which might last him through the night. Purcell looked at Crosby, knowing that Crosby feared him. Crosby had all the qualities of a dog except loyalty, thought Purcell. This simple fact explained Crosby's obsession with trees.

Crosby twirled the nipples of his booth mate. This conduct had become a kind of nervous tic when his thought turned to bloody ambushes in the Alley of Revenge or a hardcore going over the top inside HQ and knifing someone in the neck. But in truth, he also twirled nipples when lost in thought about a business scheme, or daydreaming about the perfect T-shirt which sold a million. Crosby thought talking about business might settle Purcell down, take his mind off chills, weird screams, and interior changes of HQ. But he felt inhibited talking about the T-shirt business given his jail record and outstanding debt to Purcell. It was an awkward moment. It was now or never. The debt hung like Harry's cigar smoke over the table. He fought his fear and started the conversation talking about names; this was an old hand stand-by—names that caused misunderstanding and confusion when imported from one culture to another.

"In London, I met a guy named Jim Key who had been posted to Bangkok," said Crosby. "He lasted a month in Thailand. His last name, Key, makes the identical sound the Thai word *kee*—or shit. *Kee* is normally a classifier. He didn't know that either. At first, he couldn't understand why all the laughter every time he picked up the telephone, and said, 'Mr. Key, speaking.' Finally, someone told him. He seized up. He didn't know what to say on the phone, but suddenly he hated his name. He hated that he had been burdened with a name that meant shit."

Harry Purcell saw the play action.

"*Kee kar* roughly translates as 'shit person,'" said Purcell.

"In ancient Thai it meant a slave," observed Crosby, smiling.

It was working; Harry was looking better already.

Purcell stopped and looked around the room. He felt good but remained nervous, constantly looking around the room. The Presence had not left HQ but had stopped circulating, it had desisted from sending chill waves. "Or if Mr. Key had said, 'Key, here,' a Thai might have thought he had said *kee tur* which means a 'stupid person.' And when he gave up and returned to London, the Thais would have remembered him, if they thought of him at all, as *kee pae* or someone prone to lose. They would say over lunch, 'Whatever happened to old *kee pae*?'" said Purcell.

"The Thais hated to see a shit *farang* go home," said Crosby.

"Of course, they missed the play. A *farang* who called himself Khun Shit. How could they not love such a man? Someone whose very name made them laugh. He probably never understood," said Purcell.

"They would like Khun Prick," replied Crosby.

"There was Mr. Lee which means prick in Burma. I sold him a great deal of military hardware. Some of which actually worked," said Purcell, keeping the conversation alive as the music stopped.

"Bhutto means fuck in Bahasa Malay," said Crosby.

"I once sold tanks to an Army general named Bhutto. We were at dinner in a world class restaurant in London. I leaned over and tossed a wallet under the table with one hundred thousand US inside. Then I said, 'General Bhutto, I believe you've dropped your wallet on the floor.' And he asked me, 'How much is in the wallet?' And I said, 'General Bhutto, your wallet has one hundred thousand US dollars inside.' He grinned and shook his head, 'You must be mistaken. That can not be my wallet. My wallet has two hundred and fifty thousand US dollars inside.'"

"A bribe?" asked Crosby.

"A gift among friends," replied Purcell.

Crosby was enjoying himself—Purcell was no longer in the danger zone; he was himself again, grinning, lighting a fresh cigar, and getting warmed up on old war stories.

"'Fuck' in Lao means 'to chop,'" said Purcell.

"I didn't know that," said Crosby. "So you would tell a general who wanted too much tea money that he should fuck himself and that would be a Lao pun."

"Fuck, fuck, *set lao*," said Purcell. "A phrase every Lao girl has used with her mother." Chop, chop, it is finished.

What carried the punch line of a joke in one language was only a sound byte without meaning in another. What caused sadness in one made another sick and yet in another created rage. The absence of consensus about meaning creates the ambiguity and irony that streaks through life like lightning in a monsoon sky.

From the twinkle in Purcell's eyes, Crosby knew that Harry was back from the place of dread and darkness. He rolled his cigar between his fingers, the diamond on the pinky ring flashing a rainbow of light across the whores in the booth.

Purcell thought that sound waves continued into eternity—the chill of the Presence was one of those waves passing from out of time into time and back out again. He figured one day such a disembodied voice could be recovered once the right retrieval instruments were invented. Harry wanted to patent this sound conveying instrument. He wanted to use it to recall Cortez's words as he entered the Aztec temple.

Snow had once summed up what Harry would find on calling back the past. "I can save you the trouble of a machine. Cortez said, 'Fuck, man, it's a skull bar. We've found gold!'"

At the bar Montezuma was feeling no pain. It was the best part of being dead. But this crack by Crosby was so far off the mark that, could he feel pain, then pain would have vibrated through his blue vapor-like form. What Cortez had said was nothing like what Crosby thought. Cortez had said, "Pagans. We must stop these pagans." Then he threw up his lunch on the temple floor.

4

The Massacre of May, 1992
Bangkok

Dear Richard,

Crosby and Purcell stayed late at HQ naming names while I searched for a girl named Daeng from Nan Province. Crosby gave me a full report the following morning. Purcell apparently suffered from a near seizure brought on by serious cold flashes followed by hot flashes. This might be explained by a) he is going through male menopause or b) he was consuming a large quantity of double gin and tonics at HQ. Things got out of hand over the naming game. That old hardcore version of scrabble. Crosby's conclusion was that Purcell knew more strange names with dirty meanings in other languages than any other person alive. But Crosby has always been in awe of Harry Purcell ever since the T-shirt incident.

I had my own name game that night near a university. The name was Daeng or Red and it belongs to a young Thai girl with a scar on her face shaped like a half moon. I searched the entire night for her but failed to locate even one person who had any information about her whereabouts. Things are chaotic in Bangkok with all the shooting by the Army. Who in the West would name a daughter "Red"? It is difficult to imagine. One must be careful in naming children. One must also be careful in naming the dead or the bones left behind by the dead. Harry claims the bone he gave me came from General Xue, a relative on his mother's side, and that I was in line to receive it. He never really said why I was the inheritor of the General's bone. But Harry is great on practical jokes. And the more he says he is not joking, the more you know that he is doing just that.

I still think about the bones I scooped out of the Nan River. In a cremation culture reconstructing the past from the present is done through ashes. A river of bones flows only in one direction; bones which once had names attached. What name? No Carbon 14 dating could ever say. There was no Carbon test to recover a name or a word; sounds were carried on the wind—how many knots was the wind blowing at seven in the morning 14th April one hundred thousand years ago? To ask such a question is to provide an answer as to why certain questions rarely, if ever, are raised. Such questions outstrip all ideas, concepts, theories embedded in religion, philosophy, science, art, or witchcraft to assemble information required for an answer. Such questions force us to admit the weight of what lies beyond any knowledge system; we can find old bones and Carbon date them but the flesh is gone, the wind is gone, the sound has vanished.

When Mr. Key or Khun Shit, as the Thais would hear his name, escaped to London with all that laughter ringing in his ears he understood his name anchored him to the soil of his language and customs. If he had renamed himself, he could have stayed in Thailand. What memories of his past would have gone up in smoke in exchanging names? People would have reminded him until his end that he didn't know the difference between shit and shinola. The last use of a name is to remember the dead. Mr. Key would not wish to be reminded how his memory will continue over time—after his death—as his name is passed from person to person in Thai, as the Englishman who called himself Khun Shit.

Yours,

Robert Tuttle

ps. Enclosed is a short story written not long after I met Dow, an unusual Thai woman—an engineer educated in America. Dow has pitched in to help me find Daeng.

238

5

THE WATER BOY

A Short Story
by
Robert Tuttle

It was nearly six in the evening when the water boy in dirty, ragged cut-off trousers, his shirt unbuttoned, sweat lines streaked across his chest, arrived in the compound. He kicked off his plastic sandals at the door. A ten-liter plastic bottle of water was hooked over his shoulder. He looked small under the weight. A kind of pack animal separated from the train. This was his last delivery in a twelve-hour shift. The next morning would be another day and he would start his beast of burden job all over again. His liquid eyes blinked as the maid directed him, one hand on her hip and the other pointing to a spot on the floor next to the fridge.

"Put the bottle there," she said.

As he padded across the floor in his bare feet, in a split second, a word, a gesture, the signature tune from the ice cream cart in the soi, caused a reaction in the water boy.

"One is not enough. Bring another one," the maid said.

He swiftly turned and walked out of the house. He walked down the compound pavement, picked up a second ten-liter plastic bottle, and slung it over his shoulder. He padded back to the house. After he had set it down next to the first bottle, some emotion erupted; a thread of hate and anger rose inside him, as if it were a thing about to break or tear apart inside the water boy. As if an invisible force which glued mood, attitude, and respect into a unified whole had fallen apart. The two bottles of water were perfectly lined up in a row. He had done his job; done what he'd been told his entire life. Two bottles were delivered. He had sweated to cart them from the street through the compound. Dogs had barked and snapped at his feet. He kicked out at one of the dogs and the other sank its teeth into his ankle.

Then the emotional dam burst—after his work was done. He rose up with a kind of strength which did not seem possible from his tired, slender frame. His face twisted into an angry sneer. He threw a fit of temper—*jai rawn*. With this anger, this hot heart he raced back to the fridge and grabbed first one bottle, carried it to the door, then returned for the second. He had said nothing, loading the bottles on the van again, his ankle bleeding from the puncture wound left from the dog attack. No one in the compound including the Old Uncle asked for a reason or explanation. His action was beyond reason. They watched as the water boy stormed through the compound, kicking one of the dogs which had not been involved in the attack. This foul mood storm of anger swept through the compound, filling the maids, Old Uncle, the children, and the others with silent fear. Rage out of control caused damage. And no one wanted to get in the way of the water boy. His frustration swirled, threatening to swallow them, suck them into the head wind.

A few days passed, the incident had been largely forgotten. Then the water boy's strange conduct arose in the course of a discussion between Old Uncle and Noi, his niece who had returned after four years at university in America. She had been in the compound when the water boy had arrived and departed. A few days later, she had raised the concept of patience and justice with her uncle. Noi had acknowledged that Old Uncle had more patience and tolerance than she. She claimed America had changed her; before she had been patient and the incident would not have been worthy of further comment. But now her Old Uncle's patience exceeded her own. This statement was not intended as a compliment but as a matter of fact; as if patience and tolerance were not a question of higher morality or good breeding but connected with genuine forces unevenly distributed in life.

"Do you remember the water boy?" Noi asked.

The incident returned with clarity. A small, tired boy with torn clothes, and soiled hands. "The impatient boy," said Old Uncle.

Noi said, "Yes, the impatient boy. But it isn't that easy. The water boy has no chance in life. He will never go to America for education. His life is what it is. Nothing can deliver him from his life. He sees the whole outline of how his life always will be. You can't expect a boy who understands that he lives a life which offers him no chance for deliverance to show the virtue of patience."

Old Uncle smiled and returned to tending his garden. Noi knew he had, in his own way, dismissed her. The conversation was over. She walked through the compound to the house of Khun Gerald. A *farang* who had lived more than ten years in the compound. He worked in a travel agency. She saw him sitting in a chair reading a newspaper. He was dressed in shorts. His large feet were crossed on the table, and on the table was an open bottle of Kloster beer.

"Khun Gerald, I would like to talk to you."

He invited her into his house. "Would you like a beer?" he asked. "I'd offer you water but I have none."

"You know Old Uncle. I love him as I love my own father. But he doesn't understand how I've changed. You heard about the water boy and the bottles of water he took away?"

Gerald had heard the story from his maid and a different version from Old Uncle.

"I'm troubled Old Uncle doesn't understand. Because of my father, I have had greater opportunity than the water boy. But what does this mean? My chance in life is far less than your life even though this is not your country. You see no limit to your opportunity. You have no fears holding you back. But like the water boy, I see the walls which surround me. I see stones rising into the clouds. They are higher walls than I remember before I went to America. I can never climb or go around them no matter what I learned in America. The water boy's wall is as high as the sky. I think he saw that wall when he came to the compound. He saw it here in your house. That is why I've come here. I wanted to see the wall the water boy found inside your house."

"You want to see through the boy's eyes?" asked Khun Gerald.

"I cannot. You must understand that I have greater patience than the water boy. But it is unreasonable for me to have your patience because I do not have your chance in life. Even with a university degree I can never catch up with you in my own country. Your life is huge with opportunity and this promise of deliverance makes you unable to understand. I cannot sit naked in my room reading a newspaper alone and drink beer."

He looked over his newspaper, reached forward and sipped from his beer can. "Why not?"

"You have a cool heart. You know why?"

He shook his head. Beer suds bubbled around his mouth and he remembered the one time he had made love to Noi. It was before she had left for America. Now she was back. She had changed just as Old Uncle had said that she would.

"You were born with the promise of deliverance," said Noi. "It's your birthright. It explains your luxury of patience and tolerance. Because patience and tolerance are a luxury. They are part of the wealth which comes from opportunity. Nothing stands in your way. America grants you this. You can carry this knowledge on your back to any country you wish to live in. I can possess it but I can't carry it back to Thailand."

"Why?" asked Gerald, thinking how sexy Noi looked sitting across from his chair. He no longer tried to read the newspaper.

"Gerald, when you understand one simple fact, then you can understand why you have no water. You can understand the lack of patience and tolerance in the water boy. You can also have compassion for those like me who know what is beyond the wall but can never reach that high. Noi was born to a place which she cannot leave. Mine is a world with limited chance. You should never forget that people like me cannot experience the world like you, and the pain of our knowledge weighs on our shoulders like those ten-liter jugs of water. We carry that heavy weight each step we take. We carry it for a lifetime. Set it here, someone orders us. Cart it there, another says. No, I've changed my mind, I want it downstairs. When you see the water boy and the bottles on his back, you see me. You see me forever burdened."

"Did you talk to your father about this?" asked Gerald, coming back from the fridge. He opened two fresh beers and handed one to Noi. She pressed the can to her lips and took a long sip.

"I told him what I learned in America," Noi said.

"Which was?" asked Gerald.

"No one has a right to order you to carry their water fourteen hours a day. You can choose your own life."

Gerald drank long from his beer, his eyes never leaving her breasts. "What did your father say?"

"He said Americans teach me megalomania. They make me crazy, selfish, think only about myself. In a family, everyone carries the water on their backs. No one is without this burden. If I want to walk alone, stand out from the family, then I can no longer be part of the family."

"So it's all or nothing," said Gerald. "Freedom or prison."

"Even in prison people cart water, and even in freedom people need water to drink. So how does it get into the cup?"

Gerald smiled. "Who said that?"

"My father," said Noi, with some pride. "He's wrong but terribly brilliant."

"I think you should talk with the boy," said Gerald.

She liked this idea and nodded. As she was about to leave, the maid who had listened near the door and understood little other than that they were discussing the water boy, came into the room.

"The water company fire the boy," she said. "You can't talk with him. He's gone."

Noi glanced at Gerald with an "I told you so" look.

"Why was he fired?" asked Gerald.

"He poison two dogs on the soi. Someone complain him."

The water boy had been sent away. There was no possibility for Noi to have her chance of talking to him. She looked like she might cry. "Never mind," said the maid. "There will be a new boy, you can talk to him."

6

Denny Addison had caught his second wind as he pulled himself up to the mike and waited for the music to finish. Or was he on his third wind? He made faces at the engineer in the booth behind. Addison had been tearing around the studio with his shirt off, beating his chest like Tarzan and screaming he was king of the jungle. For one moment he forgot his videocam was smashed on the staircase. No one else was all that impressed by his performance but it didn't slow him down in the department of self-praise. Addison talked low into the microphone, snapping his fingers.

"Here we are, Bangkok. For you. And just in case you've forgotten, this is your favorite 108.3 DJ, Denny Addison. That's spelled with a double 'd' for our friends who still plan to have me executed as soon as they can figure out a way to break into this bubble and drag me out. This is Radio Bangkok 108.3 presenting to you live—the revolution. It is happening live in a street near you. We are live. So far. We have music. Tons of music. We have gossip, rumors, and a countdown to doomsday. We present the news as reported by you. One rumor which came in a few minutes ago tells you just how bad things are on the streets. A listener phoned in to say she had walked on the overpass bridge above Sukhumvit Road. The concrete staircase near the Ambassador Hotel. Normally the Beggar's Patrol stations lepers and amputees at both ends. But the beggars had gone, fled the scene. At the DK Bookstore end of the bridge, there was a cat. Yes, a small white cat in a wicker basket. The cat appeared to have swallowed the beggar's quota of drugs. Its eyes were half open. But the cat made no attempt to escape. This cat curled up, chin on paws, watching our listener in a vacant kind of way. Could this cat have seen something like this in a previous life? Who knows? Who cares, you say? Now comes the resourceful part of the story. In front of the cat drugged out in the wicker basket was a Singha Gold beer can. The top had been peeled off. The beggar cat was taking donations. Talk about a breakdown in law and order. The Beggar's Patrol leaders have pulled their human beggars and have substituted animals. Sicko. Cats with missing paws will soon follow 108.3 predictions. Hey Animal Rights Activists, where are you? Hiding under the bed? There is a cat in the line of fire. Do you care? Rescue that animal. Protest. Resist. Cats begging in the street, tanks heading for a show-down, the hospitals filled with the dead and dying, and this is the City of Angels. A place where the cats have been left to beg for a meal. Now for some music dedicated to those who have been hearing the tanks rumbling past all night long. *I Feel the Earth Move.* Mr. Robert Tuttle and his gang of hardcores will immediately recognize this tune as number 127 at HQ. Scatter and reform."

7

It was one in the morning when Harry Purcell and Kleist, the German ex-tank commander who had survived the battle of Stalingrad returned to Purcell's house. They squeezed four girls from HQ in the taxi. Purcell slammed the door before the *katoey* who smeared her nipples with sleep-inducing drugs could get her leg into the taxi. HQ had a rule which barred *katoeys*. Somehow this one had slipped through. No one would have guessed—until it was too late. Either the staff at HQ were more compassionate, their guard was down, or with all the chaos, they simply no longer cared if a *katoey* slipped into the bar at the end of the universe, where killing time and buying women were the diamonds in the sky.

They arrived at Purcell's rented old mansion, an old Thai-style house made from teak off Sukhumvit Road which had survived being bulldozed for a condo project. The house had four bedrooms with wooden shutters that opened onto a large, secluded tropical garden—grounds lush with palm trees, a fish pond, a tree-house converted into a huge bedroom, and scattered throughout were cages with rare, exotic birds.

Kleist ambled ahead between two of the girls, and Harry Purcell clutched the hands of the other two girls, leading them along a path to a pond. Along the way, Purcell's two girls began to strip off their clothes and waded into the water up to their knees. Kleist splashed water on one of his girls, she splashed back. Soon everyone was hugging and kissing. Harry massaged the breasts of his two girls, watching old Kleist with his pant legs rolled up to his knees moving into the pond.

246

"Why not let the girls play?" asked Purcell.

Kleist looked back over his shoulder and shrugged.

"I think we take the girls first," said Kleist but not with a great amount of conviction in his voice. Then he cocked his head to one side, "Do I know you?"

"Purcell's the name. I think we should make our assault on Stalingrad, then take the girls as spoils of victory. What do you say?" asked Purcell.

What could the ex-German tank commander say? No? He had played the battle of Stalingrad in his mind a hundred times; sometimes he made it into the city, sometimes his tank was blown up on the outskirts. The chance of going back one more time was irresistible. Kleist turned and, sloshing his feet on the wet mud, he climbed back onto the bank.

"Yes, we go to Stalingrad," he said.

Purcell maintained a separate room filled with computer terminals, a mainframe along one wall, a huge TV screen. On one side was a cubicle built on a platform and inside was the compartment of a tank. As they walked to the house from the pond there was the distant crackle of gunfire. The killing hadn't stopped; the city remained under siege. It was the kind of starry night, and tracer-filled sky that made re-enacting the Battle of Stalingrad a giddy enterprise. The special effects on the cathode-ray screen—hooked invisibly to the computers, high grade software programs, and sound-tapes from actual battles—guaranteed that anyone inside would feel and experience every element of tank battle. Inside the room, Purcell flicked on the lights. He went over to the cubicle, opened the hatch door, and showed Kleist the way in, with a small bow of his head. Kleist looked at the helmet and gloves Purcell had handed him and then at the cubicle which looked like a gas-chamber.

"It's safe," said Purcell. "I've fought battles in the Gulf, the Battle of the Bulge, France, North Africa, and Vietnam. We have hundreds of battle programs. You can select your battle, your tank and that of your enemy. What do you say, Kleist? Have another go at Stalingrad?"

He watched as Kleist pulled the helmet over his bald head and slowly slipped on the gloves. He waddled over and climbed into the cubicle, sitting in what looked like a bamboo electric chair with straps and wires looping at odd angles, connecting to a bank of computers and terminals. Kleist eased himself in with a long sigh. A moment later, Purcell slammed the door shut, hit the main switch, hurling Kleist back through time to Russia; he was back in his command tank about fifteen kilometers from Stalingrad, where through the gun turret he saw the chunky gray skyline in the distance. Thunderous explosions rocked Kleist back in his chair. He held the joy-stick and commenced firing. Purcell watched the battle on the TV screen. He saw Kleist's flanking movement, cutting through a Russian perimeter and knocking out two tanks, one artillery placement. Two platoons of infantry turned on their heels and ran in the face of the devastating concentrated fire power from a dozen attack tanks.

An hour thirty minutes into the battle, Kleist suffered a direct hit and his tank was killed. He had made it within five hundred meters of Stalingrad. Smoke filled the screen of the interior of the tank. Kleist pulled off the helmet, coughing and hacking, his face red and his tongue, a large and bloated organ, jutting from his throat. He hated getting blown up. It was fucking depressing.

"I'm getting too old for this, Purcell," said Kleist. "And you kept changing the weapon placement and the kinds of weapons."

This was true. Purcell loved tinkering with history, injecting weapon systems which hadn't been invented until forty years after the battle. Purcell loved the battlefield frozen in a single image of death and destruction. His computer scanned the weapons, and a laser printer spewed out descriptions of weapons, shells, ammunition expended, damage assessments, casualty lists. Purcell held up the sheets of paper as they were ejected from the printer, reading the results.

"Make Mr. Kleist feel loved," said Purcell, as the girls who had been whispering in the corner, watching the TV screen and thinking it was a war film, ran forward and began kissing Kleist's bald head. They had dried themselves off with sweet smelling, fluffy towels, and sprinkled themselves with perfume supplied by Harry Purcell during the battle of Stalingrad. Purcell opened a window to the room, and a breeze fluttered the curtains. The Presence Purcell had felt in HQ drove a blade of Arctic night though his thighs, and made the HQ girls giggle, sing, and shiver—not so much from the cold of the Presence—the kind of cold that makes your guts churn ice cubes—as from their anticipation of the sexual encounter which was bound to happen next.

"Anything different, you know, out of the ordinary?" asked Purcell. The figures from the computer didn't add up; Kleist and the German Army should have taken Stalingrad hands down. They had been armed with the latest, high-tech weaponry. Yet the Russians had stopped them in their tracks.

Two of the HQ girls fondled, embraced and touched Kleist.

"Kleist, why didn't you take the city?"

Kleist's head bobbed up from between the breasts of one of the girls. He had a crooked smiled and lipstick marks all over his bald head. "Indians. Out of nowhere. I was attacked by Indians. I had green smoke coming out of cracks in my turret."

Purcell looked at the old man and the young girls wrapped in towels. Their eyes reflected the yellow flame like green cats' eyes. The stab of cold pierced his neck and Harry felt he would never swallow again. He staggered over to the window. The green vapor had cracked the Leopard-1, the top-of-the-line German tank; one that had outperformed the American Commando Stingray counterpart in almost every simulation and on every terrain. Kleist's experience was a mystery.

An M-16 rifle on automatic sounded at the other end of the soi. Purcell slammed the window shut. One girl leaned forward taking Kleist's soft member in her mouth, sucking with her eyes half-closed, and moaning quietly. The old man made one of those hospital, death-bed moans. The sound of pain rather than low-tone screech of pleasure. One of the girls tried to kiss Harry on the lips, but he pushed her away. He grabbed the computer printout and sat at the terminal, running the numbers through one of his weapon assessment programs. Nothing, but nothing came out the way it was supposed to; the numbers made the program hang up.

"The spoils of war," moaned the old war criminal, his eyes rolling inside his head. The other girls sat huddled, watching the blow-job, watching the battle screen frozen in time, and Purcell screaming at his computer.

"What's wrong? Something happened, Harry?" asked Kleist, reaching for the helmet.

"What are you doing?" asked Purcell.

"I want inside my tank. I want to find that fucking Indian," said the old man.

"How do you know he was an Indian?" asked Purcell.

"He had a spear," said Kleist. "A German tank knocked out by some asshole with a spear. And he wore a T-shirt with the word 'Montezuma's Revenge' on the front. On the back it said, 'If it floats, flies, or fucks—rent it.' I have to go back and get that fucker."

Purcell sighed. "Okay, one more chance. Knock out Montezuma and the other three girls are yours."

8

CORTEZ'S TEMPLE
by
Harry Purcell

The problem is to estimate the amount of trauma caused by all of those who died—30 million Russians alone, perished in one war. The Second World War. The Russians, like the Germans, and the Americans would settle for nothing less than precise numbers. They counted dead bodies. Counting the dead in that war led to the Cold War. The Russians recoiled into a long phase of paranoia, despair, mourning, and lived where they had counted the bodies—inside a vast landscape where bodies littered every corner. Russia was a land of ghosts who would not go away; ghosts who would not rest so long as those who had counted their bodies lived. Post-1945 Russia was filled with Presences which moved at will among the living.

Think of the trauma the Americans felt with their minor losses in Vietnam—less than 60,000 killed. Multiply that number by a factor of eighteen and you get the casualties on the Russian side in one battle—the battle of Stalingrad. Multiply it by a factor of five hundred and you have an image of Russian dead by 1945. One death is a moral outrage. In Vietnam the obsession with body counts forced soldiers in the field to count the dead. Their own and those of the enemy. How does an entire city's population deal with a horizon littered with dead people blown into pieces, heads, arms, legs, torsos shredded, a twisted wreckage of flesh? Some say they best dealt with it by not seeing it. They wore the special glasses of survival which allowed them to see only the earth, the soil, and the ground. Every body part was submerged as part of the earth, a garden of flesh and bone flowers.

There was one rule never to violate: never command soldiers to count the dead. Second, never order civilians to count bodies. Once the soldiers and civilians are enlisted in the counting enterprise, the country is doomed. To start the process of recording and seeing what is recorded signals that a corner of no return has been turned and no one can turn back to a state of innocence. No one can witness that much death and not have some sensor which holds the human mind in an integrated whole short-circuited. People can not see death of such magnitude and survive without massive trauma disrupting them for life. The Russians looked, they saw, they walked among their dead. They should have been trained to see roses. They counted until their fingers and tongues went numb. They should have seen daisy chains. The body counting gave the Russians fifty years of collective nightmare. Two and a half generations of Russians had to come and go, roil in their collective nightmare before a new start could be made. When the counters had been forgotten, the country woke up and everyone said the Cold War was over.

Cortez had counted the skulls; he had counted the dead. Did it take the Spanish two and a half generations to shake off his nightmare? Or was the Cortez off-shore body count like the American count in Vietnam—a nightmare spanning a single generation?

9

Snow had been stopped at two roadblocks. A soldier had pointed an M-16 at a spot between his eyes, smiling all the time. He decided to take the soldier's advice and not enter the zone on the other side of the roadblock where smoke and flames were visible and rifle fire cracked above the fires. He returned to HQ, a little sheepish, thinking if he really wanted to cover the uprising, he should have tried to get into the zone at some other point. Instead he returned to HQ to find a teenager who was tightly wrapped inside a sleek, black dress with a thigh-high hemline; this was the same HQer who had once bathed in a solution of Listerine. She looked gift wrapped, seeking a Christmas tree to sit under. He knew her from around the old jukebox; she had made the transition to the new jukebox without forgetting the number of a single song. Snow was impressed. Her name was Noi. Hair over the shoulders, small upturned nose, oval-shaped face and killer dimples. Snow was glad that some soldier had pointed a rifle in his face and this act had changed the course of his life, forcing him back to HQ to discover that no one had taken Noi.

Noi snuggled against Snow in the booth, sipping a watery coke, her eyes half-glazed as if she were far away. It was after three in the morning and HQ was packed; customers and girls stood, squeezed together, and the waiters, trays chest level, tried to clear a small path to deliver drinks and food. From the crowd no one would have guessed a revolution was going on in the streets. Snow whispered in Noi's ear, brushing aside her hair and earring which looked like a gold smoke ring. He had one hand on her bare leg under the table, and she giggled as he blew into her ear and massaged her thigh. Snow saw the word Listerine form and disappear like a soap bubble from Crosby's lips. She rummaged through her handbag, rattling through her assortment of knife, brass knuckles, lipstick, compact, keys to several hotel rooms, and a small bottle of Listerine. Finally she pulled out a plastic bag of chicken balls. The chicken balls were about double the size of her fake pearls, and she offered both Snow and Crosby one. They locked eyes and declined.

"They're always in a feeding frenzy," said Snow.

"As long as they stick to chicken balls, it's tolerable," said Crosby.

"What other kind of food did you have in mind?"

Crosby lit a cigarette. "Once about four years ago, a friend of mine, whose name shall remain unspoken, took a girl from the African Queen in Patpong. She had a kind of Chinese look. Very nice legs, ass and tits. I mean she was a fine product. Someone a collector would no doubt take off the market fast. Indeed, as we speak she is in France."

"Food, Crosby. The subject is food. We don't give a ratshit if she's in France or the grave. Food was the point."

The plastic bag of chicken balls was offered around and declined for a second time.

"My Thai friend took this girl—number 29—to a short-time hotel. She took her shower first. And unlike young Noi here, did not wash down in Listerine, so she was out in ten, fifteen minutes, coming out with a towel wrapped around her waist. Next, my friend went into the bathroom . . ."

"And found durian smeared over the walls," said Snow.

"No, he simply took a hot shower. Again, another ten, fifteen minutes passed, and when he emerged . . ."

"A Pizza Hut delivery boy banged on the wrong door . . ."

"Even better, he stood in the open door with a massive erection and stared into the bedroom. This Patpong goddess sat naked in the center of the bed, her ass to the side, legs curled, with mirrors on every wall and the ceiling reflecting her perfect waistline and hair tumbling down below her shoulders. She had a silky down skin without a single blemish. Her back was slightly arched, you know how the spine goes in that small curve and her breasts standing out like inflatable. . . ."

"Lilo tits. . . ." interrupted Snow, rubbing Noi's other thigh under the table.

"He took two or three steps toward the bed and noticed this goddess was eating. This girl was from Isan and had grown up on a diet of fried grasshoppers. So it would come as no surprise that she had bought a bag of fried grasshoppers from a street vendor in Patpong and stuck them in her handbag. She waited until her john was showering, opened her bag, took out the hoppers, and even though it was a short-time hotel, for a moment it was just like home. When he came out of the shower, he walked over and sat on the edge of the bed. She was watching TV. There was something odd. A crunching sound. It wasn't from the TV. A greasy food smell hung in the room. He stared at her mouth. Her beautiful jaw rotated ever so slightly, in a grinding action, like the action you would associate with milling flour, and what he watched—with some horror—his erection immediately went from north to south—was a grasshopper leg curved over the right corner of her mouth, the foot of the grasshopper extending down below the lip. As she chewed, the skinny grasshopper leg appeared to be kicking against the side of her lip, as if it was trying to climb out—'Let me outta here. You're next.' She stopped chewing and smiled at him with the leg wedged in the corner of her mouth. With a well-polished nail she delicately pushed the grasshopper leg into her mouth, chewed and swallowed. Nothing she could do after that could jump-start his member. He was more than limp, he had not just gone south, his penis had retracted inside his body. He swears this. He paid the girl and sent her off without getting laid."

"That's disgusting, man," said Snow.

"I thought you'd appreciate it."

"What would you have done, Crosby?"

"I probably would have lit a cigarette and had a think about it. But my Thai friend, he simply fled the scene. It was too much. You want your sex without grasshopper legs in the girl's mouth."

"Have a chicken ball, Crosby. It might take your mind off the past."

10

VERSION TWO OF HOW SNOW CAME TO COVER THE BANGKOK MASSACRE

A Short Story
by
Robert Tuttle

Jennifer, the high-miler who had a serious emotional attachment to Snow, decided to hole up in their Winnebago that first week in the new town. Her intention was to apply for a job—sooner or later. It wasn't much of a town. But they had exhausted their money and needed to work and save some money before setting off. She had some prior experience as a secretary—a real estate office in New Jersey—though her typing skills were not the best. The pressure was off when Snow had landed a job. Soon the cash flow would start again. After Snow's return from Bangkok, this had been his first job—in the middle of the great unannounced American depression—Snow, asking, "Hey, man, why didn't anyone tell me there was no work in America?" Jennifer replied, "You probably never asked." And Snow had to admit this was true. He had simply taken it for granted that there were always jobs, and all you had to do was apply, go to work, and collect loads of money.

They had travelled together in the Winnebago across the country, looking for work until Snow had spent his nest egg and part of the nest before finding work in Montana. It wasn't a career choice. But as a source of revenue until something better came along, minding turkeys was better than being flat broke or holding up 7-11s.

On Snow's first day working at the turkey farm a middle-aged worker named Roger came over and stood beside him. Roger had his hands in his pockets and a wad of chewing tobacco stuffed between his upper lip and gum. He looked like a Little League baseball coach. He spit a brown thick spittle on the ground every couple of minutes. Roger had been at the job in the turkey business more than nine years. He had the wild eyes and nervous, shuffling feet of a serial killer.

"Can you hear the turkeys call your name?" Roger asked.

Snow looked at him as if Roger might be armed and dangerous. When he smiled he had a brown saliva smile. He was definitely the kind of guy who hung out at HQ and believed the girls he picked went with him because they loved him. He had seen guys like Roger before, plenty of them lived hand-to-mouth in Bangkok, sleeping with young bar girls. Snow pegged Roger as someone who suffered from massive delusion. Snow played along with Roger, thinking that while he sounded psycho, he was reasonably certain that Roger was unarmed. This turkey calling your name nonsense bothered him. He mentioned it to Jennifer.

"This wando named Roger who chews brown shit from a tin said he hears the birds calling his name," Snow explained to her over dinner.

"You think he's on drugs?" she asked.

"Just tobacco. He doesn't look like the type for anything illegal unless it has something to do with guns. But life is full of sound-byte surprises."

For the next two weeks, all Snow could hear was a horizon of sound, eerie, unintelligible noise—non-stop gobbling filling every wave frequency, bouncing off walls, doors, windows, from one end of the long, narrow building to the other. Roger sniffed the air, cupped his hand to one ear, leaned into the sound wave, and smiled, nodding his head. It wasn't noise.

"Roger. Roger. Roger. That's what they are saying."

"Man, you ought to take a vacation."

"If I do, they will learn your name. That's what happens."

"You're full of shit."

The following week Roger went on vacation.

Two weeks later, it was in the late afternoon, Snow had worked his way half-way down annex building number one. The chaos of the gobbling shifted; a kind of vocal unity in the chorus of turkeys broke through. Snow shook off this rewiring of sound wave reception and kept on working. He dropped the bucket he was carrying and looked over thousands of turkeys. He blinked.

"Fuck," he said. He listened again. They were calling his name, "Snow, Snow, Snow." Roger's departure was a distant memory. They had learned his name, and now he heard it in their throats. He quit in the middle of his shift, and not waiting for his car pool ride back, he walked the three miles into town and went to where Jennifer was working at City Hall.

"We gotta get back to California," he said.

"Why?"

"Don't ask questions, we gotta go."

"I'm not going anywhere until you tell me why I have to quit a perfectly good job and why you quit your job in the middle of a fucking depression."

"Because the turkeys . . ." he broke off. Man, she's a white woman, and white women never understand the source and nature of weird sound waves.

"Because?"

"I got a freelance job in Bangkok," he said.

She looked him over, then broke into a wide smile and hugged him. Jennifer looked genuinely relieved. "God, Snow, I'm so happy for you. For a minute, I thought you had tripped the madness crosswire like that idiot Roger."

"Who?"

"You remember, the guy who said he heard the turkeys calling his name, and that sooner or later you would hear them calling your name too?"

"Oh, that guy. What the fuck does he know?"

"Nothing," said Jennifer, squeezing his head, and kissing him on the nose.

"The guy was a megalomaniac."

"How else could he hear a turkey calling his name?"

"Exactly," said Jennifer.

11

Front line
May 1992
Bangkok

Dear Richard,

It is said that if you put a seashell next to your ear you can hear the sound of the sea. Each seashell has captured the roar as effectively as any man-made recording device. And if you press a floating stone against your ear, what sound echo dwells within? Laughter, weeping, crying—what clutter of sound waves might be decoded and called forth from time? For instance, the sound of Cortez's having taken five short steps inside the temple, then the sound of his reaction which came on the heels of the sudden realization. Skulls everywhere. What was the sound of his discovery as it struck him full blast? What sound might he have heard from the 136,000 chambered skulls which lined the temple walls like seashells? Not the ocean, not a laugh, not a sigh; but the sound of mass murder with the volume turned down to zero. Would the sound have been like turkeys calling Snow's name in Montana?

In early May before the killing started the *mob picnic*—as they and the press called them, among other kinds of mobs—took to Sanam Luang by the tens of thousands. One of the demonstrators carried a sign which read: "Lose one's life, but not one's words." The *mob picnic* gathered, so the sign would have us believe, in the name of words. Protesters came to hear the words which shouted accusations against the Government and the military. The crowd applauded those words of support; and hissed the names of the leaders of the government they wished to force out of office. They created new words for themselves—*mob picnic, mob high-tech, mob nom priew.* The protesters arrived at Sanam Luang in their cars, with mobile phones, videocams, and yogurt.

"If you work a mob long enough, something happens, you start to hear them calling your name," said Snow. "A turkey sound-byte. When they start hearing it, they will leave. The Army won't have to fire a shot."

Everyone you know here was on the telephone and sending faxes, keeping the words in circulation just in case people were called upon to remember why members of the *mob high-tech* were willing to die waving their mobile phones in front of videocams held by their friends. Something had been in the air, then, something beyond the usual Bangkok air pollution, gray with dust, and infiltrated with heat waves jamming the lungs and nostrils. All those words had given a promise of hope that some meaning might be discovered in a world beyond the cars, mobile phones, videocams and yogurt. Just maybe . . . the 60s had bobbed up on the seashore of time, and Sanam Luang was a seashell that if pressed against the ear, the old mobs could be heard.

Words come with background sounds attached. The laugh track which signals when the observers are supposed to laugh—now. The applause sign facing the audience which faces the speakers who control the laugh track system. The signs light up and flash, 'Applause' blinks, meaning—clap now. When the leader spoke before Parliament in a live broadcast on TV, the background sound track was neither laughter, nor applause, but the most hated of all sounds—boos and hisses. The observers understood the signal was to boo—now. Join the *mob high-tech* at Sanam Luang. Wear your sign that worships words: "Lose one's life, but not one's words." The TV news editor was transferred. No one is ever fired. But a replacement was made because the wrong sound track had accompanied the leader's words and in the rebroadcast that evening, the boos sound track had been taken out and substituted with applause, so that a long pan shot of MPs in Parliament appeared to defy gravity like my floating stones. The MPs appeared to be clapping with their raised fists. For the first time in history the sound wave of applause had come from many clenched fists waved at the podium. And, it might have worked, but for one thing—the *mob high-tech* were all at the rally. No one stayed behind to double-check the video. Not all the boos were erased from the live version. It was not one-hundred percent applause. So a replacement was called in and taught the importance of what background sounds must accompany words.

Sound waves are more than the words on the screen. The seashell is more important than the sea. It can be carried in the pocket; stored on a shelf like a skull; or traded for something of value. The sea like the mob is an obstacle; an affront to those who wish to exercise power.

"Lose one's job, play the real sound track of dissent."

"Keep one's job, applause is reserved for your employer."

"Join the mob, search for words which can belong to you."

Yours,

Robert Tuttle

12

When Tuttle paddled his kayak along the Nan River with a cargo of bones he never thought he would be walking the deserted streets of Bangkok looking for a young girl named Daeng. He stumbled home after a fruitless night and found Ross asleep on his couch. Tuttle's maid had let him into the house. On the coffee table were bloated folders disgorging photographs and a thick envelope marked "Private and Confidential: Denny Addison." The scene spoke for itself. Ross had personally delivered the dossier on the loathsome Addison who had gained control over his daughter like a cult leader. Only Tuttle wasn't home so Ross had decided to raid the booze, and then passed out. Tuttle found him in this state, made coffee, and half an hour and three cups of coffee later, Ross had sobered up enough to explain what he had delivered and why.

"Addison is your basic asshole," said Ross, lighting a cigarette. "You think I can have a drink? I think better with a drink in my hand."

Tuttle made him a drink, noticing how several of the bottles had lost volume.

"What do you want, the bad news or the good news?"

"The good news," said Tuttle.

"Okay. Addison's had woman troubles from Manila, Hong Kong, to Singapore. And a few stops in between. His MO is pretty much the same. He becomes fluent in the native language. That gives him a real advantage, then he hunts until he finds what he calls a respectable girl. He makes her his 'babe', gets her to move into his apartment, then makes her an assistant director for one of his fucked-up documentaries. Then once she turns twenty-five, twenty-six, he trades her in for a newer model. He's been deported, banned, black-listed from four Asian countries. Two of them for life. But he's clean in Thailand. It's all in the report."

"What's the bad news?" asked Tuttle.

"I need another drink first," said Ross.

Tuttle thrust a fistful of ice into the glass and filled it with whiskey. But Ross grabbed the glass before Tuttle had finished pouring, and whiskey spilled onto the coffee table and floor.

"I guess you think I'm a messy drinker?" asked Ross, not expecting an answer.

"And the bad news?"

Ross laughed, his face turning a blotchy pink color.

"Your daughter, Asanee, doesn't turn twenty-five for another two years," said Ross. He roared again. "And there's more. He's made special films of his live-ins as insurance policies against future problems."

"What kind of film?" asked Tuttle.

"Porno," said Ross. "How else do you get lifelong bans from certain Asian countries? You have naked movies of respectable girls. So what do you want to do? You want to arrange for Addison to disappear?"

"Slow down," Tuttle said, softly. "He has a film of Asanee?"

"I didn't say that. All I said was that before he came to Thailand he made fuck films with a couple of his 'babes.' Look on the bright side, he figures he has another two years before she's too old. So he's been a little sloppy. He's thinking he has all the time in the world."

Tuttle stared at him without blinking.

"I know what you're thinking," said Ross.

"What am I thinking?"

Ross threw back the rest of his drink and slammed the empty glass down on the coffee table. "What kind of judge of character am I? Who am I to judge Denny Addison as a pervert, a whoremonger, a corrupter of local women, a man who exploits the innocent, a moveable Rocky Horror Picture Show unleashed on the face of Asia? Well, I'm gonna tell you how and why. And after you hear what I have to say, you will have no doubt as to my judgement, my verdict, the gathering of evidence in this case. My personality profile on Addison has one conclusion. Addison's a conman. He's mastered the creative closing. Only one man, an Iranian, was ever better than this guy."

"Creative closing?" asked Tuttle.

Ross nodded and smiled.

"But as the Iranian showed, sometimes your con can be too good to be true. I think Addison's history shows the same brilliant defect," said Ross.

13

HOW ROSS LEARNED
TO JUDGE PEOPLE

A Short Story
by
Robert Tuttle

Ross worked his way through college and law school selling ency-clopedias door-to-door in Council Bluffs, Iowa. Many Union Pacific Railway people lived in Council Bluffs with their families. Ross evolved a system for judging the occupants by the outside of their house. If they had an old stuffed chair on the front porch, he was guaranteed a sale. Another dead giveaway was the carpet inside the house. He rolled out a plastic stretcher and laid it on the floor and he placed the encyclopedia volumes on the surface. After the presentation, as he rolled up the stretcher, if there were tiny bits of bacon stuck to the back, the people always bought. He never knew why only bacon bits and not other kinds of food stuck to the bottom of the stretcher. If they dropped pieces of bacon on the floor, they would buy books. There was no logical explanation but it was always true. Bits of pig stuck to the carpet and stuffed, rotting chairs on the porch created this great hunger for a multi-volume set of books from a total stranger at a highly inflated price.

Some potential customers would already have one set of ency-clopedias. A few owned several sets of encyclopedias. That was

265

a better indicator of a sale than bacon bits on the carpet. These people were often encyclopedia freaks. Of course most of them also had overstuffed chairs rotting on the front porch, bacon bits on the carpet, and overgrown, dying bushes in the front of the house. They lived like pigs. But since they worked for the railway, they had money. They kept cash and sometimes they'd count out $375 in oily five dollar bills. That was a lot of money in 1962.

It wasn't always a picnic to close a sale, though. An unbalanced illiterate might sick his mongrel dog on Ross.

"We ain't reading no books," Ross would hear the madman call from the front door.

The problem wasn't so much whether he could make a sale at such houses but whether the customer would later receive credit approval.

Ross specialized in creative closings.

If the customer had a can of beer on the coffee table, he used the alcoholic closing. "You mean that for the cost of one single beer a night, you can't afford these books for your child's education? One less beer for little Billy? All Billy wants is a chance in the world. If he were old enough, he'd say, 'Dad, just drink one less beer and give me a chance to get this learning. You'll never regret it, Dad.' You won't miss that one beer. Not for your son's future."

Bingo. The alcoholic closing was fail safe. There wasn't a boozer who could swallow enough beer to wash away that much guilt.

The polio kid closing was another winner. Often the customer worried himself sick about the price. He was stone cold broke; didn't have the money. Ross always avoided using certain words such as money, budget, financial problems.

"Little Billy had polio. He couldn't walk right. He had trouble even feeding himself. But he had a desire for learning. That little boy reached out with all his will for one of these books. He stretched and stretched until he grabbed one. That's because he had the desire. And I'm not certain you desire these books. It takes a special person to have that much desire. To overcome all the odds just to reach out with all that desire."

They always signed.

Ross sometimes worked with an Iranian. Sometimes the Iranian would be the boss; sometimes Ross would play that role. This was in the days of the Shah and everyone in America loved and respected the Iranians. After the presentation, the Iranian had a unique closing that Ross had never seen anyone else ever use. The Iranian would sit opposite the couple on a lumpy couch; and Ross sat with the contract off to the side with the cap off his pen. The Iranian casually lit a cigarette.

"You can do anything you want in this world," said the Iranian. "All you must do is will yourself to want something. You can control everything in your life simply by willing it. You can will yourself these precious gifts of knowledge."

All the time the Iranian was holding the lit cigarette against the flesh of his hand. The customers sat with huge eyes, clutching one another, as a tiny screw of gray smoke rose from the Iranian's hand, and the faint smell of a substance like burnt bacon drifted across to them. Ross handed them the contract and they signed without a murmur. The problem was the company policy on follow-up. Three days later someone from the company phoned and interviewed the people about the contract. Ninety-nine percent of the customers who signed after the Iranian used the burning hand trick backed out of the deal. The shock hadn't lasted. Why was it these people changed their minds while those with bacon ground into their carpets never did? There was no answer. Only after death would the answer be revealed, thought Ross.

Ross quit selling door-to-door because he became detached; like an actor. He'd be giving the polio kid closing and suddenly he would be looking down on himself from the ceiling giving the spiel. He saw his personality fractured into parts. "I wanted to be more integrated. So I stopped selling door-to-door."

14

Cortez sat on the wheel of a burnt-out bus and watched soldiers throwing dead bodies into a burning pit. Long tongues of flames burst above the surface of the ground. The lights from several trucks and Army jeeps shined across the opening where the men worked. Montezuma had been counting the bodies out loud.

"Twelve, thirteen, fourteen, fifteen," counted Montezuma.

"I've been giving a lot of thought to TV," said Cortez.

"The studio audience loved you."

"You really think so? Or are you trying to get on my good side?"

"You have no good side to get on. Besides, enjoy while you can, soon we go back to the studio for another retake of the interview," said Montezuma. "Sixteen, seventeen, eighteen . . ."

"We've been taping forever," said Cortez.

Montezuma immediately lost count; he loved all discussions about the new machines. "You know what I like most about these breaks? The freedom to explore how counting and images work. You can change what you count. You can change how you count. You take that body number eighteen, and you cut the image in the Eye Wave Machine and put it in front of body number one, and then everyone believes that eighteen comes after one."

"That reminds me of an idea for the retaping. What about Zapruder and his film of Kennedy's assassination?" asked Cortez.

"It's been shown a thousand times on the show."

"What if Zapruder had his camera when you were hit on the head with a brick, people would still be asking the same questions. Yeah, that's the angle. Someone would add a voice-over to the Zapruder film of the Montezuma assassination: 'Did the brick-thrower who killed Montezuma act alone? Was the brick-thrower in the service of the Spanish? Was he an Indian? Was he an Aztec? Could he have been a half-breed seeking revenge for the sacrifice of a relative in Montezuma's temple? Were those objects in the hands of other people near Montezuma bricks as well?' Then we would splice in shots of the skulls in the temple; the bloody idols, the ashes from the burnt hearts, that sort of thing, to give your assassination a context."

"You wrote in *Liberation—The True Story, the Real Story* that I was killed by one of my own subjects," said Montezuma. "I wasn't looking. So how am I to know? I was the victim. You were the aggressor. Not that your position counts for much now." Montezuma gave a high-pitched laugh.

"I assumed the murderer was one of your subjects. But could I be certain who killed you? No. I had no TV cameras to record what actually happened," said Cortez. "I had conflicting information on the subject. I couldn't very well write to Charles V that I, Cortez, didn't know who was responsible for killing you."

"Think of all the hundreds of books that would have been written about me, and the dozens of films, TV movies, and mini-series," sighed Montezuma. "An eternity of work. Instead of working for eternity on interviewing you plugging your book to an audience who has never heard of you or us, and can never buy a single book to find out. Because the dead have no money."

"I'm thinking. Okay, here it is. The mystery of who killed you and why could use better special effects. It's for your own good. If we can alter how your life ended, then your death becomes far more important than your life or Aztec culture. The stone—let's make it a fist-sized diamond—used to kill you would be worth a small fortune at auction. Your face and the diamond go on T-shirts. Now, even though you're dead, you're a living legend. People will have studied every frame of the film; written doctoral theses on how and why you died, who was responsible for your death and the cover-up surrounding your death."

"And Cortez would be the villain?" said Montezuma, starting to warm up to the idea.

"Most likely. Four hundred fifty years ago who ever heard of retakes, hitting your mark, make-up, special effects, changing the script to make it politically correct, dailies, weekly box office takes? Monty, our film based on my book *Liberation* . . ."

"Stop, I know the title," said Montezuma.

"Our film wouldn't be only about the hurled stone. You took three days to die. Zapruder could have interviewed you on your death bed. Asked you who you thought threw the stone. About your theories on who your real enemies might be. Your theory of life, human sacrifice, bloody idol making as a handicraft art, that sort of thing."

"What are you really up to? Escape, isn't it? Well, it's not going to happen," said Montezuma, as the soldiers finished dumping bodies in the pit and a back hoe scooped up dirt and rock and the operator pressed the levers to dump the contents into the pit.

"This 'They'—I never had any idea who 'They' were—killed your son and daughters and all the other chiefs we had captured. Zapruder would have had a field day filming all those murders. Of course, they tortured most of your relatives and chiefs before killing them. What a film that would have made. Think if after Kennedy had been shot dead, they had killed his wife, kids, the vice-president, the speaker of the House, the Secretary of State, and the CIA director—in front of the TV. That would have been something. Just as if a TV camera had recorded a real bloodbath in Mexico, then everyone would have said about Kennedy's assassination—a bad thing, a sad thing, but realistically, folks, with no insult for the violent streak of people living at the time—what happened to Kennedy was nothing when played next to the violent and horrible Montezuma videotape which included the bloody idols and his dead relatives and advisers."

Montezuma sat silently for a moment as the Earth Moving Machines finished covering the grave. The soldiers got back into their trucks and jeeps and drove off into the night.

"You think they will get away with it?" asked Montezuma.

"Did you see any phones or TVs?" asked Cortez. "There's your answer. Events no longer exist as they did in our time. Images on tape and shown on TV define all that is real. If the movement isn't recorded for eye wave transmission, how can it exist as part of history? There is only room for captured images. What we used to call events of history—like the dumping or secret burial of bodies—fail to have force unless they are made into entertainment."

"Like when we tape before our freshly killed audience?" asked Montezuma.

"Monty, you were never any good at stand-up, even when I ordered you put in chains."

Montezuma shook his head, thinking that Cortez was right about the responsibility for events and how this limitation had caused him so much grief in the old days. Before Cortez arrived in Mexico, Montezuma had sought a reading of events—this was the function of wizards and prophets—and you could always have them and their families executed if they read the future wrong. As Montezuma remained misty-eyed—a condition arising out of materializing out of mist—thinking of the old omens of the wind blowing over a boiling lake in Mexico, one of the Thai spirits rose from the toxic waste dump and walked over to Montezuma.

"Who are you?" asked the Thai youth of about twenty.

"Montezuma," he replied. "Of course you've heard of me."

"Never heard of you," said the youth.

"And this is Cortez," said Montezuma.

"Never heard of you either," replied the boy in the universal language of the dead. "What are you doing here?"

"We have come to count and collect you. You're our guest audience for the next taping session of *Liberation—The True Story, the Real Story.* This Indian interviews me, I count you, and I tell you about my new-old book. It's our job to entertain, and your job is to be entertained. Don't worry, you only have to sit through it once," said Cortez.

"Think of us as gatekeepers. Cortez has one of those counter jobs they use for cattle. Click. Click. You're another number. Our job is to count the mob members who didn't make it. Those who did not survive the massacres," said Montezuma. "How many others down there with you?"

Before the youth could tally the number, a cluster of similar spirits appeared on the surface of the dump. Cortez and Montezuma inspected the crowd, compared numbers; Montezuma looked over Cortez's shoulder. "A rather thin audience. The numbers are the same except for him," said Montezuma, pointing at Weird Bob. "He's not a reporter. I already checked."

Cortez hated it when Montezuma was right before he had a chance to be right. All the other dead were no more than twenty-two years old. One was a young upcountry girl named Daeng; she had a half-moon-shaped scar on her face. She looked frightened. "My poor mother, can someone tell my mother that I'm all right?"

"We'll look after it," said Cortez. Shit, he thought. This was his one chance to knock a single digit off the vastly inflated number of Aztec dead. He had failed again. It was enough to make the angels weep, this constant inability to remove a single number from those he had counted in the streets and lakes of Monty's home town.

Weird Bob was the only middle-aged face among the fresh group auditioning for the part of new-old audience; and the only *farang* face as well.

"You, the one with the bad rug on your head. Yes, you, the tall guy wearing a wig no one should be caught dead in, this way," said Montezuma, blowing into a seashell. The waves of sound pushed Weird Bob back.

"But why?" asked Weird Bob.

"You aren't part of the audience. We can't count you. You must wait for the other gatekeepers," said Cortez, asserting his command.

Weird Bob, his fan rotating above his head, the red ribbon and bow fluttering, began sinking back into the toxic dump. When he was waist high, he called out to Cortez. "Who am I waiting for?" asked Weird Bob.

"The Third Hand," said Montezuma. "He'll act as your host. You others, line up, count-off down the line, and then let's go. It's time for us to begin our live taping before a dead audience."

On the way out of the dump site, Cortez calmed his new charges. "It's just a matter of time before you will no longer occupy space or time. This is a transitional phase. You're the lucky ones unlike Monty and me. You might say we pulled celebrity duty because of our past association."

"One question," said one of the Thai youths. "Back there you told the *farang* to wait for the Third Hand gatekeeper. Who in the fuck is the Third Hand gatekeeper?"

Cortez smiled at Montezuma. "That's an easy one."

Together they chanted, "The place without a gate or a keeper. The place which is not a place. The place with no tape play or sound to wave. The wait for a date which cannot be made or unmade."

PART 6
THE HUMAN CONDITION

1

"You are plugged into Radio Bangkok 108.3, and this is Denny Addison bringing you on the spot news from the City of Angels. No one can answer the big question. Is it over out there? The phone calls are telling us that the Army is pulling back. Is my brain fried or what? After four days of broadcasting from the sixth floor, I may have no brain left. Wait, one minute, I've just been passed a message. The armored personnel carriers parked downstairs have left the scene. Could this mean no more assault teams ordered to the sixth floor with orders to kill us? That's cool. I'm not endorsing these stories, you understand. I haven't personally looked out the window. Hey, what are you doing? Sorry, folks, that voice you hear in the background is Asanee. Asanee, sweetheart. Come over here and say a few words. Don't be shy."

Asanee, "Here is your camera, asshole. Whenever you get that sinking feeling you can sit on this end."

Sound byte: Plastic casing and metal crashing on a desk, footsteps falling and a door slamming.

Addison: "Martyrdom. An avenging angel. Get-even time. I survived repeated attacks by armed men in uniform, and now? Am I to be taken out of action by my girlfriend? What is this she's doing to my equipment? She looked normal, healthy and then under the pressure of the moment, she cracked and has gone mad. Was it only the pressure or could it be genetic? Or maybe it's the lack of sleep? Or could she have been intoxicated by rage and anger over some complicated emotional problem from her childhood? In the media those of us in the public eye attract the deeply disturbed who need a scapegoat. I'm a good guy for me, and a good guy for you. Not some corporate shit or dry Embassy type. Let's track through the possibilities. Could this have been something caused by her genes? Her father is a well-known resident. Robert Tuttle who made a reputation by recording for posterity the following selections at HQ: 108—*Say You, Say Me.* 129—*No Coke.* 127—*I Feel the Earth Move.* 139—*Like a Prayer.* 279—*Be My Baby.* Numbers 239 and 249—*Simply Irresistible.* 233—*Unchained Melody.*"

Sound byte: A fist slamming into a jaw, the cracking of bones, and whiney groans.

Addison: "God, I'm bleeding. Send for an ambulance."

Sound byte: Addison falling off his chair, as he passes out, and landing hard on the floor.

Asanee: "DJ Addison has fallen into his mike and must now leave the air. And soon the country. Thank you for the audition. We will call you back if we can use you. Some music from U2's *The Joshua Tree* album. *Mothers of the Disappeared.*"

Sound byte: Addison groaning and moaning in the background.

2

At dawn the violence in the streets ended. The Army pulled back. A mixture of happiness, bitterness, despair and relief ran through the crowds at Ramkhamhaeng University. It was strange to suddenly realize it was over. The time had come to disperse and go home. But what had the protesters achieved? One man screamed at the sky, tearing off his black headband. Some others cried; some applauded. In this time of confusion people milled in small groups, but small clusters split away and disappeared. Tuttle, who had failed to find Daeng, began the long walk home from Ramkhamhaeng. One of the people he had talked with earlier walked alongside him. For a few minutes neither one said anything.

"You'll find your friend now," Dow said, walking down the litter-filled street. The barrels in which fires had been lit still had embers burning at dawn. The barricades spilled into the street, and they walked around a burnt-out car.

"It ended like it started. With great speed," he said.

He looked at her, wondering what she was doing following him. Dow, who had been at the barricades for twenty hours, stuffed her hands in her jeans pockets, and walked with her head down. She had a lonely and dejected attitude; as if a shudder of gloom had squeezed her shoulders forward. He knew little about her, other than she was a twenty-nine-year old engineer; but could have passed for a student in her jeans, T-shirt, and a black pro-democracy headband wrapped around her forehead. Dow had been one of those who cried when the word came down that the Prime Minister would resign and the troops had been ordered to withdraw.

276

"It was all for nothing. People killed for what?" she asked. "Nothing. And I fucking hate that."

The metal grates were closed on the shop houses. People were sleeping on mats inside. The streets were like those of a ghost town. They walked down the center of the road—there was no traffic—and Tuttle thought about a Thai middle-class woman expressing her frustration and grief. Dow was a modern Thai woman. Using the "fuck" word was unusual even among the HQ girls. But Dow had spent her formative life amongst a rougher crowd—engineers.

"Why are you walking with me?"

"I'm fucking depressed and I don't want to be alone."

He thought for a moment. "What about your friends?"

"They don't understand," she said.

"And you think I do?"

"You risked your life looking for someone you didn't even know. Some upcountry girl no one cares about. Isn't the English word compassion?"

He looked at the street, then felt her arm thread through his own. She gave his arm a light squeeze. Her act startled Tuttle; it was out of character for a respectable Thai woman to make physical contact. Dow's character had escaped being shaped by an abiding fear of being embarrassed. Respectable Thais normally didn't trust a strange foreigner. The risk of embarrassment in front of others—family and friends—was too great. They avoided foreigners who couldn't hope to know the rules. It wasn't the foreigner's fault. The rules weren't written down and were not articulated; but among the Thais all such rules were fully understood. One of them was never to be seen to touch a *farang*. Only prostitutes would be so bold. Dow had broken one rule after another. And Tuttle found himself asking what had happened in her life to kill her fear of embarrassment.

"You're like a couvade," said Dow.

"Couvade? Is that Thai?"

"French. But it's an old, old practice in some tribes where a husband takes to bed when his wife goes into labor. The husband experiences the pain of childbirth with her. He doesn't stand apart or at another place. He doubles up with her pain of childbirth. They share the birth process. You take another's pain as your own, make it your own, and you find the truth of sharing," she said.

"I'm going home," he said. In two decades in Thailand he had never quite met anyone like Dow. Out of the blue, in the middle of a crowd, she had attached herself to him.

"I'm going home with you. If you can handle that."

Dow was definitely the next generation, he thought. On the walk back, Tuttle discovered why this outsider had attacked and criticized those who had left—something Thais rarely did with a *farang*. Dow was from an ordinary family. She had studied engineering at university in America, returned to Thailand, finding she could never really come back. Then the killings started, and for the first time, walking with Dow, Tuttle understood what had joined people together in Bangkok—they felt like "outsiders" who united to resist the generals. When suddenly the Army withdrew, and the Prime Minister promised to leave, the bond of outsideness created by a common enemy had been crushed, and the bulk of those who went into the street disappeared, faded away, leaving Dow, isolated with her American engineer's vocabulary and directness, once again standing apart.

The end of the killings did not end the pain. She remained as far outside society as before. For a brief few days she had found herself almost accepted. Once more she knew instinctively she would be cast away. She had tagged onto Tuttle, this strange *farang*, looking to rescue a bar girl. She saw something of her own futility in his action. He was her couvade. And the longer they walked and talked about what had happened at Sanam Luang, the politics in England, and her work with an oil company in Texas, the more normal she felt. She was grateful to find someone who could lessen her heartache and, for a while, fill the vacuum left when she discovered that what she had found in the crowd wasn't ever really present. Tuttle told her the story about how he had confused bones floating on the Nan River for stones, and how he had filled his kayak full with the treasures only to arrive at Daeng's village and find out he had been a floating fool. He told her about the tiny hand-carved ivory heads General Xue had braided into his moustache.

The first thing Tuttle did inside the house was to turn on the radio. He then went to the fridge and poured two large glasses of orange juice. Dow sat on the couch, looking at the Denny Addison folders stacked on the table—relics that Ross had left behind.

Then Tuttle heard his own name on the radio. Dow's head popped up from a photograph of Addison with a Filipino girl, and she looked at the radio. She saw Tuttle a couple of feet away holding the two glasses of juice. It was Denny Addison on Radio Bangkok 108.3:

"Her father is a well-known resident. Robert Tuttle who made a reputation by recording for posterity the HQ jukebox songs by their correct numbers. That's how I want to be remembered. Robert Tuttle met Asanee's mother when she was a teenager. The mother worked a coffee shop on Soi Nana. Tuttle took Bunny—dig the name—back to her hooch on Soi Sarasin. In those days, there was a *klong* which ran alongside the soi, and the shacks were built next to the water. Asanee told me her mother had one of the best hooches in the slum. Bunny and Tuttle lit mosquito coils, drank beer, and rolled around on bamboo mats. Boom boom, is the technical, scientific term for this behavior. What could Tuttle have said, 'Be my baby'? Whatever he said, he gave Bunny a baby girl. Enough, enough, my sound engineer says. Okay, let's update the latest on the end of terror in Bangkok. Reuters has reported that a compromise has been reached under which the Prime Minister has agreed to step aside. The troops have been ordered off the streets . . ."

Dow reached over and turned off the radio. She took one of the glasses of orange juice, then took a small sip.

"Why did that DJ say that?" she asked.

He didn't have an answer.

After she had drunk half of the orange juice, she put the glass down, rose from the sofa, thanked him and left. Whatever it was she had wanted from him, she had not found or she had found it and decided it wasn't what she had wanted after all, he thought. He didn't try to stop her from going. He sat alone listening to the birds outside. For about an hour, he glanced through the papers and photos Ross had collected on Addison. The heavens above seemed to have abandoned the earth below. He took the folders outside and burnt them in a clay oven. The flames crinkled the old photos, the papers turned yellow, curled up, then turned to black ash rising into the air before falling back through the bamboo and banana trees and into the uncut grass.

3

CORTEZ'S TEMPLE
by
Harry Purcell

The fabric of the human condition is flawed. Montezuma's view of the existence of three ideas—gods, omens, and legends—is a textbook illustration of the flaw. Before Cortez had touched shore the Aztec wizards—like modern journalists—had recorded lightning striking a temple, fire streaking through the daylight sky, winds boiling a lake, and a strange creature captured in a fisherman's nets. What was the response of the Aztecs? They commanded an increase in the number of human sacrifices. Orders were issued and obeyed. If conveyor belts had been invented, the carnage would have been more efficient, better organized. Primitive technology did not stop a carnage from taking place in the temple grounds, which became chambers for fresh slaughter. It wasn't killing for killing's sake. The killing was done without malice or grudge. Killings were offerings for the fear the Aztecs felt, having read the omens. This fear spawned the belief in a god who relished human hearts and blood. Feeding this god was a spiritual act of worship and this god would give them courage to face their fears.

When Montezuma first learned about Cortez and his soldiers' movements through the country, he assumed—from questioning his prophets and wizards, who read the omens—that Cortez, along with his nine-hundred-man force, were themselves none other than—gods. If you assume soldiers approaching on horseback are gods, you automatically connect with the idea that man and horse have all the power, immunities, and privileges sufficient to make them immortal. And that they have the right to belong where they want, take whatever they choose, and decide when they wish the good times to roll. No longer would priests offer hearts and blood to idols fashioned from vegetables. They had real gods to replace the idols with carrot-stick noses.

Montezuma invited Cortez and his men into the Aztec capital. Next he gave an order to round up the usual suspects for a human sacrifice in honor of Cortez. The captives were brought in, heads down, scared, watching these gods eating and knowing that they were next on the menu after the tortillas, and the Spaniards were thinking as they ate plates of tortillas that this was some nice place. All the natives were falling at your feet, they invited you into their city, gave you the city key, prepared all kinds of Aztec food (including red-deer steaks), and then had entertainers in the wings to deliver a live floor show. The Spaniards were among the first Europeans to feel, for a few hours, what it was like to be tourists. They had almost forgotten that they were warriors. In this small frame of time, they could be forgiven for the belief that they were on a package tour. Whatever their actual thoughts, their speculations suddenly changed as they watched the spectacle of Aztec junior priests with ritual knives hacking, cutting, and ripping open the breasts of the captives. They yanked out many fresh hearts and held them up, blood dripping down their hands, and the Spaniards saw more than they had ever wished for. They stopped chewing tortillas and looked at each other with "what the fuck" expressions on their faces. More hacking followed. Cups were lowered under bleeding heads and filled to the brim. The cups were then held out for the Spaniards to drink. This was never in the guidebook under the section about native restaurants. Human blood cocktails were the last thing Cortez's men had any intention of drinking.

The Aztecs were confused: why had the Spaniards failed the god test? Was the blood a little too thin? No one could accuse them of serving up day-old blood. It was fresh. The Spaniards had witnessed the cups being filled with their own eyes. Cortez's men vomited up their tortillas and red-deer steaks, screamed, cried, tore out their hair, and refused point blank to sip even one teaspoon of human blood. They showed fear in the face of blood. This was the first, unmistakable sign that Cortez was not a god. But once Montezuma had made his mistake about gods, he still didn't give up on the idea. He ordered his magicians to work spells to make the Spaniards sick or die. The cursing ceremony failed. Montezuma was at a crossroads: he could choose to believe spells were worthless against human beings or that Cortez really was a god to survive the spell. He once again could not stop his thoughts about the nature of spells and gods from controlling his action. But Montezuma could not control his fear. When Cortez made a personal inquiry about Montezuma, he fled the scene like a Bangkok ten-wheel truck driver who had crashed into a school bus. By the time Spaniards had killed a temple full of Aztec priests performing human sacrifices, Montezuma knew he had been conned. But it was too late. He was already Cortez's prisoner and held in chains. His fears and confusion destroyed his command.

Cortez questioned Montezuma about this insane notion that he and his men were gods. Whatever could have put such an idea in the head of the Aztec? At this point, Montezuma was not about to admit his captor could have ever been mistaken for a god, so he pawned off another story. Montezuma explained the Aztec legend that at a time outside the lifetime of any living men, Aztec ancestors had invaded this land and taken the land by force of arms, and many Aztecs had stayed on as an occupation force. Many married with local women. The ruler of the original invaders had returned home but his descendants had refused to come away with him. Guilt and more guilt was felt by the Aztecs. They had rebuked their old ruler. This made them fearful. They lived in a state of perpetual fear and anxiety, waiting to pay the price. They believed that sooner or later the great lord would come back again and they would be destroyed. Cortez, said Montezuma, was a case of mistaken identity—he was wrongfully thought to be that great lord or at least his representative.

Spaniards versus Aztecs was the Purcell family's first important battle. The Purcell fortune rested on understanding that fear was often irrational, largely misunderstood, and sometimes destructive. All an arms dealer required was sympathy with his client's plight.

All clients for weapons worried about the same fate—the arrival of the alpha males who appeared in the form of strangers from another land or arose from within their own ranks—who would challenge their command, their gods, and seize their gold and women. Why have the Purcells worked so closely with manufacturers to name battlefield weapons after powerful, deadly animals—Cobra, Leopard, Hawk, Stingray, Wildcat, Tigershark, Hornet, Sea Wolf? It is the human condition to fear jungle animals. To fear an alpha wolf attack in the middle of the night. How far removed is our species from jungle survival? Weapons must have names which inspire confidence. What comes from the jungle are strangers hungry for land and command. Arming men with Cobras, Leopards, Hawks, and Stingrays puts the terror of the jungle on the side of command. Commanders have always been jungle fighters. The Purcells' insight into the use of lethal weapons with animal names and the fear inherent in the human condition ensured their order books would always be full.

4

WHORE TIME

A Denny Addison Documentary
Running time: 32 minutes
Black and White

There is a sitting room with bare wooden floors. The sofa is covered in red upholstery. Inserted into the wood panelling are two French doors with the louvers painted blue. Seated on the sofa is a whore named Roon. Roon has large exposed breasts and is smoking a cigarette. She is wearing long black boots which lace up the front. On her left wrist is a fake Rolex watch. Roon, who has worked on Soi Cowboy for five years, looks to be in her mid-20s.

"Roon, you know why I want to make this film?" asks Addison off camera.

Roon nods her head as she stubs out her cigarette inside the neck of an empty Singha beer bottle.

"Because you pay me two thousand baht to tell you about whore time."

"Right," says Addison. "So tell me about whore time. Whatever comes to your mind. You don't have to think. Just talk to me like you did in the bar."

"Okay, remember, I say to you how sometimes *farang* angry with me because I tell him I go to his house. I make appointment with him. He come to bar on Saturday night. He say, 'Roon, you make appointment with me. Can you do that?' I say to him, 'Yes, I can make appointment with you. Yes, I know your house. I go there before, two, three times.' Then he say, 'Thursday, can you make appointment at eight o'clock? You come to my house then. Can you do that, Roon?' I say, 'Yes.'"

All the while Roon talks she threads the lace up the front of one of her boots. Her slow gentle touch shows the pride in making each loop perfect.

"Then on Thursday, what happened?" asks Addison off camera.

"I not go to house of *farang*. I stay in my room and sleep. The next night he come to the bar very, very angry with me. His face red and I think maybe he will hit me. He say to me, 'Roon, you are a bad person. You promise to come to my house. You make me appointment. I wait and wait. I think you come. I not sleep all night thinking maybe Roon have accident.' He say, 'Why you not phone me and say you not come? Why you lie to me and say you come when you know you won't come?' Then I get very angry with him. I want to kick him. But I say to myself, *jai yen, jai yen*. Keep a cool heart. Then I tell him what I say to you at bar. *Farang* not understand how Thai girl think. Why he angry with me? I not go make appointment I lose five hundred baht. That is very much money. Someone steal five hundred baht from me, I think I kill him. So I not go to make appointment I punish myself very much. I hurt myself, stealing my own money and throwing it away. And where is my money? It's in the pocket of *farang*. He's angry with me? Why? He has my five hundred baht. I say, why he angry? He have Roon's five hundred baht that I steal from myself and put in his pocket."

"And you call this whore time?" asks Addison.

Roon is working on the lace of her other boot.

"*Farang* say that. He say to me, 'You talk whore time, Roon. Whore think about time like you think. I think maybe I have relationship with Roon. I think you liked me. I think you like appointment with me. But I was stupid man. I not understand whore time. Now Roon tell me I punish her because she not come. Roon say I owe her five hundred baht, keep in my pocket, but never mind can keep, because Roon not make appointment.' I think he not understand how Roon think. He not like I break appointment. I not like not have his money. I think each person have hurt. But my hurt is more hurt because when you have money you not hurt so much as when you lose money."

"But you were not late for our filming today," says Addison.

She smiles into the camera.

"Cannot."

"Why doesn't whore time work here?"

"Five hundred baht, Roon live on whore time. Two thousand baht I live on *farang* clock time, sure."

5

The night after the killings ended Crosby arrived at HQ wearing a T-shirt advertising a brand of condom called "Tigers." There was a cartoon of a soldier with a condom over the barrel of his gun, and printed underneath was written: Suit up in a Tiger before going into battle. Crosby slipped into the booth with a beer in one hand and a big smile on his face. He waved a piece of paper at Purcell and Snow.

"I passed," said Crosby.

"The war's over and they've allowed you to stay. Fixed your residency permit problem," said Snow. "So you don't have to move to Liberia."

Before Crosby could straighten out what was on the paper, Mae, an old-time HQ favorite performed a back flip onto Crosby's lap (worthy of a 9.8 score card rating), wrapped her arms around his neck and planted a kiss on his lips. Mae was a little drunk, and had the sour smell on her breath of someone who had been drinking all day.

Purcell resumed his discussion about guns. Before Crosby had arrived they had been in a heated debate about the relative merits of small and large bore handguns.

"You're an expert on handguns?" asked Purcell.

"Hey, man, anyone from America qualifies as an expert on handguns. We have as many gun-runners as lawyers. Gun-runners provide a useful function in American society," said Snow. Guns in the United States—a conversation topic which ranked in popularity right up there with sex and rock 'n roll for the former turkey farm employee.

"What is the offensive weapon of choice?" asked Purcell.

Purcell was no fool; he played to Snow's ego. It was this kind of grass-roots research which had been a Purcell family tradition. It was the man on the street who had to use the guns which generals bought for protection. It was the man on the street who was sent into battle.

"Let's say, a kid goes to school and wants to pop another kid," replied Snow. "He packs an offensive handgun. The kid goes for a .22. Easy to carry. Easy to conceal. The shooter walks over to the other kid and pops him. The .22 is ideal. Because there's not much sound. The dead kid drops to the ground and the shooter walks over to the water fountain, takes a drink, then strolls off for his next class. No sense interrupting his education. I know what you're gonna say, 'Yeah, a kid thinks a .22 is an offensive weapon. But what about the big boys?'"

"In America they think like children," said Purcell, his long pure-white hair making him look like a combination of God and Santa Claus.

"Unlike Europeans who hit middle age by their sixth birthday. All I can tell you is the mob in New York and Chicago are no different from the mob in England or Hong Kong. Their best gunmen use the same weapon for a hit. A standard .22 pistol. But if what you want is defensive stopping power, then you go for a .357 magnum. If someone is coming at you in a pick-up, you want fire power that goes through doors and glass and cuts him down behind the steering wheel. Pack a .357 magnum."

"Maybe you bought a customized surface-to-air rocket kit for your caravan? Or did they come as standard equipment?" asked Crosby, as Mae shot off his lap and headed toward one of her regular johns.

"Get out of here, Crosby. It's not a caravan. It's a Winnebago inhabited by me and a half-dozen Miss Lilos along with a current list of all hot 900 numbers. But to answer your question. I keep a stock of both offensive and defensive weapons."

Purcell watched the show, thinking Kleist might be coming soon and they could go back for another shot at Stalingrad.

"One in each hand?" asked Crosby.

"It depends on the drugs I'm taking," added Snow with a wide smile. "There are guns for uppers which aren't to be confused with those used with downers."

"I've always wanted to sell T-shirts to Americans," said Crosby. "Cartoons of guns, cars, bunkers, underground weapons depots, and computerized radar screens."

"You're a card, Crosby. Unfortunately not all your holes got punched in the right sequence. So your personal understanding of life came out slightly warped."

Purcell spotted the piece of paper Crosby had been waving until he was cut down by the beer-guzzling Mae. He spun it around and glanced at it. He had been thinking it was time to leave. Then he remembered what Crosby had said the night before about getting his test results. Purcell slid the paper over a Kloster beer bottle Mae had left. Snow had arrived from America with his HIV negative certificate from the family doctor, and challenged everyone else to produce their clearance or explain why not. The HIV negative certificate had become like a sexual .22; it was an offensive weapon, one that gave confidence to walk up beside someone near the jukebox and pop the question. "You wanna go with me? One purple, okay?"

"You made it to the clinic," said Purcell, looking Crosby straight in the eye.

It was a spooky look and Crosby's head snapped back. A smile appeared slow-mo on his face; the pained look like that on the lips of zebra pulled neck first into the dirt by a lion on a National Geographic TV Special.

"HIV . . ." said Crosby, pausing.

Snow swallowed hard. "Yes . . ."

"Negative," added Crosby.

"Crosby, if you are HIV negative then AIDS must be a government conspiracy to make us crazy; keep our feet on the ground and off the bed. A way to scare the fuck out of us. You are the original bareback rider of HQ. You have never used a condom."

"I only take the clean ones," said Crosby.

"You crazy shit. You come off like a teenage bar girl. He looks clean, so he must be healthy. How a girl looks has nothing to do with what is in her blood."

"I tested negative," Crosby said again, with some pride.

"When did you go?" asked Purcell.

"At eleven this morning. I said, 'Don't take my blood unless you can give me the results today. I don't want to sit around waiting all night thinking about the possibilities.' I guess I'm not the first one who has told them that. The nurse said, 'No problem, roll up your sleeve and phone us back this afternoon.'"

"You made sure it was a new needle?" asked Snow.

"I watched her unwrap it myself," said Crosby. "And sure enough by three this afternoon they had the results. Negative."

"Where did you go?" asked Purcell.

"To a clinic on Silom Road," he sighed and was silent for a moment. "Two hours later I started thinking about my test. My negative score. The first time my negative score made sure I graduated. And I started going a little weird. I said to myself, what if . . ."

"What if, what?" asked Snow, the veins sticking out of his neck.

"What if the doctors at the clinic were told by certain officials, when a *farang* comes in for an AIDS test, tell him to call back in two, three hours and tell him the result is negative. You know how the Thais hate confrontation, weeping *farang*s and generally giving out bad news. The *farang* would immediately blame the Thais. I got this shit from one of your whores, what are you going to do about this? I'm gonna die. Your whores killed me. I'm going back to America, crying in the press, suing your ass and then finding me an offensive handgun and coming back here to even the score. Then I said to myself, would the Thai doctor, educated in the West, do such a thing? They have Western values—ethics—it comes through their education. They know it is wrong to lie; and that a doctor must tell his patient the truth. But telling the truth is not the only factor. There is pride in culture and country. There is image. If you tell the truth, and bring disgrace on your people, then you lose a ton of face as well. So what has the truth earned you? From a Thai perspective, not a whole lot. By lying, however, you see nothing but happy, smiling faces. Everyone is feeling *sabaay, sabaay.* No one is angry, raising their voice, crying, wailing, gnashing their teeth. Let the poor sod go back to his own country, with instructions to get re-tested in six months just to make sure. Let an American doctor break the news to an American; and an English doctor to an Englishman, and so on. So I'm negative, so they say. But am I really negative, or is being negative part of some larger conspiracy?"

Purcell sighed, watching Crosby, his hands shaking with fear.

"You ever think of a career in the arms business?" asked Purcell, turning to Snow.

"Get out of here," said Snow.

"You have all the right qualifications."

"Such as?"

"Massive paranoia and a child's pure vision of offensive and defensive weapons," replied Purcell.

6

DAENG'S HALF MOON

A Short Story
by
Robert Tuttle

Not long after she was born in a bamboo hut beside the Nan
River, her father bestowed on her the nickname Daeng. The
literal translation into English of Daeng is red. The color red has
special power and influence—the color which deflects fear and
demons. The Chinese gold shops throughout Bangkok are painted
red. Phalluses planted in the beach of Pattaya are painted red.
Red is the lightning rod attracting prosperity and wealth. Red-light
districts attract men from across oceans. Red is the color painted
on brothel window lights. Gold is wealth; a large, bold, erect phal-
lus a sign of fertility and prosperity; a red light beacon hitting the
walls of lust. Her father loved his child the moment he laid eyes
on her. This beautiful new child promised to bring him wealth
and prosperity. As a child, Daeng was noted for her beauty. Nan
Province had many beautiful girls so to have a beauty which rose
above the crowds of beautiful children was a special omen for the
entire family. Her reputation spread among other villages. One day
just before Chinese New Year, a merchant came in a boat with two
other men. The merchant was from Phrae, the capital of a nearby
province also called Phrae, and ran a successful Chinese restaurant.
He asked the headman about this young girl named Daeng whose

reputation had reached his ears, and the headman took the merchant to the family house.

The father greeted the merchant and invited him to drink inside the house. After the drinks were laid out, Daeng's mother brought Daeng who was about twelve years old up the stairs and into the main room.

"Yes, she is as beautiful as they say," said the merchant.

The father beamed with pride.

"She is the light of my life," said the father.

They drank to Daeng who then went off and sat in the corner, with her knees pulled up under her chin. She watched the stranger drinking with her father, and the way he glanced back at her.

It seemed to Daeng that her father and the merchant talked for hours. When the merchant removed a leather pouch from his belt the room was silent. He counted stacks of purple bank notes, carefully laying them out on the floor. There was a piece of paper folded into three parts. The merchant had put on his eye glasses and began to read the paper. Only then did Daeng see the mood swiftly change on her father's face. The way his eyes narrowed, his jaw clenched hard like a fist ready to strike; even his breathing changed from the steady, even stroke to a sound she recognized as choking anger. As the merchant started to read, her father held up his hand and shook his head. The merchant smiled the kind of smile of someone reacting to trouble and fear. When the merchant began to read again, her father snatched the paper from his hands and tore it into shreds. Her mother, who had been standing slightly behind the father, shuffled across the room and sat next to Daeng.

"You will leave now," said the father.

The merchant removed the large stack of purple bank notes and pushed them back into this leather pouch.

"You will be sorry for this attitude. I offered you twenty thousand baht. I raised it to twenty five thousand baht. That is more than twice what any other family receives. And you are too arrogant to take this money. I curse you. From this day nothing but misfortune will strike you, your family and your daughter."

If the two men who had accompanied the merchant had not been waiting outside, Daeng was certain her father would have struck the merchant. Instead he ordered him out of the house. At the top

293

of the stairs, the merchant turned, pointed his finger, shaking it at her father, mother and Daeng. "You will all suffer for this. You waste my time. You waste your daughter for nothing. You are fools and your life will come to ruin. I promise you, it will be smashed by the curse."

Then the merchant from Phrae was gone in his boat.

No more than two weeks later, Daeng had walked to the river where she was attacked by a village dog. The four-year-old large white and brown dog had bitten others before, and on more than one occasion, villagers had threatened to destroy the animal, and each time the owner, a cousin of the headman, was able to hide the dog until the hard feelings had subsided. On this occasion with Daeng, the dog attack occurred precisely at the spot where the merchant had docked his boat. She had tried to run. But she fell, and the dog's teeth sank deep into her face, tearing the flesh away from the bone. She felt the sharp sting of teeth, the blood, and the shock of pain caused her to pass out. When a villager found her, some boys were sent running to Daeng's house. Her father ran to the river, saw his daughter and burst into tears. He lifted her and carried her back to their house. While her mother cleaned the wound, her father took a needle from the family sewing kit and after twelve stitches had closed the wound into a perfect half moon.

After he had washed his hands, he went down the stairs and walked straight to the house where the dog was kept. He went inside without taking off his sandals and found the old woman cowering in the corner, her arms wrapped around the dog. Daeng's father pushed the old woman away, and wrapped a rope around the dog's neck. He pulled the dog across the wooden floor, down the stairs, and down the dirt path to the river. The dog howled with fear as Daeng's father pulled him, all four paws dragging against the rope. A group of villagers gathered and watched as Daeng's father pulled the dog to the edge of the river. He then tied the rope to a boat. He turned back and looked at the crowd, then without saying a word, launched the boat, jumping inside as it left the bank. He rowed toward the center of the river. The dog paddled as best it could against the river currents. The wild-eyed fear of the dog and the wild-eyed hatred of the father locked in a stare down on the river. The father paddled and paddled until the dog's eyes finally disappeared below the water line. Even then the father did not stop. He continued rowing back and forth in front of the village and the villagers, dragging the carcass of the drowned dog, until Daeng's mother came down to the river bank and told him to come home, that his daughter was calling for him. When he returned to shore dragging the wet, drowned dog, one of the villagers said he had made a mistake by turning away the merchant. He left the dog's carcass on the river bank. No one in the village claimed it or buried it. Flies and worms appeared after a few days, the body bloated and burst. The stench hung over the village for days. The villagers said the father had brought a curse onto himself and the entire village suffered in fear and silence. Now who would want his daughter? Who would offer such a large sum of money for a damaged girl? He struck the man who said these things, and without looking back at the man who lay in the dirt, he returned to his house.

He found Daeng crying. He dropped to his knees and comforted her. She suffered the agony of one who had experienced great pain, worry, and had to accept the loss of her beauty.

"I'm sorry your Daeng is no longer beautiful," she sobbed.

This broke his heart and he sobbed with her.

"I will buy it back," he said.

A couple of months later he found work through a broker who sent men to work in Saudi Arabia. He announced his plan to save money to have her face restored, her beauty restored, her innocence brought back, and the curse ended.

Daeng pleaded with her father not to leave the village. He sat beside her, wiped away her tears. "I will always be there for you. I will take care of you. I will come back. You'll see. Nothing could stop me from seeing my daughter again. No curse can stop me."

He was away for nearly three months, and had paid back the broker's fee when he suddenly took ill and died in Saudi Arabia. A one-page letter was sent to the broker from Saudi. One of the broker's employees delivered it to Daeng's mother. The letter said that the father died of a heart attack in the desert. They had no money to bring his body back to Thailand. He was buried in the sand. They sent home his personal belongings. Among them was a photograph of Daeng in her school outfit.

"Don't worry, mother, I will take care of you," said Daeng.

Her mother wept until the letter was soaked in tears. Her daughter's beauty was gone; her husband dead. What was she to do to survive? How would they live now that everything in her life had changed for the worse? She blamed the merchant's curse. She blamed herself for not overriding her husband's decision not to let Daeng go and work for the merchant. So many of the daughters had gone and for so much less. The merchant had been right—her husband had been arrogant and selfish, and now who was left to suffer?

The next time a man came to the village, the mother did what the father would not have allowed. She sent her daughter away from the village in the company of an agent who said she would work in a Bangkok restaurant. He promised it would be a respectable restaurant and gave the mother two thousand baht. She signed a piece of paper but she couldn't read. She didn't know what it said, and the agent said it wasn't important. Just a receipt for the money she had received. When the boat left, the mother cried bitterly. Now she was alone—it was her husband's village and she had no relatives living there—and the villagers, including her husband's relatives, avoided her. They were afraid this curse might not be finished and might drag others down like the father had dragged the dog under the river. The isolation and loneliness overcame the old woman. She waited for a sign. Some way of undoing what her husband would have never allowed. Then she had her chance when she saw a *farang* who had docked on the same spot the merchant who made the curse had used. She showed him Daeng's picture. She offered him the money she had taken from the agent and had never had the heart to spend. The *farang* looked up from the photograph and promised to find her daughter, and return her to the village. He refused to accept the money paid to the mother for Daeng's services. Her blood-red money. It was on that thread of hope, a man, who like her husband would not take money for his Daeng, that she passed the hours of each day.

7

The first thing Crosby said when Snow came into HQ was, "So the war's over."

Snow snarled. "It's in remission. It's not like baseball. War ain't over even when it's over. It just goes to sleep for awhile, then rears up like a monster to bite your ass just when you start to relax."

"Is that the sound of fear?"

"Fear is your friend," said Snow, with a crooked grin on his angular, unshaven face. "An ex-Green Beret friend told me that in Jakarta. In jungle combat, fear is what keeps you alive. When you learn to be unscared is when the trouble starts." He was talking to Crosby and didn't see someone come up from behind him.

"I agree with everything Snow just said. Paranoia is your right hand man," said Ross, who was drunk when he wandered into HQ.

"Hey, man, pull up a chair," said Snow.

"What do you mean pull up a chair? You're sitting in a booth."

"So I am, so pull up a booth."

Ross looked confused, dazed, as he looked around at the girls, and then he sat down hard beside Snow.

"What were we just talking about?" asked Ross.

"Fear, paranoia . . ." said Crosby, who gestured for the waiter to bring Ross a drink.

"Now, I remember. What I wanted to say, Snow, was you let me come up behind you. I could have killed you by sticking an ice pick through the back of your neck."

"Hey, I saw that on *Star Trek*. Klingons with ice picks."

"I'm serious. Soldiers survive on fear. Lawyers prosper on para-noia. You never want a lawyer who doesn't think whatever deal you are doing someone is out to get you—your money, your wealth, your women. You go to a lawyer because you fear people you do business with will hurt you, inflict pain, and hunt you down even if you are honest. You worry about the day when your back is turned, and they gun you down."

"Are you serious, man?" asked Snow, glancing over at Crosby who showed no expression one way or another.

"Of course, I'm serious. My role as a lawyer is to educate clients about the dangers of business. How to fully develop their paranoia to succeed in the modern world, to teach them the kinds of conspiracies which others will unleash against them, and the kinds of conspiracies they can employ to confuse, defeat, and generally fuck up friends and enemies," said Ross, stopping to gulp down the drink the waiter had set before him. Before the waiter had gone two steps away from the table, Ross ordered him to immediately bring another Old Granddad and soda. "What were we . . ."

"About people waiting to gun you down," said Crosby.

"Or smash into your car and kill you. Or say terrible things on the radio about you. Like that evil asshole Denny Addison."

Ross had captured the attention of Snow and Crosby, who liked the stark simplicity of his world view.

"My first experience with a girl was in a slum on Soi 22," said Crosby.

"Slum girls always make you sentimental," said Snow.

"I hope they cure AIDS before they cure poverty," said Crosby.

"That would be a bummer," replied Snow.

"You have no idea the damage this has caused my client," said Ross. "You're not taking it seriously."

"It could have been worse, Ross," replied Crosby, raising a Kloster to his lips.

"How?" asked Ross.

Crosby lowered the bottle.

"In the early 80s, Tuttle, Snow and me went over to Pratunam—meaning door to the water—where girls waited in long boats. If you were a local you paid forty baht."

"Or eighty baht for the *farang*," said Snow. "Yeah, I remember the boat girls. They existed long before the boat people."

"They rowed you out into the *klong* and under the bridge where they tied the boat up to one of the pilings. Then the girl hiked up her dress and you had your go," said Crosby.

"All I can remember is the evil, sick smell of the *klong* and the movement of the boat, the noise of long-tail boats, the overhead traffic. Only Crosby could ever finish the act in the boat. The rest of us sat with limp dicks wondering what combination of vile substances and noise could stop Crosby."

"You see, Ross," said Crosby, "Addison could have broadcast the boat girl story. The slum girl story is nothing. It's common as pollution in Bangkok. But taking boat girls is something altogether different. People would have remembered that one."

Ross was about to lose his temper. His face flushed and he clutched both fists around his glass, then quickly drained it.

"The law of libel doesn't rest on associating another with the lowest form of perversion," said Ross.

"Okay, man, Addison's an evil punk."

"It's obviously right for a T-shirt," said Crosby, making a note on his pad.

"Are you stealing that?" asked Snow

"Which one?" asked Crosby.

"The last one. That Addison's an evil punk. Ross said it first, right, Ross?"

"Did I? I could have. But then again, someone else might have. It's likely public domain. And it's the truth. So it's neither copyrighted nor libel. That will cost you another drink, Crosby."

Ross had their close attention and didn't notice that Tuttle had arrived, and was standing a couple of feet away, talking to one of the girls from the old days.

Tuttle came over to the booth, and Ross looked up and smiled at him, trying to place him. "I remember you. You're my client. And I left important files for your consideration."

"They were destroyed in a fire," said Tuttle.

Ross's jaw opened. "Destroyed? A fire?"

"An unfortunate accident. But you will be glad to know there were no injuries."

Ross rocked back in the booth. "How can we nail this asshole if all the evidence has been destroyed? This is a major setback."

"Send me a bill, Ross," said Tuttle. "The case is closed."

"You haven't seen Purcell around?" asked Tuttle.

"He and Kleist took some girls out last night and no one has seen them since. Maybe they dropped acid in the bunker," said Snow. "I'm not that impressed with Purcell's knowledge on weapons. He knows almost nothing about guns."

"You've got to be joking," said Crosby, coming to Purcell's defense. "His family invented guns. He specializes in Main Battle Tanks. Not your average handgun."

"Maybe Purcell's part of a conspiracy," said Ross. "Maybe he burnt the files on Addison. HQ attracts some people who have these strange ideas."

"Or some pretty strange people changed by the chemicals they use," said Snow, looking over at Ross and then arching an eyebrow at Tuttle.

"Yes, yes," shouted Ross. "I may be paranoid and thus you may wish to discount my views. One more thing I think you should know. I distrust non-paranoids. In my experience they are living in a cartoon world."

"Why are you looking for Purcell?" asked Crosby.

"To ask him if he established contact with Montezuma," said Snow.

As Tuttle left the booth, *Simply Irresistible* started up on the jukebox. This was the paranoids' theme song. It was the only song which appeared twice on the jukebox—numbers 239 and 249. At the double numbering—the shadow and the substance—the corkscrew of green vapor spun out of the jukebox and slipped through a ceiling vent just as Ross tilted his head to finish his drink.

8

Twenty-four hours before the Hell's Angel had crashed into Snow's Winnebago and Jennifer the high-miler had flipped pancakes in the skillet with no intention of sharing them, Snow sat inside the shopping mall beneath a potted palm tree and read a letter from Richard Breach.

April 1992   London

Dear Snow,

Many people who have been held hostage experience grave difficulty in getting their life back on track. You may well suffer from what is called the Stockholm Syndrome. A person held hostage feels an enormous bonding with his captors. The basis of the relationship alters in subtle emotional ways until the hostage no longer feels he is a hostage but that he belongs to the cause for which he has been kept. Sometimes the captors remove his chains and give him a gun and they go out hunting for cash or new hostages. The reason it is called a syndrome has to do less with the initial abnormality of shifting loyalties than with the later period, after the hostage has been "released" or "rescued," when the hostage misses his prison and wardens. The hostage ends up fearing his rescuers.

In your case, it is more complicated. You were your own hostage and Thailand was your captor. George, you harbored delusions—how else can one describe the desire to become a Lahu Godman? Freud might have called this displacement. I anticipate that you will argue Freud never lived in Bangkok. Like most deluded thoughts, your thoughts, in the story, started as a practical joke. You had an instinctive insight that with magic tricks—and of course you knew the limitations of tricks—you could reshape the loyalties and relationships in the Lahu village. They would worship you, George Snow, and hand over their virgins, best food, and present you with the remote control panel to their TVs. Your mistake was not realizing that religion and magic are the same coin turning over and over in the air. It is arbitrary which side the coin comes down on: heads is religion and tails is magic. Flip the coin in the air again a century and a half later and the reverse occurs. When you walked into the Lahu village with your backpack filled with store-bought magic tricks, a coin was flipped. You convinced yourself that you had conned them into thinking that you were a god. And as a Lahu Godman you were not performing magic but religious rituals. In any other century but ours you might have gotten away with the act for years; no other century had the village headman and shaman getting ripped on Mekong and watching American TV. In the end, you were nearly killed because it was a false flip of the coin: you could not claim religion or magic. You made a fool of people who had lived their entire lives together, and how can you feel a strong sense of belonging to people you view as foolish?

You are back in California and have become involved in what from the outside is a "normal" relationship with a woman of your own age, education, and class. She is a female mirror in which you are examining your life since leaving Thailand last year. She wants children; and you say that for the first time in your life you consider that a real possibility. It no longer sends fear through your soul. Children are the ultimate relationship which always belongs to us.

To what you belong, and to where you belong are questions beyond the scope of a letter, a conversation, a dream, and maybe a lifetime. I wish you luck in finding an answer which you find satisfactory.

Yours,

Richard Breach

9

Snow slammed the door of the Winnebago—a whoof of air waves flying back at Jennifer. He slipped his American passport into his back pocket where he had stashed his turkey money—a wallet containing $145 non-disclosed dollars which still called his name in the middle of the night, and five credit cards. Otherwise, he decamped with the clothes on his back. After stabbing the biker, Snow calmly walked through the shopping mall, out the other end, across the vast paved lot to the street, changed his clothes inside the Winnebago, then took a taxi to the airport where he booked a cheap one-way flight on Korean Air to Bangkok via Seoul. Snow had left LA before the Hell's Angel and his friends could find him.

Somewhere over the Pacific, the cabin lights were switched off, and Snow swore that he heard turkeys back in Montana calling his name. An echo of a thousand bird voices. Snow. Snow. Snow. He curled up in his seat with the airline paper-thin blanket and the pillow shaped like a bloated water bug. He patted his wallet. The turkey money was untouched. The high point of his life had been the three days that the Lahu had held him as their "guest" until Harry Purcell's friend, Richard Breach, had arrived with a letter from Harry, enclosing five hundred dollars to secure his release.

The headman remembered Harry Purcell—a *farang* with much white hair and black, black bushy eyebrows—as did the *maw pii*—the shaman—from those days when Purcell had researched his book *Magic Hilltribe Rituals*. He had returned years later when doing work on *Cortez's Temple*. Snow sometimes wondered if Purcell had been perverse enough to bleach his hair white. They talked about Purcell with affection and fear. They believed he possessed magic. He had arrived up the mountain in a pick-up carrying a hundred kilos of rice, several pigs, and chickens. He turned the entire lot over as a gift to the Lahu village. The villagers fell on their knees. They loved Harry after that; and confirmed that much had changed. The girls had gone to Bangkok; their young men dreamed of Reebok racing shoes and fresh white shoe laces. Harry had made them laugh and sing and remember how it had been before the development plans. Before money had discovered Thailand, and all the girls had fled to Bangkok. A time when there had been a vast jungle canopy and a culture which rarely touched a foreign presence. He told them of ghosts, of ancient massacres in Latin America, and how his family had armed entire continents.

Harry had arrived in the village with more than sleight of hand magic; Harry Purcell's charm was based on more than the wonder of conviction, language, history, and taking pleasure in the details of their life. He had stripped to the waist and helped them dig a new well. Three days until nightfall, Harry had stood shoulder to shoulder digging with them. Four feet down they discovered human remains. Bones. Harry emerged with a skull perched in his upright hand. The right side, just below the eye socket had been smashed in from the blow of a blunt instrument. The villagers had been sinking a well straight through the ancient remains of some ancestor. But Harry knew better. He kept the bones and carried them back to Bangkok. There were people waiting for the bones, who wrapped them, and sent them to America for tests. One fragment he had held back and later gave to Tuttle who sent it to Richard Breach in England. He knew what Tuttle would do, and he planned for it. And he understood the consequence of handing a bone from that part of the world to Tuttle. When the test came back establishing that the bone was four hundred fifty years old, the sting of green vapor filled his nose. What kind of magic had Purcell performed on that bone? What kind of magic had those bones performed on Harry?

Snow raised the plastic shade on the window. The plane was flying from the past to the future. The sun never set on the flight from LA to Bangkok. So many men had taken that journey; some had never returned, some tried to return and couldn't; still others heard in the dead quiet of the night over the Pacific, some inner voice calling their name.

10

She wore a tiny blue hat and a red jumpsuit. Her tiny hands were bunched at the knuckles, leaving dimples. She slept with her mouth slightly open, Dow rocking her gently. Tuttle came down the stairs to his living room dressed in jeans and T-shirt. He stopped halfway down as he saw Dow with the baby. Her eyes rose to meet his.

"I thought I would never see you again," said Tuttle.

She rocked the baby, adjusting its jumpsuit.

A glass of water had been laid out by his maid. She was nowhere in sight. The Thais had an instinct for when to disappear, melt into the background without a sound.

"How long have you been down here?"

"Twenty minutes," said Dow. "Not long."

"My maid should've . . ."

"I told her not to disturb you. I wait. No problem. *Jai yen.* Cool heart," said Dow.

He came down the stairs and sat opposite Dow. He never took his eyes off the sleeping child.

"Your baby?"

Dow shook her head as the baby's eyes opened. Emerald green eyes, the shade of Asanee's eyes. The baby had a *farang* father who had fled the scene or was unaware of the child with gemstones for eyes he had left behind in Bangkok.

"After I left your house, I go to Soi Cowboy. I found the Crazy Eight bar, and talked to Daeng's friends. They had heard nothing from her. They were worried. I said that was normal. Who the fuck

306

wasn't worried with all the killing and people who disappeared? Then one of the girls told me about Daeng's baby. A *luk kreung.* Her name's Oon. That means 'warm' in English. But, of course, you speak some Thai, so maybe you know this. And I said where is this baby? Daeng had left her with a friend in Klong Toey. No one knows who the *farang* father is. So I took a taxi and found the shack. Six people and one baby inside. I told the woman there that the baby's father had sent me to get the baby. What are they going to say? No? I gave the woman five hundred baht. And she gave me the baby. I said to myself, 'Why am I such a crazy girl to do this thing?' Then I have my own answer. You are the man who came out looking for this girl. The couvade who had gone into labor. So here's the baby. I think maybe you had a reason for looking. Maybe Oon, Daeng's baby, is the reason and you didn't want to say. I can understand that. So I ask myself, 'What can I do?' I will come and show you the baby. It is up to you. If you want to throw her away to the slum, wash your hands, why not? It happens all the time. You wouldn't be the first *farang* to walk away, and certainly not the last. Then I'm confused about what you want. Who you are really looking to find, and I wonder if you know."

Oon was sucking her thumb and drooling down her hand.

"She won't bite you," said Dow.

Tuttle reached forward and touched her cheek with the back of his hand, and immediately the baby's face clouded up in a storm about to break.

"Are you sure this is Daeng's baby?"

Dow sighed, reached for her water and drank slowly. "How can anyone be sure of that? The bar girls who worked with Daeng said so. But I suppose in their profession they learn to lie. But why would they lie to me? What money could they make from lying about the mother of this baby?"

"You think I'm the father?" asked Tuttle.

"There are many kinds of fathers."

She sat on the couch with her legs curled underneath a cushion, her eyes watching him closely. It was early morning and she was shaky from the sleepless night with Oon in her room, the confrontation with people in the slum who were suspicious of her taking the baby away, and the uncertainty of what to do, where to go if it turned out she had made a mistake. There was a basic decency about Tuttle which had eased her feeling of terror. Given the turmoil in her life, she had stopped trusting. She had forced herself to make this effort; this last-ditch chance to reclaim something she couldn't put a name to which they had fought for in the streets. In every life there was a moment of truth. This was her moment, the baby's and that of Tuttle. It had been one thing to search for Daeng—but what he had been found was altogether different from what he had gone looking for. A decision was required. A delay of days or weeks was not an option; it had to be agreed upon. Dow's impulsive, reckless act in showing her hand had resulted in making Tuttle show his own. He felt that he had every right to reject what was being offered. It was a high stakes game, and he had to read his hand and know that many lives would be changed no matter what he decided. He could not deliver them from the world; but he could seek deliverance for himself in a household formed by accident, in the shadow of death, in the midst of a rescue operation for a dead girl.

"Oon's grandmother lives alone in a village. I remember her face as she stood on the bank of the Nan River," said Tuttle. "'Find my daughter, Daeng,' she called after me."

"You will send Oon to live with her?" asked Dow.

"I don't know. I don't want to."

"Then don't," said Dow.

"It's not that easy. What if Daeng never turns up?"

"You're afraid of that?" she asked.

"You don't know what you are asking," said Tuttle.

A wave of terror crept through Dow, making her throat tighten as if hands had suddenly been clasped around her neck.

"What were you looking for, Khun Robert? A story? A documentary? Material? This is a real flesh and blood fucking child and you started something. Are you able to see it to the finish?" asked Dow.

"That's crazy," said Tuttle. "The Thais would never let me keep this child."

"Is that why you are afraid?"

"Can I hold her?" asked Tuttle.

"I didn't think you were ever gonna ask." She handed Oon to Tuttle, who sat back in the chair, cupping the baby in his arms.

"How old is she?"

"Seven months," said Dow.

"Her mother never mentioned a baby," said Tuttle.

"Because she didn't want her to know. A baby with green eyes in a small village—what is different can cause a problem."

"Yeah, I guess so," said Tuttle.

"So do whatever you want."

The baby began to cry. Tuttle bent his head down, looking at the baby in his arms. He gently rocked her back and forth as he wished he had the chance to do when Asanee had been a child.

"It's okay," he whispered. As the baby stopped crying, he said, "You're exhausted, Dow. It's hard for you to think straight in your shape. Let me handle this."

"Not good enough," she said.

She nodded at the baby.

"You can come and visit Oon whenever you want," said Tuttle.

"I guess I can go now, Tuttle" she said, rising from the sofa. No other Thai woman had ever called him by his last name. She walked to the door and slipped on her sandals.

"See you around," said Tuttle.

She nodded and left the house.

Tuttle closed his eyes, thinking about caring for Daeng's child; wondering when Daeng would come to reclaim what was hers, and what he would say at that time. No sooner had he decided to keep the baby than he began to worry that he would lose her. He wondered if Dow had been right, more right about him than he had been about himself—he had been delivered what he had been searching the streets of Bangkok to find. When the baby shifted her head he saw in her left earlobe a tiny half moon of gold earring. He smiled and he knew he had found what he had been looking for.

11

A couple of months later Tuttle leaned his elbow against the wooden gate and pushed the buzzer on the wall between the gate and the entry door. Harry shouted from inside the complex for Tuttle to let himself in; the key was under a potted plant to the left of the door. He found Harry Purcell rocking himself slowly in a hammock strung between two wooden posts on his porch. Below in the garden, a small fire crackled, tongues of flame and ash rose into the heavy, hot Bangkok air.

"Rumor is you have accumulated a large number of women in your small house," said Harry Purcell, lazily rolling his head to the side.

Tuttle held up three fingers. "Dow, Asanee, and Oon. Oon's nine months old."

"Very domestic," said Purcell.

Tuttle watched the fire and shrugged off the comment.

"Where you headed?" Tuttle asked

"The Gulf. Not to golf, as Snow said."

"Snow is a funny kind of guy," said Tuttle.

Purcell sighed, flashed a big grin. "And he's as bright as hell. You know what he said the other night? 'There are two ways for a journalist to become a legend. He either gains access to those who are inaccessible and tells their story or he becomes inaccessible to those who enjoy the absolute power of access.'"

"You could make him a legend, Harry," said Tuttle.

His black eyes sparkled as if they had been painted on with black lip-gloss. "Next time I download another computer virus hosting ghosts."

"You still haven't said where you're off to next," said Tuttle.

"First Manila. Then to the Straits of Hormuz to transact a little Balkan business. The Balkans have been a family cash cow for centuries."

Harry Purcell was scheduled after the Philippines to continue on to the Middle East where a ship waited for him in the Strait of Hormuz. The ship, crammed with state-of-the-art telecommunications equipment, was anchored off Banda Rabbas. Once on board, he would finish the last minute details of an arms deal with a general who was an old family friend and inaccessible enough to make a newsroom of Snows into a legend if they could tell his story. The general's order was for tanks. Lots of tanks. Tanks were profitable, efficient killing machines.

"Before I left, I wanted to give you something," said Purcell. "Maybe you better sit down first."

Tuttle knew before Purcell could say another word. He had asked Harry Purcell for a personal favor; Daeng was listed as one of the missing, and he asked Purcell to use his influence with the military to find out if she was being held.

"She's dead, Robert. Don't ask me how I know or who told me. It doesn't matter. How can you live in that house with all those women and not know what happened to her."

"Where, how. . . ?"

Purcell raised his hand. "It's enough to know."

"How can you deal with this kind of person, Harry? Someone like you. No one forces you to do it. Why, Harry, why get their dirt, other people's blood on your hands?"

"I once asked my father the same questions."

"And?" asked Tuttle.

"He said, 'You either sit across from them at their table or you put your neck under their boot.' There's always been a moral vacuum at the center of power and wealth. When that vacuum fills with morality, the power is lost. Then the morality bleeds away, and a new vacuum arises, more generals, new weapons, more killings. We live in a world where fear and terror are the rule, and the smart killers never count their dead. Hope is necessary. As are most illusions. They allow us to live by what we believe rather than according to what we actually see happening. It is our survival instinct to have this hope. Without it the generals would have no way of inspiring fear. The threat to hope is their ultimate weapon. Their ace up the sleeve of their uniform. Now you have my answer and my father's. And the answer about your young Daeng."

Purcell climbed down from the veranda and went down to the pond. At first Tuttle watched him, then followed his path, drawn by the smell of smoke. As he approached the pond, he saw a small fire. Burned pieces of paper circled around the base of the palm trees, and a large half-burned page landed at his feet. He reached down and picked it up. On the page was the word "headhunter" near the blackened edge. Then he saw the title page—*Cortez's Temple.*

"What are you burning, Harry?"

"Rubbish."

Tuttle walked around the fire, kicking dirt onto the pyre. But it was too late. The fire smoldered, thin columns of smoke rose from the papers and left a melted down clump of plastic computer diskettes—including the ones with the Battle of Stalingrad. He shook his head, as the dirt and smoke blew back into his face. The fire had gone out. But everything had been consumed; nothing—no paper, notebook, diskette—looked remotely salvageable.

"Why did you do this?" He was angry.

"Why shouldn't I do this?"

Harry sat beside the pond, putting his bare feet into the water and kicking them up and down, splashing like a child.

"Why not?" repeated Harry.

"I deserve a better explanation."

Harry wasn't certain if Tuttle had any such right. Friendship carried obligations but rarely rights. He looked up from his splashing. "Did I tell you that the Presence had gone, vanished, left? The Purcells appear to be ghost-free for the first time since 1519. Whose ghost? Montezuma? Da Vinci? Cortez? All three of them in some unholy trinity? Who can ever know? But during the killings in Bangkok an old family ghost was banished. I can go back to the family trade without looking over my shoulder for the ugly, disgusting green mist. You know, Kleist took Stalingrad. Four nights in a row he led German tanks into the streets of Stalingrad. He buried his own ghosts. Not one of my simulated Commando Stingray tank turrets blew up. He was even better on the Leopard-I's. On average his victory saved more than half a million lives. Not small change in the life-saving department."

"What did it achieve? They did die. You can't reverse history by refighting old battles."

"You know what Kleist said?"

Tuttle shook his head, he really had no idea what Kleist could have come up with which would have sent Harry Purcell off the deep end to destroy his family chronicle.

"You never finish burying your dead until you honor them and their suffering. And that can only be done with a victory. Even a simulated one," said Purcell.

"He's crazy," said Tuttle.

"Crazier than the people who put 136,000 skulls in the Aztec temple?"

Tuttle sat on the grass. He watched the goldfish swimming in the pond. He felt the heat from the fire. He felt tears swelling in his eyes, as he understood that Daeng would not be found, and that no matter how many stairs he climbed to the end of the universe he would never understand where, by whom or why.

He wanted to blame Harry Purcell; his body pumped with rage, his heart thumping in his chest. He knew the killers. He even defended them, sold them weapons. Purcell crossed his feet at the water's edge, watching the fish swim closer for a nibble at his toes.

"'Harry, you're sacred. Like God.' That's what Kleist said. A tree worshipper, as Snow calls the Germans," said Purcell in a near whisper.

"You only have white hair like God, Harry."

"And I don't walk on water," whispered Purcell. "Keep out of the temples," he continued after a pause. "That's what I think Cortez said moments before he died. And on my death bed, if I'm so lucky to have one, I would whisper pull down and destroy the temples. There is no 'sacred.' The sacred is the junk bond of the spiritual world. It promises great leverage but in a bankrupt scheme. Others have tried to sound the alarm to bring forth this message before. They failed because the audience doesn't want to listen to the real story, the true story. But I thought that Harry Purcell would show them a thing or two. Where my ancestors had failed, I would prove the root of evil led straight from that temple door. Then something happened, Robert. The entire weight of the book collapsed on itself when old Kleist said, 'Harry, you are sacred.' The temple, the temple. It's not just a building or a shrine. It's the power to strike fear which is sacred. With it you make others bring you any number of skulls."

Later, as the evening wore on and a bottle of wine was finished, Harry Purcell finished packing a single carry-on case. Everything else he threw onto the fire, the flames reflecting off the pond. Robert Tuttle did nothing to stop him. It was as if Harry knew he wasn't coming back. He was travelling light and dressed in pure black silk. On the last trip down the wooden stairs, Harry handed Robert Tuttle an ancient silver object shaped like a cigarette pack.

"A parting gift," said Harry Purcell. "Besides, it won't burn. Or make its way through the airport metal detector."

Tuttle opened the box and looked inside. "What is it?"

"An ivory bead carved in the likeness of General Xue," said Harry Purcell, lighting a cigar. "My mother said that it was sacred. It passed from mother to son for almost three hundred years. Keep it for Daeng's daughter. Have her wear it around her neck. A gift of face. We Purcells aren't in the gift business. So it's time to dispose of some old relics."

Harry Purcell thumbed the tip of his cigar. The lines around his eyes wrinkled as he smiled; as if he were thinking about another time, another place—a joke retold passing through his head. As he sucked his cigar, he sat on the edge of the veranda and stared at the heap of ashes below.

12

It was Snow's last night in Bangkok before heading back to California, his half-interest in the Winnebago, and his relationship with Jennifer. He checked into HQ around midnight, and found Crosby with two girls huddled behind a stack of T-shirts and well into his third Kloster beer. The TV played to a small audience of girls along the far wall. The jukebox blared with number 139—*Like a Prayer.* The waiter everyone called the Old New Kid brought Snow a large cola with ice.

"Purcell's left. Selling Hawks to mullahs. Tuttle is changing nappies . . ."

"Diapers," interrupted Snow.

"And now Snow's flying to the arms of an old white woman who refuses to cook him pancakes."

"The world's going to hell in a hand basket," said Snow.

"Have you seen Tuttle's new old lady?"

"The butch-looking engineer who uses 'fuck' as a noun?"

"Yeah, that's her," said Snow. He liked it that someone other than himself was taking heat on choice of female partners. "You don't really think that he does it with her?"

"Hey, man, we can't all charm nice girls like these two." Snow looked between the two hardcore hookers seated like temple lions on either side of Crosby.

"These are my sales staff," said Crosby a little defensively.

"Is that Kleist over there?" asked Snow, looking toward the bar. "What the fuck's he got on his head?"

"It's a wig," said Crosby. "I suspect some Nazi-hunter must be in town, checking around for the usual suspects."

Ross came over in the middle of the conversation, cleared his throat, his hands folded around an Old Granddad and soda. He sat next to Snow. He stared at one of his fingernails, then sighed.

"Mr. Snow, during your time in HQ have you ever seen or heard of anyone who has been restrained by age or decency, or from doing anything they really set their mind on doing or could pay someone else to do for them? If it's in their interest, it gets done. Even if it means buying new hair. If it's not new hair, then maybe it's murder. Either you have the power to make something happen or make someone disappear or you don't. That's what the massacre was about. You can write that for one of your newspapers, and quote me as a usually reliable source."

"How about if I attribute that wisdom to Old Granddad?" asked Snow.

"That's really hardcore what you just said." Ross belched and waved for another drink.

Crosby pulled a fresh, new T-shirt from the pile and unfolded it on the table. On the front was printed: The Target is the Bullet; and on the back: The Bullet is the Target. A black and white image of a young woman demonstrator's face with a target around it was on both the front and back. It was Daeng's face, a scanner had been used to attach a black pro-democracy headband to cover her forehead.

"Purcell paid for this lot," said Crosby. "I've got another two thousand in my godown."

"You never paid off the first loan from Harry," said Snow.

"This is the payment."

Snow arched an eyebrow. "He said that?"

Crosby nodded. "Take one. One hundred baht. Take another for your high-miler. The money goes for a fund for the families of the missing."

"Tuttle got to him," said Snow with conviction.

But he was wrong.

"Dow pitched the idea to Harry," said Crosby.

"God, Tuttle's sleeping with a political activist. He'll have dog heads thrown over the wall of his compound," said Snow.

"Funny thing," said Crosby. "Tuttle didn't know about the T-shirts until after Harry Purcell gave him one. I would have loved to see the expression on his face."

"And Tuttle's living with a woman's libber," said Snow.

Ross had waited long enough and shouted across the room.

"Bring me an Old Granddad and soda or I'm taking hostages."

A moment later the Old New Kid brought him the drink.

"Dow's hardcore like Tuttle," said Snow.

"You'll be back, Snow," said Ross.

"So will Purcell," said Crosby. "And Tuttle. The hardcore never can change. They just rest for a while and then come back to HQ. Like war, Snow. They have no other place in the universe. HQ will always be here, and so will we."

"Hardcore evolution has produced one Crosby. Could there be others as insane as this Crosby?"

13

Montezuma stared bleary-eyed into the lens; it had been a short, yet emotional killing time. "We wish to welcome our Thai audience to the show tonight. We are pleased to have General Hernan Cortez as our special guest on tonight's show. He is here with us to speak about his new-old book *Liberation—the True Story, the Real Story.* What he likes to call the ring within the ring story of history."

Cortez smiled as the applause sign went on. None of the Thais clapped their hands. They booed. But a Sound Wave Machine wiped the boos and replaced them with the sound of clapping.

"Thank you for your warm welcome. Some nights I'm co-host. Some nights I'm the guest. Some nights the victim; other nights the hero. Monty and I go back a very long way. And we have a secret."

"One that Cortez hasn't told you," said Montezuma, looking out at his first audience of Thais since 1976.

"What he means is—how long does a night last?" asked Cortez.

"What I mean is, Cortez has told me he has a surprise. Can you believe this loser who hasn't surprised himself once since 1519 has something to tell us we don't already know?" asked Montezuma.

"How many worthless souls must be saved before Cortez is released? What is the number?"

"Give or take, a quarter of a million," said Montezuma, yawning.

"Give or take," said Cortez, throwing his head back in laughter.

318

"We wish to introduce some of our special guests, Lek, Noi, and Weird Bob. In his last life Weird Bob won an electric fan for being the tallest man in Bangkok," said Montezuma. "And we ended up taking him even though it was not our job."

"What Monty means is that this white guy took the prize off the short locals."

"Who was the woman I was supposed to save?" asked Cortez.

"Ten bonus points for the right answer," added Montezuma.

The red neon applause sign flashed.

"You there in the back row. The girl with the half-moon- shaped scar."

The girl stood under the intense beam of a spotlight.

"*Chun*," a thin, unsure voice rang out. Everyone else among the dead looked at her and couldn't believe what they saw.

"In English!" said Montezuma who had never spoken a word of English until a stone bashed his head.

"Okay, me," said Daeng. "I got shot."

"So you are dead. Officially not rescued," said a smug Montezuma, arms folded over his chest.

"But my daughter, Oon. She's ten months now," said Daeng "She got rescued. She's not dead, thank God."

"Safe!" roared Montezuma, flames shooting from his ears. "Your worthless whore's daughter was saved? By whose authority? So this explains why all my channels have been blocked."

"I signed the betting form just before the window closed," said Cortez. "I laid down a double or nothing bet. I went for the jackpot. A game of chance. What were the chances of Daeng's daughter surviving the junkyard? How in a million years would she ever be rescued? I bet the whole half a million. I won. The partnership is over, Monty."

Cortez was gone. His chair was empty. The audience looked at the Aztec who played for time, fumbled with some papers, afraid to look up at the TV camera.

"Lucky bet," said Montezuma, gloomily.

"I'm sorry if I did something wrong," said Daeng.

Montezuma was still sulking when he called her onto the stage.

"You know anything about show business?" he asked.

She shook her head. "Well, neither did Cortez. After four hundred fifty years he finally got rid of the curse. You want to try? It's up to you."

"What do I do?" asked Daeng.

Montezuma put a hand on her knee and a charge of electrical energy nearly knocked him off the stage.

"Why did he win?" asked Daeng.

"He bet on hope. A fool's bet at best."

"But he won," she said.

"Stick with me, kid. You won't see that dark horse winning for a few more aeons."

She thought about this proposition. She looked back at the crowd which suddenly had a greenish steam rising from lifeless forms spilling out of the chairs. "And if I don't want to stick with you?"

He had no choice but to tell her the truth.

"Then it is back to 1519 for me and it starts all over again, because I've learned nothing. I get my skull cracked again, and try to fill it with some meaning one more time. But you wouldn't want that. Would you? Please, pretty please."

When she smiled, the smile of hope, the half-moon scar straightened on the side of her face, and a second later Montezuma had vanished. And when she saw her father walk toward her she knew whatever curse had been cast was now forever lifted.